ADVANCE PRAIS

M000074885

"*Red Sparrow* meets *The Kite Runner*.
Beautiful, so well-written and a compelling story."

— HOLLY LYNN PAYNE, AUTHOR OF *THE VIRGIN'S KNOT*,
THE SOUND OF BLUE AND *DAMASCENA*

"*The Missing Peace* has a cinematic quality to both the prose
and the way the story moves between different characters and
countries that I found wildly engaging. The setting was
described with an aerial quality and an eye for detail
emphasizing its sweeping scope."

— MASIE COCHRAN, SENIOR EDITOR AT TIN HOUSE

"Joyce's novel is one that overflows with vivid particulars.
The thrills come in seeing how all the aspects of this
multifaceted world will eventually come together.
This gripping spy tale offers entertaining
and realistic details."

— KIRKUS REVIEWS

"A great story, powerful characters
and a plot that rings devastatingly true."

— FRANK VIVIANO, *NATIONAL GEOGRAPHIC* JOURNALIST,
SAN FRANCISCO CHRONICLE WAR CORRESPONDENT
AND AUTHOR OF *BLOOD WASHES BLOOD*

"The world is a better place for having authors like Mr Joyce.
His style is smooth and articulate. At times it is wonderfully
cinematic. No small feat with the written word."

— THOMAS HENRY POPE, AUTHOR OF *IMPERFECT BURIALS*

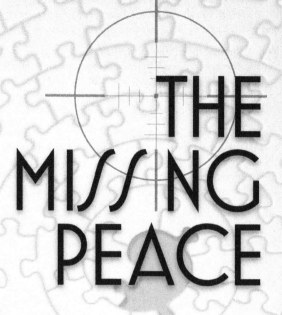

THE
MISSING
PEACE

TOM JOYCE

HERETIC PUBLICATIONS
Washington DC

First printing May 2021

HERETIC PUBLICATIONS

Print: ISBN-13: 978-1-7329372-3-9
eBook: ISBN-13: 978-1-7329372-0-8

Registration Numbers:
US Copyright Office: 1-8747395831
WGAw: 2050845

Printed in the United States of America
Set in Adobe Jenson Pro, Montserrat and Mostra
Cover photo by Ruhumun Izi
Cover and interior design by
Tom Joyce/Creativewerks

For Mama Hope and the TNWs

AUTHOR'S NOTE

IN AUGUST 1961, construction of the wall that bisected Berlin also marked the birth of the Cold War spy novel in which the Union of Soviet Socialist Republics, our former ally against Hitler's Third Reich, was portrayed as a "Godless Evil Empire" bent on destroying cherished Western values. 28 years later, Mikhail Gorbachev's radical *perestroika* changed the face of Soviet politics and that iconic wall came down. Overnight, we lost both our literal and literary nemesis.

At least until September 2001, when the same "freedom fighters" we had enlisted in the 1980s to disrupt the Soviet occupation of Afghanistan suddenly became freedom's worst nightmare. While we were inventing reasons to invade sovereign nations, sorting out the "good Muslims" from the bad ones and debating the legal definition of torture, Russia, our estranged partner in a global "War on Terror," was rekindling a nationalistic obsession with empire as it rebuilt an arsenal of very real weapons of mass destruction and mass deception right under our noses.

Make no mistake, the Cold War is alive and well.

Written in the wake of our post-9/11 paranoia, *The Missing Peace* is a political thriller draped in the lingerie of romance, mystery and adventure inspired by the classic works of Eric Ambler, John Le Carré, Len Deighton and Graham Greene, translated into a 21st Century vernacular and extrapolated to the edge of credibility.

In our confusing era of "fake news," fiction is all too frequently conflated with fact. *The Missing Peace*, although a work of fiction, is constructed around a core of factual material. So, for readers who enjoy drilling down into background data that would only slow the narrative and drown dialog in contrived and tedious exposition, I've included *factual* footnotes, rather than a glossary, for quick reference. While some readers may consider this convention unorthodox for a novel, I'm of the opinion it is far less disruptive than having to resort to Wikipedia—or WikiLeaks—for clarification.

I began writing this novel in the summer of 2009, inspired and alarmed by extensive travels in the Middle East and Central Asia. While my description of places, events and technology are consistent with that period, things have changed considerably since then.

Istanbul, crossroad of Europe and Asia, has become a target for both terrorism and draconian crackdowns by Turkey's leadership. Dushanbe, Tajikistan' capital city, has undertaken some impressive public work projects, including a much-improved airport terminal paid for by an influx of narcotics money. Either the landmines have been cleared from the roadside in Gorno-Badakhshan or the graphic warning signs have been removed to promote tourism. Sadly, the situation in Afghanistan has greatly deteriorated. The security in Badakhshan Province is more precarious than it was a decade ago. The Taliban, incentivized by Russian money and American compassion fatigue, and *Daesh*, the bogus "Islamic State," have both ramped up their offensive against government troops. Luckily, their fanatical corruption of Islam has not yet spilled into the Wakhan Corridor, one of the last pristine mountain frontiers on Earth, or threatened its gracious Isma'ili inhabitants—so far.

Many people smarter than me contributed their time and expertise to help make this book both plausible and readable. Technical consultation in multifarious disciplines, translation assistance, and editorial suggestions were generously provided by: Tamim Ansary, Dani Beit-Or, Emily Bower, Kathy Butler, Glenn Carroll, Michael Carroll, Tom Cammarata, Maisie Cochran, Peter Engler, Byron "Blitz" Fox, Edward Henning, Scott Henning, Gene Hern MD, Nicholas Joyce, Lyudmila Kirillova, Gorgali Khairkhah, Vassi Koutsaftis, Hildy Manley, Svetlana Marochnik, Gary McCue, Bill McGinnis, Lisa McMahon, Eleanor Bingham Miller, Yakov Okupnik, Teddy Piastunovich, Thomas Henry Pope, Amy Rennert, Peter Alan Roberts, Omid Safi, Carey Sublette, Adrian Summers, Ruth Schwartz, Shayesteh Talai, Shai Tamari, Lisa Tracy and Frank Viviano.

As any writer knows, the work of crafting even a short story, let alone a novel, is a combination of creative enthusiasm, existential despair and editorial drudgery. But even in the bleakest of moments, encouragement and inspiration always came from a close family of extraordinary literati and fellow travelers: Cyn Cady, Chris Cole, Amanda Conran, Tanya Egan Gibson, Josh Gibson, John Philipp, Jill Rosenblum Tidman, Maya Lis Tussing, Dave Winton, the late Major Jon Wells, the always-enthusiastic gang at Peri's and our dearly missed mentor, Stephanie Moore, the one and only "Mama Hope."

A very special thanks to Terry Irving, Holly Payne and Krystyna Srodulski for their astute critiques, skillful editing and unrelenting faith in my work. Truly, there are not enough words to thank you all.

Tom Joyce—Washington DC, December 2020

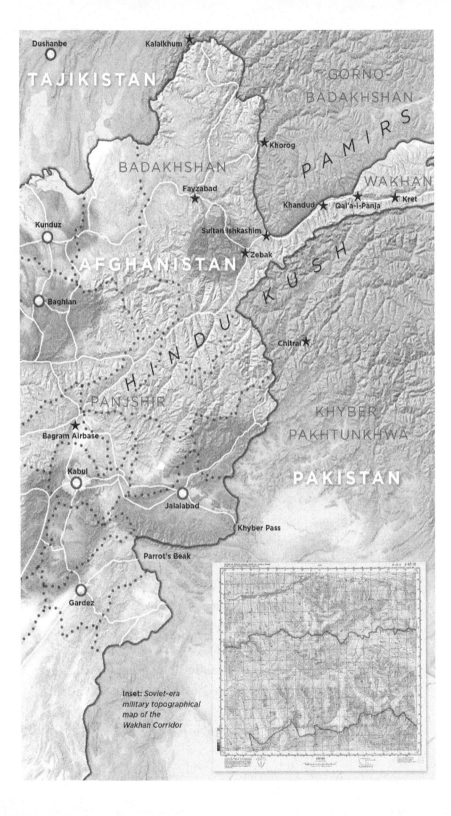

TAJIKISTAN

Dushanbe

Kalaikhum

GORNO-
BADAKHSHAN

BADAKHSHAN

Khorog

P A M I R S

Fayzabad

WAKHAN

Khandud Qal'a-i-Panja Kret

Kunduz

Sultan Ishkashim

AFGHANISTAN

Zebak

H I N D U

Baghlan

K U S H

Chitral

PANJSHIR

KHYBER
PAKHTUNKHWA

Bagram Airbase

Kabul

PAKISTAN

Jalalabad

Khyber Pass

Parrot's Beak

Gardez

Inset: *Soviet-era
military topographical
map of the
Wakhan Corridor*

THE MISSING PEACE

TUESDAY, 14 FEBRUARY 1989 • HINDU KUSH, AFGHANISTAN

....

THE AIR SMELLED OF OZONE, tasted metallic and felt like the edge of a knife. Somewhere behind the pilot's eyes, a memory ignited, jolting him back into consciousness. He heard no sound of life in the aft cabin, nothing but the violent wind scouring a fractured canopy somewhere above him, until his own voice began to play back like a damaged tape recording in his ears.

Yuriy…pozhaluysta…skazhite mne…

He could neither feel nor move his crushed legs beneath the gunship's instrument panel. Hands shaking, the pilot lifted his helmet's sun visor and saw the drying blood spattered across his flight suit. It belonged to Alyushin, his weapons system officer, who had been decapitated by his own gun sight on impact.

He closed his eyes, drifted and waited to die.

…please…tell me…these are not…

Images teased his brain. He could remember gliding over the jagged peaks east of ancient Kapisa and a golden dawn breaking

above snow-choked passes of Nuristan as he banked his helicopter
northward toward the distant border of the USSR. Was it just
a dream? No. He remembered now. After ten bloody years, after
15,000 comrades zipped into body bags, the Limited Contingent
Soviet 40th Army was finally withdrawing from Afghanistan. He
was going home. To Leningrad. To his family.

But something had gone terribly wrong.

Sounds and images flashed like tracer rounds across the pilot's
closed eyes: the warm sodium glow of Bagram's hangar, Alyushin's
crisp salute, Stas' prescient warning, Yuriy's duplicity as the eight
commandos of Spetsgruppa Alfa* loaded a dozen meter-long cases,
each stenciled with a blatant lie, into his gunship's cabin.

He remembered a strange key. Six latches. A bullet-shaped
cylinder bearing a red star. An urgent plea to his commander...

Yuriy, please tell me these are not *what I think they are.*

...and Yuriy's astonishing response...

Just get them to a safe place, Dmitry Mikhailovitch. For God's sake!

The pilot heard himself praying now to that God in which he
never believed. He prayed the Sukhoi Fencer flying high-altitude
support would quickly follow protocol and destroy his disabled gunship before the *döshman*, the faceless "enemy" he had been killing for
a decade, found him. Or his cargo of "meteorological equipment."

As he waited for an Aphid missile to end his pain and absolve him
of his guilt, the pilot struggled to pull the leather glove off his trembling
right hand. Numb fingers fumbled to unzip the breast pocket of his
jacket, search within and extract the engraved metal disk his flight
mechanic had pressed into his palm before lift-off. He fisted it tightly,
squeezed his eyes shut again and heard Stas' insistent voice.

---

* **Spetsgruppa Alfa**—a Soviet KGB [*Komitet Gosudarstvennoy Bezopasnosti*] Committee for State
Security elite paramilitary, the Spetsnaz [*Vojska Spetsialnogo Naznacheniya*] Special Purpose
Forces were originally a GRU [*Glavnoye Razvedyvatel'noye Upravleniye*] Military Intelligence unit.

Please, sir! Take it for your daughter.

The burnished silver heirloom calmed him like morphine as he watched himself from above, walking with a light, happy gait along Dekabristov, his long legs warming with the brisk movement. He could hear snow crunching beneath his civilian shoes, his footsteps tapping lightly on the granite stairway up to his flat and Maryna's cry of anguished relief as the front door cracked open. He could feel the warmth within radiating toward him, inviting him into his wife's welcoming embrace, her tears of joy wet on his cheek. He could almost taste her mouth as they kissed for the first time in over a year.

Pápa!

An excited voice warmed his ears as the little girl pattered barefoot across the polished wooden floor and flew into his open arms. How tall she had grown. He could feel his hand clutching Stas' still-frozen gift in the pocket of his overcoat, the silver broach engraved with calligraphy that formed the shape of a proud lion looking back over its shoulder. He watched himself display the heirloom in his open palm like a glittering sweet as his daughter's amber eyes widened with excitement.

The last thing the pilot's imagination heard was Sonya's delighted laughter in the wind as his dream of Leningrad faded into a lace of ice crystals on the shattered canopy above him.

INTERPRET

....

"It has been generally agreed here and abroad that the major danger from nuclear weapons in the dissolution of the former Soviet Union comes from the wide dispersion of the smaller, easily transportable tactical warheads."

— Reginald Bartholomew, US Undersecretary of Defense for International Security Affairs, at a meeting with the Soviet Delegation in the autumn of 1991

....

SUMMER HEAT CARESSES HER SKIN as she crosses Garden Street into Cambridge Common. Bare-chested boys hurl softballs and toss Frisbees across its tree-lined green wedge in the muggy afternoon as girlfriends lounge on blankets by the barbecue. Sweat mingles with slow-burning charcoal, freshly cut grass and the promise of rain. Eight years dissolve.

Walking the Common's shaded brick path and breathing in the humid, deciduous scent of her interrupted youth, Sonya Aronovsky feels almost relaxed. Here, the world still looks, smells and tastes exactly the way she wants to remember it: like rowdy boys in sleek boats cutting a wake up the Charles, like grilling burgers and cold beer, like Danny's warm, salty skin after a race.

Here, there is nothing to remind Sonya of her *real* life.

Through Johnston Gate, Harvard Yard remains an academic anachronism. Clusters of visiting applicants still stroll the elm-shaded quadrangle of brick façades, slate roofs, and white steeples, regaled by student docents in *veritas* T-shirts. Still guarding the battlements of University Hall, a bronzed John Harvard slumps in ennui as kids polish the toe of his left shoe for luck with their scholarship applications. Pausing on the diagonal walkway, Sonya remembers how much she loved this indulgent ivory tower, and how much of her closed down when she had to leave its cloistered world of long-winded lectures and late-night liaisons for the hard realities of a life under constant siege.

Her leather knapsack is slung over one shoulder and the sleeveless linen blouse beneath it is glued to her body in the sticky heat. She has dressed conservatively in a knee-length skirt, her short blonde hair brushed back off her forehead and only the bare essentials of make-up. She has spent most of her life hiding inconvenient emotions behind a fortress of cool professionalism, but at this moment Sonya is unable to ignore the fluttering stomach that reminds her why she has come here.

Across Francis Street, Harvard Divinity School's Center for the Study of World Religions hides its Brutalist face from the Gothic disdain of Andover Hall beneath a green Ginkgo canopy. Sonya approaches the slatted gate, finds a number on the call box directory and punches it into a chrome keypad. The amplified voice that answers brings a flush to her face. She pretends not to recognize its owner and buries her feelings along with everything else in the world she has ever loved.

"I have an appointment with Father Callan," she announces.

"Back door," Danny's voice replies without a hint of emotion.

The gate buzzes open and Sonya places one Ferragamo sandal in front of the other, focuses on navigating the blacktop driveway as her pulse races. Even graduate students have abandoned the campus for the Independence Day weekend. The only sound she hears is the chirp of nesting robins. A footpath leads her to a pair of green doors beneath the bank of second story windows overlooking a lawn dotted with dogwood.

Sonya hears his footsteps even before the aluminum door clicks open. Her eyes touch first on his hand, its sinewy, suntanned skin feathered with golden hairs, then on his wrist and the stainless-steel divers' watch his mother had given him as a graduation gift. Despite Sonya's resolve to remain detached and in control, she cannot help but remember. Everything. When her eyes reach his face, she can almost feel his strong arms around her body again.

"Long time, Sonny."

She smiles at the memories his nickname evokes and prays the flush in her face is not as transparent as it feels. He has to be almost forty by now, even more chiseled than she remembered him. His short, sandy hair is still as unkempt as it was on those autumn afternoons when he sculled the Charles River as if nothing else in the world mattered. But his sharp blue eyes are set deeper into a filigree of creases, not really laughter lines, more as if life has finally convinced him of its seriousness. For some reason, she expected him to be dressed in clerical black, a white Roman collar beneath his square jaw. Instead he wears a navy camp shirt, khaki cargo shorts and sandals, almost as if he wants to remind her of how it used to be.

"You look different," he says. "I mean, *good*. More..." He seems embarrassed to be staring at her. "The short hair works for you."

"Better in the heat." She smiles awkwardly. "So, should I be calling you 'Father' now?"

"Only if you're seeking pastoral counseling."

"We're safe, then." Sonya brushes quickly past his curiosity. She can feel his eyes following her movements all the way up to the second-floor landing. "You're teaching here permanently?"

"Since they gave me an office, I'm practically living here."

Danny escorts her down a narrow hall where a faint odor of mildew rises from the carpet. "Inter-faith studies focused on Central Asia are not quite as popular as interpretive hip-hop in post-modern America, but my classes are always full. Students are particularly interested in Afghanistan. Go figure! Maybe a morbid curiosity about innocent people we're bombing back to the Stone Age."

"Yes, I was one of those students. Once upon a time."

"As I recall."

Danny's shortened Bostonian vowels sound odd to her after an eight-year absence. In the Hebrew Reali School she attended as a child, Sonya was taught to speak "proper" English, instead of the harsh colloquial patter of settlers from Brooklyn. Her mother never lost her Russian accent, but Sonya could pass for a well-heeled Chelsea schoolgirl as easily as she could an American Millennial.

She enters Danny's tiny office, a microcosm of his eclectic mind. All around the room, hundreds of books are arranged on his shelves by alphabetical category: anthropology, archeology, art history and so on. Between the shelves, he has hung a framed intaglio broadside of Saint Francis of Assisi's prayer: *Lord, make me an instrument of Thy peace*, and a brocaded Tibetan *thangka* depicting a blissful figure meditating on a lotus flower. He once told her it represented the quintessence of human compassion. Hanging in the only other free space on his wall, Sonya recognizes an Arabic calligraphic illumination of the opening salutation from *Al-Qur'ân*: *In the Name of the One, the Compassionate, the Merciful...*

The theme of Danny's academic pursuits dovetail so seamlessly with his inspiration. Sonya cannot help but smile at his endearing naiveté, but she is happy to see he still allows himself one secular conceit: the 2004 Red Sox pennant hanging proudly above his desk.

Sonya drops her knapsack and sinks into a worn armchair. She watches Danny crack the seal on a tin of expensive tea and carefully spoon fragrant leaves into the basket of an iron Japanese pot. It is so like him, going out of his way and spending more than he should to accommodate her tastes. She feels uncomfortably self-conscious, considering the way she left things eight years ago.

"Needless to say," he says anyway, "I was surprised by your letter. However, you really could have benefited from a Catholic school education in penmanship. And maybe even a good thrashing from one of our Sisters of Mercy."

Sonya purses her lips and crosses her legs impatiently. "When you've finished my handwriting analysis, Father Callan, I'll explain why I wrote that letter."

Danny unplugs the hissing plastic kettle, pours boiling water into his teapot, settles into his creaking desk chair, and strains unsuccessfully to appear relaxed. "Forgive me, Sonny. I promised to listen to your story, not reopen old wounds." He pours tea through a strainer into two cups bearing the Society of Jesus monogram. "Hope you still like Russian Caravan."

"*Horoshaya pamyet*," she suppresses a smile while appraising his inquisitive stare. "Good memory."

"Your letter said something about a family heirloom?"

"Actually, something I found in my mother's flat."

"And how is Maryna these days?" Although he remembers her mother's name, likely stores it in the same place he keeps historical minutia, Danny never met Maryna Aronovsky. And never will.

"She died three years ago."

"Sorry." He draws a breath and awkwardly shifts his emotional transmission into condolence gear. "I hope your mother finally found the peace she was looking for."

Danny knew that Maryna had been a dedicated peace activist in Israel, much to Sonya's chagrin. It had been so like her mother to redouble her efforts after Hezbollah began launching missiles from the Lebanese border in July 2006. "Katyushas hit a hospital in Safed and killed a couple Arab kids in Nazareth," she explains. "Mother was appalled that they would shoot at their own people, even if they *were* Israeli citizens. So, she went straightaway to the Galilee to patch up all the wounded in Nahariya." Sonya lowers her eyes. "Hezbollah barraged the town and hit Kibbutz Sa'ar where Mother was based."

Recoiling from the memory, she assesses his reaction. "Ironic way to find peace, wouldn't you say?"

He says nothing.

"Couldn't bring myself to pick through Mother's flat after cremating what was left of her. So I had everything boxed up and put into storage. Last year, I moved back to Haifa and sorted through it all. In a shoe box where she kept my father's letters, I found this."

Sonya flips back the unbuckled flap of her knapsack and withdraws a short carbon fiber tube. She unscrews the cap and carefully extracts a mottled piece of vellum. Danny clears a space on his desk and she gingerly spreads the fragment out for him to examine. Rough-edged on three sides and cut cleanly across the bottom, faded sepia calligraphic strokes are inscribed in neat lines across its surface.

"Looks like a Persian Ta'liq script," he says.

"Quoting an Arabic *surah*. But I can't read what's underneath."

Danny bends toward the vellum in amazement. "A palimpsest?"

"Appears to be." She lifts a manila envelope from her knapsack and unwinds the tie-string. "A colleague at the Technion had an analysis done using Multi-Spectral Imaging." She extracts a sheaf of digital prints and hands them to Danny, explaining as he reads.

"He said MSI employs lens filtration to favor various wavelengths from infrared through the ultra-violet range," Sonya says. "The images get converted into digital stacks with an algorithm that enhances characteristics unavailable to the red-green-blue spectrum of visible light."

"Right. Separates the spectral signature of older ink embedded in the vellum from newer ink on its surface," Danny confirms.

Sonya watches his face intently as he shuffles through a half-dozen gray-scale images showing portions of the under-text at various sizes and resolutions.

"These strokes look familiar," he says, "but the surface text is creating too many gaps to read what's underneath."

Danny glances up at her, obviously intrigued. "We need to show this to Cyrus."

....

"**HE SPECIALIZES IN FORENSICS**," Danny explains as they walk west on Brattle Street. "Cyrus made a name for himself identifying stolen artifacts and forgeries."

"You suspect this piece is a forgery?" Sonya asks.

"Didn't say that. But Multi-Spectral Imaging has limitations and Cyrus has connections. He consults with anonymous high rollers that buy and sell antiquities. I'm going to need some technical back-up to decipher the text underneath."

Cyrus Narsai's antebellum home in West Cambridge sits well back from the road on a manicured green lawn. A pair of arching maple trees frame its Greek Revival portico. White Ionic columns support its peaked pediment and gabled roof. Cyrus appears at his front door flanked by tall sidelight windows and Danny shakes his hand.

"Sorry to interrupt your work, but I thought you might want to meet a young lady with an old manuscript."

"And that's what I so love about you, Danny Boy," Cyrus replies. "You exploit all my weaknesses at once without making me feel the least bit guilty."

"Just remember to make an act of contrition, Cyrus."

When Danny introduces Sonya, Cyrus' silver-streaked Van Dyke shifts from laughter to lecherous grin. "We're shoe-less here," he says as Sonya feels his hand escort her into his vestibule. "These damn pine floorboards scratch if you breathe on them."

Cyrus' pristine floor is finished in a dark stain that makes the white leather sectional seem to levitate in front of his ceramic fireplace. The décor is elegantly sparse: framed black and white Man Ray photographs hang from rails between shelves of hard-bound art books, antique Persian rugs protect the soft planking and a Chihuly blown glass sculpture on a black marble pedestal splashes primary colors onto the room's otherwise neutral canvas.

When she slips off her shoes, Sonya stands eye-to-eye with Cyrus. Slender and fit, he has smooth olive skin and a shock of salt-and-pepper hair styled to look as if it has not been. Over faded jeans, he wears an unironed white linen shirt, sleeves rolled and the front placket open far enough to reveal an antique gold coin hanging in a trimmed thicket of silvery hair. As he pours iced ginger lemon tea into hand-blown glasses for his guests, Sonya unscrews her tube, carefully extracts the rolled vellum sheet and lays it on his glass coffee table.

Cyrus barely glances at the manuscript before launching into a lecture, clearly delighting in the sound of his own voice.

"You can make parchment or vellum from any number of animal hides. Scribes preferred calf, sheep, or goat," he explains, rubbing a thumb against two fingers. "The very best vellum, translucent and thin as a condom, came from an unborn calf."

Cyrus crinkles his hawkish nose and hands Sonya a frosty glass, taking the opportunity to appraise her figure. "Greek scribes liked goats because they were plentiful and, well, receptive, I guess." His left eyebrow twitches. "One goat will give you two sheets of roughly 12-by-15 usable inches. You rule out your lines with a blunt point, and then write your text with a reed pen using ink made from crushed oak galls: small, abnormal tree growths formed by insects, and rich in tannic acid. *Archie* was written on goatskin."

"Who's Archie?"

Cyrus looks hurt. "Sorry, love, Archimedes Palimpsest. I thought Father Callan might have mentioned that." Cyrus unfolds his reading glasses. "In the 1840s, a scholar named Constantine Tischendorf visited the Metochion of the Holy Sepulcher in Constantinople and got his hands on a single page from a 13th century *euchologion*— that's Byzantine for prayer book. He recognized it as *palimpsestos*, a technique often used by Greek scribes. Literally means 'scraped again'. Well, what had been scraped off the sheets of parchment in this prayer book included treatises from *On Floating Bodies, The Method of Mechanical Theorems*, and the *Stomachion* by Archimedes. Old bugger used to write his notes on papyrus, which were made of reeds and never survived the various conflagrations of the Dark Ages. Luckily, they were copied over the years onto more durable material like parchment and vellum. This particular collection was probably penned in the 10th century. A Greek Orthodox priest cut up those sheets to make his prayer book in 1229."

"Why would a priest cut up one of Archimedes' manuscripts?"

Cyrus' brown bedroom eyes caress Sonya over the top of his reading glasses. "Because in those days, advanced mathematical treatises were about as valuable to the Christian kings of Europe as a rabbi with leprosy." He cocks an eyebrow. "And God knows, vellum wasn't cheap! The good friars recycled whatever they could.

"Now, Tischendorf never recognized the mathematical formulae as Archimedes' work. John Ludwig Heiberg figured that out when he visited the Metochion in 1906. Guy must have had extraordinary eyes to see the under-script without ultraviolet light.

"Eventually, the *euchologion* ended up with a French collector and was sold for a large sum at Christie's in 1998. I was brought in to authenticate it for the collector who purchased it and arrange for the Walters Museum in Baltimore to fund its conservation."

Sonya looks around Cyrus' opulent home. "And the rest, as they say, is history."

Danny hands him the envelope of digital prints. "Sonya's already had MSI run on this piece."

Cyrus' fingers glide lightly over the pages. His eyes scan back and forth from the photographs to the vellum's mottled surface with a detective's scrutiny. "That script hiding beneath the Ta'liq calligraphy looks like Sanskrit, but the letter-forms are unusual."

"That's because they're Kharosthi," Danny says.

"I'll be damned! Those Semites got around, didn't they?" Cyrus arches another sardonic eyebrow at Sonya, then turns his attention back to Danny. "You think this is Gandharan?"

"Hard to say. There's a lot of dropout. I can't make out enough of the under-script to tell."

"We'd need to do XRF imaging to be certain," Cyrus suggests.

"Anybody closer than SSRL?"

"There's a geek at MIT who might give us some downtime on his EDAX…"

Sonya sighs. "Can we default to English, please?"

Cyrus chuckles as he settles in beside her on the sofa. He fans the prints out across her skirt and finds every excuse to touch them as he speaks. "The problem with reading a palimpsest is dropout caused by the more recent overwritten text. But we've found a way around this using high energy, short wavelength photons."

"X-rays," Danny translates with air quotes.

"Fascinating," Sonya exhales like an ingénue impressed.

"Some of the photons excite individual atoms in the inks, which generate secondary, or fluorescence X-rays, each with its own unique wavelength and signature. Now, since the fluorescence from an iron atom is different than a calcium or potassium atom, you can map the atomic structure of each ink and literally read beneath the surface."

"And this is how you were able to authenticate *Archie*, right?"

"Exactly!" Cyrus beams with Sonya's appreciation. "The Stanford Synchrotron Radiation Lab had the most sophisticated equipment at the time. But there are new-generation Micro X-Ray Fluorescence Analyzers that will do the job *if* the mapped area hasn't been too badly debased." Cyrus' hand lingers on the prints in Sonya's lap. "Even so, this *could* take a while."

Danny rolls his eyes as he carefully slips the vellum back into its tube. "How long are you in town, Sonny?"

"I've got a meeting in Manhattan on Monday, and a flight out of JFK on Wednesday."

"Any chance your geek can spare some time tomorrow?" Danny asks Cyrus.

He shrugs. "Fourth of July weekend…but what the hell! It's certainly worth a call." Cyrus' eyes spill over Sonya like warm oil. "Intriguing challenge," he muses, scanning the swell of her blouse below its open collar. "Let's plan to map out a strategy over dinner tomorrow evening, shall we? Fireworks optional."

"**OH MY GOD,** I *so* need a drink!" Sonya exhales her tension as she drops into a beige leather banquette at Om. The softly lit cocktail lounge on Harvard Square opens in the summer to sidewalk tables. Opposite the bar, a three-by-three-meter Tibetan painting dominates the room. Sonya stares at the triple-faced, multi-armed, demonic deity astride a giant lotus, encircled by a halo of stylized flames. On closer inspection, she realizes the creature is locked in sexual union with an equally ferocious female, their four eyes bulging in coital bliss. In their otherwise disengaged hands, the Tantric couple brandishes fiery weapons and human skulls filled with a roiling orange fluid.

"Those Buddhists like it rough, don't they?"

"Black Mahakala and his consort, Kali, drinking *amrita* while performing *yab-yum*," Danny replies as if she were still one of his students. "Symbolic representation of insight joining with skillful means. Uncle of the owner here is a master *thangka* painter."

"He looks skillful alright! Girlfriend seems a bit clingy though. Sonya pretends to scrutinize the menu their waitress has brought. "How are the Lemon Drops here?"

"Haven't a clue," Danny mutters, scanning the list of exotic drinks with complete disinterest. "What's on tap?"

"Stella," the Goth waitress with the eyebrow ring announces.

"She'll do."

Sonya crosses her legs, smooths her linen skirt and relaxes into the banquette, simultaneously amused and annoyed by Danny's attempt to look at anything and everything except her.

"So, Professor, where do you think this piece of goat skin that didn't end up as a condom came from?"

Danny tosses the menu onto the table between them and stares past Sonya at the intricate *thangka*. "The under-script appears to be

Sanskrit but written in an alphasyllabary derived from Aramaic called Kharosthi, consonantal and diacritically augmented but reads right to left with a typically Semitic vowel order. Commerce on the Silk Road bred polyglots, so alphabets were often borrowed from foreign languages."

"You can bet we Semites charged interest on our vowels."

Danny suppresses a laugh, scooping a handful of peanuts from a dish on the table. "Kharosthi script was also used to write Gandhari Prakrit. And it so happens that the oldest South Asian manuscripts discovered are Gandharan Buddhist texts found in Eastern Afghanistan. Where did Maryna get this thing?"

"I was hoping you could tell *me*."

"You said she kept it with letters from your father?"

"That's right," Sonya buries her eyes in the menu.

"So..." Danny taps his fingernails impatiently against his jaw. "Would it be safe to assume your father *gave* it to her?"

She glances over the menu's edge. "Making assumptions is always dangerous."

"What are you not telling me, Sonny?"

"You don't trust me, Father Callan?"

"Don't bullshit me."

At least that gets her some eye contact.

"I find it hard to believe you were just dying to visit the old *alma mater*," Danny continues. "After all these years, after...everything." He looks away. "Not even a phone call or an e-mail, just an old-fashioned letter with a stamp on it. Why, Sonny?"

Goth girl brings their drinks, and Sonya washes the taste of Cyrus' unrelenting come-on out of her mouth with a sip of citrus-infused vodka. Her eyes drift across the narrow, bustling alley to Winthrop Park. Students lounge on benches with their laptops beneath the maple shade, pirating WiFi from Peet's and Grendel's Den, smoking cigarettes and drinking macchiatos. Long before the trendy restaurant in which they sit was approved by the Cambridge planning commission, she and Danny spent many lazy summer afternoons in that shaded park—he, absorbed in arcane books, and she, trying every trick in her repertoire to distract him from them. It only took eight years of separation to find one that worked. The irony is not lost on her.

Sonya searches through her knapsack, finds a lipstick, twists the end and extracts a tightly rolled strip of vellum from the tube. She flattens it out for Danny's inspection and his eyes narrow as he scans the crude Cyrillic letters scratched into its surface with what appears to be a charcoal implement:

РАЗБИТ НО ЗХИВОЙ. ГРУЗ В БЕЗОПАСНОСТИ.

"I didn't want anyone but you to see this piece of the puzzle," Sonya admits. "I suppose Cyrus would go apoplectic if he knew I'd cut it off the manuscript."

"And I wouldn't blame him." Danny inclines his head toward the rough-edged strip. "What's it say?"

Sonya runs a fingernail below each of the words as she translates. "*Razbit no zhivoy*—'Broken, but alive'—*Gruz v bezopasnosti*—'Cargo is safe.'"

His brooding blue eyes ask the tacit question and Sonya decides to lay her cards on the table.

"I know this will sound absolutely crazy, Danny," she admits with a restrained but genuine touch of vulnerability. "I have reason to believe my father may still be alive."

TUESDAY, 16 JUNE 2009 • KYIV, UKRAINE

....

THREE WEEKS BEFORE her arrival in Boston, Sonya Aronovsky emerged from the Palats Sportu Metro station dressed in a gauzy, raw cotton shirt knotted at the waist over a pale-blue T-shirt, faded denim miniskirt and sandals. Her short-cropped hair, deep sun tan and the leather knapsack slung over her shoulder, would have led any casual observer to assume she was just another university student returning from one of the Crimean beach clubs, exactly the impression she wanted to give. Emerging onto the plaza, she was surrounded by a pack of pan-handlers, most damaged veterans of Afghanistan and Chechnya. Sonya deftly dispersed a handful of Hryvnya single notes, and slipped undaunted through the indigent gauntlet.

In sweltering heat beneath an overcast sky, Sonya climbed to the crest of a hill overlooking the sprawling Dnieper River port and caught her breath atop the earthen battlements of Kyivs'ka Fortetsya. Pensive figures in lab coats strolled the massive fortification past a cluster of fat tourists posing for mobile phone snapshots beside antique cannons. During the *perestroika* era, the red brick barracks hugging a semicircular parade ground had been re-purposed into a hybrid military hospital and museum. But the fortress, she knew, was once a notorious prison where the *narodniki*, partisans who opposed the Czar's "Russification" of Ukraine, had been sent for execution. It felt as if ghosts lingered in the stones.

Sonya found the pre-arranged bench on the battlements, crossed her legs and turned to the old soldier beside her arrayed in his ill-fitting hospital trousers and a sweat stained T-shirt. Beneath bushy brows, his eyes were marbled with cataracts. His lungs wheezed like a steam radiator. He smelled of mothballs and stale tobacco, and his skin was rice paper stretched over alabaster. As he combed gnarled fingers through a brush of white hair, his face contorted into a grotesque cough.

Regaining his breath, Yuriy Pashkovsky spoke slowly to Sonya in Russian. "*U menya rak legkikh* [I have lung cancer]." His milky eyes scanned the erstwhile parade ground as he informed her the prognosis was three-to-six months.

Pashkovsky laughed bitterly. "Life plays cruel jokes, young lady. My grandfather was a Zaporozhian Cossack who fought against the Ottomans, Poles and Bolsheviks. He remained loyal to the Czar even in exile. I, on the other hand, joined the glorious Communist Party and gave forty years of military service to the Union of Soviet Socialist Republics." The name seemed distasteful in his mouth. "Remember them?" He made a limp gesture toward his surroundings. "So, *this* is my reward, spending my last days rotting in a shit-hole where Ukrainians were hanged or shot, without so much as a final cigarette. Grandfather would be pissing his pants and laughing at the irony, don't you think?"

"*Ya mozhu otsenyty ironiyu, polkovnyku* [I can appreciate irony, Colonel]." Sonya replied in perfect Ukrainian. "My great grandmother lived in Minsk during the *pogrom* of 1905. Your grandfather probably burned her house."

A dry cough sounded like glass grinding in the old Cossack's throat. His watery eyes were fixed somewhere in the distance as he resumed the conversation in his native language. "I had great respect for your father and considered him a friend despite our difference in rank. War is a great leveler. We sometimes drank vodka together, and he spoke about your mother. A doctor, as I recall. Mostly, he talked about you. I remember he once showed me a Polaroid photo. You could not have been more than three or four at the time."

A stocky, tight-lipped nurse pushed a withered octogenarian in his wheelchair over the cobblestones past their bench. She inclined her head stiffly while the blanketed veteran mouthed an inaudible plea for help, as if he were about to be kidnapped by aliens.

Sonya observed some disorientation in the Colonel's eyes and wondered whether he suffered from dementia as well as cancer, wondered if she could trust his memory of those soul-crushing years in Afghanistan. She questioned him with a soft determination.

"You sent a letter to my mother about ten years ago. There was a piece of old vellum inside the envelope, something written in Persian script with a single line in Cyrillic scratched at the bottom. Do you remember that, Colonel?"

He shrugged at the cannons.

"Can you tell me what happened to my father?"

"How much do you know?"

"My mother was told his helicopter crashed somewhere in the mountains of Afghanistan. That he was listed as 'missing in action, presumed dead.'"

"All true."

"The Russian Federation made lots of excuses why they could not release any information to us. I thought you might be able to tell me what happened that day."

"That day…" The Colonel sucked in a shallow breath as his eyes narrowed in memory. "…we were the last garrison to withdraw from Afghanistan by air. Marshal Yazov ordered me to transfer millions in assets to that Pathan bastard, Najibullah," he snorts in disgust. "Meanwhile, the gallant General Gromov was pushing his armored convoy toward the Friendship Bridge, leaving us with that cunning Tajik, Massoud, breathing down our necks at Bagram. I had not slept in three days. No one was thinking clearly. Our systems were breaking down and things that should have been a priority were slipping through the cracks. To make matters worse, the KGB was hounding me relentlessly because Kryuchkov could not risk the Americans finding out we had brought those infernal war…"*

Pashkovsky halted mid-sentence, blinked and winced as if he had just said too much. He turned toward Sonya for the first time. "Your father volunteered to fly some sensitive cargo to Chirchik on that day. I sent along air support in case he took fire from the hill positions. We had already lost too many of our gunships to shoulder fired missiles the Americans supplied to the *döshman.*"

Sonya watched his face intently. "You confirmed that he was shot down?"

"The Hindu Kush has swallowed armies, you know."

---

* **Dmitry Timofeyevich Yazov**—last Marshal of the USSR before its collapse; **Mohammad Najibullah Ahmadzai**—former head of Afghan State Intelligence Service and president of Afghanistan; **Boris Vsevolodovich Gromov**—last Commander of the Soviet 40th Army in Afghanistan; the **"Friendship Bridge"** over the Amu Darya [Mother River] built in 1982 at Termez, Uzbekistan—the main supply line for Soviet troops entering Afghanistan; **Ahmad Shah Massoud**—Afghan/Tajik military commander during the Soviet occupation; **Vladimir Alexandrovich Kryuchkov**—7th Chairman of the KGB

"And aerial reconnaissance…"

"Found nothing."

"But there must have been a radio distress signal…*something*. I was told he flew one of the Hind attack helicopters. Surely they were equipped with GLONASS, weren't they?"*

"We called them *krokodil*," he laughs. "And no, Frontal Aviation ditched anything it considered unnecessary weight on combat missions." A wracking cough sent spasms through the Colonel's body.

"That piece of vellum…where did it come from?"

His eyes shifted toward the parade ground. "I was told a herdsman left it at a border checkpoint. That was at least six months after we had pulled out of Afghanistan. There was nothing to identify where it came from."

"But you *knew* who wrote that line at the bottom."

The Colonel coughed up phlegm as he shook his head helplessly. Sonya began to find him as distasteful as rotting meat.

"My father found a way to tell *you* he was still alive. You searched for him, didn't you?" She clutched the old soldier's spindly arm with a fierce grip that caused him to wince in pain. "Well, *didn't* you?"

His eyes glazed over with guilt. "The KGB took control. It was out of my hands."

"You said he was your friend…"

"You don't understand, young lady. Your father was missing in action. The KGB had closed the inquiry and there was not a fucking thing I could do about it." The Colonel's eyes squeezed shut for a moment and a painfully slow tear rolled down his sallow cheek. He licked his parched lips as if searching for water.

---

* **Hind**—NATO's designation for the Soviet Mil Mi-24 helicopter gunship series.
 GLONASS [*Globalnaya Navigatsionnaya Sputnikovaya Sistema*] Global Navigation Satellite System—Soviet-era radio-based alternative to GPS

"When I retired from service, I tried to locate your mother. The Jewish Agency said she had already immigrated to Israel and forwarded my letter with that scrap of vellum to her. I suppose it was a sentimental gesture..."

"*Sentimental?*" Sonya's eyes flashed at him like magnesium flares. "You thought you could absolve your guilt by sending my mother her husband's last words? Ease her grief by admitting he kept your fucking 'sensitive cargo' from falling into enemy hands?"

"And thank God for that!" He conceded, gasping for a breath. Sonya looked down at the Colonel's trembling fingertips, still stained orange from nicotine, clutching the wooden bench slats like a thin alibi. He groped for her arm in pathetic desperation.

"Did you bring what I asked for?"

Sonya could not bear to look at him any longer. She probed her knapsack, found a white tin of Balkan-Sobranie cigarettes, still sealed in cellophane, and placed it between them on the bench. As his gnarled fingers tried to snatch the tin, she held it firm against the wood slats.

"What was my father transporting for the KGB, Colonel?"

Pashkovsky wiped his mouth and withdrew his hand, straightening his bowed spine, still the good soldier. But his eyes refused to meet hers as she confronted his long-buried lies.

"I'm very sorry to say my memory of those days has faded, young lady. There is nothing more I can tell you."

Sonya pushed the cigarettes across the bench toward the dying Cossack like a service revolver loaded with his final redemption.

After a moment, she stood and nodded curtly. "You've told me quite enough, Colonel. *Shalom.*"

FRIDAY, 19 JUNE 2009 · GLILOT MA'ARAV, ISRAEL

....

SHLOMO LEVI LOOKED UP from the *Russia Today* program on his ThinkPad as the Institute's* Head of Operations pushed through a heavy security door into the sterile meeting room. Head shaven and dressed in a crisp, short-sleeved white shirt with a knitted black tie, "Holiday," as he was ironically code-named, entered like a petulant bull and planted his stocky frame in a leather chair at the far end of a smoked glass conference table. As the louvered blinds closed and the door locked behind him with metallic reassurance, his boss appraised Shlomo's colorful Kahala print shirt, unkempt hair, moth-eaten beard and the fragrant remains of his grilled lamb *shwarma*. Through thick progressive lenses, Holiday's magnified eyes never blinked. He reminded Shlomo of a crocodile waiting on a riverbank for a thirsty deer to drop by.

"*Tzahara'eem tovim, Mar Levi* [Good afternoon, Mister Levi]." Holiday raised his hands and grunted. "You've got fifteen minutes."

Shlomo closed his laptop, pushed his lunch aside and tapped a random cadence on his Coca Cola can. "Sir, you are no doubt aware the 12th Main Directorate of the Soviet Union's Ministry of Defense was responsible for control and custody of more than 21,000 tactical nuclear weapons deployed at 600 bases before the USSR collapsed."

His boss' reptilian eyes revealed no sign of the impatience he was surely suffering.

Shlomo continued, undaunted. "A high-ranking GRU officer, Stanislav Lunev, defected to the West in 1992. When Helga[†] debriefed him, Lunev freely admitted the KGB had their own cache of

---

* The Institute for Intelligence and Special Operations [*Ha Mossad le Modi'in ule Tafkidm Meyuchadim*] is headquartered between Tel Aviv and Herzliya near the Glilot Ma'Arav Interchange.
† **Helga**—Mossad's code-name for the US Central Intelligence Agency

TNWs, small, plutonium-based, fusion-boosted, linear implosion devices yielding about one kiloton. They were designed as enhanced radiation anti-personnel weapons, or 'neutron bombs,' designated RA-115-01. The warheads could be fired from a 105-millimeter howitzer, measured less than a meter in length, weighed about 25 kilos, and were easily transported in a hard case or backpack. Lunev claimed that an unspecified number of these devices, once stored secretly at Ukrainian arsenals, were still unaccounted for."

Holiday rubbed the bridge of his nose beneath steel-rimmed glasses. "So, they had a lousy accounting system. What else is new?"

"Lunev's story was later confirmed by General Alexander Lebed, commander of the Tula paratroop division in Afghanistan, who went on to become Secretary of the Russian Federation Security Council until his 'untimely' helicopter crash. Lebed was politically sidelined by Yeltsin after he told a US Congressional Committee that half of these so-called 'suitcase nukes' had gone missing after the breakup of the Soviet Union. Our good friends at Helga said Lebed admitted privately that he knew at least twelve of these weapons had been deployed by the KGB to Afghanistan in 1988, a hedge of last resort against direct American intervention there. It might have caused a cataclysmic escalation of events, but apparently not even Gorbachev knew about them. When the Soviets finally agreed to withdraw their forces, the weapons were supposed to have been removed. However, according to both Lunev and Lebed, there is no record of them ever returning to either Ukrainian or Russian inventory."

Holiday frowned. "We've heard these rumors about suitcase nukes for years, Mister Levi. Nobody has ever seen one. And even if they *do* exist, I'm told they don't have much of a shelf life."

"Actually, sir, these weapons were designed to last a long time in deep cover," Shlomo replied, referring to the hand-written notes on a green file folder beside his laptop. "Most likely manufactured at Arzamas-16 in Nizhny Novgorod Oblast, the model RA-115-01 Permissive Action Links were powered by a low-maintenance radio-isotope thermoelectric generator operating on the alpha decay of plutonium-238. That's a non-fissile isotope with a half-life of about 87 years. Their cores were extremely well shielded, but without maintaining a constant level of tritium more than half will have decayed over time, reducing neutron emissions and gamma radiation."

Shlomo looked up earnestly. "The good news is that *if* these nukes still work, they won't be as dirty as originally intended."

"Small consolation," his boss conceded.

Shlomo idly tapped a ballpoint pen against the back of his hand. "We have reason to believe the TNWs disappeared somewhere between Bagram and the border of the former USSR twenty years ago, on the final day of the Soviet withdrawal from Afghanistan."

"And your evidence?"

"The former base commander of Bagram, a Ukrainian Colonel, now in hospice in Kyiv, confirmed that a helo carrying 'sensitive cargo' for the KGB went missing in the Hindu Kush as the last troops were pulling out. In the chaos, no wreckage was ever recovered, and no information released to the pilot's family. FSB* still considers the incident highly classified."

Holiday squeezed his fingers into a meaty fist and mimicked Shlomo's tapping with his watchband against the glass tabletop. "Where did you come by this so-called intelligence?"

Shlomo shifted uneasily in his chair. "An off-line conversation with the former commander."

---

* **FSB**—[*Federal'naya Sluzhba Bezopasnosti Rossiyskoy Federatsii*]—Russian Federation Security Service, formerly the internal security and counter-intelligence directorates of the Soviet KGB

"There is no such thing as an 'off-line conversation' in our business, Mister Levi." His vegetarian boss sat back in thought and scowled at Shlomo's *shwarma*. "It's still more Russia's concern than ours. We've got bigger problems in our own backyard—Iran, Lebanon and Syria, for instance—not to mention our good neighbors in Gaza. The Radical Front, remember?"

"Exactly!" Shlomo leaned into his argument. "Whether or not these nukes actually exist, a credible rumor that they do, word on the street that we are actively looking for them, could give us the leverage we need to eliminate a big problem in our own backyard."

Propped on his elbows, Shlomo met Holiday's skeptical stare. "Assad stockpiled VX and Sarin through his Russian benefactors, before we intercepted them, and no one believes he has given up on acquiring nukes just because we leveled Al-Kibar.* Putin wouldn't dare supply them, but when you've got a motivated buyer with deep pockets, and a gray dealer like Wild Boar..."

"Ah, so it's Wild Boar again. He keeps you up at night, doesn't he?"

Shlomo felt his face flush with anger. "Well, nobody gave a shit when that Ukrainian bastard sold Kalashnikovs to *shwartze* kids in Sierra Leone. But now, he brokers SCUDs and Katyushas that mysteriously turn up in Beirut and Damascus, paid for by Tehran and deployed by Hezbollah. His *ksharim* have more twists than my mother's *challah*. But, since he's an Israeli citizen with clean Turkish end user certs, we haven't been able to give him so much as a parking citation. So, we can sit on our thumbs, bide our time and hope he slips up...or we can play Grass Widow with him."†

---

* **Al-Kibar**—a plutonium reactor built in a canyon at Dir al-Zor, Syria by North Korean technicians in 2006 and destroyed by an Israeli Air Force strike in 2007

† *Ksharim* [knots]—digital records tracking social, business and financial connections among terrorists and criminals. **Grass Widow** is a technique used by IDF special ops units to bait terrorists into exposing themselves for "interception" [assassination].

Holiday raised an eyebrow. "Specifically?"

"We grease his stairway." Shlomo smiles slyly. "What if Wild Boar were to get wind of a dozen, off-inventory tactical nuclear warheads just waiting to be salvaged and someone who can lead him straight to the cache?"

His boss looked unconvinced, but Shlomo raised a conciliatory hand. "And what if an anonymous third party were to make him an offer he couldn't refuse? Big stick. Juicy carrot. Cash deposit. Minimal risk. What do you suppose a cocaine and call girl-obsessed gun-runner would do if he thought he could retire like a rock star?"

Holiday peered over the top of his glasses. "This is beginning to sound like a personal vendetta, Mister Levi."

"We've been tracking Wild Boar's activities for the past decade." Shlomo slapped the fat green folder beside his laptop. You've read the dossier. As long as this fucker's in business, I won't sleep well. And neither should you or the Prime Minister. If that makes it 'personal' then so be it."

Lips drawn tight, his boss reminded him, "A katsa* is only as good as his last accomplishment, Giraffe." Shlomo knew he was being taken seriously when Holiday addressed him by his code name. "It took the Institute a long time to rebuild credibility after Amman. Don't fuck this up."

"I won't…as long as I can pick my own team."

Holiday rubbed his square chin warily. "Just whom did you have in mind?"

---

* **Katsa** [instrument]—an acronym for *ktsin issuf* [collection officer] with the division of Mossad called *Melucha* [Kingdom], formerly *Tsomet* [Junction], organized under the Institute's Head of Operations to recruit and run field agents

FRIDAY, 19 JUNE 2009 • HAIFA, ISRAEL

....

SHLOMO PARKED HIS SILVER A4, lifted a shopping bag from the rear boot and walked to a white marble balustrade overlooking the Mediterranean. From the Yefe Nof Balcony on Har Ha'Karmel, he looked down on a green cascade of 19 terraces that terminated 500 meters below at Haifa's bustling port. Midway down the Persian Garden, cypress sentries saluted a rose-gold dome enshrining the remains of 'Ali Muhammad Shirazi, messianic progenitor of the Bahá'í religion. Beyond, the glittering shoreline arched like a scimitar toward the medieval Christian stronghold of Acre. Further north, a mantle of cumulonimbus threatened thunderstorms over the sectarian schizophrenia of Lebanon.

A gentle sea breeze fluttered like sensual fingers through Shlomo's loose shirt as he spotted a raven-haired woman by the wrought iron gate just below the balcony. Approaching close enough to smell her musky vanilla scent, he dropped the shopping bag beside the woman's wedge-heeled sandal and watched her smile obliquely.

"*Ma koreh, Giraffe* [What's happening, Giraffe]?"

"*Akol tov, Akrav* [It's all good, Scorpion]." He slipped a packet of Noblesse cigarettes from his shirt pocket and tapped one out for her. During military service, everyone smoked them in the field. The ritual was Shlomo's nod to their shared past.

Scorpion held the cigarette between her lips. Shlomo flicked his Zippo while eyeing a band of olive skin with a gold navel piercing exposed between her black tank top and white chinos.

She tapped the shopping bag with a polished toenail. "Gershon Bram. I like your taste."

"I know *yours*." Expensive shoes were her guilty pleasure.

"Holiday's going to ask the PM for a green light to run Grass Widow on Wild Boar," Shlomo said. "But after your unscheduled visit to Ukraine, he wants me to tighten your reins." He lit his own smoke, squinted down at her and exhaled through his raptor-like nose. "Consider them tightened."

Beneath Scorpion's thick bangs, wide sunglasses hid her eyes, making it difficult for Shlomo to focus on anything but a plump cherry mouth pouting above her angular jawline and a distracting décolletage that swelled with each breath.

"You know, I so appreciate a *katsa* who watches my back instead of my boobs." Scorpion blew a playful stream of smoke up at him.

Shlomo suppressed a laugh and motioned toward the shopping bag between them. Instead of fashionista footwear, the sack contained two twist-tied manila envelopes and a gray carbon fiber tube, 33-centimeters long, with a screw top. "I had one of our techs run a digital analysis on that document. He says there's something else written below the script on the surface. Hard copies of his scans are in the envelope, but he hasn't got the bandwidth to trace it to a source right now. No small task, apparently."

"I have someone in mind."

"*Sayan** or civilian?"

"Civilians make better cover."

Shlomo shook his head. A *kidon*† was expected to maintain a low profile, but this one made a habit of pushing the envelope way beyond postal regulations.

"Wild Boar is a fucking psychopath," he reminded her.

---

* *Sayan* [Assistant]—someone recruited from the international Jewish Diaspora community to work covertly with Mossad
† *Kidon* [Bayonet]—a deep-cover operative of the *Komemiute* [Combatants], a unit of Mossad's *Metsada* [Fortress] division that conducts special operations, kidnappings and targeted assassinations

"Just my type."

Shlomo leaned into her. "Listen to me. *I'm* calling the plays, understood? You follow operational protocols. No improvising. Any civilians you involve are potential liabilities. We clear on this?"

Scorpion lifted her sunglasses, propped them on top of her head and brushed strands of fine black hair off her cheek. Gazing up at Shlomo with ingenuous amber eyes, she smiled at his earnestness. The gambit probably worked well on most men, but Shlomo knew too much about her, a lot more than her shopping habits. He knew what Scorpion was capable of doing. He knew what *really* happened at that wedding banquet in Amman.

Her white-tipped fingernail gently prodded his chest where the curly hairs peeked out above the top button of his Kahala shirt. "You know I'll get the job done, Giraffe."

Scorpion crushed the lipstick stained cigarette beneath her cork heel and lifted the shopping bag with two fingers. "And you can inform Holiday that the Colonel in Kyiv will not present a security problem."

"Meaning?"

She threw a final rejoinder over her shoulder like a pinch of salt. "I've heard Balkan tobacco is contaminated with all sorts of nasty stuff these days. Probably fallout from Chernobyl."

Shlomo watched Scorpion ascend the marble steps as the setting sun painted her receding silhouette with a rosy hue.

"*Shabbat Shalom,*" he muttered to her lingering scent, shivering at the thought of what Scorpion might do if she were ever really angry.

....

SONYA STEPPED OUT OF HER SHOWER and briskly toweled her wet hair into a spiky flaxen crown. The expensive wig she wore for assignations with her *katsa* was uncomfortable on hot summer nights, a small annoyance offset by the naughty pleasure she took in playing *bat leveyha*, an agent-escort her macho colleagues crudely referred to as a "swallow." Sonya found the soft-core, dress-up performance art an amusing counterpoint to her usual professional role as *jada'it*, a woman tough enough to compete with men when push came to shove. So, when those arrogant bad boys joked about her sexual orientation, Sonya just smiled and kept them guessing.

Massaging her scalp, Sonya stood naked in front of the bathroom mirror, surveying her body as if it were a topo map. She inspected her muscle tone and flattened her fingers against the gold piercing in her navel. Lifting her breasts, she frowned. Weight training and Krav Magá had kept her body ripped, but in another five years she would require reduction surgery, just as her mother had. Sonya had to smile at the irony. In her profession, tits worked better than a taser on most of men she had to deal with.

Except for Giraffe.

Shlomo Levi had always been an anomaly. Cute, in a boyish way and a bit of a nerd. But at least he smelled good. Like chocolate. Sonya enjoyed testing how far she could push her *katsa* before he pushed back. She recalled the time he had briefed her on an operation in the parking lot at Stella Maris. A group of unidentified civilians had wandered too close so she decided to run a *maulter*—an unplanned security contingency—by giving Giraffe a hand-job in the front seat of his Audi to authenticate her cover.

Only time she ever saw him lose his cool. Or break a sweat.

Acting and casual sex came easily to her, and was so much less complicated than falling for someone. Besides, Sonya had no time for a romantic relationship when her country was under siege by fanatics who exploited their own peoples' misery. That reality informed not only her work, it shaped her world view, her *weltanschauung*, to

borrow one of those Kraut philosophical terms her mother had
bandied about with liberal friends at peacenik fundraisers.

Sonya's pre-9/11 life was locked away in the same repository
of memories as her childhood in Leningrad, another sweet dream
from which she had been rudely awakened when those towers in
Manhattan came crashing down. The only remnant of Russia was
her mother's *dreidel* collection, displayed on the narrow glass shelves
tucked into an alcove of Sonya's living room. She had pulled them out
of storage during Chanukah last year, her small attempt to reconnect
with a tradition her mother had abandoned for peace protests. The
little four-sided spinning disks, diamonds, boxes, and pyramids were
made of sterling silver with intricate filigree, ceramic, wood or brass
inlaid with blue and white *cloisonné*. The ones called *sevivon* were
emblazoned with a Hebrew acronym that meant: "A great miracle
happened here." She smiled at the memory of Golda Meir's quip
about Moses having led "God's Chosen People" to the one spot in
the Middle East where there was no oil. Some miracle.

Lifting her right leg with a dancer's precision, Sonya rested it on
the bathroom sink, pumped lotion into her palm and smoothed it
along her muscled calf. Like her father, she had been a competitive
runner, until the breasts she inherited from her mother had gotten
in the way of sports.

She could have written a book about her mother's eccentricities,
but her father remained a mystery, just another missing soldier in
a war no one wanted to remember. When Maryna learned the KGB
had classified his disappearance, she feared for her own security.
Despite all the talk about *glasnost*, her mother knew all too well how
precarious it was for even a secular Jew to remain in Russia. Taking
advantage of Gorbachev's open window, they had arrived in Haifa
just in time to celebrate Sonya's 11th birthday.

She remembered sunlit walks through the HaEm Garden with her 80-year-old great uncle, Reuven, and his compelling stories about the founding of Eretz Yisrael. Barely a thousand Jews had lived in the Turkish-controlled port of Haifa at the end of the 19th century, he told her. The *Harat al-Yahud*—Jewish Quarter—expanded up the northern slope of Mount Carmel with the first and second *aliyah* from Eastern Europe and Russia. Reuven had come in on the second wave. As hard as it was in Palestine, it beat the hell out of pogroms in Minsk, he assured her with a rasping, tobacco scented laugh.

Trained as an emergency room physician, her mother quickly found work at the B'nai Zion Medical Center. Two years later, Maryna bought a small flat on Sha'ar Halevanon with a stunning view of the Mediterranean coastline to the north. On a clear day Sonya could see as far as the green hills of Lebanon. Uncle Reuven had told her the people there hated Jews, She wondered why.

Sonya had an aptitude for languages. She learned Belarusian and Ukrainian from her mother, Yiddish from Reuven and picked up Hebrew from her neighbors in Haifa. In school, she mastered proper English, salted with American trash talk, and conversations with her schoolmates became a linguistic mash-up of international colloquialisms. Maryna always encouraged her to integrate into Haifa's homogeneous Levantine culture. So, by the time Sonya was 14, she could speak Arabic like a street vendor.

During the first *intifada*, Haifa remained an open and mostly tolerant city. Influenced by her mother's politics, Sonya had sympathized with the Palestinians—as much as any blonde Russian Jew could. But the liberal worldview Maryna instilled in her shifted radically with military service.

Patrolling the streets of Jerusalem in fatigues, a Galil assault rifle slung over her shoulder, Sonya watched an impenetrable wall rise

between her and the Arabs who hustled a meager livelihood in the
souq near Damascus Gate. Even though she spoke their language,
their eyes always reminded her that she would never understand
their resentment.

During her 28-month stint in the Israeli Defense Force, Sonya
acquired skills her mother would have considered abhorrent. Firing
an M89SR sniper rifle and watching its 7.62-millimeter rounds
punch through a target at 400 meters had aroused her in a curious
way. She later read in one of Maryna's medical journals that shooting a firearm can excite the same neurotransmitters in the brain as a
passionate kiss. Sonya found the gun a more predictable thrill.

Deployed at 18 to the West Bank, her linguistic talent had been
an asset to AMAN, IDF's intelligence wing. In Hebron, still seething
three years after the Purim uprising that followed an American
settler's mass-murder of 29 Palestinians in the mosque,* Sonya's
fluency in Arabic proved useful at "Stalk," Aman Unit 504's secret
interrogation facility. She learned to play good cop/bad cop with
al-Qassam† prisoners, track the movements of HAMAS operatives
from the rooftops and even read their lips through her rifle scope.

It was the bird woman in Khan Yunis that finally asphyxiated any
moral ambivalence Sonya retained from her mother's liberal politics.
She felt not the slightest remorse when an Apache helicopter rammed
Hellfire missiles down the throat of some monster who had sent a
child *shahid* [witness] across the Green Line strapped into a vest
sewn with ball-bearing-packed pipe bombs. But this woman with
the birds seemed different, the loving way she handled, fed and spoke

* **Purim Uprising:** In February 1994, Baruch Goldstein, an American physician and follower of
Brooklyn zealot, Meir Kahane, entered the Masjid Ibrahimi—built over the Cave of the Patriarchs
in Hebron—opened fire with two assault rifles, killed 29 Muslims in prayer and wounded 125.
Survivors beat Goldstein to death and a bloody uprising ensued in the West Bank.
† **Al-Qassam** [*Izz ad-Din al-Qassam*]—military branch of HAMAS [*Haqamat al-Muqamah al-
Islamiyya*], an offshoot of the Egyptian Muslim Brotherhood, co-founded by Shaykh Ahmed Yassin.

softly to them, from what Sonya could see perched above the city streets. Yes, she was one of Yassin's soldiers, dedicated to the obliteration of Sonya's adopted country, but there was something about the bird woman—something unexpectedly human—that made Sonya hesitate to follow her "intercept" instinct.

Her hesitation had cost two callow IDF soldiers their lives when they stopped to admire the woman's birdcage and failed to notice her moving for cover. After her Semtex-packed cage cratered the street, the soldier's scattered remains had to be scraped off the walls and cobblestones by a ZAKA* team, then carried away in plastic bags for a reverent burial while Sonya watched helplessly through her scope. In a moment of impotent remorse, she had cried for those birds.

Never again would she make a mistake like that, finally certain that the only way to prevail against ideological fanatics was to become more ruthless than they were.

Sonya pulled a white T-shirt over her head and finger-combed the spikes out of her hair before walking barefoot into her kitchen. She plugged an electric kettle into the outlet, brewed a cup of Russian Caravan tea and carried it into her living room where tall windows framed the lights of Haifa's port below. She never closed her curtains.

Maryna had adored the sleek, modernist leather furniture of Mies van der Rohe and Le Corbusier, on which no one was ever comfortable sitting. It was her mother's way of reminding herself—and everyone else—never to get too comfortable in life. Despite Sonya's concession to an overstuffed IKEA sofa, she had taken Maryna's lesson to heart.

Contentment was not in her vocabulary.

---

* ZAKA [*Zihuy Korbanot Aso*]—Disaster Victim Identification, Orthodox Jews that assist ambulance crews with first aid and clean-up of human remains after a terrorist attack or natural disaster

Following the intensity of military service, Sonya had craved the rush of adrenaline to avoid what seemed to her like a black hole of existential despair. At first, she channeled her manic energy into academics. At the University of Haifa, she focused on *Arab-Israeli Relations* and *Political Economy of the Middle East* with the same laser-like discipline she had applied to breaking down and cleaning her G'lilon carbine blindfolded. However, attempting to rationalize—let alone *understand*—the incessant conflict between Abraham's progeny proved to be as boring as it was impossible. A new class, *Terrorism and Responses*, bypassed the labyrinthine "why" and went straight to the pragmatic "what now?"

A classmate and former AMAN comrade with a penchant for Russian history had re-purposed her future. Sonya found the tall, gangly Shlomo Levi brilliant and oddly attractive, perhaps because she also felt like a social misfit. They dated for a while, Russian movies followed by tepid sex in his tiny apartment, but fucking Shlomo was never as interesting as listening to his frequent political rants. One particular diatribe she remembered as a watershed moment.

"Did they teach you about the Okhrana in Saint Petersburg?" Shlomo had asked while idly drumming his plastic dining utensils against the cafeteria table.

She lit her hand-rolled cigarette. "You mean Leningrad?"

Shlomo laughed. "In case your memory needs jogging, the Okhrana—Czar's secret police—were the bastards that converted an obscure novel into *Protocols of the Learned Elders of Zion*. A Russian Orthodox priest published it as non-fiction in 1905, and the Okhrana circulated it as a transcript from some 'top-secret' rabbinical conferences dedicated to exterminating Christians, then used it to incite their pogroms. Hitler quoted from it to grease the wheels of his Final Solution. The *Protocols* were exposed as a forgery decades ago, but that piece of shit is still used by imams and mullahs to justify the destruction of Israel. You can buy the fucking thing on Amazon."

Shlomo drank Coca Cola all day long, and his caffeine-fueled rhetoric made up for the passion he lacked elsewhere. She wanted to laugh at him, but instead had squinted through her tobacco smoke with disdain, the way her liberal mother would have done.

"Idiots will believe anything, Shlomo. What's your point?"

He stopped drumming and leaned into her with fire in his brown eyes. "That this is never going to stop, Sonya. Until *we* stop it! Until every Jew stands up and says, '*Never again!*' Despite their attempts at political correctness, the rest of the world still thinks we control every fucking government, bank and media conglomerate. They think we killed Jesus, have horns and drink children's blood. And when push comes to shove, when it comes down to a choice between Sa'udi oil or a secure Jewish state, where do you think our so-called allies will ultimately stand?"

She considered that for a few seconds before responding with a sarcasm that masked genuine alarm. "And what exactly do you suggest I do about all that, *poputchik* [fellow traveler]?"

"Thought you'd never ask," her future *katsa* had replied, and ten years had sped by in a wild blur she could never have anticipated.

Tucking her legs into the sofa's cushions, Sonya opened one of the envelopes Shlomo had given her. It contained a dossier on Viktor Volodymyr Kaban. In Ukrainian, his surname meant "wild boar," so some Institute analyst had thought it clever to assign him that as a code name. Scanning Kaban's profile, Sonya decided the moniker was aptly chosen. An INTERPOL mug shot, taken when Kaban was arrested in Milan five years ago for soliciting prostitutes, showed a pig-like nose dominating a puffy face and short brown hair bristling like a razorback. His cold eyes seemed only capable of intimidation.

When the USSR dissolved in the early 1990s, Ukraine found itself with a stockpile of unsecured weapons that had been abandoned by the Second Soviet Army. Economic chaos quickly led to partnerships between freelance arms merchants and unpaid army officers who plundered a weapons surplus intended for a force of 800,000. While most international arms sales are legal transactions between corporate entities and nation states, "gray" brokers profited handsomely by selling weapons illegally to regimes under international embargoes, or to the insurgents fighting them.

Viktor Kaban was one of those gray dealers. He had shipped inventory through Turkey to Sarajevo and Kosovo, covered his tracks with complex financial transactions, bribed customs inspectors and produced bogus end-user certificates with false destinations for his cargo. But he attempted to circumvent the wrong corrupt official in Saint Petersburg while learning the ropes. For that breech of etiquette, Wild Boar spent two years in Kresty prison, where he was rewarded with the *v krugu vorov*, a half black, half white circle tattooed on his ring finger, his seal of approval by the *Vory v Zakone* — "Thieves-in-Law." The Russian mafia apparently liked his *chutzpah*.

Wild Boar's prison stint at Kresty opened lucrative doors. He began smuggling weapons to Sierra Leone in exchange for "blood diamonds," and as a result of his new *vory* connections, Kaban's business expanded into New York. He established himself with the Russian-Jewish scions of Brooklyn and bought an opulent condo in Brighton Beach. As one of the many wealthy Ukrainian expats who could prove Jewish heritage, he also claimed Israeli citizenship, refurbished a medieval apartment building in Yafo, and pumped a lot of shekels into Jewish charities to legitimize his public status.

In private, Viktor Kaban had an erratic temper and a sizable appetite for cocaine and vodka. He liked rough sex with prostitutes, sometimes beat them up when he was high, and was suspected of having brutally murdered several informants with his bare hands. The US State Department and CIA looked the other way because Wild Boar, and others like him, quietly filled the vacuum created by the official prohibition against doing business with Russia's military export office, Rosoboronexport. SHABAK* also tolerated his business activities, until he sold some Katyushas to a broker with ties to Damascus. That earned him a slot on the Institute's Red Page, their euphemistic "negative treatment" list. However, because of his preferential Israeli citizenship, Kaban would have to be "intercepted" quietly, in a way that would not implicate Sonya's employer.

She tossed Kaban's dossier onto her coffee table and reached for the second envelope. It contained a sheaf of black and white digital prints made from the vellum Colonel Pashkovsky had thoughtlessly sent to her mother, that mottled scrap of hide on which her father had scrawled his last declaration of loyalty to a comrade that had thrown him to the wolves.

Sonya appreciated irony more than the Colonel knew. One bit she had neglected to mention was that traces of the radioactive metallic element ^{210}PO had been found in cigarettes for years, possibly the tobacco industry's dirtiest little secret. Increasing the curies by a factor of 10,000 or so resulted in a much quicker death than the old Cossack bastard deserved. The Technion "ghoul" that fashioned those lethal smokes and the shielded tin in which Sonya had transported them, told her a single dust mote of Polonium-210 was 250 million times more toxic than cyanide and had a radionuclide that became undetectable in only 138 days. It had to be ingested or inhaled because its alpha particle could not penetrate the skin. Best of all, there was no antidote. Ironic indeed.

* SHABAK [Sherut ha-Bitachon ha-Klali]—Israeli Security Agency. Shin Bet is the short form.

Sonya examined the Multi-Spectral Imaging print-outs Giraffe had given her. A palimpsest, they had determined: the translucent, mottled vellum had been scraped clean and written over many centuries ago, probably somewhere in what is now Afghanistan. But in order to determine exactly where her father had found it, she needed to have the manuscript translated and analyzed by an expert. As talented as her ghouls were, they did not have those special skills.

Fortunately, Sonya knew someone who did.

She unscrewed the carbon fiber tube, extracted the 20-by-25-centimeter square of vellum, the color of old ivory, and picked up a pair of sharp fabric scissors. Carefully, she cut off a narrow strip on which her father's last message had been scratched, rolled it tightly and slipped it into an empty lipstick tube. The rest, she returned to its safe container.

Sonya carried her tea to the teak writing desk in her bedroom, flipped open a thin laptop and Googled Harvard Divinity School's Alumni Association, logging in as a member of the class of 2001. Locating the name and address she wanted, Sonya searched her desk drawer for a box of A4 stationary. E-mail and phone calls left electronic trails, but handwritten letters had only a postmark to identify them. She picked up the slim Mont Blanc fountain pen her mother had treasured, cleaned its golden nib with a damp tissue and snapped a fresh ink cartridge into the barrel.

Sonya's hand hesitated over the watermarked sheet, butterflies fluttering in her stomach as she remembered his face. Considering how she left things eight years ago, he had every reason in the world *not* to respond. But then, he could never resist a mystery.

Dear Danny, Sonya began. *You were probably not expecting to ever hear from me again…*

....

REVEREND DANIEL CALLAN, SJ watches the steeple of Dunster House salute the rising sun. Wearing faded Boston College swim trunks and a gray sleeveless T-shirt, Danny waits on the sloping quay of the Weld Boathouse in oblique morning sunlight as Carl Keogh selects a key from the crowded ring chained to his belt.

Carl flips the brim of his Red Sox cap backward to avoid hitting his head on one of the jutting oar riggers inside the bay, then sniffs the air as if he is sampling its barometric pressure.

"Gonna' be wicked hot today, Father. Thunderstorms comin' in later, though. Good mornin' to be out there on the Chuck."

Danny follows Carl into the boathouse through a red brick archway where racks of sleek sculls hang like medieval weaponry. He strokes a black carbon fiber hull and whistles softly.

"Whose Fluid Design?"

"Bert Peterson's," Carl selects a pair of composite oars for him from the rack. "He was racin' singles last weekend against Newell. Caught a crab, and nearly broke a fuckin' rib. What a 'pissa, eh?"

"Ol' Chowderhead should leave his stock portfolio on the dock when he races," Danny laughs as he unhooks the padded sling from a yellow Emacher K12 racing single. He hoists the 34-pound wing-rigger by the gunwales, balances its sliding seat on his head and carries his scull down to the edge of the Charles. Kicking off his Tevas, he slips an oar into the dockside lock, tightens down the screw nut and swings into the molded seat, both oar grips secure in his left hand. Danny tucks his feet into Velcro shoes fixed to the foot-board then pushes away from the dock. He squares his blades, digs his legs and back into a long stroke, feathers his oars and listens to the flats skitter over shimmering green water. A few more pulls and his Emacher slips silently into deep shadow beneath the Anderson Bridge. Its granite arch hangs over him like the memories he has never been able to shake.

Danny knew he was in dangerous waters, even as he recited the liturgy from his Breviary that morning. Every year on the Feast of Saint Thomas the Apostle, he remembers Reverend Dominic diDesio, the chain-smoking priest at Saint Mary's who called him "Doubtin' Danny." Inspired early on by Descartes' methodological skepticism and Diderot's assertion that incredulity is "the first step toward philosophy," the first targets on which Danny trained his incredulous sites were the Jesuits who tried to sell him on their dogma. Rather than slapping him down, "Father Dee" had encouraged his questions and challenged him to take the gloves off.

"Our walls have stood against attack for two millennia," Father Dee once assured him as he lit an unfiltered Pall Mall. "You think you're the only punk who ever doubted the Faith?"

During "Jesuit boot camp" at Boston College and his Novitiate at Weston, Danny's doubts crystallized into certitude as he devoured the soul-searching of other rebellious punks like Augustine of Hippo and Thomas Aquinas, brilliant minds that had meticulously sorted through their own doubts and constructed an intellectual fortress around Church doctrine. Danny took refuge in *De Civitate Dei* and *Summa Theologica*, found comfort in the notion that some part of him was eternally safe and secure.

Then came his doctorate at Harvard Divinity School and a teaching position at the Center for the Study of World Religions, where a singularly distracting member of the student body had pushed him right back to the brink of doubt.

"Want to make God laugh?" Father Dee had chided through a cloud of smoke. "Tell Him you've got your life all mapped out."

God, Danny discovered, will be quick to remind you that you are still a punk-ass Southie with a long way to go before you can call yourself a spiritual warrior.

Then, just to prove it, He will throw you one hell of a curve.

....

THE FINAL DAY OF THE 2000 Head of the Charles Regatta was October 22nd, an unseasonably warm Sunday afternoon. Danny, who first pulled an oar at Boston College in the 1993 New England Championships, placed in the top five for Club Singles on Saturday and he was feeling cocky, showing off his Dot Ave colors to those "Barneys" from the People's Republic of Cambridge. Sunday was the main event: Directors' Challenge, Quads-Men. 26 teams put in at DeWolfe and Danny pulled the 5000-meter course with the *Canonical Four*, his master's crew from Harvard Divinity. His boat tucked into the tight Eliot Bridge turn at just under 14 minutes, placing the

C-4 in second position for the finish. Twenty meters downstream from the Cambridge Boat Club, a black Vespoli, manned by the aptly named *Wrecking Crew*, cut his bow and everybody went swimming.

The tall blonde girl stood out in the crowd on the boat house lawn as Danny washed up on the beach. It was impossible not to notice her. Or her laughter.

At the traditional post-race ripper on the old boat club's upper deck, the smell of grilling hamburgers and spilled beer hung in the Indian summer afternoon. The tall girl parted the crowd carrying two red plastic cups of Sam Adams. Females usually made Danny uncomfortable, but this one set off every fire alarm in the building. Her shoulder-length mane of loose golden curls was back-lit in late afternoon sun, and she approached him the way a lioness courts its mate before playfully sinking her teeth into his throat. Danny became an ice-sculpture when she handed him one of her beers, wary but fascinated by the probing intelligence immediately apparent in her amber eyes.

"Boys are so predictable," she told him.

"Say what?"

"You could have avoided that collision, you know."

She was obviously not American. Her accent sounded proper English and her sentences ended in a period rather than a question mark. The girl wore a Navy-blue hoodie, zipped in front, but not high enough to cover the plunge of a distracting white bikini top, and khaki shorts covering very little of her runner's legs.

"And I'll bet I can tell you exactly what was going through your head the moment those guys cut you off."

"Take your best shot."

She leaned close to his ear, close enough for Danny to smell the musky fragrance of afternoon sun and vanilla body lotion on her skin. "Ramming speed!" she said, her mouth opening into a perfect white smile as she emitted that same laugh he had heard on the beach. It was the sound of delight in life's unpredictable serendipity.

"*Exactly* what I would have been thinking," she added. "Should have been born a boy, I guess."

"That would have been such a waste," Danny replied before he could stop himself.

Her sharp nose crinkled as the irises of her eyes turned golden in reflected light from the Charles. "*L'chaim!*" She touched the rim of her cup to his. "I'm in your class at CSWR. *Culture and Faith in Central Asia.*"

Danny slapped his forehead in embarrassment. "Sorry. Didn't recognize you out of context." He extended a hand. "Danny."

She took it with a firm, boyish shake. "Sonya." But there was nothing masculine in the way her wide eyes assessed him. "So, in addition to a back-handed compliment master, you're a Jesuit priest."

"Novice, actually." Feeling exposed, Danny cleared his throat. "I'm at HDS on a fellowship. 'Proto-Indo-Aryan Languages and the Collision of Eastern and Western Spiritual Traditions Along the Silk Road.'"

Sonya nodded earnestly. "Yes, collision is obviously something at which you excel, Professor."

Danny laughed as a phalanx of burly jocks pushed through the noisy crowd, splashing beer on his dingy canvas bobos.

"Mind if I ask a personal question?" She didn't wait for him to protest. "What does a Catholic priest—sorry...novice—find so fascinating about Indo-Aryans?"

"What a relief! I thought you were going to ask if I'm gay."

Sonya's mouth parted as her eyes probed his. "That never crossed my mind. It's obvious what you like, but...not what you want."

Danny felt the sweat rolling down his side. "Guess I'm not as transparent as I look."

"Transparency is not the same as clarity, Professor." Sonya held his uneasy gaze. "What we want…and feel…can be misinterpreted."

"Then let's strive for clarity."

"Agreed." Sonya shook his hand and held on to it. "Would it be misinterpreted if I invited a man of the cloth to my birthday party?"

Danny glanced down at their hands and she let go.

"I'm right off Arsenal Square," she said. "Won't be a big crowd. No presents."

He took a sip of beer to wet his dry throat. "Date?"

"I was hoping."

Danny's face flushed. "I mean, *what day* is your birthday?"

"The 31st." Sonya's calculating eyes sparkled like warm honey. "Sorry, I'm being wicked, aren't I?"

"I'd expect that from someone born on Halloween."

....

THERE WAS NO CROWD and no birthday party at the graduate students' housing on Garden Street. Only Sonya wearing a provocative black dress and waving two tickets for the Boston Ballet. She even paid the cab fare.

Danny was completely out of his league. He had never been to a ballet performance, and was surprised to find himself almost as captivated by Balanchine's choreography as he was intoxicated by the smell of Sonya's hair and the scent of vanilla on her skin.

After the performance, they walked from the Wang Center to Teatro, where Danny insisted on paying for dinner even though he could not afford it. Seated in a banquette near the open, bustling kitchen, Sonya informed the waiter with exaggerated sophistication,

"I'm twenty-one today, so let's have some wine. Do you have anything from the Golan? No? Something French then."

Sipping Coteaux du Languedoc, reminiscences about her childhood in Russia competed with clattering dishes and random conversations caroming off the marble walls and vaulted ceiling.

"It was called Leningrad in those days, you know, and the winters
lasted for-*eeeevvver!* My mother used to take me to the Kirov Ballet.
Stunning productions of *Flames of Paris* and *Fountain of Bakhchisarai*.
I just adored Pushkin, imagined how wonderful it would be to dance
like Zakharova. That was when I was still a skinny little girl."

"Hard to imagine."

"Once upon a time," she glanced coquettishly over the rim of her
glass. "Mother and I emigrated to Israel when I was ten."

"She was divorced?"

"A widow," Sonya's eyes plunged into her wine glass but quickly
emerged to change the subject. "Were you in the army?" she asked
brightly. "*I* was in the army. Compulsory service, you know. Only
a couple years ago, I was carrying a big rifle and marching every
morning with a platoon of girls in Jerusalem. I liked shopping the
Arab section. Good produce, but you have to really bargain for it."

"I know," Danny replied. "I spent a month there last summer, at
the Studium Biblicum."

"Isn't that the place they call 'Flagellation Monastery'?"

"Not a very inviting name, is it?" Danny forced a laugh but felt
himself slipping into a reminiscence she had set in motion. "Both my
father and brother served in the Marine Corps. I broke with tradition
when I enlisted in a different branch of service."

"Feeling radical, were you?" Sonya's gleeful laughter told him
the wine was taking effect. "Why didn't you join the SEALs or something? You look fit enough."

"I knew I could never kill anyone."

She suddenly grew serious. "Sometimes, you have no choice."

"I don't believe that."

Sonya tapped her dinner knife against the tabletop, tension exaggerating the dimples in her jaw. "Well, why don't you ask your father and brother about that?"

Danny took a long sip of the red wine and drew a slow breath, looked straight into Sonya's eyes and answered with restraint. "My brother, Pete, was stationed in Beirut. One of the casualties of the barracks' explosion in '83." Danny's voice wavered and his eyes closed. "Pop just couldn't let it go. I think he was eaten up by guilt for not having been there to save his number one. Didn't seem to care much what happened to number two after that. Eventually drank himself to death like so many other emotionally wounded warriors."

Danny paused to meet Sonya's challenging eyes in the candlelight. "Short of suicide, we don't get to choose how we die. But we always have a choice about how we live."

"Is that why you decided to become a priest?"

"Look, I was 13 years old, angry as hell," he admitted. "I tried to keep it in the boxing ring but ended up bringing it to the street. There was a priest who saw I was about to skid. Tough little dago from SoBro." He laughed at his unintended slang. "That's South Brookline."

Then Danny told her about Father Dee, who pulled no punches and never glossed over the uncomfortable truth about religious conflict, from the "Holy Crusades" to the sectarian slaughter in Beirut. Father Dee gave Danny some context for his brother's death. He spoke with hagiographic reverence about Ignacio de Loyola, the Basque knight who founded the Society of Jesus. Inspired by Francis of Assisi's writings while recovering from crippling battle wounds at Pamplona, "Iñigo" lived the rest of his life as an exemplary instrument of peace, an embodiment of the spiritual warrior. Father Dee taught Danny a lot about warriorship, that anger will take you down quicker than fear, and that the toughest struggles are always the ones you have with yourself.

Sonya listened attentively and by the time he had finished, her eyes were ignited by passion and wine. "That all sounds very noble, Danny, but let's face it: your brother died because a Muslim that also considered himself a 'spiritual warrior' thought he could buy his way into heaven by killing a slew of Christian infidels."

"Point taken. What better reason to devote my life to peace?"

"You sound so like my mother," Sonya bristled. "But over here you have that luxury, don't you? Some people have to fight every damn day for survival. Americans talk a lot about peace but you just don't understand what it's like to have your backs to the sea. Canadians and Mexicans aren't trying to wipe you off the map."

"Okay, truce!" Danny forced a grin, raised both his hands in surrender. "I didn't mean to drop a bomb on your birthday dinner. Let's sidestep the geopolitics and order some food, shall we?"

She sipped her wine, sighed deeply. "I'm sorry, Danny. I grew up reading both Dostoevsky and Wiesel. For a Russian Jew, looking on the 'sunny side' of life is no easy task."

He laughed when her fingers drew air-quotes around the cliché.

"Even an Irish Catholic finds it hard sometimes…*Sonny*."

"Oh, I don't doubt *that*." Amused by her new moniker, Sonya's face dimpled into that deliciously wicked smile, the sensuous shape his torment would assume from that moment on.

Danny blushed at his unintended double entendre and buried his embarrassment in the menu. "More wine, please."

After dessert, a Metro cab dropped them at the south end of the Anderson Bridge, where under-lit arches reflected onto the Charles like luminous footprints. They strolled onto the bridge's sidewalk, bantered about baseball and classmates she found obnoxious. Music from Halloween parties in Cambridge blended with the white noise of traffic on Soldiers Field Road.

At mid-span, cool air rose up from the river, a reminder they were only hours away from November. Danny paused to lean against the granite balustrade as Sonya hugged her bare shoulders. She balanced unsteadily on her high heels as he removed his wool blazer and laid it over her shoulders, allowing his hands to rest a moment too long—long enough for her to pivot gracefully and nestle against his chest. He felt her breathe deeply and her breasts swell against his solar plexus as she looked up at him with ingenuous eyes, her smell overpowering his sense of purpose and discipline. Pretending that neither of them knew what both were thinking, Danny began to feel his heartbeat entraining with hers. His face felt hot and his mouth dry.

"I promised myself I wouldn't kiss you," he heard himself say.

Sonya took his left hand between both of hers. "Funny, I was just thinking that kissing is actually more intimate than sex," she confided. "Offering your mouth…the very portal of your survival to someone. It's an immense act of trust, don't you think?"

"Or would you say…faith?" Sonya looked up at him, her playful smile a sensual counterpoint to the gravity of her words. "We definitely shouldn't kiss…" Her eyes held his in anticipation.

"Definitely," Danny replied, listening to the word shatter into meaningless syllables as Sonya took his thumb into her wet mouth and sucked it, her lips and tongue gently ministering to the fighting scars of his youth and lost innocence.

DANNY SHOULD HAVE SEEN IT COMING. Or maybe he had.

Thinking back on that night, watching his self-righteous moral resolve crumble like an old church missal, Danny remembers hearing very clearly in his head, like a distant Gregorian Chant, the tortured prayer Saint Augustine of Hippo wrote in his *Confessiones* 1,600 years ago:

Lord, grant me chastity and continence—but not yet.

....

CARLTON CHIN IS SLUMPED into a knock-off Barcelona chair near the reception desk at Massachusetts Institute of Technology's Bioinstrumentation Engineering Analysis and Microscopy Laboratory, deep into a tortilla wrap and Mango Bebida from the Mexicali Burrito Company on the BEAM Lab's ground floor. Emerging from a security elevator Cyrus introduces Danny and Sonya to the hungry post-doc.

The hipster engineer confesses he had been planning to spend the long Independence Day weekend crunching on a Fluorescence Spectrophotometry paper for the *American Journal of Physiology*, until Cyrus called with an unusual request sweetened by an irresistible bribe.

"Sox versus Mariners." Cyrus slaps two tickets to Fenway into Carlton's outstretched palm.

Danny shakes his head gravely. "Hernandez is pitching for Seattle tonight, and Ichiro's on a 27-game hitting streak. Where's the Gator when you need him?"

"Seriously bad news for the Dominicans," Carlton daubs *pico de gallo* from the MIT identification badge dangling on a lanyard around his neck. "Francona should activate that Japanese pitcher he optioned last March. Wakefield can't carry it all by himself."

The young engineer's eyes are cartoon large behind his titanium-framed glasses as he appraises Sonya's sleeveless V-neck tee. "Sooo… where's our specimen?"

Sonya holds up the carbon fiber tube and flashes Carlton her girl-with-a-flat-tire-on-the-roadside smile.

"Let's have a look at that new EDAX," Cyrus impatiently checks his gold Rolex so everyone can admire it. He wears a striped dress shirt, casually rolled at the cuffs and tucked into crisp linen trousers. His shoes are real alligator and his belt matches. One of these days, Danny decides, he will ask Cyrus to take him shopping for a new black suit. He bought his last one at Banana Republic during the Clinton Administration. Not that it makes much difference, since he only wears it paired with a Roman collar and as seldom as possible. Poverty is a vow Danny always had less trouble with than obedience.

Or chastity for that matter.

Carlton leads them past glass cubicles with a view of the *Sim-City* landscape on Main Street, where tiny architectural-drawing poplars dot patches of green and separate one austere concrete slab from another. They thread a maze of office dividers and wall-mounted whiteboards covered with work-flow diagrams, then pass through a gray Formica kitchenette.

Carlton uses his key card on a door that opens into a window-less, air-conditioned room. He flips a light switch to reveal a vinyl table holding a CPU tower, LCD monitor, keyboard, digital printer, six stacked hard drives and a beige machine the size of a dorm room refrigerator. Above its vertically striated door, an access key and three buttons protrude from an inset electrical panel. A cylindrical red light emblazoned with the international radiation symbol glows beside its conical turret.

"Meet *Orbis*," Carlton introduces his new toy, pats its sloped roof as he turns the key.

"That cute little thing is an X-ray chamber?" Sonya asks.

Carlton snorts, bends over the PC keyboard and fires up his screen. "This bad boy's fitted with three collimators and a thirty-mic, ultra-high intensity poly-capillary. It's got video co-ax sampling *and* kicks ass at XFR micro-spot analysis."

"Sweet!" Sonya rolls her eyes at Danny, and sinks into a black ergonomic desk chair beside Carlton. Sonya crosses her legs and touches her fingertips together in a thoughtful bridge, tapping them against her lower lip. "Remind me again, what's a…collimator?"

Cyrus sees his opening. "It isn't possible to focus short wave-length radiation through lenses alone," he explains, employing his cupped left hand to simulate a lens. "So, a curved mirror is used to filter a stream of X-rays and allow only those traveling parallel to a specified direction through to the target." After posing as a beam simulation, his right hand comes to rest on her shoulder. Sonya's lips form an appreciative "O" and he winks condescendingly.

Carlton grasps both handles and opens the bay. Danny carefully removes the vellum from Sonya's tube and places it on the targeting panel as she peers over Carlton's shoulder. He lifts the catch on a 12- by 16-inch vacuum sample chamber, aligns it, resets the glass lid, clips it shut and gently guides the frame into a lead-lined cylindrical port in the machine's belly. Snapping the door shut, he presses the green button, slips back into his desk chair and begins to tap out commands on his keyboard. The soft whir of the precision-calibrated runners is followed by the hum of an optical scanner working its program.

"*Orbis* does Energy-Dispersive X-Ray Spectroscopy," Carlton explains. "When any periodic element gets zapped by a high-energy beam, it fluoresces, you know? Gives off a lower energy radiation. That's its signature. So, we'll do a step scan and digitally map your doc by progressively rastering an electron beam over one small area after another. In other words, we'll create a pixel-by-pixel image of its chemical elements."

"How long will it take to map?" Sonya asks.

Carlton leans back and finger-combs his streaked hair, leaving the cowlick standing at attention. "Resolution is determined by beam size and the relative response of each element is determined by how long the beam lingers, right? Wavelength-Dispersive Spectroscopy would give you a more detailed mapping, but EDS is *way* faster. Basically, you're trading quality for speed."

Sonya glances up at Cyrus. "That's so typical of men, isn't it?"

Danny suppresses a laugh as Cyrus slides his hand off Sonya's shoulder and feigns keen interest in the logarithmic intensity scale displaying elemental peaks and valleys on Carlton's screen.

A mortised square in the right corner shows a gray-scale X-ray image with a calligraphic stroke appearing lighter against a black background. Danny bends toward the LCD monitor as Carlton punches key commands adjusting the primary beam filters and the lighter pen stroke turns blood red. "There's your ferrous sulfate, bro."

"That would be the Ta'liq script," Danny confirms. "Iron gall ink. But the under-text hardly shows. Stronger potassium signature, you think?"

Carlton lifts his face toward the screen to get a better angle through his thick progressive lenses. He taps a few more commands. "We got sulfur...traces of hydrogen, chlorine, iridium, and...*whoa!* A butt-load of carbon."

"Can you filter for carbon density?" Danny asks.

Carlton's fingers tease out the older script that had been scraped off the vellum's surface centuries ago. A very different stroke begins to resolve in green against the negative background.

"I'll bet it's *masi!*" Danny's voice jumps an octave in excitement. "Burnt-bone bound with tar or pitch. Sometimes they used charred almond husks mixed with cow's urine."

Sonya's eyes reflect the green light from Carlton's monitor as she looks up at Danny.

"Who are 'they'?"

....

"REMEMBER THOSE GIANT STATUES the Taliban dynamited at Bamiyan?" Danny lifts a mug of reheated coffee from the microwave. Carlton, needing some time to work his digital alchemy without distraction, had shooed everyone into the kitchenette.

"Who could forget?" Sonya grimaces as she sniffs an open carton of milk she found in the refrigerator, replaces it quickly and opts to drink her Earl Gray black.

"They were carved by the Kushans," Danny says, "a confederation of five Indo-Aryan tribes that migrated from Western China into what's now northeastern Afghanistan. They absorbed the remnants of Alexander's army and the Persian population that had settled in the area, adopted the Greek language and Zoroastrian religion, then pushed south into Pakistan and conquered the Gandharan Empire. The fifth Kushan king, Kanishka, took a shine to Buddhism and had texts that were originally written in Gandhari Prakrit—a Middle Indo-Aryan dialect—translated into Sanskrit using Kharosthi script borrowed from the Persian Achaemenids."

Cyrus rummages through a basket of herbal tea bags. "You think this vellum is really Kushan, Danny boy?"

"Well, it's definitely Sanskrit, and the characters are Kharosthi, not Brahmi. One of the earliest ink manuscripts ever found is the Khotan *Dhammapada*, written around the 2nd century in Gandhari Prakrit with Kharosthi characters."

Cyrus appears skeptical. "But that was on birch bark, as I recall."

"Right, *bhojapatra*. Doesn't decay or decompose. That and a cool ground temperature is why the Gilgit Manuscript* survived so well. Do you remember that cache of documents discovered in clay pots on the southern edge of the Tarim Basin? They were written on *ajina*, a vellum made from antelope or tiger hide."

Cyrus leans back in his chair and whistles softly, "If this piece is from Kanishka's library, it could be worth a bloody fortune."

"Let's not jump to conclusions," Danny cautions. "First, I've got to figure out what it says. Then we'll know more about its origin."

Cyrus checks his expensive chronograph. "I've got some business to handle this afternoon. You working tonight on that translation?"

"That was my plan." Danny replies, sensing Cyrus' scheme.

"Excellent." Cyrus places a hand on Sonya's bare shoulder. "In the meantime, you and I have a dinner reservation at a trendy little spot on Mass Ave. Pick you up in front of your hotel at eight."

"How shall I dress?" Sonya asks, never taking her eyes off Danny.

Cyrus pauses at the hallway door, raises a Mephistophelian eyebrow and one corner of his silvery Van Dyke. "Surprise me, love."

---

* **The Gilgit Manuscript** was unearthed in 1931 at Napaur in Jammu-Kashmir. The box contained four sutras written in the 2nd century CE on birch bark in Pali, Sanskrit and Prakrit.

CURBING HIS BLACK 911 CARRERA S in front of the Sheraton Commander Hotel, Cyrus finds Sonya waiting impatiently beneath its red awning wearing her little black dress. The brushed silk fabric clings to her sleek figure and below the hemline, her long athletic legs cascade into spike-heeled pumps that ought to be registered as lethal weapons. Over the plunge of her spectacular cleavage, Cyrus notes a glittering amber pendant suspended on a silver chain. Sonya's short hair is fluffed and angelically back-lit by the marquee lights, bangs tousled across her forehead. A post-coital Joan of Arc, Cyrus muses while breathing an anticipatory prayer of thanks.

Sonya slips gracefully into his Porsche's beige leather seat. "You're five minutes late."

Cyrus pulls out onto Garden Street and accelerates. "Sorry, love. Mass Ave is a bitch tonight."

"Thought you had lots of experience."

"With Boston traffic?"

"Bitches."

Cyrus executes a double-take just in time to catch Sonya's red lips pursing wryly.

The Temple Bar opens onto the frenetic hum of Massachusetts Avenue. With Sonya towering at his side in her stilettos, Cyrus greets the hostess by name; then follows her metronomic bottom to a booth lit softly by a shaded table lamp and cooled by a Kipling-inspired ceiling fan. On the brick wall behind the semi-circular banquette, a mirror allows Cyrus to keep tabs on regulars crowding the copper bar. It amuses him to watch the black clad, young urban professionals sipping their Bee's Knees, Brass Monkeys, and Molokai Mules. Even more so because they rarely notice the impressionistic mural hanging above their heads as if it were mocking their pretentious social rituals.

As Sonya scans the menu, Cyrus casually rolls the cuffs of his Missoni dress shirt and orders drinks from the hunky waiter. "Ask Shane to make me a Ketel One Martini, two olives. Sonya?"

The young Latino wears a tight black T-shirt; his glistening hair is moussed to a peak and a trimmed soul patch accentuates his pout. Sonya assesses the waiter's biceps and asks demurely, "How are your Lemon Drops?"

"How do you like them?"

She smiles up at him. "Big and strong."

Cyrus makes a mental note to have Shane check the kid's green card. When the drinks come, he orders Sesame Ahi Tartare and Blue Hill Bay Mussels as starters, then scans the wine list. "A Sokol Blosser will pair nicely with those." Cyrus leans back, drapes his arm across the rolled lip of the banquette and watches Sonya's eyes appraise him over her pale-yellow drink.

"So…what's your story, Ms. Aronovsky?"

"Well, a steamy romance is always amusing, but I generally prefer non-fiction."

Cyrus forces a smile while rotating the stem of his martini glass in a puddle of ice melt. "Let me try a different approach…"

"Small talk, take two," Sonya smiles sweetly.

He enunciates slowly. "What exactly *is* your line of work?"

"Not unlike yours, Mister Narsai." Sonya crosses her legs giving him a better look at the cut of her calf muscles. "I arrange things for people. Broker deals. Antiquities mostly. Quite an inventory coming out of the Middle East these days."

Cyrus nods thoughtfully as his tongue hunts for something lodged in his teeth. "And how do you know the good Father Callan?"

"Danny taught one of my classes."

"So, you really *did* go to Harvard?"

"Once upon a time." She smiles demurely.

Cyrus extracts two plump olives impaled on a toothpick from his shimmering glass and devours one. "Brilliant guy, Danny, but I always found him an odd candidate for the Jesuits. Makes me think he's hiding from something. What's your take?"

Sonya curls a thin strand of lemon rind around her index finger. "I think everyone has a fatal flaw, Cyrus," she says. "Danny's is idealism. Yours is women."

He feigns a pout while inching closer and gently fingering the pendant hanging from her necklace. Antique Roman glass, exactly the color of her eyes. His cannot help but drift to the terrain below. "I'm beginning to think you don't feel safe around me, Sonya."

She glances down at his reconnoitering hand but does not pull away. Sipping her drink, Sonya levels those unflinching eyes at him. "Cyrus, the fucking crack of dawn isn't safe around *you*."

He laughs and returns to his widowed olive. The waiter brings appetizers and wine as a cluster of loud lawyers deluge the bar.

Sonya probes a poached mussel. "But, I have to confess I do find you attractive…in a Faustian sort of way. Must be the vodka."

"Try the Pinot Gris, love. It might just open your mind to new literary possibilities."

Sonya leans into the table. "Let's not be foolish about this, Cyrus. I have a rare manuscript and a good idea of where a lot more can be found. You know people who are interested in collecting things like that and can pay handsomely for them. That seems to me like the beginning of a mutually profitable arrangement. Don't you think?"

He considers it for a moment. "Are you suggesting a…merger?"

"Something like that."

Sonya turns her attention to the appetizers. A pink tongue peeks between her lips as she pries an oval bivalve from its black shell and

displays it on her fork like a trophy. The mussel's labial palps pucker
suggestively as she extends it toward Cyrus' mouth.

"Would you like a taste?"

....

IN THE LIBRARY at the Center for the Study of World Religions,
half-a-dozen reference books and a sheaf of digital prints are spread
like an unsorted hand of solitaire over a distressed oak trestle table.
Father Callan sips cold coffee and ignores the remnants of a chicken
salad sandwich. Bending over his Mac Book, he is so engrossed by
an enlarged section of the EDAX spectroscopic scan that he fails to
notice it is nearly midnight.

Before heading out to Fenway Park, Carlton Chin saved digital
maps of Sonya's vellum on a thumb drive. The high-resolution, tagged
image file scans, filtered for ferrous sulfate, potassium and carbon
signatures, had enabled Danny to read each character of the Kharosthi
script through the scraped surface and over-written Ta'liq calligraphy.

On a pad of lined yellow paper, Danny had carefully copied each
of the characters and diacritical marks on one line then noted the
probable meaning below in transliterated Sanskrit, constructing a
series of phrases in English:

fathers, mothers...melted by
fire/flame of desire/bliss
teacher/guide is not different...deity
enlightened mind gives teaching/initiation
fashioned into thunderbolt
comes out from mother's (lotus)?
the initiation chair/seat

Two hours earlier, his eyes blurred from fatigue, Danny sent his first cut at a translation of the under-text to Arthur Heinrick, a colleague at the University of Washington's Early Buddhist Manuscripts Project. He noted the *svastika* symbol appearing after the final character, a typical Sanskrit/Kharosthi convention designating "eternal auspiciousness."

At 11:56 pm, he receives Art's reply:

Great to hear from you, Danny. Your text appears to be one of the *Kalachakra* initiations. Here's a recent translation:

Through making this supplication, all the Conquerors,
Fathers and Mothers and so forth, become absorbed,
are melted by the fire of bliss,
and enter by way of the crown protrusion of the lama,
who is the same as the principal deity.
Emerging from the vajra pathway,
the mind of enlightenment
initiates you as a Vajra Mind Deity.
You emerge from the Mother's lotus
and sit on the initiation seat.

But there's one big problem: the *Kalachakra Tantra* didn't appear in India until 1027 CE– in Bihar or Bengal– around the time the Ghaznavid and Ghorid Muslims invaded. Kharosthi script, however, fell out of use by the 4th century, maybe survived in remote backwaters until the 7th century at the very latest. So, the timing is way off.

Hate to say it, Danny, but I think your manuscript is bogus.

Caveat emptor,
Art

WELL PAST MIDNIGHT, Cyrus drops Sonya at her hotel and watches her walk the red carpet to its entrance, one stiletto heel in front of the other, flexing each gluteal muscle for his viewing pleasure. Cyrus is a man who appreciates detail—the Lagerfeld tag in Sonya's little black dress, for instance—and the fact that she is not wearing panties underneath. Even more than her sartorial sex appeal, Cyrus appreciates her probing, intelligent eyes, the sharp Slavic nose that flares when she laughs and the sexy little mole that draws attention to her mouth.

"Pillow lips," he muses aloud, remembering her good-night kiss and stroking his Van Dyke as if it were another part of her anatomy.

It takes him only seven minutes to drive to West Cambridge from the Common. Cyrus parks his Porsche in the garage, raises its convertible top and enters his house. A bottle of San Pellegrino is chilling in the fridge. He pours a glass, kicks off his shoes and moves into the living room. Relaxing into the Roche Bobois sofa, he unbuttons the front of his shirt and his left hand idly reaches for the gold coin minted by his Achaemenid namesake, Cyrus the Great. Touching its worn surface, he recalls how smooth Sonya's antique glass necklace had felt between his fingers and how much smoother her breasts looked beneath it. Meanwhile, his right hand thumbs an encryption sequence on a Global System Mobile Com Blackberry.

"Archie-One secure," Cyrus officiously informs a voice-activated system. A series of clicks and intonations greets his ear before a human voice answers.

"Hi Courtney," he says. "I need a make on a twenty-something female... That's very funny. If I could have gotten it on Match.com, I wouldn't be wasting your time, now would I...

"Surname: Aronovsky, first name: Sonya. Hair: blonde. Eyes: I'd say hazel...no, more like amber. Height: five-eleven in stocking feet. Alumnus of Harvard Divinity School in the past decade or so...

Haven't seen her passport, love, but I'd wager she's Israeli. Says she's booked on a flight out of JFK this coming Wednesday, so you can start with that…

"Not entirely clear. She wants my help brokering an old manuscript…Well, nothing specific but I think she's a pro. I'd just like to know *whose* pro before I take her bait."

·······························

IN HER ROOM AT THE SHERATON, Sonya slips out of her dress, showers in tepid water and lies naked on the cool sheets of a king-size bed. VAIO in hand, she logs on to her Facebook account and scrolls through her *Friends* menu until she finds Golda Solomon, whose profile photo is the silhouette of a wide-hipped, curly-haired girl in an ill-fitting sarong beneath a palm tree on a tropical beach. In the "Write Something" box, she types:

> **OMG! Met the cutest guy tonight! Perfect date for your party.**

Sonya hits the *post* button and sends the message to Giraffe.

After serving with IDF and AMAN, Shlomo Levi became a *katsa* with the Institute's Melucha division. The first field agent he recruited was Sonya. Employing his signature arsenal of flattery and guilt-tripping, Shlomo campaigned to convince Sonya that her military intelligence background, European features, language skills, aptitude scores and academic focus were tailor-made for undercover work.

She resisted for a while but soon realized he was right.

Sonya's incentive package included a Fulbright scholarship to Harvard Divinity School's Center for the Study of World Religions because, as Shlomo always said, there is no more defensible "legend," no better alternative identity for an intelligence operative than the truth.

Neither Harvard, nor anything else, went quite as planned.

In late summer of 2000, Sonya arrived in Cambridge and spent the happiest year of her life—under cover in a way she never expected. Falling in love with a man who wrestled with angels had not been on her curricular agenda. But she had brought it all on herself. Pushing a seemingly innocuous flirtation too far, Sonya ended up the victim of her own seduction. She had never met anyone so comfortable in a body and simultaneously, so tortured by a spiritual vocation. That dichotomy was both Danny's Achilles' heel and the fortress she could never penetrate.

Any fantasy Sonya might have nurtured about a happy ending was abruptly cancelled on September 11, 2001, when she was recalled from HDS on Daylight Priority, the Institute's highest state of alert, and enrolled at the Seminary, the grueling training academy for its Special Operations Division, Metsada.*

There was no time to mourn the loss of her American dream.

The Institute was undergoing reorganization and the Head of Operations thought Sonya was made of the right stuff—a cross-cultural Zionist with initiative, brave but smart enough not to be fearless, aggressive but not foolhardy, and a natural at deception. She had been field-tested with Unit 504, psychoanalyzed, interrogated and given the Institute's seal of approval. Her Russian passport, linguistic fluencies and Semitic eyes made Sonya a valuable asset. Like the Biblical Judith, she quickly demonstrated an uncanny talent for infiltrating the enemy camp and smiting its leaders.

Amman was the *pièce de résistance*. Holiday had made a deal with the devil and Sonya became his pitchfork. A dozen high-value targets were intercepted before they could send any more children under the

* The Seminary [*Ha Midrasha*]—the high-security Mossad training facility for **Metsada** [Fortress], Special Operations Division near Herzliya, officially the Prime Minister's summer residence.

wire strapped into *shahid* vests. Unfortunately, *nezek agavi*, another euphemism for "accidental damage," had been quite high. Had the GID, better known as Mukhabarat,* not decided that it would be in their best interest to quietly work *with* Israel to avoid further embarrassment to the monarchy or risk a Palestinian uprising, the incident might have created a diplomatic nightmare.

Further impressed with Sonya's *chutzpah*, Holiday assigned her to his former unit, an elite group that had evolved from the Mifratz, post-partition vigilantes with a reputation for killing Arab *fedayeen*,† Nazi war criminals and rogue German scientists. They had joined forces with the commandos from AMAN's Unit 188 and SHABAK's *Tziporim*—"Birds"—to become Caesarea, the operatives that hunted down the Palestinian Liberation Organization's "Black September" terrorists responsible for the planning and massacre of Israeli athletes at the 1972 Munich Olympics.

Called *Komemiute*—"Combatants"—Sonya's unit targeted the commanders, controllers, financiers and suppliers of any terrorist organization dedicated to killing Jews. They were "sleepers" who stayed sharp and awaited orders to deploy to do what they did best. In her case, it was "low-signature interception," targeted killing that left no incriminating evidence. She regarded her work as an art form and approached each assignment with a creative eye for detail.

Holiday buried his lethal weapon in deep cover and arranged an Arabic translation grant for her at the University of Haifa to corroborate her legend. Then he assigned Giraffe as Sonya's only contact with the Institute. Like the other *kidonim*—"bayonets"—she was known

---

* GID—General Intelligence Directorate, or **Mukhabarat** [*Dairat al-Mukhabarat al-Ammah*], the Jordanian secret police
† **Mifratz** [Gulf] was formed by commanders of Irgun Zvai Leumi [National Military Organization] and Lehi [The Stern Gang]. The *fedayeen* [those who self-sacrifice] were Jordanian and Egyptian militia that infiltrated Israel to kill Jewish settlers.

only by the code-name her boss had assigned: "Scorpion." Sonya was never quite sure if it had been an arch reference to her astrological birth sign or his personal assessment of her natural disposition.

Sonya rented a tiny apartment near the Technion, lived alone, worked mostly from home, and made no close friends except for a few technicians who hacked through encrypted firewalls and developed lethal toys for the Institute. The "ghouls," as they were disdainfully called, had all graduated from the elite Talpiot program, but were considered too eccentric to work with Unit 8200.* They fascinated Sonya with their focus and intensity, popping Adderall, washing it down with strong coffee and practicing their alchemy into the wee hours, chattering incessantly—and instructively—about the details of their deadly work. Sonya learned a lot from the ghouls.

Six months later, Israel invaded Lebanon and her mother was killed at Kibbutz Sa'ar.

She had balked at moving into Maryna's flat, but Shlomo convinced her it made sense to live in a more secluded neighborhood. Sonya put her mother's Barcelona chairs into storage and furnished the place in cheap IKEA comfort. She settled into a quiet academic ennui broken only by rare assignations with Giraffe. Life became predictably dull and boring.

In retrospect, Sonya decided the black depression she experienced that winter was probably a delayed reaction to Maryna's death. She read up on post-traumatic stress disorder, a clinical diagnosis popularized by American shrinks. To an Israeli, it was just life under siege. Business as usual.

Coming down from the intense, agitated high of field work, there were days when she could not bring herself to leave the flat or even get

---

* Many candidates for **Unit 8200**, Israeli Signal Intelligence National Unit [ISNU], come from the **Talpiot** program, an elite IDF group training in advanced math, physics and problem-solving.

dressed, days when the wind-driven rain on her window seemed to penetrate her skull, drill deep into her brain and suck out her life force. Anxiety over isolation, her inability to trust or confide in anyone, shrouded her in terror during the early morning darkness and left her exhausted during daylight hours.

Eventually, the harsh pendulum swing between anxiety and depression led Sonya to consult a psychiatrist friend of her mother's, someone outside the Institute's purview. She was diagnosed with Bipolar-II and began treatment with Lamotrigine and Cognitive-Behavioral Therapy. The anti-convulsive drug helped her sleep but affected her coordination; the shrink just bored her to tears. So, she read all the peer-reviewed literature on her "disorder" and decided to manage her own treatment.

Sonya cut off her thick locks and started working out five days a week at the university gym. Cardio kickboxing, martial arts and weight training helped to elevate her serotonin levels.

As her body got harder and her sleep patterns normalized, she ramped off her meds and went shopping.

Sonya spent two-month's salary on a fine black hairpiece, the hottest outfits and the sexiest shoes she could find at Gershon Bram. She considered getting some body ink but tattooing still had bad connotations, even for a secular Jew. She settled on a gold piercing in her naval. Her undercover training had already taught her the importance of disguise and she concluded that, if she were going to be tagged and treated like some sort of venomous creature, she should damn well look the part.

The first time Sonya tucked her spiky flaxen hair beneath that sleek, raven wig, applied mascara to her eyes and painted her lips crimson, she had appraised herself in the mirror and laughed with naughty pleasure at the "bad girl" that stared back at her.

In retrospect, Sonya suspects her former shrink would change her clinical diagnosis to "dissociative identity disorder." But she no longer gives a damn what pathological labels mental health mavens might append to her behavior because she alone knows the truth.

It is "Scorpion," her dark alter ego, that keeps her sane.

....

FATHER CALLAN CANNOT SLEEP after reading Art Heinrick's reply. The possibility that Sonya is playing him has crossed his mind more than once in the past 36 hours and Danny cannot think of a single reason why he should trust this woman after her parting shot eight years ago. He remembers her terse e-mail of September 15, 2001 as if he were reading it now, its syntax dispassionate, every calculated word carved in dry ice:

Danny, I don't want to see you again, or get into why. It is about me; please respect this. I do wish you well.

Before he could even ask her what she meant by that, Sonya had cleared out of her room, taken a taxi to the just re-opened Logan airport, and boarded the first plane for Tel Aviv. It had all happened that quickly, a non-anesthetized emotional amputation.

Pacing the worn library carpet at CSWR, Danny runs scenarios through his head before returning to his office. He rings Sonya at her hotel room but there is no answer. Then he remembers her dinner date with Cyrus and decides not to try her mobile number. There are details he prefers not to know.

And yet, no torture in life is worse than *not* knowing.

....

DANNY HAD NOT SLEPT the night of Sonya's 21st birthday, either. He remembered feeling her soft lips on his, even as he reread that passage from Saint Ignatius Loyola's charter for the Society of Jesus, desperate to distract himself from the throbbing below his belt.

> *Whoever desires to serve as a soldier of God*
> *beneath the banner of the Cross in our Society…*
> *after a solemn vow of perpetual chastity, poverty*
> *and obedience, keep what follows in mind…*

"Chastity" meant *abstinence*. He knew that when he had signed on as one of God's Marines. Loyola's Spiritual Exercises had emphasized "indifference," the conquest of physical desire, the regulation of his life so that no decision would be made under the influence of attachment to material comforts or to pleasure. Iñigo believed detachment was freedom from ego-driven appetites. But Danny knew that he was *far* from detached and began to think he was no "soldier" worthy of the title. He had failed miserably at mortification, proven that he was just as weak as any other man tempted by the sight and smell of a beautiful woman.

And Jesus! She *was*. If he had petitioned the Almighty for the perfect companion, an Eve soft and strong and wicked smart, the answer to his prayers would be Sonya.

Although not technically a virgin when he entered the Novitiate, Danny assiduously avoided exploring why his attempts at physical intimacy had been disastrous. He professed First Vows before embarking that summer on pilgrimage to Jerusalem, and made a silent retreat prior to beginning his intensive *lectio divina*, "divine reading" and meditation upon Holy Scripture prescribed in preparation for Tertianship, the final formal graduate studies in the Society of Jesus.

Soon, he would be expected to take Perpetual Solemn Vows. Walk the walk. Put up or shut up. He would be expected to obey, to *abstain*. And what was his alternative, anyway? Washing out of the Society? Losing his position at HDS for having inappropriate relations with a student? Disgracing his family's name in the Town? Danny winced at the thought of his mother having to listen to fat Mrs. Murphy's gossip at the Fish Market on Dot Ave.

For Christ's sake, the girl's not even a Catholic!

Sonya was not just a game-changer; she was a threat to everything he had worked so hard to become.

The evening after her birthday, All Saints' Day, Danny had met with his Spiritual Director, the Reverend Sean Devlin, SJ, at the Jesuit Seminary Guild. Father Devlin welcomed him into the comfortably furnished library, sat him down on the burgundy leather sofa in front of a stone hearth, and made a pot of strong Irish tea. Danny's attention was again drawn to a cartouche beneath the mantle bearing the monogram attributed to Ignatio Loyola, inscribed within the quadrants of a cross: AMDG—*Ad majorem Dei gloriam*—"For the greater glory of God." How, Danny had always wondered, could any human aspiration presume to add glory to The Supreme Being?

"Sean, you ever have…doubts?"

"Every damn day, Danny." Father Devlin's voice still bore a trace of County Cork. Beneath a shock of white hair, his ruddy face glowed with years of good humor, sacramental wine and stronger spirits. Danny had come to consider Sean a friend as well as his mentor. "You don't think we all have 'em, bucko? You don't think our Lord had 'em right up until the moment they nailed his feet to the cross?"

Danny laughed. "By then, it was too late for him to back out."

"By *then*, Christ had accepted what he'd come on Earth to do."

Danny considered that superhuman altruism as Father Devlin poured tea into bone China cups. "I envy him, Sean. I never knew what I was born to do. And I've never felt complete..."

"Complete as what?"

"As a man. I can't pretend that part of me doesn't exist."

Father Devlin's smile hardened into a tight line. "None of us can, Danny. But we've all taken a vow to sublimate it, to offer up our lives to something higher than our libidos. That's what discernment is all about, *discretio*, and that's where the Grace of God comes in. We don't do this alone, you know. It's not just about muscle and determination. That's ego talking! You need to be clear on that."

Danny poured milk into his cup and summoned his courage. "You're right, Sean. I know I can't begin Tertianship until I've gotten clear on that." He took a deep breath; spat it out before his courage folded. "I need to take a leave of absence."

"What are you saying, Danny?" Father Devlin's blue eyes clouded over as he slouched into his wing chair. "Be straight with me, bucko."

"It's a woman, Sean."

His mentor appraised him quietly and then sighed, in what sounded like relief. "Well...it could be worse." Danny cringed at the innuendo. "You slept with her yet?"

"Not yet." He focused on his scuffed shoes. "But you have no idea how much I want to."

Father Devlin glanced up from his teacup. "Oh, I think I do. I'm not a damn piece of stone, you know." Sean drew a slow breath and held it while he considered his words. His face suffused with blood as he exhaled. "But here's the deal; I *am* still your advisor. If you're bent on this hiatus, I can only sanction it as an extension of your Spiritual Exercises. I want you to continue with the *liturgia horarum* and your meditation, especially your daily examination of conscience. Will you do that, Danny?"

He nodded, and Father Devlin leaned into his admonition. "Most importantly, I want you to supplicate the Holy Spirit every day for intercession. Ask him to guide you through this crisis of faith. He will, you know."

Danny pushed aside his empty cup and stood to leave.

"He'd better, Sean."

....

SONYA FOUND A B&B and Danny borrowed a car for the weekend from a college buddy in Charlestown. The coastal village of Rockport was practically deserted but they had not come to sightsee. The Linden Tree Inn near Mill Pond Park looked cozy, the room comfortable and the big bed inviting.

They checked in mid-afternoon and Sonya repaired to the bathroom for a quick shower. She emerged wrapped in a white terrycloth robe, while Danny waited awkwardly on the edge of the bed still dressed in his thrift store civvies. Sonya unclipped her wooden barrette, shook a thick knot of hair loose and let it fall like spun gold around her shoulders.

"I'm not very good at this, Sonny," Danny told her, torn between his honorable reputation and the erotic promise standing in front of him like Bathsheba before King David.

Sonya moved slowly toward him as he stood to meet her eyes. Her scent alone gave him an erection. She reached up and gently touched the hair at his temples. "Relax, Professor." Then she cradled his face in her hands and kissed him softly, very slowly, savoring the taste of his mouth. She closed her eyes and whispered into his lips, "Let me take it from here."

Sonya opened her robe, slipped it off her shoulders and let it drop to the floor. Danny stared unrepentantly. He had never seen anything like her, except in a centerfold. But this was no paper goddess; she was warm, breathing and very real. Sonya watched with pleasure as he drank her in, then took his hands and brought them to her lips, barely kissing and slowly licking his fingertips. As she guided them to her breasts, he let his fingers spread over their fullness and gently thumb her nipples. She purred and led him on an exploration of her silky skin, urging one hand lower, holding it firmly in place between her parted legs, and shuddering as he touched her as he had never before touched a woman.

Eventually, Sonya undressed him, almost reverently. She lifted the coarse woolen sweater and T-shirt over his head and slowly traced a line from his throat to his chest with wet kisses. Her tongue circumscribed the silver medal that hung in the cleft of his chest as if she craved the salt on his skin. When she slipped his leather belt past its buckle and opened the zipper of his jeans, Danny's breath caught in his throat.

He stroked her glistening hair as she slid down his body, running her hands up over his tense hamstrings to the small of his back. Her fingers took hold of his waistband, lowered his shorts as her warm breath escaped in a sigh of anticipation. When she knelt before him, as if in prayer, Danny knew the Holy Spirit surely had His work cut out for Him.

"I WOULD KILL FOR A CIGARETTE."

Sonya had stretched her long legs diagonally across the disheveled bed and nuzzled into the triangle of hair in the cleft of Danny's chest as he relaxed in the golden autumn sunlight angling through their cottage window.

Hands behind his head on the pillow, Danny laughed. "Not on my watch, Sonny."

"And by the way, you're a liar," she said.

He tucked his chin into a tacit question.

"You told me you weren't very good at it."

"I just meant…I mean…I don't have much experience."

"A guy like you must have had a slew of girlfriends."

"And what do *you* know about a guy like me?"

Sonya raised herself on an elbow, her eyes serious. "I know you're a gorgeous, conflicted man, Danny, an idealist who wants to save the world, even if it means neglecting your own needs. Hence, your choice of professions." Sonya gave a smug little grin as she fingered the silver medallion on his chest. "*And* your heroes?"

"That's one of my mother's, actually. Saint Christopher."

"Protector of travelers, isn't he?"

"Ma got pissed when Christopher's feast day was removed from the Calendar of Saints. *Nobody*, not even the Pope, was going to tell her who she could venerate. When Pete joined the Marines, she gave him the medal… 'to keep you safe,' she said." Danny's eyes squeezed shut. "My brother had this on when he died in Lebanon. Came back with his body. I've been wearing it ever since. Unofficially, of course."

She pursed her lips and nodded. "Another thing I know about you…you've been living in your brother's shadow, trying to prove to yourself you're as good a man as he was. You've never gotten over his death, have you?"

Danny felt the memories accreting around him like winter fog. He took a deep breath and decided to tell her the whole story.

"When I was five years old, Aunt Gertrude predicted that Peter would become a priest. In an Irish-Catholic family, that meant I had to choose between lawyer and cop. Gert made the pronouncement as if it were some kind of unwritten holy law."

At least, Danny thought, Pete would now have to be the upstanding member of his family, and whether Danny opted for the Bar or the Force, both gate-way drugs to the Boston political arena, no one would ever expect the same display of piety from him as they would from his big brother. As fate would have it, Pete turned out to be the opposite of pious.

"He was sent home from Saint Mary's so many times for fighting that the old man stopped asking why. In a Marine Corps family, fighting was expected, and as long as you didn't give any lip to the nuns, you remained in dad's good graces."

Meanwhile, Danny watched from the sidelines, trying to learn vicariously from his big brother what *not* to do.

In high school, Pete played football and rugby, hung out with the hottest girls and developed a legendary reputation as a bad-ass. "He was like some kind of superhero, Sonny. It's a big deal when your brother's the toughest kid in the Town. You hold your head high and nobody dares give you shit. But it went beyond that. I watched him take some major thrashing from my old man, just because he was the oldest. It was Pete's job to get his ass kicked first, so it would be clear to me where the line was drawn, you know? ' Marine's code, Pee Wee'—both he and Pop called me Pee Wee— You take it for your brother, Pee Wee, and smile like it's an honor. More it hurt, the better. That's what *I* learned about idealism."

"You idolized him," Sonya replied.

"I assumed Pete would eventually come to his senses, like Saint Augustine had. But my brother's transformation took everyone by surprise. *Nobody* saw it coming."

Danny paused, breathed deeply at the painful memory and then spat it out.

"Pete's best bud was Sid. They hung out together all the time, slamming beers, cruising Dot Ave for a scuffle. The hoodsies *loved* them, two good-looking bad boys who had the whole wicked town by the balls. They could've had any girl they wanted."

Sonya nibbled Danny's ear as he spoke. "Mmmm, I'm getting wet just thinking about them."

"All they wanted was each other, Sonny."

Danny could hear the breath catch in her throat as she waited for him to continue.

"When Pop found out, he nearly beat my brother to death. Next day, Pete signed with the Marines and the old man never said good-bye when he left for Parris Island. Sid hit the Jameson's hard. One summer night, he drove his Camaro off the Fish Pier just past Stavis'. My brother found out when he got back from boot camp. Never talked about Sid after that."

Sonya sighed. "Were you afraid it was...genetic?"

"Sonny, I was afraid I'd never be able to show my face again south of Somerville. I was afraid my crew would find out that Pete wasn't really what they all thought he was, and I'd be the one who'd have to uphold the family's honor."

Danny choked back the guilt, felt his throat and chest tighten as he continued.

"Day it happened, we heard about it on the six o'clock news: 241 Marines killed in a barracks explosion at the Beirut Airport, turned into hamburger while they slept by a truck full of TNT. 241 medals sent off to parents, wives, lovers, brothers;...241 brave soldiers, one who happened to be the guy you most admired in the whole world except for one tiny little flaw in an otherwise legendary reputation. Pop looked like he'd been shot through the chest. Mom was on her knees on the kitchen floor, apron soaked with grease from the chicken she'd dropped. They just *knew*.

"I was 13-years old at the time, and all I could think about was the horror I'd have to face if some reporter found out that one of those 241 big, bad jarheads was queer." He let a slow breath escape from the emotional vortex in his chest.

"So, yeah, I had sex with a few girls after that, more to prove to myself it *wasn't* genetic. But I never let any of them get too close, never really had a girlfriend, let alone a lover. Tell you the truth, it felt more like mutual self-abuse. I accepted Pete's death long ago, Sonny. It's his *life* I haven't gotten over."

Sonya brushed his cheek tenderly. "So that's why you decided to become a priest? Oh Danny, whose sins are you atoning for? Yours or your brother's?"

"Mine are far worse." He looked out the window. "I still hate myself for the relief I felt when he died."

When he glanced back, a single tear had crept from the corner of Sonya's eye. She quickly wiped it away with the side of her hand, as if embarrassed by her display of sentiment.

"If you try to take the sins of the world onto your own shoulders, Danny, it will kill you," she said. "One of our rabbis found that out the hard way 2,000 years ago."

"You don't have to worry about that, Sonny. I am nowhere near as brave as your rabbi was."

He pressed himself hard into Sonya's body, kissed her mouth as if he were trying to draw the breath from her lungs. As twilight painted their sheets in primrose, they made love again, this time with a violent urgency, and forgot the world until sun licked the morning frost from the window above their bed.

....

IN RETROSPECT, the following year had a bittersweet Dickensian quality, certainly one of the best and worst of Danny's life. On leave from the Society of Jesus, he moved from his Kirkland Court residence into an attic space in a Queen Anne that belonged to the parents of one of his rowing pals at Harvard. Danny continued to teach at the Center for the Study of World Religions and lived frugally on his small stipend.

With her Fulbright, Sonya always had enough money for them to go out for a pizza or grinder and get away to a secluded spot every so often. Between getaways, they met clandestinely in his room. She enjoyed the intrigue and illicitness of their assignations, creatively acted out her sexual fantasies, sometimes in ways that shocked Danny and left him breathless, but always kept him impaled on the horns of a delicious dilemma. She was both the intimate partner he never dreamed was missing from his life and the sweetest drug he could have ever imagined.

On a gusty Thanksgiving Day, Danny took Sonya down to his old neighborhood in South Boston, where his mother still lived in the bottom flat of their Dorchester Avenue triple-decker. Danny's cousins and a few of the old Townies dropped by for the stuffed bird, mashed spuds, and Brussels with bacon. Beer flowed, and all the boys lusted over the hottie he had lured "down channel," as the hoodsies used to say. Kathryn Callan welcomed Sonya into her home and held her tongue, but Danny knew he had broken his mother's heart when he scrubbed the Novitiate for a Jewish girl.

At the semester break, Sonya flew home to visit her mother in Haifa. On New Year's Eve, he bussed through frigid slush to meet her return flight at Logan. The moment she appeared at the customs gate, her suntanned face glowing beneath a golden halo of curls, Danny knew he was hopelessly in love, even though his bliss had been purchased with a broken vow. Since he was destined for the Inferno, he figured he might as well enjoy the fall.

The summer saw mornings of labor on post-doc publications followed by workouts at the Briggs Athletic Center. On some days, he and Sonya pumped iron, on others they wailed on the heavy bag together. Danny was impressed with her physical prowess, especially how hard she could punch. He taught her how to scull, and they spent most weekends sprawled on green boathouse lawns, grilling plump burgers and sipping local micro-brew with exuberant rowing crews in the late afternoon sun. The smell of her warm skin and damp hair, the weight of her body against his naked chest after a good sweat and a well-earned cold one was about as close to heaven as Danny imagined he would ever get.

But heaven came crashing to earth eleven days into September.

They had met for their ritual coffee at Peet's on the morning of the World Trade Center attack. He had expected Sonya to be more vocal and politically opinionated than usual. Instead, she seemed uncharacteristically detached from the events that had shocked the rest of the world.

Danny conceded that it sometimes took a cataclysm of Biblical proportions to wake people up. "God works in strange ways, Sonny. International sympathy is focused on us because of this catastrophe. It changes everything, the whole paradigm of hegemony. If ever there were an opportunity to broker a peace deal in the Middle East, it's now, don't you think?"

He would always remember that look she gave him, eyes hard as any he had ever seen on the streets of Roxbury.

"You've no idea who you are dealing with," Sonya said. "None of you Americans do. The monsters that engineered these attacks don't *want* a peace deal, and they will make damn sure one never happens. It doesn't take much, really: a few lengths of lead pipe filled with triacetone triperoxide stitched into a vest packed with ball-bearings, and a cheap mobile phone trigger. Just strap it onto some kid programmed to think he's got a garden full of virgins waiting for him in Paradise and put him on a packed commuter bus in any city you please. I've seen the results with my own eyes, Danny. You can't negotiate with fanatics who believe they've got nothing to lose. You can only exterminate them—*before* they get on that bus."

He stared at Sonya as if she had just unzipped her skin and emerged as some alien life form.

"But you are dead right on one count, Professor," she added. "This *does* change everything." She tapped out a cigarette and lit it just to spite him. Sonya's eyes glared granite hard as she blew smoke toward Grendel's Den. "Absolutely *everything*."

....

DANNY OPENS THE TOP DRAWER of his desk and stares at a sheet of ecru stationary. An elegant Crane's Crest watermark lies beneath Sonya's public-school scrawl.

> Dear Danny,
>
> You were probably not expecting to ever hear
> from me again. And I guess I wouldn't blame you
> for not responding. Truth is, I have been so
> heavily involved in tragedies here at home that
> there has been no time to think about anything else—

*except how upset you must have been,
considering the way I left things.
You really did deserve better than that,
and I would like to explain what happened
if you will allow me.*

*I'll be in Boston for a few days in early July
and would very much appreciate your counsel
regarding a family matter. I will call your office
when I arrive, and hope you are willing to see me.*

*Until —
Sonny*

From the get-go, Sonya has pushed his curiosity through the firewall of better judgment. But what possible reason would she have for faking the authenticity of an old manuscript? Technical forgery of that caliber requires an extraordinary level of skill and knowledge. Anyone that good would never make such a blatant mistake on the historical timeline, unless… Unless it is *not* a mistake.

Danny dashes back to the library with his laptop, makes a pot of strong coffee and types KALACHAKRA into the Google search engine. In Sanskrit, the term means "Wheel of Time" and the Tibetan *Blue Annals* lists about twenty translations of the work. All of them agree on its origin:

At the Great Stupa of Dhanyakataka, on the full moon in the year following his "awakening," the Buddha was asked by Suchandra, *dharmaraja* of a kingdom called Shambhala, to teach him how a monarch might bring enlightened rule to his subjects. Suchandra subsequently wrote down the Buddha's exposition in 60,000 verses. This "Mother Book" [*Mula*], written in Shambhala's "twilight tongue," is now lost to posterity. However, the seventh *dharmaraja*, Yasas, wrote a summary in Sanskrit Sragdhara metre, shortened to 1,030 verses, called *Kalachakra Laghutantra*.

Shambhala is described as homeland of the highest spiritual teachings, and *Kalachakra* is the outward reflection of its ancient shamanic tradition that clearly emulates Zoroastrian eschatology: the continuous cycle of time and archetypal struggle between darkness and light. Buddhist interpretation suggests that the world around Shambhala will succumb to barbarian armies of darkness until liberated by the forces of light.

All well and good, except Art Heinrick claimed the *Kalachakra* did not appear in India until 1027 CE, even though Tibetan tradition maintained it was much older, predating even the Bön culture.

Danny finds himself fixated on this chronology: Sakyamuni, the historical Buddha, supposedly lived and taught in Magadha during the 5th century BCE. If some special initiation had been given to King Suchandra, and assuming that each of Shambhala's monarchs ruled for the period of time their legend claimed, Danny calculates that King Yasas would have penned *Kalachakra Laghutantra* during the 2nd century CE, placing it during King Kanishka's reign over the Kushan dynasty in Gandharan India and Bactria.

Was this "twilight tongue" of the original *Mula* a cognate of Sanskrit? Or was it some proto-Aryan language originating to the west of India, where twilight appears on the horizon each evening?

And what about Shambhala? This mythical land situated to the north of the Himalaya, sheltered within a ring of ice mountains, free from famine, sickness and aging, where peace reigned eternally, was the obvious model for Shangri-La in James Hilton's *Lost Horizon*.

Scanning reams of scholarly commentary, his eyes blurring with fatigue, Danny discovers to his amazement that Estêvão Cacella, a Portuguese Jesuit missionary, described a place called "Xembala" while he explored Asia in the early 17th century. Father Cacella's account so intrigued his contemporaries that finding this mythical kingdom became an obsession for many European adventurers.

Helena Petrovna Blavatsky, eccentric founder of the Theosophical Society, declared that Shambhala was home base of the Great White Lodge, ascended masters that "dictated" her *Secret Doctrine*. In the early 1920s, the artist and Theosophist, Nicholas Roerich, received support from the Soviet Cheka to search for Shambhala in Tibet. Nazi Shutzstaffel Reich Commander, Heinrich Himmler, mounted several full-scale Tibetan expeditions to locate Shambhala, which he believed to be the racially pure Aryan homeland. This explained why Adolph Hitler had chosen the Bön *svastika* as the Nazi logo.

Neither the Russians nor the Germans ever found any trace of Shambhala, probably because they had been looking too far to the east. A dozen possible sites for an Aryan homeland have since been proposed by scholars, from the Andronovo Complex in Siberia to the Tian Shan in Kyrgyzstan. More recently, linguists identified a Proto-Indo-Aryan language originating in a Bronze Age civilization designated BMAC—Bactria-Margiana Archaeological Complex— an area along the Oxus River comprising Turkmenistan, southern Uzbekistan, western Tajikistan and northern Afghanistan. Balkh and Merv were its thriving city centers.

Danny feels excitement cutting through his exhaustion. The BMAC is *exactly* where the Kushan tribes settled when they migrated to the west from Khotan in Xinjiang—toward the twilight.

....

DANNY AWAKENS ON A STIFF SOFA in the library at 8:15 am. He cracks the blinds, blinks painfully at the morning sun and splashes cold water on his face in the men's room.

At 8:30, Danny jogs down Francis Street to get blood pumping through his stiff muscles and leaps up the steps of the red-shingled Ignatius House on Sumner Road. He grunts to Fathers Morrison and Ciccone in the kitchen, pours himself a cup of tepid coffee, and ambles up the stairs to shower in his shared bathroom after Father Silvera has finished shaving. None of his brothers of the cloth even raise an eyebrow because Father Callan has a reputation for burning the midnight oil, a habit which has resulted in some very impressive academic publications and mitigated their disdain for Danny's unorthodox method of conducting God's work.

Although he has no obligation to say daily Mass, canon law requires all ordained priests to pray the Divine Office as the core of their spiritual discipline. Alone in his room, Danny cracks open his Breviary containing the service for each day of the year, makes the sign of the cross and raises his right thumb to his dry mouth. From his single dormer window, he can see the U-shaped brick edifice of Kirkland Court where he lived in a 4th-floor dorm during grad school—before Sonya arrived in his life.

"Lord, open my lips…"

As he speaks the words, the taste of Sonya's mouth, the smell of her just-washed hair, the feel of her skin taut over the muscles of her legs, torments him like demons from the *Purgatorio*.

He squeezes his bloodshot eyes closed, and with an act of sheer will banishes the shadow of his past sins before bowing in reverence toward the wooden crucifix on his wall.

"Glory be to the Father, and to the Son and to the Holy Spirit…"

As he recites the *Liturgia horarum*, canonical "Liturgy of the Hours" obligatory for all ordained Roman Catholic priests, at the periphery of his awareness, like heat lightning on a muggy summer night, Danny senses a dark impulse he has not felt in a very long time.

Jealousy.

At 9:00 am, Danny phones Sonya in her hotel room.

"Do you have a car?" he asks.

"No." Her voice sounds deep and sleepy.

"Rent one."

....

"DID YOU SLEEP WITH CYRUS?"

Danny's clipped question shatters the serenity of what would otherwise have been a relaxing 90-minute drive from Boston to the bucolic college town of Northampton. He refuses to look at her, unsuccessfully attempting to mask his agitation.

Sonya laughs insensitively at his misplaced jealousy. "Have you come to hear my confession, Father Callan?"

Danny grabs her arm quickly and unexpectedly. "Do *not* fuck with me, Sonny!"

She suppresses her defensive tactics, holds her breath and waits to hear just how far Danny is prepared to go. His passionate outburst is surprisingly exciting and her breathing quickens as the electricity of his rough touch flows through her like a warm current, terminating in the delta between her legs. She has not felt this kind of raw sexuality in years. In fact, not since the last time he touched her. It triggers a cascade of detailed memories—how the muscles of his arms flexed as he held himself over her when they made love, how his back arched and his buttocks contracted when he came inside her. She can almost smell his delicious scent as if it were anointing her again.

Danny stares into her eyes and relaxes his grip with a weary sigh. "I just want to hear the truth from you."

She pulls to the curb and stares defiantly at him. "I did not have sex with Cyrus, although I did tease him unmercifully. Sorry, I know he's your friend, but he had it coming."

"Believe me, I'm not feeling protective of Cyrus."

"Well, *what* then?" Her eyes soften, probe his.

Danny looks away like a petulant schoolboy. "Sonny, that story you told me about your father…is it true?"

"Yes, as far as I know. He went MIA when the Soviet army pulled out of Afghanistan. It's still classified information in Russia, Danny. Those bastards won't even tell me what happened to my father twenty years after the fact. I finally located his commanding officer in Kyiv. He said my father's helicopter disappeared in the mountains, somewhere north of Bagram Airbase. The wreckage was never found. But the message he scratched into that piece of vellum appeared at a border post six months later—after the KGB had classified his mission…" Her face suffuses with anger. "After his fucking commanding officer had written him off."

Sonya remembers the pleasure she took in passing Colonel Pashkovsky that tin of toxic cigarettes—instead of the benign one she had brought—and vaguely recalls a cynical quip Oscar Wilde made about revenge being best served cold. She wishes she could have watched that pale Cossack bastard light his final smoke.

"Twenty years, Sonny," Danny reminds her. "What makes you think he could have stayed alive in that hostile environment—even if he *did* survive the crash?"

She looks at the steering wheel, shakes her head. "I never even considered the possibility until I found that note in my mother's things. To be honest, Danny, I have no proof. It's just a feeling… an intuition I've had since he disappeared…as if he's been trying to reach out to me. He was very resourceful, my father, but, what if he were really hurt? Captured and held in some shit-hole village all these years? It *has* happened, you know." A single tear slowly follows the contour between her cheek and nose. "If I don't at least *try* to look for him, I couldn't live with myself." She turns back to face Danny with a savage resolve. "But I need to know *where* to look."

Danny directs Sonya's attention to the overhead sign routing them onto US 90 West. "Somewhere north of Bagram," he says. "It doesn't get any rougher than the Hindu Kush, Sonny."

Sonya pulls into the middle lane and merges with highway traffic. "Or any more dangerous," she concedes. "Look, I brought that vellum to you because I hoped you could help me narrow the search coordinates, Danny. I had no one else to turn to."

His bloodshot eyes close as he leans back against the headrest. She glances over and sees him smiling for the first time that morning.

"They're narrowing," Danny says. "Wake me when we cross the Connecticut River."

....

STARS AND STRIPES FESTOON Northampton's Main Street from the railway overpass to the old courthouse. The New England college town is already infused with the smell of barbecuing meats and exploding firecrackers. A short walk from the Haymarket Café, where Sonya and Danny stop for coffee and croissants, Bashir's Oriental Rug Shop is shaded from the wilting summer heat by a luminescent green parasol of maple trees. In its window, *katchli* and *kilim* tribal rugs are displayed beside a brass samovar, a tasseled Turkoman saddlebag and an antique daguerreotype depicting turbaned Pathans leading a caravan of overloaded Bactrian camels through a mountain pass. A flyer is taped to the glass door announcing that the Northampton Islamic Art Museum is open by appointment only.

Inside the shop, two ceiling fans blend muggy air with the scent of old wool. Neat stacks of intricately patterned throw rugs are dwarfed by a palisade of eight-foot rolled carpets, while a few of the more-pricey specimens hang like muted abstract art on the white brick walls. Sonya hears the soft clatter of spoons in the back of the shop, and the high-pitch lilt of a man's voice.

"*Karwan-I-Ruus guftee, baleh* [You said Russian Caravan, yes]?"

To Sonya's surprise, Danny responds, "*Baleh, amoora…ah… bisyar khush dara* [Yes, that's her favorite]."

A short, slight man wearing a loose raw cotton shirt and a black scally cap turned backwards on his head appears with a burnished copper tray, three gold-rimmed glasses and a double spouted teapot. His skin is bronze and his neatly trimmed beard white as a lamb's pelt. Beneath thick, dark brows, the man's eyes shine like polished hematite, and his smile seems to reflect sunlight into the shop. He sets the tea service on a pile of rugs, takes both of Danny's hands in his own and looks up into his face like the father of a prodigal son.

"*O mardeh Khoda* [Ah, the Man of God]! Good to see you again, my friend."

"Is that Farsi?" Sonya asks.

"Dari," he says. "Old Persian. Father Daniel is getting pretty good. When we first met, he couldn't speak a word."

She looks at Danny with surprise. "When was that?"

"March '02," He says. "I was invited to accompany the director of the Society for the Preservation of Afghanistan's Cultural Heritage to Rabatak Pass. Archaeologists had found Kushan inscriptions there but the site had since been bulldozed and looted. Bashir happened to be in Mazar-i-Sharif to buy inventory at the time. When I found out we were practically neighbors, he graciously offered to be my interpreter."

"I offered to be his spiritual bodyguard," the little man corrects with an ingratiating smile.

Sonya scrutinizes the rug dealer's face. "You're Afghani, then?"

"No such creature," Bashir trills a laugh as he pours tea into three small tulip glasses. "But useful for buying a rug."

"An Afghani is a unit of currency," Danny explains.

Sonya persists. "So where *do* you come from?"

"Before the Greeks called it Bactra, Balkh was one of the oldest cities in the world—home of Zoroaster. 'Mother of All Cities' it was called, because its children gradually migrated west, south and east to become Persian, Baluch and Pashtun. Those who stayed or went north were called 'Tajik'—and not very respectfully, I might add. About 800 years ago, my ancestors fled Balkh to Bukhara, trying to stay out of Genghis Khan's way. Their strategy did not work so well." He points to the unmistakable Mongol heritage in his eyes and laughs with self-deprecating delight, then hands Sonya a steaming glass of tea on a copper saucer.

"Does that help you decide if I am a good Muslim or a bad one?"

"Why do you ask that?"

"Because I can see in *your* eyes the mark of Ibrahim's tribe. And I would guess it is the branch that settled in the Negev rather than the Hijaz."

Sonya scrutinizes her host with the cool detachment she once employed interrogating Palestinians in Hebron. Bashir seems completely ingenuous, lacking even a tinge of apprehension or subterfuge. She decides the little man can be trusted, sips her tea and immediately recognizes the smoky fragrance of Lapsang. "Russian Caravan."

Bashir inclines his head. "Your favorite, of course."

Sonya smiles, places a hand over her heart and thanks him in classical Arabic. "*Shukran, lak ya sidi.*"

"*Al'afw, habibti* [You are welcome, my dear]," he answers in kind with a pleasant laugh. "Would you like to see my treasures?"

She and Danny follow Bashir to a three-panel Shaker door, which he unlocks. Sonya descends the creaking stairs into an air-conditioned cellar as their host dials up track lighting on the low ceiling. Exquisite Ottoman miniature paintings, hand illuminated pages from medieval Qur'âns, and antique Tekke prayer rugs are displayed on the whitewashed brick walls. Bashir sits quietly on the stairs as his guests admire his esoteric treasures.

"Look," Sonya takes hold of Danny's arm and points to a Persian manuscript, "It's a page from Rumi's *Masnavi.*"

"An 18th century copy," Bashir admits. "But pretty, don't you think? Mowlana—who you call 'Rumi'—was born near Balkh, but his family was cleverer than mine at escaping Mongols."

Sonya glances at Bashir. "Are you Tasawwuf?"*

He smiles. "I am neither a Sufi nor an Afghani. Just one open heart looking into another."

"Hearts can be deceived." Sonya replies, feeling her face flush.

Danny touches her arm. "Show Bashir your vellum, Sonny."

She lifts the carbon fiber cylinder out of her knapsack as Bashir unlocks another door. In the center of an adjacent room, completely

---

* **Tasawwuf** [one of the woolen clothed]—a Sufi, or practitioner of Islam's esoteric "inner path"

surrounded by floor-to-ceiling bookshelves, Sonya carefully unrolls her manuscript on a worn oak library table beneath a brass lamp, then taps the tube and reveals the strip she cut from the bottom.

"We think this came from somewhere in the northeast of Afghanistan," Danny tells his friend. "Her father used it to get a message out of the country."

Bashir scrutinizes the vellum's mottled surface, carefully matching up the excised strip with its crude Cyrillic letters scratched in charcoal over the faded Ta'liq calligraphy. "Why would he do that?"

"Because his helicopter crashed in the mountains, somewhere between Bagram airbase and the Amu Darya River." Danny hesitates. "Her father was a Russian pilot during the war."

Sonya expects his disdain, but instead Bashir looks at her with compassion in his eyes. "Your father was lost, *habibti?*"

"That's what I'm trying to find out."

"Think he might have gotten help in one of the villages near the border?" Danny asks.

"It is possible. The Soviets controlled all of Badakhshan and Wakhan Provinces. They built roads for their tanks, and bridges across the rivers. Also, they distributed food and clothing to the villagers at their posts, when they were not planting land mines."

Sonya points to the characters inscribed on the vellum. "These first lines are Arabic, a *surah* from Al-Qur'ân. 'And the cattle, He has created them for you; in them there is warm clothing and numerous benefits, and of them you eat.'"

Bashir nods appreciatively, unfolds narrow readers and scans the manuscript, running his bony fingers from right to left, just above each line of text, careful not to touch the surface. "*An-Nahl*—The Bee.'" Bashir chuckles. "It is quoted here in the context of an old fable: the 'Debate of Animals'. Do you know it?"

Sonya shakes her head.

Bashir walks to one of the bookshelves and scans the titles. "The King of the Djinn holds a debate between the animals and humans on a remote island to decide who should have dominion there. The nightingale, the jackal and the bee all give passionate and eloquent presentations, nearly defeating the humans. But one points out that Al-Llâh has given only to human beings a chance for eternal life, so men should rightly rule over animals. The Djinn King cautions that the very same law which gives men dominion promises severe punishment if they mistreat the animals."

"Sounds like a fanciful explanation for the *halal* dietary laws," Sonya remarks.

"Which, of course, came from Jewish *kashrut*." Bashir pinches a smile as he carefully extracts a battered leather book from the packed shelves. "It is interesting to note that this fable appeared in the *Rasa'il Ikhwan al-Safa'*: a collection of treatises written in the 10th century by a secret brotherhood in Basra." He winks playfully at Sonya. "Sufis. The Tasawwuf often ran afoul of conservative Sunni clerics and had to teach anonymously for their own protection. But in this case, what is important to note is that passages from the *Rasa'il* were often quoted by a famous Isma'ili missionary from Khurasan."

He carefully leafs through the yellow-edged pages of the book. "Nasir-i Khusraw was a scholar and financial secretary to the Seljuk *emir* in Merv before making his Hajj pilgrimage. In those days, the journey to Mecca was long and arduous, so Nasir spent seven years traveling. In Egypt, he became attracted to the Isma'ili tradition. His later writing and poetry reflected this eclectic philosophy. When he returned to Merv, the conservative Sunni elite branded him a heretic. Nasir was forced to flee into the mountains of Badakhshan, where he spent his last decade writing and teaching in exile. His work had a lasting influence on their culture, and to this day the Pamirs of Afghanistan and Tajikistan are dominated by Isma'ili."

Bashir stops on an illuminated page. "It is quite possible that your document is a verse from Nasir-i Khusraw's *Diwan*, a collection of poems written in the structured meter of traditional *qasida*. Did your father read Persian?"

"I have no idea."

"From what you have told me, I think he would have empathized with Nasir's misfortune. Look, this is a couplet Nasir wrote while in exile." Bashir translates the text: "'Pass by, sweet breeze of Khurasan, to one imprisoned deep in the valley of Yumgan, who sits huddled in comfortless tight straits, robbed of all wealth, all goods, all hope...'"

Sonya feels the slow irritation of a tear inching down her cheeks as Bashir recites the verse, as if her lost father is reaching out to her through this cagey little rug dealer, who is obviously so much more than that. She quickly wipes away the evidence of her emotional lapse, looks up, and notices Danny watching her. He seems uncertain how or whether to respond.

Finally, Danny turns to Bashir and asks, "So, where would a Russian pilot have gotten his hands on a treasure like this? And who might have helped him deliver it to a Soviet border post?"

Bashir shrugs. "For these questions, Father Daniel, I have no answers." Just as hope begins to bleed from Sonya's heart, he adds, "But my cousin, Murad, might."

"And where would we find your cousin?" she asks quickly.

"Ishkashim," Bashir's eyes sparkle in the lamplight, "On the Afghanistan side of the Amu Darya. I am sure he would be willing to help—*if* you can get there."

Sonya takes the little Afghan's hand in gratitude, "*Insha'al-Llâh* [God willing], we will get there."

SATURDAY, 4 JULY 2009 · MANHATTAN, NEW YORK

....

NATHAN SPEKTOR PUSHES THROUGH a pair of red steel doors
inset with diamond-shaped windowpanes, steps into a dingy black
and white checkerboard linoleum lobby and suddenly imagines that
he has just been transported to Moscow during the height of the
Cold War.

With all the subtlety of a Soviet-era bordello, the KGB Bar is
sandwiched on the second floor between a repertory theater and
a comedy club. Its embossed tin ceiling is painted black in a futile
attempt to hide the exposed ventilation and sprinkler systems. The
red walls are festooned with a Soviet flag, Cyrillic *Daily Worker* posters
and a gilded mirror flaking from behind as if it feared its own reflection. A fake bronze bust of Tolstoy stands guard over Art Nouveau
shelves laden with exotic vodkas behind a bar yellowed by decades
of heavy shellacking.

Stationed with the Consulate General of Israel near UN headquarters in Manhattan, Nathan has spent more than a few evenings
exploring East Village theater district bistros and watering holes with
thirsty visiting dignitaries. He is certain his old army buddy with an
obsession for Soviet-era culture—if that is not an oxymoron—will
love this place.

Evening light from 4th Street seeps through gaps in the heavy
red drapes, allowing Nathan to locate his tall friend sequestered in a
corner booth, nursing a Baltika porter. An empty shot glass keeps it
company and from appearances, it hasn't been the only one.

"*Ma koreh, ach shely? Harbe zman* [What's up, bro? Long time]."
Shlomo Levi stands unsteadily, clasps Nathan's hand. "Remind me,
was it Hebron or Gaza?"

"Gaza, bro." Nathan wedges his stocky frame into the red booth. "You should remember. I almost flattened your ass cornering that Mark IV in Netzarim."

"Merkavas always had shitty brakes," Shlomo slurs. "So, look at you now, wiping diplomats' asses."

Nathan runs stubby fingers through his short, curly hair and scans the room for potential action. "Manhattan rocks, bro! Tons of women looking for single straight guys who aren't being investigated by the Security Exchange Commission." He signals the tattooed waitress with dyed red hair and a tight black T-shirt emblazoned with the hammer and sickle. "Whatever my friend is having."

"Three shots of Kubanskaya and a Baltika back?" she winks conspiratorially at Shlomo.

"Just one shot for now. But keep checking in." Nathan slips off his new Bergdorf necktie and rolls his French cuffs. "Did I not tell you this place is sick, bro? And speaking of all things Russian, what ever happened to that incredible blonde you used to date in Haifa? You know, the one with…" He makes a gesture as if weighing two imaginary cantaloupes.

Shlomo responds with a dismissive wave. "*Zonah!* Those Russian cunts are all schemers. Couldn't trust the bitch as far as you could throw a fucking camel."

"Harsh, bro!" Clearly, the alcohol has only pissed off whatever bug Shlomo already had up his ass. Nathan eyes the waitress and decides on diplomacy. "You *so* need to get laid. I'll bet that fly little *kussit* with the red hair would do a great Lewinski on you, bro. I can feel the love."

Shlomo downs his porter and smacks the bottle against the table. "I don't need love, I need a fucking life!" He leans toward Nathan and belches, eyes fluttering at half-mast. "My boss is delusional.

He's convinced—are you ready for this?—there are Soviet-era nukes stashed somewhere in Afghanistan, just waiting for al-Qaeda to snatch them up. *Ta'ase li tova* [Give me a break]!"

Shlomo makes a lewd gesture with his middle finger.

Nathan raises an eyebrow. "No shit!"

"I suggested he call that lying, drug-dealing fuck, Karzai, and remind him about Entebbe."

Nathan laughs as he eyes the redhead. "Things could be worse, bro. Being a jumper* has its advantages. Am I right?"

"Believe me, I'd rather be sniffing *kussyot* than making nice with some Persian cocksucker?"

"So, what's *that* about?"

Shlomo shrugs. "Big shot art dealer. Says he's got the dope on where these Russian warheads are gathering dust, right? Like my mother used to say: 'and fucking *chazzirim* can fly!'"

"Your mother had a mouth on her."

The gamine waitress returns with two shots and another bottle of porter. Nathan fists a twenty, tells her to keep the change. This time, she winks at *him*. He sips the shimmering vodka and leans closer to Shlomo, scanning the room for faces that might recognize his and ears that might be tuned to their conversation.

"So, what does this art maven know from nukes?" Nathan asks his glassy-eyed friend.

Shlomo throws up his hands. "Fuck knows! I'm supposed to meet the *putz* for tea at the Algonquin on Monday. Hear what he's got. Probably knows a guy that knows a guy who fucked some general's mistress. Waste of fucking time, but nobody listens to what *I* think anymore."

---

* **Jumper**—a Mossad *katsa* [collection officer] stationed primarily in Israel and the Middle East that makes short-term forays into other countries to work with *sayanim* on assignment

Shlomo seems to drift off until a thought brings him back. "Hey, we should work together again, bro! Your uncle's a big *macher* in Little Odessa, right? Maybe he can pull some strings, talk to a few people, get me into the consulate as a *kaisarut?*"* We could have some fun again! Remember when we busted that Amnesty International caravan of Norwegian chicks making a video at Rafah Crossing?"

Nathan grins at the memory. "Good times!"

"Hey, remember that scene in *The Brothers Karamazov?*" Shlomo bends forward with an open mouth, grabs his shot glass off the table with his teeth and quickly tosses his head backward, draining the vodka in a single swallow.

"Slow down, bro..."

"If I had Yul Brenner's *beitsim,* I'd eat the fucking glass."

"You are one crazy motherfucker," Nathan laughs.

Shlomo remembers something and his face lights up. "Hey, look what I found in a pawn shop over on First Avenue this afternoon?" He reaches beneath his loose Kahala shirt and slips an automatic pistol from the waistband of his jeans, laying it on the table next to his empty shot glass. "Tokarev TT-33. Ugliest sidearm ever made. Pure Bolshevik art."

Nathan leans instinctively over the weapon to hide it. "Put that fucking thing away, bro! This is Manhattan. You can't just pack heat here like it's downtown Tel Aviv."

"Why not?" Shlomo taps his empty shot glass against the pistol's wooden grip. "New York is a dangerous place." With a straight face, he snatches the pistol up from the table with surprising speed, points it at Nathan's chest and pulls the trigger. A jet of butane flame bursts from the muzzle and curls harmlessly upward.

* *Kaisarut*—Mossad Intelligence liaison officer with Israeli Embassies and Consulates

"Got a smoke, bro?"

Nathan would probably have pissed himself were it not for the woody he still nurses fantasizing about that cute redhead waitress going down on him in the men's room.

SATURDAY, 4 JULY 2009 • MASSACHUSETTS TURNPIKE

....

CRUISING THE INTERSTATE at seventy miles-per-hour under a moonlit summer sky, Sonya sighs at the ironic hopelessness of her carefully orchestrated reunion with Danny. Their relationship reads so much like a Russian novel: Danny is still as unavailable as Count Vronsky, and she still as conflicted as Anna Karenina, though not quite ready to throw herself in front of a moving train. It is rare that she allows herself time to indulge in such romanticized thinking, but there is another hour of highway to Boston and a rather large elephant in the car with them.

"I apologize for my behavior this morning." Danny is slumped uncomfortably in the passenger's seat, his long legs cramped beneath the plastic glove box. He sounds exhausted and vulnerable. "I had no right to interrogate you...or touch you that way."

"No harm done," Sonya assures him, remembering that touch with an excited shiver. She also remembers how his sinewy body always relaxed diagonally across her bed after her mouth had feasted on him, how his eyes had closed peacefully in unconditional trust.

"I've been trying to imagine what it must be like," he says, "not knowing if your father's still alive. I'm sorry I doubted you, Sonny. I was thinking of myself and..." When he hesitates, she glances over at him. "And how it felt when you left."

That elephant. "I guess I owe you an explanation," she says.

He shakes his head, grimaces as if the wound is still raw.

"I'm truly sorry I hurt you, Danny. I didn't know how else to handle things at the time."

"I must have read your e-mail a thousand times. 'It's about me,' you said. But it wasn't just about you, Sonny. It was *never* just about you."

"That's not what I meant. I just thought it was the best way…"

"To break my heart?"

"Hearts mend…eventually."

"Or, you can always hide it behind a stiff white collar, right?"

"You never took that collar off, Danny. I know you tried, but your vocation was stronger than your feelings for me. And you were so naive about the world, such a dreamer about peace on Earth and the goodness of Mankind."

"What else besides faith in human decency can save us from extinction, Sonny?"

"Human beings are shit, Danny. You wouldn't believe the things they are capable of doing to each other in the name of their gods. Your life has been so sheltered from all that, a cloistered world of academia and piety that sees everything through rose-colored glasses."

"And how did yours get tinted black?" Danny pauses, looks away, and when he speaks again, long-suppressed emotion seeps through his clerical armor. "I was in love with you, Sonny. I was ready to give up everything."

"And that wouldn't have been fair of me to ask, because I had nothing to give back to you under the circumstances."

"What circumstances? Why *did* you leave?"

"I had no choice. Every IDF reservist was activated the morning of 9/11, recalled to Israel as soon as we could get on a plane. There'd been an alert that an attack on the US was imminent."

"Wait…are you saying you got an alert *before* the planes hit?"

She nods. "A lot of Israelis working or studying abroad back then stayed connected through an instant messaging service called Odigo. The company had an office two blocks from the World Trade Center in New York. We all got an alert about two hours before it happened. Possible attack on US cities was all it said."

"Holy *shh…!* You could have told me."

"It might well have been a false alarm."

"I mean afterward. After you knew you were being recalled."

Sonya feels a flush in her face and moisture in her eyes that cause the taillights ahead of them to blur into soft focus. "I guess I was a coward, Danny. I couldn't bear to look in your eyes and tell you the dream was over. All I can do now is ask your forgiveness."

He stares through the windscreen. "As a priest, it's my duty to grant you that, Sonny."

"And as a man?" She concentrates in silence on the road ahead, awaiting Danny's answer.

He deftly changes the subject. "We'll need Carbon-14 analysis to authenticate your vellum."

Sonya glances at him as oncoming headlights illuminate Danny's sad eyes.

"You'll help me then?"

"I'll try."

SATURDAY, 4 JULY 2009 · CAMBRIDGE, MASSACHUSETTS

....

SONYA FLIPS OPEN HER LAPTOP to check e-mail and finds a Facebook notification from Golda Solomon. *Missing you at my 30th,*

Golda has written above a yellow box that contains a reply link. Sonya clicks on it, logs in and sees a mobile phone photo of three young women with little umbrella drinks at a party in some unspecified tropical location.

She saves the grainy image to her screen and opens it with an encryption program hidden deep in her system folder. In a dialog box, Sonya keys the 27 digits that give her access to a list of discrete co-sign transformation coefficients used in .jpg compression. She finds Giraffe's tongue-in-cheek message embedded in the code:

Hook is baited. Attach lure and go fishing.

Sonya smiles, lapsing into a rare moment of nostalgia as she remembers old Sasha Krasny's unkempt hair swirling around his head like a snowdrift as he lectured in his classroom at the International Policy Institute for Counter-Terrorism in Herzliya.

After 9/11, the technical sophistication of covert communications changed considerably. Multiple layers of secure data encryption became standard operating procedure over the Internet. The most common was TOR—The Onion Router—an open-source software developed by the US Naval Research Laboratory. TOR was employed by the military of many nations, insurgent groups, terrorist cells, white supremacists, drug traffickers, child pornographers and free-lance assassins because its user anonymity and multiple layers of encryption were relatively secure—until its protocols became an inevitable target for status-seeking hackers.

But Sasha was old school, a former KGB counterintelligence officer. He taught his students to follow the four basic "Moscow Rules"—One: assume any technology will eventually let you down. Two: trust your instinct but question what your eyes and ears are telling you. Three: stay within your cover profile but vary your pattern frequently. And four: never hesitate to employ misdirection, illusion and deception.

Sasha told his students how, back in the day, operatives from SMERSH, counterintelligence arm of the Soviet GRU, had used invisible ink to smuggle information safely to their Red Army handlers. He contended that the best way to hide anything secret was to put it in plain sight, where no one would *ever* think to look. Like Histiaeus, the tyrant of Miletus, who had shaved the head of his trusted servant, tattooed instructions for the Ionian Greeks to revolt against their Persian overlords on his courier's scalp, then sent him off to relay the secret message after his hair had grown back. Sasha called it the first recorded use of steganography.

The basic idea had not changed in 2,500 years. But now you could send massive amounts of encrypted data using Voice Over Internet Protocol, or embed messages in digital .jpg and .mpg files that no one would think the least bit suspicious.

Sonya deletes Giraffe's encrypted post from Facebook and signs off. She picks up her mobile, dials a number, and speaks wistfully. "What are you doing?"

"Sipping an 18-year-old from Speyside and listening to Gavrilov dominate the Rach Three," Cyrus replies. "How about you?"

She laughs at his unapologetic pretension, realizes she is actually beginning to like this man despite her better judgment. Then, in a moment of weakness, she thinks that she might abandon her game entirely—if only it were Danny's voice at the other end of the line.

But the thought passes. It always does.

"I can't sleep," she tells Cyrus.

"I have just the remedy," he assures her.

....

ARRAYED IN CASSOCK, ALB AND AMICE, Danny recites Sunday Mass then strips down to his shorts and T-shirt for a jog to the boathouse. Gliding over the black water, he again dissects the incongruities of Sonya's manuscript with each pull on his oars, and re-sifts the known from the hypothetical in an attempt to refute his personal inferences and cognitive biases. In the end, the conclusion he continues to reach is nothing short of breathtaking.

He docks his boat and dials the Sheraton Commander on the clubhouse phone. Unable to reach Sonya there, Danny calls the mobile number she gave him.

"Where are you?"

"Up early...It's a beautiful morning." There is hesitation in Sonya's voice. "Can you meet for breakfast? Cyrus' place around ten?"

Danny feels his throat tighten. "There are better places to eat."

"I want you to tell him what we learned yesterday. He could be an ally."

"Yeah, ally with benefits, if Cyrus has anything to say about it."

"Look, if it will help me find out what happened to my father, I'll *give* Cyrus the goddamn piece of goatskin." He hears her sigh deeply. "You said you'd help."

"Okay, Sonny. I'll meet you there."

Climbing the steps to Cyrus' portico at 9:30 am, Danny swallows the suspicion that has been roiling in his gut all morning. He has dressed in clerical garb, a starched Roman collar tucked into a short-sleeved black shirt, not because it is Sunday but to remind himself that he is an ordained priest in the Society of Jesus. And confronting Cyrus without decking him will take a special dispensation from the Holy Spirit, who has not been much help to him so far.

Danny lingers for a moment beneath the white Doric colonnade, inhaling the scent of freshly mown grass and squinting into the dappled shade beneath a cool canopy of maple boughs in the wilting heat. Somewhere, on the other side of this crisis of faith, there *has* to be peace. If only he can hang tough, remain a soldier true to his vows. His prayer mitigates the rage in his belly and comforts his aching heart as he forces his finger to depress the doorbell.

"Danny boy!" Cyrus' cheeks are pink and stylishly unshaven, his hair freshly moussed like a model in a men's cologne ad. "I've got some sinful croissants in the oven." Danny contemplates how sinfully satisfying it would be to break that aristocratic Persian nose with one good shot.

"Make you an espresso?"

"A double," Danny grunts.

Sonya is a sphinx in mint T-shirt and white chinos. She sits coolly on the leather sofa, her short hair artfully tousled and still damp from the shower. Danny tries to avoid looking at her but cannot manage it for long. He stands rigid in the center of the room, his judgmental eyes locked on hers as Cyrus' voice waxes cleverly from the kitchen.

"Sonya tells me you had an interesting field trip yesterday. Too bad you missed the fireworks here in town. Boston Pops did their annual blowout on the Charles." Cyrus raises his voice above the pressurized hiss of an espresso machine, "Neil Diamond was the headliner this year. Makes me feel old just knowing who the guy is." Carrying a tray with a golden croissant and white demitasse cup, two cubes of raw sugar and a tiny spoon arranged beside it on the saucer, Cyrus enters his living room singing, *"Sweet Caroline, good times never seemed so good…* Take a load off, Danny Boy. I know it's Sunday, but you look so damn stiff in that collar."

Danny takes the cup from Cyrus and lowers himself onto the leather ottoman of an Eames chair. As he stirs sugar into the thick coffee, Danny notices no one else is eating. His host slides onto the sofa beside Sonya, and if he were uncertain before, Danny can sense by their body language alone that they spent the night together.

"So, I'm dying with suspense," Cyrus grins, rubbing his hands briskly. "What did you find out about our manuscript?"

Danny tosses back his espresso in a single gulp, ignores the croissant lest he choke on it and sets the tray on Cyrus' glass coffee table. He takes a deep breath to steady his voice.

"The scans Carlton made enabled me to read enough of the under-text to run a rough translation past Art Heinrick at the Early Buddhist Manuscripts Project. I followed up last night with Leo Van Camp, who chairs the Committee on Inner Asian and Altaic Studies here at Harvard. Based solely on their input, I'd have to conclude this piece is a forgery and we're both being conned."

Cyrus' grin flat-lines as Danny presents a dispassionate analysis. "The Kharosthi text is an initiation verse from the *Kalachakra Laghutantra*. Because of its apparent references to Muslim invaders, most scholars believe it was composed in 11th century India, about five centuries after Kharosthi fell completely out of use. In fact, the mistake is so blatant, you'd have to conclude one of two things: first, despite the technical proficiency of linguistics, calligraphy and materials employed, our forger never bothered to do a Google search."

Sonya remains inscrutable, never drops her eyes from Danny's and never reveals the slightest waver of confidence.

"And the second?" she asks.

"That's the only reason I'm here," Danny replies coldly.

"Your document is written in Classical Persian and Arabic using iron gall ink on a piece of vellum that was recycled in the Greek method of surface scraping. The original text appears to be a Buddhist tantric initiation in Sanskrit using the Semitic Kharosthi alphabet and ink made from burnt bone and cow's urine. So, the first question I ask myself is: why would any forger worth his salt produce a technically perfect palimpsest using the wrong alphabet?

"An authenticator would routinely run Carbon-14 to determine how long the vellum has been around and Polymerase Chain Reaction analysis to confirm the hide's species by reconstructing the genetic code from DNA strands. The EDS test we ran with Carlton told us what the inks were made from, but not when the document was inscribed. The best method for determining that is history. You correlate the artifact with others of verifiable vintage or found in a location already *terminus ante* or *post quem* dated."

He took a breath and continued, "The Kharosthi script doesn't jibe with the text, which calls its authenticity into question. But it dawned on me that the key to this document's provenance is actually the Ta'liq script, what was written *over* the Kharosthi. That's why we went to see Bashir Bokhari yesterday, someone I know has more than a theoretical expertise in Persian art and literature."

Cyrus bites anxiously into his croissant and wipes puff pastry flakes from his Van Dyke. "So, what did your guy say?"

"That the Persian over-text appears to be the work of an Isma'ili scholar and poet from Khurasan, which means it most likely originated in the far northeast of Afghanistan where the Isma'ili sect has thrived for 800 years. After examining the vellum, Bashir thinks it may have come from Badakhshan Province, where this poet lived and died in exile."

Cyrus frowns. "But we've still got that 500-year discrepancy on the Kharosthi script."

"That's true," Danny says. "*If* the *Kalachakra* originated in 11th century Bihar or Bengal as a Buddhist response to Muslim invasions, which is what most scholars believe. But what if it didn't?"

Danny pauses, shifts his weight on the leather ottoman. "What if the prevailing theory is wrong? What if there *is* an earlier source, just as the *Kalachakra* claims?"

"You're making the hair on my arms stand up." Cyrus replies.

"Got a World Atlas?"

Cyrus pulls an Oxford edition off the bookshelf and sets it on the coffee table between them. He and Sonya bend over the book as Danny locates the spread displaying Central Asia.

"Commentary on the *Kalachakra* states that its source material is an initiation given in the 5th century BCE by the Buddha to the King of Shambhala. Giuseppe Tucci, one of the founders of modern Buddhist studies, reckoned the Shambhala legend referred to an actual kingdom in Eastern Turkestan, what's now the Xinjiang Uyghur Autonomous Region."

Danny's finger circles an area ringed by mountains, the Tian Shan to the north and east, the Kunlun Shan to the south, and a knot of peaks to the west where the Himalaya, Karakoram, Hindu Kush, and Pamir ranges converge. He taps the northern edge of the Taklamakan Desert on the map. "This was the Kushan homeland. They were driven out of the Tarim Basin by rivals, migrated west and conquered Bactria. Under Kanishka's reign, they re-conquered their homeland in the early 2nd century. And here," he taps the southern edge of the basin, "in Khotan, at the Buddhist ruins of Gosnga Vihara, is where the Kharosthi *Dhammapada* manuscript was found."

Sonya's eyes widen. "You're saying Shambhala *did* exist?"

"I'm just saying that all the translations and commentaries on *Kalachakra* claim it originated in Shambhala and imply that it was distilled into its present form around the 2nd century. That coincides with Kanishka's reign. I'm saying your vellum could have originated in Balkh, maybe at Nava-Vihara, a vast Buddhist monastic complex that was destroyed by Umayyad Arabs in the 8th century. It could have been rescued by a fleeing monk and stashed for safe keeping in some remote retreat in the Pamirs, where the cold, dry climate preserved it. It could have been exhumed centuries later by a Tajik scribe that knew squat about tantric texts but had mastered a scraping technique handed down by his Greco-Bactrian ancestors. And he could have used the recycled vellum to record the verses of a revered Isma'ili poet using Ta'liq script with iron gall ink."

Danny pauses to let Sonya and Cyrus consider the implications. "I'm saying there's a reasonable possibility you've got something here that refutes all the conventional theories."

Cyrus leans back on the sofa, whistles softly. "Sweet Jesus! This thing could be priceless."

"*If* it's not a fake."

"You're not a very convincing *advocatus diaboli*, Danny Boy." Cyrus claps his hands together. "Okay, let's assume we've got a winner. We should have C-14 results by Thursday if we get a sample of the vellum over to Geochron first thing tomorrow morning." He turns to Sonya. "Then, you and I will hop a Metroliner to Manhattan and meet with your fixer."

Danny feels as if he has been jabbed with a needle. "Your 'fixer'?"

"An associate from Saint Petersburg who can arrange access and transportation," Sonya explains. "I contacted him yesterday after we visited Bashir. We'll need to get in and out of Afghanistan safely, and an expedition like that requires financing. Cyrus has offered to provide that. After all, Danny, based on what you've just told us, can't we reasonably assume this is only one page from a much longer manuscript? There could well be a whole cache, right?"

In that moment, Danny has no idea who the woman he once loved so fiercely has become. And no clue what she is *really* after.

"Someone I once trusted told me that making assumptions is dangerous." He stands to leave, no longer able to confront Sonya's poker face. "Guess I should have listened."

SUNDAY, 5 JULY 2009 • BRIGHTON BEACH, NEW YORK

....

A YOUNG WAITRESS BAGS five orders of *vareniki, kupatu* and sweet *penek* as the Petrenko twins man their usual positions like six-foot-eight-inch Tighthead Props at a rugby match, itching for a scrum. Kyrylo's mass blocks the front door on Coney Island Avenue, and Marko's the kitchen entrance behind the cash register. Beneath short-sleeved polo shirts, they carry identical, and illegal, polymer Glock 25s tucked into Kydex belt holsters, so they can exchange 15-shot .380 ACP magazines in a pinch. Their employer sits inconspicuously at a table beneath a kitschy painting of village life on the Ukrainian steppe while his chiseled blonde bodyguards wait for him to finish a bottle of malty *kvass* and tip the strawberry blonde waitress $20. She accepts the money with a cautious smile.

Everyone in Little Odessa knows who Viktor Volodymyr Kaban is. A lot of the *zlodiy*—the Ukrainian mob—came to Brighton Beach thinking they would be welcomed as oligarchs by expatriate countrymen because of their reputations and money. Many did not live long enough to enjoy the approbation. But everybody knows Viktor is untouchable, if not why.

The "why" is because Viktor Kaban never takes sides. He has no political ideology and no nationalistic loyalty. He was born a Jew in the Ukrainian city of Odessa, survived the USSR's institutionalized anti-Semitism and hard time in the Russian Federation's brutal prison system. He became an Israeli citizen when the opportunity presented itself and feels about his new country exactly how he felt about Ukraine. Both are good places to do business.

Viktor carries passports from six countries and does business with anyone who deposits cash into his accounts in Istanbul or Vaduz. He never questions allegiances or cares about the final destination of his merchandise as long as the end-user certs are impeccable. It was rumored that the BM-21 Katyushas he brokered to a business associate in Peshawar were deployed against American forces in Afghanistan, but no one in Washington can link him to that. Nor to the 9K72 SCUDs, purchased from a now-deceased General at the Vinnytsia 48th Ammunition Arsenal, which somehow turned up in Syrian hands. It is not his concern how inventory is used. Or

by whom. And, despite the show of public outrage made by oppor-
tunistic politicians, six countries still consider Viktor a valuable
resource when weapons need to find their way to destinations with
which said countries cannot afford to be associated. Hence the passports, and the reason he never has to wait for an order of *vareniki*
anywhere in Brighton Beach.

Lunch tucked under his arm, Viktor nods to the twins who take
their usual positions fore and aft. Kyrylo, always in front, slows to check
windows of the laundromat, locksmith, and travel agency before they
pass beneath steel girders supporting the B-line "L" tracks. Crossing at
the intersection, two barrel-shaped Chechen women, dressed in long
overcoats and colorful *hijab*, carry overloaded plastic shopping bags
past an ice-blonde supermodel wearing a *Juicy* tank top and pushing
a baby carriage. The three women do not seem to notice each other,
as if they exist in mutually exclusive parallel universes. Viktor finds
this disconnected community amusingly predictable.

A thickset young man with a buzz cut and soul patch beneath
his lip stands at the corner of Brighton Beach Avenue by the Subway
sandwich shop. His arms are crudely etched with blue stars, crosses
and Cyrillic banners advertising his tenure in Kresty prison. On his
back, above the sweat-stained sleeveless T-shirt, the *zolotiye-kupola*
tattoo depicting Saint Michael's golden-domed spires proclaims the
zlodiy has survived three stint at Kresty. As the *Juicy* blonde mother
passes by, he blows a jet of smoke and mumbles just loud enough
for her to hear, "*Na koliny, sheleva* [On your knees, slut]."

Viktor nudges the man from behind and snarls, "*Zakriy pel'ku,
zhopa* [Shut your mouth, asshole]! That's my niece."

The young hood spins around to confront his own reflection
in Viktor's dark glasses. He looks up in terror at the twins towering
like granite gargoyles on either side. For a moment, his unshaven face

goes slack as a death mask until Viktor's tight mouth splits into a savage grin.

"Only kidding, Pavlo," Viktor admits with a shrug. "I would fuck her myself."

Pavlo forces a laugh, but Viktor can tell he has almost shit his pants. "Someone was asking for you at the pub earlier," he says. "That *pereguznya* [polecat]…from the consulate."

"What did the little shit want?" Viktor asks.

"Just to know if you were in town," Pavlo plucks the burning ash off his cigarette and saves the half-smoked butt behind his ear. "Said he had some business with you."

"And *you* said…?"

"I only told him I would pass it on."

"So, now he knows I am here," Viktor snarls. "Maybe you should not talk to anybody but little sluts, Pavlo. Maybe you should just stick to pouring pils and keeping your fucking ears open." The twins never take their steel-gray eyes off the panicking hood.

"On my mother's grave, I swear I told him nothing!"

Viktor lightly taps Pavlo's unshaven cheek several times, "Relax, Pavlo. When you see the *pereguznya* again, tell him I will be at the chessboards after lunch."

....

ZOYA KABAN FINDS THE GHETTO MENTALITY of Little Odessa petty and predictable, which is exactly why her big-shot son moved her into a penthouse at the Oceana overlooking Riegelmann Boardwalk. Viktor equates predictability with control, and never misses an opportunity to demonstrate that. He spends a month in Brighton Beach three times a year before making his business trips to God-knows-where. Zoya misses the Black Sea, but on her balcony, she can at least console herself with a panoramic view of the Atlantic Ocean and the swooping roller-coaster tracks of Coney Island.

Her opulent condo glitters in afternoon sunlight. White beams angle across an open atrium above the massive fireplace. Overstuffed love seats float like soft marshmallows above antique rugs from Azerbaijan and bleached oak flooring. As always, she has exotic flowers arranged in vases to splash color around the room and impress her few visitors.

While the giant Petrenko twins wolf sausages in the kitchen with Vitali, Zoya's current brutish minder, she and Viktor sit in wicker furniture on the double balcony beyond a wall of sliding glass doors eating the lunch he brought. She loves Café Glechik's *vareniki*, but reminds her son that her *borsht* is still superior to theirs. He nods dutifully, bites into a wedge of *penek* and sneezes because the Stargazer Lilies always irritate his sinusitis. Zoya cannot smell anything over her cologne.

Despite Viktor's insistence, she refuses to learn English. *"Lena Lyubisch hoche, schob ya do nei pryihala v Miami tsiyeyu zymoyu* [Lena Lyubisch wants me to visit her in Miami this winter]." She draws a gauzy sage pashmina across her slender torso as if some phantom breeze is chilling her to the bone.

"Miami is a bad place," Viktor blows his nose into a satin napkin. "The Cuban drug people are always making trouble. Why not invite Mrs. Lyubisch here?"

"Because I hate it here in winter. The rain never stops. I want to go where it is warm."

"Okay, I will have Vitali drive you down to Miami."

"I do not want to go with Vitali. He frightens everyone, and he eats like a pig."

Viktor sighs. "Okay, I will find someone else to take you."

"I feel like I am in prison, Viktor. If I had known it would be like this in America, I would never have let you bring me here."

"Yes, yes, I know. You tell me this every time I come to visit. Do you know how much this 'prison' costs me every month?" He throws his napkin on the table next to a half-eaten slice of cake and pushes his chair back. "I am going down to the boardwalk to play chess."

Zoya turns her eyes toward the sea like Penelope awaiting liberation. She knows Viktor hates it when she puts on that wistful, long-suffering face. He says that allowing her to wander as she pleases would pose an unacceptable risk. His enemies might try to get to him through her and that would be very bad. "For business," he adds.

Viktor leans over to kiss Zoya's rouge darkened cheek. "We can go to Primorski for supper if you like."

"Georgians are pigs," Zoya waves a dismissive hand. "Take Vitali."

....

BENEATH THE ARCHED SHELTER across the boardwalk from Café Volna, elderly men wearing garish T-shirts, baggy shorts, and duckbill caps gather around concrete chessboards, kvetching about anything that has changed in the past two decades. They sit for hours on the steel and wooden slat benches, smoking cigars and insulting each other in Russian, Ukrainian and Yiddish. When not engrossed in a game of chess, the contestants perch like a tiding of magpies, gossiping about their neighbors and arguing politics until it is time for supper. Viktor finds them all incredibly boring but predictable. And he does enjoy the games.

As the twins take positions diagonally, at either side of the shelter so they can maintain eye contact, Viktor nods to a few of the regulars, walks to the rear bench, and sits beside a young man wearing an unmarked baseball cap and sunglasses.

"How is your uncle?" Viktor asks in English.

"He's good," Nathan Spektor replies. "Thanks for asking, Mister K. And your mom?"

Viktor shrugs. "She does not leave her apartment these days with all the crime on these streets." He leans closer to Nathan and lowers his voice confidentially. "Only this last week, I heard a *shwartze* was caught selling crystal meth. Right *here* on the boardwalk. The police found his body near the airport."

Viktor pauses for effect. "His head was missing."

Nathan squirms on the bench. "Dude had it coming, I guess."

"Chechenskaya Obschina,* everyone says," Viktor stares conspiratorially at Nathan. "You cannot blame them for wanting to protect the community from an animal who sells poison to children."

Nathan shakes his head sympathetically. "The world's sure going crazy, Mister K."

Viktor slings an arm over the bench back, smooths the wrinkled front of his blue linen shirt, and hopes no one will notice that he dripped some of his lunch onto the placket while arguing with his mother. "So, what can I do for you, Nathan?"

"I wanted to pass on some information, Mister K."

"What will it cost me?"

Viktor watches sweat drip from Nathan's pink cheeks onto his Izod tennis shirt. "Friends are in from London next weekend and I'd love to get some good Bolivian…but only if you think this information is useful, Mister K."

The young consul turns toward Viktor without noticing the twins easing their right hands under their respective shirts and resting them a heartbeat from their Glocks.

* **Chechenskaya Obschina** [Chechen Community]—a liberation movement founded in Moscow by Khozh Ahmed Noukhayev that became a drug and weapons trafficking mob, the Obschina are now reputedly controlled by the Russian FSB.

"Last night, I hooked up with an old IDF buddy. Dude works for Mossad now. And drinks a little too much, you know?"

Nathan laughs and Viktor laughs along with him.

"Not a good combination," Viktor concedes.

"So, something came up during our conversation that I thought you might want to know."

"You are a *mensch*, Nathan," Viktor says. "I am all ears."

MONDAY, 6 JULY 2009 · MANHATTAN, NEW YORK

....

A BONE-RATTLING TAXI RIDE from Penn Station ends on West 44th Street beneath "Old Glory" hanging limp above the Algonquin Hotel's monogrammed awnings. As Cyrus pays the fare, a doorman spots Sonya's long legs and red-soled stiletto heels emerging from the Yellow Cab and hustles to the curb.

"Dorothy Parker never got that much attention around here," Cyrus remarks.

"If only she'd worn Louboutins," Sonya smiles appreciatively as the doorman takes charge of her rolling suitcase. She is dressed for business in a fitted linen suit, her hair swept back conservatively. Clearly, Sonya understands that in a world still dominated by sexually frustrated, rich, white men, her formidable figure will trump business acumen in their pathetically predictable minds, or at least hide it in plain sight. Her calculated and liberated pragmatism makes Sonya even more attractive to Cyrus.

In the Algonquin's wainscoted lobby, where HL Menken held court during the Roaring Twenties without the aid of air conditioning, a long-legged man with a shock of dark, curly hair and a sparse beard sits in a striped Edwardian rollback chair nursing iced tea. He is strategically positioned between one of the dark mahogany columns and the far wall of the lobby where a mirror allows him to monitor the front door. Cyrus notes that the man faces narrow sidewalk windows, their panes etched to exclude prying eyes, and a ceiling-high fern shields his back from the rest of the room.

Sonya clasps his hand and shakes it like a man. "*Sergei, spasibo chto prishol* [Sergei, thanks for coming]."

"*Priyatno pomoch'* [Pleasure to help]." He switches to heavily accented English. "Sit please, sit."

Cyrus flags down a waiter on cruise control and orders Perrier with lime.

"Tea with milk," says Sonya. "Russian Caravan, if you've got it."

She introduced Cyrus to her colleague and they make small talk about the sticky weather in Manhattan, long TSA lines at JFK and the subsidized price of petrol in Saint Petersburg, until the waiter returns with hot water and a tea caddy. Sonya frowns at the assortment of pre-packaged bags, settles for Earl Gray, and shifts into business mode.

"Sergei, we want to get into Afghanistan. Safely. Ishkashim, on the northern border with Tajikistan. We have a contact there. After that…we're not yet sure where."

"Getting into Kabul, no problem," Sergei replies thoughtfully. "Outside Kabul, *big* problem. Taliban and drug lords control roads. Safest way through Tajikistan. I will check requirements for visa with consulate here in New York and local contact in Dushanbe to arrange transportation."

Sergei narrows his eyes ominously. "Since civil war, everyone in Tajikistan in drug business. Much corruption." Then he rubs his fingers together and shrugs lightly. "But, no problem; I can fix."

"Let me guess," Cyrus interjects, put off by Sergei's batik-print island shirt. "A stack of Rubles in the right palm?"

"Euros." Sergei corrects. "In *right* palm, yes. Wrong palm, you spend long time in jail trying to reach American Embassy on dead phone line." He scratches his beard thoughtfully. "Roads outside Dushanbe not so good. You will want Toyota Land Cruiser, not Russian vehicle. Worse than British. How many traveling?"

"Depends." Sonya taps her fingernails against the porcelain teacup. "I had hoped to have someone who could translate for us in Afghanistan, but…" Cyrus raises an inquisitive eyebrow. "Danny's being recalcitrant," she explains.

He snorts a laugh, "That's an understatement. The tension at breakfast yesterday morning was thicker than my espresso. What *is* it between you two?"

Sonya sips her tea, crosses her legs and sighs. "We have…history."

"You mean the good father had a moral lapse?"

"It was a long time ago, Cyrus. As you know, I was in Danny's class at Harvard. He was just a novice then."

"Obviously, that collar hasn't prevented him from carrying a slow-burning torch."

"Danny may be a hopeless idealist, but he's a good man. I hoped he'd forgiven my schoolgirl crush, but I suspect I hurt him rather badly," Sonya sighs. "Young and oblivious."

Cyrus grins skeptically "You're quite the opposite of 'oblivious,' love. You strike me as a woman who knows exactly how to get what she wants. By whatever means necessary. I suggest you make the good Father Callan an offer he can't refuse."

Sonya glares over the horizon of her teacup. "I have a better idea, Cyrus." She sips the last drop and sets the porcelain cup decisively into its saucer. "I think *you* should make him that offer—partner. You're the one holding the aces."

"You mean the checkbook."

"Danny's program at CSWR always needs outside funding." She flashes him an exaggerated smile and turns to Sergei. "We'll have a head count for you by end of the week."

Sergei nods and crosses his legs. "And I will have numbers for you by then."

"Don't forget to add that line item for *bhaksheesh*." Cyrus quips, but his droll humor is lost on the taciturn fixer.

....

SONYA TIPS THE BELLMAN, closes her door and only has to wait five minutes for the knock.

Cyrus stands in the hallway, hands tucked into the pockets of his taupe gabardine trousers, that lascivious smile she has come to know so well beaming through his trimmed Van Dyke.

"Just checking to see if your accommodations are as nice as mine," he says. Sonya steps aside and waves an admissive hand. He follows her gesture into the room and strolls directly to the king-sized bed, then runs his hand over the monogrammed "A" on a throw pillow. "Well, at least it's not scarlet."

Cyrus plops down on the satiny duvet, kicks off his alligator loafers and swings his feet up. "Nicely appointed, but I do miss the eccentricity of the 1920s. Things weren't as commoditized in Menken's day."

"Not everyone is as critical as you, Cyrus."

He strokes his lower lip. "I like to think of myself as discerning."

Sonya waits until he has settled in before she repairs to the bathroom, fluffs her hair and freshens her lipstick in front of the ornately framed mirror, where she can monitor his anticipation. Unbuttoning her blouse, Sonya slips it off her shoulders and hangs it behind the bathroom door. She unzips her skirt, lets it fall to the tile floor and, one at a time lifts her peep-toe Louboutin pumps out of the puddle of fabric. In the mirror, she observes the effect her pale mint brassière and string panties are having on Cyrus' respiration. His eyes widen and she detects a flush in his cheeks.

Sonya pivots on one heel like a lingerie model and stands, legs and lips slightly parted, in the bathroom door, fingering the tiny bow at the plunge of her lacy décolletage. "I trust your sponsor is as discerning as you are, Cyrus. We may need a *lot* of Euros in the right palms before we can get our hands on that cache of manuscripts… But just imagine what we might uncover."

Cyrus relaxes his lean body and slowly unbuttons his white dress shirt. "My imagination is already running wild, love."

Sonya takes her time circling the bed and stops where Cyrus can enjoy an unobstructed view. He scans slowly upward from the gold stud in her naval to her cleavage. But unlike most men, his eyes come to rest on hers, and for just a moment, an instant of mutual recognition, she knows that he really *sees* her, and she him.

"My God," he says like a boy about to unwrap a birthday gift, "you are magnificent!"

Sonya is surprised by the attraction she is beginning to feel for this sophisticated older man who worships art, artifice and hedonism. In his unapologetic excess, he seems completely genuine. Then, as if caught off-guard in an unanticipated nanosecond of vulnerability, his shield rises, his sexy mouth curls into that supercilious smile and he becomes "Cyrus" again.

"Let's discuss our game plan over *petite filet au jus*…in an hour or so," he says.

Sonya runs her fingernail through the trimmed hair on Cyrus' chest, traces a slow line from the antique coin he wears like a trophy down to his flat belly.

"First the *amuse-bouche*," she says. Her finger hooks his belt buckle and deftly flicks it open.

MONDAY, 6 JULY 2009 • SOUTH BOSTON, MASSACHUSETTS

....

BULLETS OF SWEAT FLY as Danny slams a double right uppercut into the well-worn heavy bag, imagining it is Cyrus' ribs he is pounding into hamburger. He usually stops at Peter Welch's gym on Dot Ave every Friday evening. It relaxes him before eating supper with his mother and confronting her hopeless bookkeeping. But today, he just needs to blow off steam before he blows his cork.

The regulars know Danny from the old days and never try to edit their salty language just because he is a priest now. Within the cavernous warehouse gym, the sound of leather slapping leather, of speed bags chattering and fighters grunting, the smell of perspiration and perseverance takes him back to his roots. No matter what tragedies or challenges the world hands him, Danny always feels safe here, on balance and in control, attributes conspicuously absent since Sonya reappeared in his life four days ago.

It threw him for a loop seeing her standing at his office door, her blonde mane shorn in that shaggy, boyish cut. She looks more like a professional athlete now, her curves more sculpted, her arms and legs more taut and sinewy than he remembered. And her dimpled jaw seems harder, more set and determined. But Sonya's eyes still electrify him. And her mouth...

God! He has to stop thinking about her this way.

She is down in Manhattan now. With Cyrus. Meeting with her "fixer" and probably sipping champagne. Knowing Cyrus, it is expensive champagne. *Really* expensive. And Danny has only himself to blame for whatever else Cyrus has on his agenda.

Which leads him to wonder what Sonya has on *hers*. He wants to believe that story about her father, but his gut tells him there is more to it. Something she is hiding, something dwelling in the dark shadows that surround her shuttered life. He knows from experience how masterful a manipulator she can be. Even so, even though his guard had been up and anticipating her sucker punch, she still managed to hit him again where he is most vulnerable.

Danny tries to beat these thoughts out of his mind, focus instead on the bag and his vocation, on Loyola's *Spiritual Exercises*. But what bleeds into his consciousness as he pummels the heavy bag is the *First Principal and Foundation:*

> *All the things in this world are gifts from God,*
> *Presented to us so that we can know God more easily*
> *and make a return of love more readily.*

The reminder washes over him like a cold shower until he feels ashamed of his jealousy and anger. This is not how Iñigo would conduct himself, not the way of a spiritual warrior.

Danny stands back from the leather bag swaying on its heavy chain. The white noise echoing off the concrete walls and rafters calms him as sweat rolls off his chin and drips onto the medal of Saint Christopher that has worked its way out of his wet dago-tee.

He lifts the silver oval with the curled tip of his Everlast glove and remembers everything it represents. All the loss and pain, all the hope and faith that followed. He brings the protector's medal lightly to his lips and then tucks it back into his salt-stained shirt, next to his heart.

"Man up, Pee Wee," Danny mutters to himself as his fist drives hard into the heavy bag.

MONDAY, 6 JULY 2009 • MANHATTAN, NEW YORK

....

AS A WARM SHOWER CARESSES the sensitive Brazilian-waxed skin between her legs, Sonya rinses dried semen off her belly, closes her eyes and smiles. She has to admit Cyrus is indeed a discerning man and quite capable of using his silver tongue for more than just pretentious banter. She even managed to get off, but only by imagining it was Danny who was pleasuring her. Forbidden fruit is always more satisfying than the low-hanging variety.

She dries off, rubs vanilla-scented lotion on her skin and wraps herself in a plush terrycloth robe. Before dressing for dinner, Sonya slips the VAIO laptop out of her leather knapsack. Just about the time Cyrus was climaxing on her gold belly button stud, "Golda Solomon" was posting another photo on her Facebook page.

Two short, round women in loud colored shorts and floppy beach hats pose in front of a roller-coaster. The tag below reads: *Me and mom cruising the boardwalk at Coney Island.*

Once decrypted, the .jpg reveals Giraffe's instructions: time, place, crew and required method of rendition:

07-07, 18:00. Last stop B-Line. Black Yukon + 3. Deliver 2 dry

CYRUS' GSM ENCRYPTED BLACKBERRY rings just as he steps out
of the shower in his room at the Algonquin. He wraps a bath towel
around his waist, punches in his security access, and listens to the
digital intonations before a familiar voice answers.

"It's been three days," Cyrus reminds his contact in Langley,
Virginia, while pouring ice water from a carafe. "Good thing the fate
of the free world isn't at stake."

"Nothing is 'free' anymore," the woman replies. "Least of all the
goddamn world. And I *have* been working on a few other things,
mon chér."

"Of course, you have, Courtney. Forgive the sarcasm. So, what
have you found out about the mysterious Ms. Aronovsky?"

"An open book. At first glance, anyway."

"Yes, I found her very forthcoming as well." Recalling his pre-
meal *hors d'oeuvre*, Cyrus peeks through the gauzy curtains onto the
midtown Manhattan rooftops. The muffled sound of rattling taxis
rises up from 44th Street.

"Only thing is: I don't believe a word she says. What did you
find out?"

"Born: 31 October 1979, Saint Petersburg, Russia; father: Dmitry
Antonov, Major, Soviet Frontal Aviation, MIA Afghanistan 1989;
mother: Maryna Aronovsky, ER physician, died near the Lebanese
border in a Hezbollah missile attack, 2006. Immigrated with her
mother to Haifa, 1990; attended Hebrew Reali School. IDF service,
'96 to '99, worked with their intelligence wing in the West Bank and
Gaza; University of Haifa, 1999; Ofakim honors program in political science and Arabic. Fulbright, Harvard Divinity School in 2000;
qualified as a Mensa. PhD in poly-sci, University of Haifa, 2005.
She currently holds a translations and research grant in the Islamic
History Department there."

"Impressive resumé," Cyrus muses. "But I could have gotten all that from her LinkedIn profile. What about *your* sources?"

"We know she had a brief affair with one of her professors at HDS—a Jesuit—and left the US on September 15th, 2001, after the World Trade Center attacks. Apparently, she's been leading a quiet academic life ever since. Travels occasionally in the Middle East and Europe. Speaks five languages fluently, a few others passably. Treated for depression after her mother died. No significant relationships, male *or* female. Shops for expensive shoes at Gershon Bram in Tel Aviv. Want to know her dress size?"

"Already do, *chéri*. Did you check with Military Intelligence or the Shin Bet people?"

"They have nothing on her, *mon binôme*."

"Nothing?"

"It raised my eyebrow, too."

Cyrus whistles softly. "I guess I'll have to be a lot more careful about what I expose to Ms. Aronovsky."

"I know that will be difficult for you."

He laughs. "Thanks, Courtney. I owe you dinner at 1789 next time I'm in DC."

"You're making my mouth water, Cyrus. Better score a big deal."

"Believe me, I'm working on it."

A MATTE BLACK GMC YUKON cruising up the zinnia-lined driveway of the Oceana Condominiums looks to the gatehouse guard as if it has been recently salvaged from a junkyard. Raucous music rattles its dented doors and smoky tinted windows as the guard approaches the driver's side, stands with his hands on his hips, and sucks in his belly. He scans the Yukon's cluttered interior, glares at the wiry, unshaven driver wearing a short-brimmed fedora, dermal punch earlobe piercing and a pentagram tattooed on his neck. The guard does not need to know what those Cyrillic letters beneath it spell. He has had enough experience with the local *vory* to know what they mean.

A cigarette hangs from the driver's lips, ticking like a conductor's baton to the music, as his hands keep time on the steering wheel. Beside him, a lanky girl with black, bobby-pinned hair, nose and eyebrow piercings, and dark lipstick, wears a loose patterned skirt, mesh stockings and a tattered slip layered over her faded tank top. Hoop bracelets hang on her wrists, a garish crucifix around her neck. The girl turns down the volume on her scuffed iPod and tells the guard in a heavy Russian accent, "My boyfriend have new car!"

"He should take it to my cousin's body shop for a face lift."

The driver blows a stream of smoke out the window and grins at the guard, his gold front tooth glinting in the sun. "Family discount?"

The girl trills a vapid laugh, rattles off something in Russian to the driver and suddenly remembers why they are there. "Oh, sorry, I bring dinner for Mrs. Kaban." She holds up a paper bag, and opens it for his inspection. "From Café Glechik."

"Who ordered it?"

"Mister Viktor order for his mother. *Vareniki.*"

The guard phones the Kaban residence from his booth, steps back to the Yukon and chops directions into the air. "Bang a right, then an immediate left. Down the ramp and follow the signs to elevator B. The old lady's a cheapskate, so don't expect much."

....

ZOYA DOES NOT HEAR THE INTERCOM buzz because she is watching her favorite TV program: *America's Funniest Home Videos.* She cannot understand a word Tom Bergeron says, but the little dogs doing flips and peeing everywhere make her laugh, unlike Vitali, who never does anything but grunt, eat and fart. Vitali is sequestered in his room, where he is supposed to be monitoring the hallway surveillance cameras. But Zoya knows he is watching pornographic videos when he is not consuming every morsel of food in her kitchen.

Viktor, as usual, is out somewhere "doing business," which means he does not want her to know *what* he is actually doing because it would only upset her.

Out of the corner of her eye, she notices her bodyguard in his dingy white T-shirt lumbering toward the front door, mumbling something about the hall camera being broken. When Vitali turns into the vestibule, Zoya hears the locks snap back and the front door open. There is a muffled exchange in Russian followed by a sharp thud, as if someone has hit the heavy steel door. The next thing she sees is Vitali sprawled on the hardwood floor in front of the kitchen. He groans, gropes at his chest and then lies still. A man wearing black clothing and a balaclava over his head kneels to check the pulse at Vitali's throat. Then a second masked man appears and helps his partner drag the inert bodyguard into the hallway.

A tall girl dressed like a gypsy and carrying a large handgun appears in the vestibule, hopping gracefully over Vitali's sliding torso. She enters the living room just as Zoya locates her purse and fumbles for the little Beretta Viktor always insists she carry. Zoya tries to remember which way the safety catch is supposed to go, but the gypsy girl is on her like lightning, effortlessly twisting the pistol out of her hand. She jams the long barrel of her own weapon beneath Zoya's chin, leans close to her face and narrows her evil amber eyes.

"*Yakscho zakrychysh, abo skazhesh hoch slovo, ya zupyniu tvoie sertse* [A single sound from you and I will stop your heart]," the gypsy threatens. "If you cooperate, you won't be hurt."

Zoya's heart pounds in her chest like an unbalanced washing machine as the gypsy pulls her wrists behind her back, binds them with a zip-tie and gags her with a balled-up handkerchief and duct tape. Cotton balls are stuffed in her ears and taped into place.

The last thing Zoya sees on the wide-screen TV before a black hood drops over her head is a middle-aged woman attempting to lower her immense bottom into an inner tube before she capsizes with a tsunami-sized splash into a swimming pool.

IN THE PARKING GARAGE by elevator B the two men in black secure Kaban's mother beneath a false deck in the Yukon's cargo bay next to her unconscious bodyguard. Dov, the gold-toothed driver, aims a wavelength-agile military gun sight laser attached to a golf scope monocular at the surveillance camera covering the elevator while Scorpion stands watch. The Keshet *yaridim* did their homework thoroughly, from Zoya Kaban's favorite take-out restaurant to the number of surveillance cameras their *neviotim* would need to neutralize.*

"Ein tzorech be'kiyul meduyak [Precise calibration isn't necessary]," Dov had explained to Scorpion as they approached the Oceana with his team concealed in the plywood shell beneath bags and cardboard boxes of recyclables in the Yukon's cargo space. "The beam randomly changes color from red to green to blue, so filtering is useless. The camera sees only a white-out, as if its iris is stuck open."

"Don't tell me how it works," Scorpion replied brusquely while adhering two faux rings to her left eyebrow. "Just make us invisible."

Past the guard booth, Scorpion had transferred a Cap-chur CO_2 pistol from Dov's glove box into her restaurant take-out bag, along with two 12.95-millimeter injection darts—each containing 300 micrograms of fentanyl. Just one was enough to put the bodyguard on ice until they arrived at their destination.

Scorpion is relieved that Kaban's mother decided to cooperate, because the second dart would probably have killed her. And Giraffe's instructions were to "deliver dry," meaning unscathed. Her *katsa* knows she has never been comfortable with irregular rendition, but Holiday demanded zero casualties until they have Wild Boar where they want him.

* **Keshet** [Rainbow]—Operational division of Mossad overseeing *yaridim,* security teams that conducts surveillance and *neviotim,* break-in specialists that install listening devices

The *neviotim* slip out of their balaclavas, gloves and coveralls, stuff their gear into an athletic bag and climb into the backseat of the Yukon.

"Everything set at the drop?" Scorpion asks.

"Good to go." Dov slows as they exit the garage, and the two men jump out with their kits. Walking casually around the corner, dressed in summer street clothes and chatting idly to each other in English, they reach the tree-lined sidewalk exit to Brighton Beach Avenue unnoticed, just as the Yukon stops on the opposite side of the gatehouse.

Dov flashes his gold tooth at the fat guard. "You were right," he says with a sneer. "A lousy two-buck tip."

TUESDAY, 7 JULY 2009 • RED HOOK, NEW YORK

....

THE TEXT MESSAGE COMES from Zoya's mobile at 7:30 pm. Viktor calls Vitali's number immediately to determine if it is a prank and hears his mother's trembling voice tell him it is not. Checking with the Oceana security office, he is informed about a food delivery to his residence, reported by the gatehouse guard, and an "unrelated" surveillance camera malfunction in the garage.

"You fucking idiots!" is his summary response.

At 8:15 pm, he and the twins cruise down Smith Street over asphalt worn away to reveal the old cobblestones of Kings County. Kyrylo parks the Mercedes S550 beside an abandoned brick warehouse next door to Brooklyn's erstwhile I & E Tire Company. The street lamp is burned out above a rusted chain link fence crowned with razor wire, but there is still enough light for Viktor to see that a padlock has been severed with a bolt cutter and the narrow gate left slightly ajar. Behind the fence, a stretch of macadam between the warehouse and a corrugated aluminum building is veined with cracks and sprouting weeds from every fissure. The pavement terminates at the Gowanus Bay inlet, fifty meters past the gate. Beyond, the Hamilton Avenue overpass hovers behind barges waiting to be filled with gravel. Weathered wooden pallets are stacked alongside the brick building, and the gray steel shutters sealing its tiny windows look rusted closed.

Marko discovers a side door has been jimmied, and Viktor sends him in for a look. Three minutes later, his massive shoulders fill the warehouse door frame as he motions all clear.

The twins snap xenon tactical lights and screw suppressors onto the barrels of their Glocks then scan the musty darkness of the long-abandoned building. On the bare cement floor, their footsteps echo off the wooden joists three stories above their heads. Battered workbenches and the corpses of rusted machinery appear like apparitions as their beams illuminate the perimeters. Twenty meters in, Victor is able to make out a dim, fluctuating light source about waist-high. Another ten meters and he recognizes it as an open laptop computer displaying a dissolving montage of galactic clusters. In front of the bench where the PC sits, three folding metal chairs are waiting. As Viktor approaches the glowing Andromeda Nebula on the screen, an electronically altered female voice addresses him in Ukrainian through the laptop's speaker.

"*Natysnit' bud'yaku knopku* [Touch any key]." When he hesitates, the voice reassures him, "Don't worry, Viktor. It will not explode."

The twins simultaneously sweep a 360-degrees arc around the warehouse with their tactical lights. Viktor taps the space bar on the Toshiba's keyboard and its screen-saver vanishes to reveal a Skype webcam feed. Two grainy, blindfolded figures are seated side-by side, their mouths sealed with duct tape—Zoya, wearing her florid house-dress and pashmina, and Vitali slumped forward in his white under-shirt, his broad torso taped securely to the chair. A tiny green diode above the screen and a mortised video image of his own eerily lit face tells Viktor he is also on camera.

"Where is she?" Viktor roars.

A bright spot of red light pricks his black piqué Polo shirt—directly over the heart. Kyrylo sees it first, freezes, and Marko follows his lead.

"Eject your magazines and clear your breeches immediately," the woman's voice commands. "Place your weapons on the bench beside the laptop and sit down."

The only thing Viktor detests more than appearing foolish is feeling helpless. But the laser gun sight convinces him acquiescence is preferable to the alternative. He nods to the twins and they disarm as instructed.

"Who are you?" Viktor growls.

"RA-115-01," the screen voice says. "Mean anything to you?"

He shrugs impatiently.

"A plutonium-based, linear implosion, anti-personnel weapon with a yield of one kiloton, which can be transported in a suitcase or backpack by a single man. There is word on the street that you are interested in acquiring twelve of these devices that went missing in Northern Afghanistan just before the Soviet Union collapsed."

That fucking *pereguznya* has been talking out of school. Viktor snorts in disgust. "You are delusional. Who the hell are you?"

"Unimportant. All you need to know is that we are prepared to offer you fifty million US each for these weapons. We don't want to engage in a bidding war."

Viktor laughs. "Look, I am not an idiot. Those things would be worth more than fifty million on the street. Maybe four times that."

"Only if they include activation codes. We want to buy the whole inventory as is."

"If you've got that kind of money, you must be representing a big player."

"You don't need to concern yourself with political affiliations or end-user certificates, Viktor. You only have to get the cache out of Afghanistan. We'll take it from there."

Viktor leans forward in his chair, his face crimson. "You invade my home, threaten my family, place my reputation at risk. Why should I do business with you?"

"Because we know what you do, Viktor, and where you do it. Not just here in Brooklyn, but at your apartment house in Yafo; your villa in Bebek; oh yes, and that private club in the Aksaray where you audition your girls. A display of mutual trust is in everyone's best interest."

"So, you take my fucking mother hostage?" The veins in his neck swell with rage.

"To get your attention, Viktor. To let you know we are serious."

"What if I do not *want* to do business with you?"

"Then you will put more than your reputation at risk."

He rubs his jaw, looks down at the red dot on his chest. "Alright, I will think it over."

"Don't think too long," the altered voice warns. "Your mother is waiting in the garage. Our good faith gesture. There's a mobile phone taped to the back of her chair. We will call with instructions." The transmission ends, the red laser dot disappears and Victor lets out a sharp breath. Sweat runs down the back of his shirt and pools at his waistband.

A green EXIT sign high on the rear wall of the cavernous warehouse flickers on. The twins rise slowly from their chairs, scan the perimeter, reload their magazines, chamber rounds, and move with Viktor toward the illuminated exit sign. Behind the door is a vacant garage, and in the middle of the oil stained floor, Zoya and Vitali are bound into metal chairs. A battery-powered LED work light is alligator-clipped to a short aluminum stepladder in front of them, and a laptop identical to the one in the warehouse sits open on its top step.

Viktor unties the black cloth that covers Zoya's eyes, and carefully removes duct tape from her mouth and ears. Her hands and feet have been fastened with plastic zip-ties to the chair. Marko whips out a spring-loaded tactical knife and slaps it into Viktor's outstretched hand like a surgical nurse. He snaps it open with a flick of his finger and carefully cuts the bonds around his mother's thin wrists and edema-swollen ankles, rubbing her hands and feet to stimulate recirculation.

"Viktor," she whimpers, "Victor, what is happening? Who are those gypsies?"

"It's okay. You are safe now," he tries to reassure her. "I promise you, this will never happen again." He turns to Kyrylo. "Take her out to the car and stay with her."

With a hand around her tiny waist, the enormous bodyguard lights Zoya's way out of the garage. Viktor glares at the PC, observing the wrathful image of his own face on the screen. The watcher has blocked her own video feed. Viktor pulls the ladder closer to the still-drugged Vitali, his massive body secured to the small folding chair with zip-ties and duct tape.

Gripping Marko's knife, Viktor stands behind Vitali, slaps his cheek several times to rouse him. "Wake up, you lazy fuck! You let them take my mother, you Georgian pig. My fucking *mother!*" He glances toward the laptop screen as if cueing the eavesdroppers to pay attention, then viciously jerks Vitali's head backward and screams into his blindfolded face. "Do you know how weak that makes *me* look?"

Viktor's knife hand moves quickly from left to right, slicing open Vitali's throat with the razor-sharp serrated blade. Arterial blood drenches the neckline of Vitali's T-shirt and spatters across the concrete floor to mingle with the dried oil stains. The bodyguard lows like a steer in an abattoir beneath his gag as he becomes conscious of what is happening to him. His torso thrashes involuntarily against the bloody gray tape that binds him for nearly thirty seconds before he dies.

"You stupid, fucking Georgian pig! You should be grateful I gave you such a quick death," Viktor grunts, wiping the knife blade on the cloth draped over Zoya's chair. He thumbs the lock mechanism and snaps it closed before tossing it back to Marko. Then Viktor notices the Samsung flip-phone taped to the chair back. Using the blindfold to cover his fingers, he pries it free and brandishes the mobile toward the PC screen.

"Okay, I have thought it over," he theatrically informs the invisible eavesdropper. "Here is *my* good faith gesture." Viktor pulls the dead bodyguard's head back and shoves the little phone into Vitali's gaping trachea as blood oozes around its clamshell case. "Leave your message with him."

Viktor wipes his hands on the cloth and adds, matter-of-factly, "You know, the Obschina would have castrated this fat fuck and left his cock in his mouth as a calling card. But, as you can see, I am a civilized man. So, if you want to do business with me…" He grins at the screen one last time. "Make a fucking appointment."

Viktor snaps the PC laptop closed and tucks it under his arm, leaving the LED in place to illuminate his handiwork. Marko leads him quickly through the dark warehouse, but when they pass the workbench the other laptop is gone. Viktor looks nervously around, wipes sweat from his forehead, straightens his collar and returns to his Mercedes.

Slipping into the back seat beside his mother, he notices that she is shivering beneath her pashmina in the muggy night air. But he cannot bring himself to place a comforting arm around her shoulders. Viktor hates her for all the trouble she has caused him.

"Where is Vitali?" Zoya asks with chattering teeth as Kyrylo pulls away from the curb.

Viktor stares out the window at nothing. "He was incompetent. I decided to let him go."

As Zoya regains her composure, a smile of satisfaction transforms the smeared lipstick on her mouth into a clownish rictus. "I never liked Vitali," she sighs.

NATHAN SPEKTOR'S UNCLE thought it a safe bet when he lent his nephew the cash for a refurbished flat on Rutherford Place and East 15th, directly opposite Stuyvesant Square. After all, nobody ever lost money on Manhattan real estate. A quiet neighborhood cooled by silver linden and English elm, Nathan's place is only a stone's throw from Beth Israel Medical Center and an easy walk to the Israeli Consulate.

Stretched out on his leather sectional in NYU sweat shorts and a T-shirt, Nathan has been watching the Season Three finale of *Lost* on his Blu-ray. Jack Shephard has just driven to a funeral parlor accompanied by the edgy strains of Nirvana's "Scentless Apprentice" when the intercom buzzes. Nathan swears at the untimely interruption, lowers the volume on his Bose sound system, and shuffles to the intercom, singing: *"Hey, go away, go away, go away!"*

Eyes still glued to his flat screen, Nathan punches the button and barks, "Who is it?"

"Nathan, I have a package from Bolivia. Should I leave it on your doorstep?"

Fear reddens Nathan's skin as he opens his front door to find Viktor Kaban and one of his twin bodyguards—he can never tell which—filling the narrow hallway. "Mister K. What a surprise! I wasn't expecting…"

Even Viktor's smile inspires terror in Nathan. "We were in the neighborhood, and I thought I would just drop off the party favor for your guests this weekend."

"That was sure nice of you, Mister K, but you shouldn't have gone to the trouble." Nathan offers a weak smile as his visitors press past him into his living room. "Can I…get you anything? I've got some nice Pinot…couple beers in the fridge, I think."

"No, no. Do not go to any trouble," Viktor stands with his hands in his pockets, scanning Nathan's bachelor accouterments. "Nice place. You must be doing well." He grins, slips a plastic zip-lock bag from his pocket, and gestures to the glass-top coffee table on which Nathan has been eating supper. "Let us sample the candy, shall we?"

Nathan's sharp laugh exposes his nerves. "It's a school night, Mister K…"

"Sometimes, it is worth being late for school," Viktor shrugs as his menacing eyes twinkle. "Just a little taste."

Nathan clears the Chinese take-out containers, steering awkwardly around the mountainous blonde bodyguard who seems to be in the way no matter where he stands.

Viktor taps out a small mound of white powder onto the tempered glass tabletop. "We must be sure this is good enough for your guests." He unclips a tiny utility tool from his key chain, pries out a knife blade and cut the cocaine into two lines. "Besides, Nathan, I am very grateful for the information you gave me on Sunday, and the pictures you sent last night."

Nathan's perky assistant at the Israeli Consulate had surreptitiously captured a half-dozen images of Shlomo Levi and his guests with her iPhone in the lobby of the Algonquin Hotel, which Nathan promptly forwarded to Viktor. "Shoshanna likes to think she's some kind of Jewish Lara Croft," he explains with a manic laugh. "Any excuse to get out of the office, you know?"

Viktor slips a $100 bill from his money clip and rolls it tight. "Nathan, I would like to know more about your Mossad friend who drinks and talks too much."

Nathan sets his half-eaten dinner on the kitchen pass-through and tries to look preoccupied. "Not much more to tell, Mister K. He wants to relocate to the States, maybe get into a less stressful gig. Asked me to talk him up at the Consulate."

Viktor motions for Nathan to join him, and his bodyguard's body language makes it clear Nathan needs to comply. Viktor hands him the rolled Franklin and gestures toward the sugary lines on his coffee table. He bends over hesitantly to sample the blow as Viktor suggests, "Perhaps I can make your friend an offer."

"Wow, that's awesome, Mister K! I will be sure to pass that on to him." Nathan pinches his right nostril shut, sniffs hard through the rolled bill, tosses his head back and wipes his watering eyes as he slides back on the sectional sofa.

"*Whoa!* This stuff rocks!"

"I would like to meet your friend," Viktor says cheerily, lifting the banknote straw from Nathan's tight fingers. He lowers his face toward the remaining crystal line and it quickly disappears up his nose. Viktor snaps erect as the drug infuses his bloodstream. His puffy eyes open wide and his brush-cut hair seems to crackle with the electricity Nathan feels surging through the room.

"Tonight."

"Mister K., I don't think…"

"Why don't you give him a call." It is clearly not a request.

....

WHEN NATHAN INSISTS THEY MEET right away, Shlomo Levi has a very bad feeling. A potential job, Nathan says. They need to talk about it before morning, but *not* over the phone. He's paranoid. Says he doesn't trust AT&T. Thinks the NSA is screening his calls.

Shlomo has known for quite some time that Nathan is in Viktor Kaban's pocket, exchanging information and favors for cocaine. He also knows that the best way to leak a rumor—say, about suitcase nukes—is to pass it through a *mabuah*, an unwitting courier with a big mouth. His corrupt, coke sniffing army buddy has been set up to grease Wild Boar's stairway, pave the way for that offer he cannot refuse. However, the *neviotim* leader just reported that Zoya Kaban's rendition did not go as anticipated. Her erratic son has proven to be as unpredictable as he is frustratingly untouchable.

Shlomo now realizes he has miscalculated badly. Because, even if Kaban is convinced the nukes are legitimate and available, he has graphically demonstrated that he will not be pressured into brokering them to an unknown buyer, not even on threat of losing his mother. Shlomo should have anticipated that. But it is too late now, and time to engage damage control.

If he refuses to meet with Nathan, his pipeline to Kaban will be capped and the operation set back for months, if not permanently. Holiday will be pissed and, rather than jumping with the Kome-miute, Shlomo will find himself shaking down foreign diplomats at the Institute's "sexpionage" flat in Arlington, Virginia. So, even though it is totally against his better judgment, he feels there is no alternative but to meet with Nathan.

Before he leaves his room at the Larchmont on 11th Street in the West Village, "Golda Solomon" embeds a Facebook message for Scorpion within a .jpg of a seagull with a bagel clutched in its beak:

Proceed upstream. Await fishing permit.

When Nathan opens the door to his flat, his eyes are bloodshot and his movements nervous. Two men sit in his living room and Shlomo immediately recognizes Kaban from his INTERPOL photo. He is a bit heavier than he appeared in the mug shot from Milano, but his narrow eyes, upturned snout, and the bristling gray hair of his namesake are unmistakable.

Shlomo also recognizes Wild Boar's bodyguard, one of the infamous Petrenko twins—the "Dancing Bears," as they are called at the Institute—whose muscle mass seems to dwarf Nathan's sofa. He knows the Petrenkos served with Spetsgruppa Vympel* during the devastating invasion of Grozny and were reputed to have been part of a death squad operating throughout the Caucasus before they were recruited by Wild Boar four years ago.

Not expecting to be shaking hands with a man who has just literally cut his own employee's throat, Shlomo's gut impulse is to find a quick excuse to bail. Instead, he decides to hold his cards close to his chest and bluff. He smiles with professional decorum as Nathan makes the introductions.

"Mister Shlomo Levi from Tel Aviv, Mister Viktor Kaban and his associate..."

---

* **Spetsgruppa Vympel**—Special Group Pennant was formed by the Soviet KGB to conduct assassinations and renditions of terrorists and drug dealers. It now operates under the FSB.

"Marko." Kaban inclines his head toward the bodyguard, who nods curtly. "His English is not so good and I am still a novice at Hebrew. It is very nice to meet you, Mister Levi. I am an old friend of Nathan's uncle. He's a very important man in Brooklyn's Jewish Community, you know."

"Indeed." Shlomo sits on the sectional sofa across from Marko.

"It is such a small world, Mister Levi. You and I are almost neighbors," Kaban grins effusively. "I bought a run-down Arab building in Old Yafo when the Amidar housing agency was subsidizing redevelopment. Converted it to apartments and artists' ateliers."

"You're in the art business?"

"Import-export. Heavy equipment. And you?"

"Just a civil servant."

"Nathan says you served together in IDF."

"Hebron and Gaza."

"Military intelligence, Nathan says."

"For a while."

"You sound like a man with useful talents, Mister Levi."

"Call me Shlomo."

"Ahh, like the King—Solomon!"

"My mother hoped I'd be rich as well as wise."

Kaban laughs a bit too effusively, but maintains eye contact with Shlomo, as if anticipating his next move. "Nathan says you like vodka. Do you have any vodka, Nathan?"

"Some Stoli in the freezer, I think." Nathan says.

"*Urla*," Kaban sneers. "Latvian crap. Oh well, it will have to do. Let us drink to King Solomon's wisdom and future wealth."

Nathan does as he is told, fetches a frosty bottle of Stolichnaya and four small tumblers from the kitchen. Kaban fills three with the shimmering liquid. Marko's glass he leaves empty.

"Designated driver," he chuckles.

The tension in the room is thicker than the humidity outside. Shlomo has never been much of a drinker but knows he must uphold the precedent he set at the KGB Bar to avoid arousing Nathan's suspicions. Tonight, he does not have the option of bribing a flirtatious redhead waitress to stack empty bottles on his table and fill his shot glass with ice water instead of vodka.

Shlomo lifts up his tumbler and toasts *Budmo!* and *L'chaim!* with Kaban and Nathan as Marko remains rigid, observing every movement like a Rottweiler waiting for an attack signal. After the second shot of vodka, Shlomo no longer feels his teeth on edge.

"I hear you are thinking about a career change," Kaban ventures.

Shlomo scowls convincingly at Nathan. "That was supposed to be confidential."

"Please," Wild Boar assures him, "you are among friends. And it so happens *I* can offer you a job. The benefits will be much better than your civil servant's position."

"What sort of job?"

"Importing heavy equipment, of course."

"From?"

"Afghanistan." Kaban pours another round, plays his hand. "I think you know what I am referring to."

Nathan averts his eyes as Shlomo feigns outrage. "You told him about *that?*"

"Please," Kaban says, "we are all speaking in confidence here. I am putting my cards onto the table for you. I hope you also will be candid with me. *Za vashe zdorovya!* Your health!"

Shlomo frowns, sighs heavily as if the cat has already escaped the bag, tips his glass and peers into its empty bottom. "I don't know exactly what Nathan told you, Mister Kaban."

"Please! Call me Viktor."

"As I told Nathan…Viktor, I am quite skeptical about this rumor. But, assuming the information I received is even partially accurate—and that is a very *big* assumption—I would never want 'heavy equipment' of that nature to fall into the wrong hands. My country's security would be severely threatened. You understand, don't you?"

"Of course!" Kaban looks mortified by Shlomo's implication. "I, myself, am an Israeli citizen now. I would be bound by honor and conscience to do business only with a friendly buyer, one that can guarantee safety and security. And you, Mister Levi, would be handsomely rewarded for your consultation." Kaban leans in, holds the bottle of vodka suspended over Shlomo's glass.

"We do understand each other, yes?"

"I think we do," Shlomo nods and Kaban pours. Things seem to be looking up.

....

COCAINE AND VODKA USUALLY whet Viktor Kaban's appetite for pussy, but all he can smell now is the sweetest score of his career. This Shlomo *shmuck* with the chin fuzz and Hawaiian shirt on the sofa across from him might just be his key to the kingdom.

He has never known anyone in his business that has seen, let alone bought or sold, a suitcase nuke. Since the Soviet Union collapsed, there have been a flood of rumors, but not a single one has ever turned up. If one ever *did*, the big seven in the Nuclear Club would pay almost anything to ensure such a weapon never falls into the hands of some jihadist group. Viktor reasons that if the Mossad is taking this rumor seriously, it *must* be credible. Ergo, if he can get his hands on even one of these weapons, let the bidding war begin!

He could live like a Sa'udi prince for the rest of his life, buy that island he saw for sale near Marmaris off the Turkish coast and build a villa there. He could hire his own army, wall his whining mother up in a fortress for the rest of her life so no one would ever again make the mistake of trying to extort him through her. He could finally tell the Americans and their Israeli bitches to go fuck themselves. They would all be kissing his ass, bidding up the price for his merchandise just to keep it off the street.

Viktor still wonders about those *lyudej*, Zoya's "gypsy" kidnappers. They were good enough to knock out a surveillance system and neutralize a professional bodyguard. Why the hell would they think *he* knows where these suitcase nukes are stashed? Maybe Shlomo, the tall, skinny spook that has wandered serendipitously into his web, knows more than he is letting on. Viktor is not about to let this drunken fly out of his sight until he finds out.

Then, just as he is basking in the heady glow of fantasy, something goes terribly wrong, shortly after their fifth toast.

Nathan has apparently given up the idea of going to the consulate in the morning. Already coked up and pissed on vodka, he plays loud music on his stereo and mouths off to his old army friend about the "real" problem Israel faces.

"...700,000 of those blood sucking Haredim! And most of them refuse to work. 'Those who fear the Lord' fear lifting a fucking finger to press an elevator button on *shabbat!* But they don't fear making babies and collecting welfare. Tell me why those fuckers should be exempt from military service when every high-school girl is expected to bleed on the front lines? What the fuck was Ben-Gurion thinking anyway?"

Nathan paces the room as he rants, then searches through every drawer in his desk until he finds a plastic bag of foil-wrapped hashish and a tiny brass pipe.

"This Leb Red is epic!" Nathan says. "Take the edge off that blow."

"I *like* the edge," Viktor protests, but Nathan continues to unwrap and crumble the pressed cannabis resin into his pipe. Viktor is not paying very close attention because he has been trying to read a text message from a business associate in Istanbul regarding a bribe demanded by some Turkish Black Sea Coast Guard officer to bring three new girls in from Moldova. These tedious details are always such a distraction.

He hears Nathan mumble to Levi, who sits beside him on the sofa with heavy eyelids, that he needs matches. "You bring that Bolshevik lighter with you, bro? Hey, wait till you see this, Mister K. You are gonna love…"

Viktor almost misses what happens next while trying to read the messages on his Blackberry. Levi reaches beneath his garish shirt and it looks as if he has a semi-automatic pistol in his hand. It must look that way to Marko, too, but since the bodyguard has not been able to follow their conversation in English, his reaction is quite different than Viktor's.

Marko always takes cues from his brother in tense situations, and lacking Kyrylo's direction he has acted impulsively on occasions. Tonight, after all the stress and bloodletting at the warehouse in Red Hook, Marko is wound tight as a mainspring. He is also surprisingly agile for a man of his size. In the blink of an eye, before Viktor can even process what is happening, Marko reacts properly to what he perceives as a clear threat, reaches across the coffee table, jams a throw pillow over Levi's face and pumps two soft rounds* from his silenced Glock into it.

---

* **Soft rounds**—developed for sky marshals, these frangible, polymer-tipped, hollow-point bullets are packed with tiny pellets that expand on impact, limit penetration, disintegrate on harder surfaces and eliminate ricochet.

Levi's head explodes beneath the pillow. Blood and bits of skull splatter Nathan's face as a shell casing lands beside him on the sofa like a copper insect. The *pereguznya* hyperventilates as Levi's body spasms, goes limp and the antique Russian pistol drops from his dead hand.

"What the *fuck?*...It was just a lighter, Mister K! Oh fuck! *Fuck!*"

"*Scho tse ty zrobyv, khlopchyk* [What have you done, boy]?" Viktor growls at Marko. "He was fucking Mossad!"

Viktor leaps to his feet and paces elliptically around the sofa, trying to clear his head and consider his next move. He orders Marko to get the shower curtain from the bathroom and restrains an urge to pummel Nathan to death. Instead, Viktor places an avuncular hand on his shoulder.

"Listen to me now. You will need to clean up this mess, boy. Are you listening?"

Nathan stares straight ahead, shaking uncontrollably.

"You must burn this pillow and use hydrogen peroxide on yourself and everything in the room to destroy DNA," Viktor instructs. "Report Levi missing first thing in the morning. Tell the police where you work, and who he works for. That will get their attention...Say Levi told you he was meeting with some Chechens in Brooklyn, but he did not say why...Tell the police his phone is no longer working, and you are worried. Do you understand, boy?"

Nathan nods, but his eyes have already glazed over in shock. Viktor glances at Marko who is examining Levi's Tokarev replica. He pulls the trigger and a gas flame shoots out and upward from its muzzle. Marco looks perplexed and almost embarrassed. He has probably never killed a man for trying to light a hash pipe.

"We will take care of the rest," Viktor assures Nathan as a patch of urine spreads slowly over the crotch of his shorts.

....

FROM NINE TO FIVE, Dov Reznik is home alarm systems specialist at Radio Shack in New Hyde Park, Jamaica Queens. His earlobe piercing is authentic, but the *goyim* tat on his neck was removed with mineral oil when he returned home from his night gig.

Dov is not often called in as a *yarid* or *neviot*, but his precision under pressure placed him on Keshet's A-list. He worked with Shlomo Levi on several occasions, but had never seen the tall woman with the black hair before. He was told only that she is *kidonim* and that means it is better not to know anything more about her. Bad things always happen around those people.

Dov gets the call from his NYPD contact while explaining the Simon XT control panel operations to a particularly querulous customer. He hands the kvetcher off to another salesperson, and tells his manager he has a family emergency.

Soft rain falls as Dov's '99 WRX hugs the asphalt of Union Boulevard, threads the Cross Island and Belt Parkways at 70 miles-per-hour, bypasses John F Kennedy International Airport, and exits at 119th Avenue. Lefferts Boulevard dead-ends at JFK's long-term parking, where an open gate festooned with razor wire and signs barring unauthorized persons is blocked by two Port Authority squad cars and an unmarked cruiser. Lieutenant Len Shapiro, one of the Brooklyn *sayanim*, wears a blue windbreaker over his wiry frame and an NYPD ball cap. He waits for Dov in the gray drizzle.

Shapiro motions to the cruiser. "Jump in." Dov slips into the back seat behind the safety cage and Shapiro rides shotgun as they turn onto a narrow road running parallel to Bergen Basin. The uniformed officer behind the wheel drives them past a low white building flying stars and stripes. Beyond, in a sodden field of gravel, a fleet of orange earth moving equipment lumbers like steel dinosaurs clawing at the grit. Two hundred feet past the Port Authority's training facility, the paved road ends at a sand pit, where a Crime Scene Investigation mobile unit is parked. Near a thicket of brush growing along the fence, rubber-gloved technicians comb through a yellow-taped site like archeologists on a dig. Shapiro flashes his shield and leads Dov to the dismembered corpse.

He barely recognizes his former colleague. Only the blood-stained Hawaiian shirt wrapping what remains of Shlomo Levi's head provides a clue to the collection officer's identity. Dov soldiered with the IDF through the second *intifada*, cleared the wreckage of bombed-out shopping malls and assisted ZAKA teams as they bagged scattered body parts. He is no stranger to brutality. But this just seems...gratuitous.

"Watchman found him this morning," Shapiro scrapes the sole of his shoe in the sand as if trying to wipe away his disgust. "A guy from the Israeli Counsel General's office named Spektor reported Levi missing about an hour ago. Said he was an old army buddy in town on official business. Supposed to meet with some Chechens yesterday. Spektor says he didn't know why." Shapiro shrugs and gestures toward the corpse. "The style is consistent with Obschina hospitality, alright. There was another execution in Red Hook last night. Caucasian John Doe duct-taped to a chair, throat cut, cell phone jammed in his gullet. Probably a snitch. Don't know if there's any connection, but I thought you'd want to be advised before we make an official report."

"Thanks Lieutenant," Dov cups his hands to light a cigarette. "Appreciate the heads up." He slips a Blackberry Storm out of his pocket. "Mind if I take a few shots?"

"Knock yourself out. Just keep them off fucking YouTube, will you?" Shapiro mutters, turns back toward the squad car, then adds, "And tell your people in Tel Aviv to stay the fuck off my turf. We got enough corpses in Brooklyn."

Dov stops at Mr. Lo's before returning to work, thinking he should try to put something in his stomach. While waiting for the takeout, he attaches three photos of Levi's corpse to a text message using Advanced Encryption Standard:

Giraffe retired 8 July. Suspect Chechen mob. Advise.

WEDNESDAY, 8 JULY 2009 · BRIGHTON BEACH, NEW YORK

....

ZOYA KABAN IS STILL SEDATED after her ordeal with the "gypsies," and Viktor still hung over from Latvian vodka chasing Bolivian cocaine. With Marko brooding in the back room and drizzling rain blending a gray sky into a gray Atlantic beyond his balcony windows, Viktor tries to clear his head and focus. He has Kyrylo put all of Zoya's flower vases out on the balcony so he can breathe, and then he sinks into the plush living room sofa with a cup of strong Illycaffè.

On his laptop, Viktor re-examines the photos Nathan's assistant took in the lobby of the Algonquin Hotel. The *pereguznya* had e-mailed them while Viktor was talking to him on his secure line Monday evening. The images are not terribly sharp but clearly show a well-dressed man and woman seated around a coffee table, having a conversation with a disembodied pair of gray trousers.

"These long legs are Levi's?"

"Yeah," Nathan had confirmed. "Shoshanna said he was sitting behind a pillar. Made it impossible to get a clear shot of him without giving herself away." The little shit had an annoying laugh. "That's Shlomo's style alright. Once a spook, always a spook."

No longer a spook, Viktor muses with a lingering dread.

The other man in the photos looks fit and suntanned, with a hawkish nose, dark hair salted with gray and a trimmed goatee. The Persian art maven, he had guessed correctly. The shots were taken from across the room so Viktor cannot make out much detail in any of the faces, but the woman with the Persian man has boyish blonde hair. She looks young, attractive and controlling. Maybe a lesbian. Certainly, all business.

"The art maven's secretary?"

"Probably polishes the Persian's *schmeckel*," Nathan suggested.

They both had a good laugh, but Viktor is not laughing anymore.

He now has two corpses to deal with. No one will give a damn about Vitali. But Levi was Mossad, as well as Viktor's pipeline to a potential fortune. Since the deceased spook is now in pieces near the airport, made to appear the victim of a Chechen vendetta, only this nameless couple in the photos can provide a clue to the whereabouts of those missing suitcase nukes. Levi told Nathan that the Persian supposedly knew where they were, and Zoya's kidnappers confirmed the location. But Viktor can't afford to show his hand yet. He needs a professional to suss out the situation discreetly. Someone well connected, but with no sticky loyalties. Someone he can really trust. For the right price.

He finds the number he is looking for, dials it and wonders where in the world it will be picked up.

WEDNESDAY, 8 JULY 2009 • KATHMANDU, NEPAL

EDDY THOMPSON AND TWO PLEASANTLY STONED Australian girls have just begun to tear into a fragrant *chatamari*—Newari pizza —and several liters of San Miguel lager at the Third Eye when the Thuraya satellite phone clipped to Eddy's belt begins to vibrate.

"Sounds like your strap-on wants a chat, mate," says the buxom redhead named Roz.

"Sorry, ladies. Got to grab this." He pushes back from the table and moves to a railing on the rooftop terrace, where multi-lingual white noise rises up from the streets of Thamel Marg to obscure his conversation. To the west, twilight transforms the brown hydrocarbon haze behind Swayambhunath into a primrose veil strung with haloed pearls of light. Eddy tucks an unfiltered Silk Cut between his thick Fu Manchu moustache and arrowhead soul patch, lights it with a well-worn Zippo and takes the call.

"Hello, Payload," Viktor Kaban says.

"Well, fuck me!" Eddy laughs. "How's it hanging, Vik?"

"As it always hangs, Eddy."

"Still parked in my home town?"

"Yes, but the weather in Brooklyn is lousy this time of year. I am leaving on Sunday for Istanbul. Where are you?"

"Wining and dining a couple of Aussie chicks in Kathmandu," Eddy replies. "Got back this afternoon from rafting the Kali Gandaki and the girls just want to have fun."

"Sounds exhausting," he laughs hoarsely. "Tell me, Eddy, are you available for a private excursion?"

"Depends. Where to?"

"A hunting party in northern Afghanistan. You know that area well, do you not?"

"Well enough," Eddy squints into the twilight and brushes a speck of tobacco from his moustache. "Hunting trips are expensive, Vik. Especially in *that* neighborhood."

"Of course. You know I always pay well for exceptional service."

Eddy eyes Roz provocatively licking Newari pizza sauce from her fingertips and joking with her friend, Susie. Their lusty laughter is punctuated by glances in his direction. The girls' flight to Bangkok does not leave until late afternoon tomorrow and Eddy is already anticipating an interim threesome. He blows a jet of smoke into the sultry evening. "What kind of game we hunting, Vik?"

"A Persian peacock and a long-legged Russian gazelle."

"Sounds intriguing," Eddy says. "Tell me more."

WEDNESDAY, 8 JULY 2009 · NEW HYDE PARK, NEW YORK

....

IN HIS CRAMPED WORKSPACE, Dov Reznik sits on a swivel stool with a carton of won-ton soup, surrounded by racks of PCs used for equipment installations. As he cracks open his fortune cookie, one of his personal laptops, the Toshiba T100 he used the night before, suddenly chimes a Skype request from its mate: the one Wild Boar took from the warehouse in Red Hook.

Dov answers without activating his own webcam. On the screen, he sees a square faced man with a pug nose and brush-cut gray hair back-lit by a bank of windows. Wild Boar stares into the camera as if trying to penetrate through the machine into Dov's mind.

"*Ty tam* [Are you there]?" he asks. "Can you hear me?"

Dov taps an IM ping.

Yes.

Wild Boar reads it on his screen and smiles.

"I have changed my mind," he says. "I have decided to do business with you after all—whoever you are. But the price is now $100 million for each piece of equipment I retrieve. You will need to confirm by noon tomorrow. Then I will give you contact instructions and where to wire the deposit. Is that clear?"

Clear.

He types the confirmation and watches Wild Boar's hideous face disappear. On the blank screen, Dov's imagination projects the image of Levi's bloody head wrapped in that gaudy Hawaiian shirt, as if it has been burned into his photoreceptors. He tries to shake the grisly mental picture by glancing down at the little white strip of paper bearing his cookie fortune:

Where curiosity leads, adventure will follow.

Dov dials a long string of numbers on his mobile, waits for a tone, then says, "*Ani tzarich chibur me'uvtach* [I need a secure line]." He tells the voice that answers, "We have Daylight in New York."

....

BUILDING THE FIRST ALL-JEWISH CITY on 12 acres of sand dunes surrounded by Arabs and ruled by Ottoman Turks always seemed like a risky real estate investment to Sonya. But naming it after the biblical Tel Abib—"Mound of Spring"—was pure marketing genius. Crossing the tree-lined Sderot Rothschild into the heart of the White City, she has to admit the *chutzpah* paid off.

As she turns into Mazeh Street, Sonya can almost hear Uncle Reuven's gravelly, didactic voice explaining how the Nazis decided Bauhaus design was as "un-German as the degenerate, communist, social liberals that espoused its aesthetic ideas." Consequently, Jewish architects who studied at Dessau with Walter Gropius flocked to the Levant, built 4,000 structures in the International Style and transformed those bleak sand dunes north of the ancient port of Jaffa into an artistically vibrant garden city, while Albert Speer was busy encasing Berlin in concrete *kitsch*.

One of those original white Bauhaus buildings, formerly the headquarters for the newspaper, *Ha'aretz*, was reincarnated as the Hotel Diaghilev. Sonya always stays there when she has to overnight in Tel Aviv. She likes the artificial tree sprouting soccer ball leaves and the golden cardboard sofa dominating its atrium lobby. She likes the spacious rooms with their wild video installations, comfortable beds and black sheets. She likes walking to one of the nearby cafés in the morning then relaxing with her coffee in a wicker chair on the hotel's radiused balcony overlooking the thick canopy of green *ficus sycomorus* and flowering red *tze'elon*. It might have been one of those relaxing mornings except for her visitor.

The Institute's Head of Operations sits on her balcony dressed in a blue polo shirt, his face an expressionless granite façade behind clip-on sunglasses. A short, powerfully built man with a bald head and practically no neck, her boss is probably as old as her father would have been, and annoyingly parental in his judgment of her.

Without looking up, Holiday asks, *"Ze yofee'a al heshbon ha'hot-za'ot shel'cha* [Is this going to show up on your expense account]?"

Sonya sets two cups from Café Hilel on a low glass table beside him. *"Ha cafe alay* [The coffee is on me]," she says, taking a chair opposite her boss. "To what do I owe the honor of your personal interrogation?"

"If I were going to interrogate you, Scorpion, I'd have picked a less-expensive venue."

Sonya laughs. "This place reminds me of my mother—liberal intellectuals milling around the modern art, earnestly debating the latest peace proposal over a glass of white wine. She'd have felt right at home here."

"Your mother was Shalom Akhshav,* as I recall."

* **Shalom Akhshav** [Peace Now] was organized in 1978 by IDF soldiers and reservists, and grew into a national popular movement.

"More militantly so after Rabin's assassination."

Her boss grunts. "After the Oslo Accord, Yitzak became some kind of *sabra* folk hero to every peacenik in the country. It eventually killed him."

"All this time I thought it was a Mizrahi zealot with a Beretta."

"Young people forget Rabin was one hell of a soldier before he became a politician. In sixty-seven, he commanded the forces that took the Sinai from Egypt, and East Jerusalem from Jordan. I was there to see it."

"Along with Moshe Dayan, as I recall."

"You know those bullet holes in the wall near Damascus gate? More than a few of them are mine. When the Hashimites begged for an armistice, everyone believed we'd finally live in peace. I remember how we celebrated in the streets." He breaks into uncharacteristic song: "*Shalom chaverim, shalom chaverim. Le'hitra'ot, le'hitra'ot, shalom, shalom.* [Have peace my friends, have peace my friends. Till we meet again, till we meet again, have peace, have peace.]"

Two bright green parrots circle noisily overhead, accompanying Holiday's nostalgic interlude. "We were so naive then, believing that peace was even possible." He chuckles bitterly.

Sonya stares past the balcony's safety glass into the treetops, where the parrots blend into the green canopy. "My mother died believing it."

"When your neighbors act like nails, the only tool you need is a hammer." Holiday pauses, drills into her with his sardonic voice. "You and I understand there is no such thing as peace—only brief gaps in the hammering. If you ever start believing otherwise, you'll end up like Rabin, Scorpion—*and* your mother."

Her boss pries the plastic lid off his cup. "What happened in New York?"

"Didn't Giraffe give you a debrief?"

"I want to hear it from you."

Sonya sets down her cup. "Giraffe contacted a *sayan* at the New York Consulate—former IDF named Spektor with a big-shot uncle in Brooklyn who knew Wild Boar. Giraffe heard Spektor exchanged information with Wild Boar for cocaine, so he decided to set him up as a *mabuah*. He planted a rumor about the Soviet suitcase nukes, then staged a meeting at the Algonquin Hotel with myself and the *molich** I recruited in Boston. Giraffe assumed Spektor would be watching and report back to Wild Boar. Once the seed was planted, Giraffe decided to convince our target he was being stalked by a motivated buyer." She reaches for her coffee. "It didn't go as planned."

"Continue," her boss replies.

Sonya recounts the details of Zoya Kaban's rendition in Brooklyn and Wild Boar's brutal retribution at the Red Hook warehouse. "Giraffe's instructions were to return to Haifa and await confirmation that Wild Boar had taken the bait. I was looking forward to doing my laundry, believe it or not."

Holiday sighs heavily and stares into his coffee cup. "Apparently, Giraffe's scheme got traction after all. Wild Boar contacted one of our *neviotim* on that laptop you left at the scene. He now wants a good faith deposit: $2 million in US dollars at Akbank in Istanbul for working capital, followed by $25 million in an account at the Lamda Privatbank in Lichtenstein."

Sonya purses her lips in approval. "Game on!"

"He might just be testing the water, and it's far too much good faith to show a player as unpredictable as Wild Boar. We need to make him sweat a bit more."

---

* *Molich* [walker]—someone recruited unknowingly to lead an operative to a target

Holiday shifts gears. "I should not have let Giraffe bring you into this operation so soon. It exposed you needlessly."

"He needed a *bat leveyha* and I was the logical choice."

"Why you?"

"Because I have the perfect legend and look good in a dress."

Sonya decides to tell her boss about the vellum manuscript her father had gotten smuggled out of Afghanistan and how she had tracked the Ukrainian colonel who sent it to her mother. "I found him through a Soviet veterans' data base," she explains. "It was more than just a morbid curiosity. I needed to know what really happened to my father, and why the KGB stonewalled my mother's attempts to find out. I never expected the meeting would reveal what it did. So, I reported our conversation to Giraffe and that was the genesis of his plan to bring down Wild Boar."

"Are you saying it was *you* who started this game?" Holiday's disapproving eyes burn through his sunglasses. "And what if your Ukrainian Colonel has reported the conversation to Moscow, to one of his old comrades now working for the GRU or SVR?"*

"Unlikely."

"How can you be so sure?"

"He had terminal, cancer," Sonya says. "Didn't last long."

"You confirmed his death?"

She meets his hard stare. "I administered negative treatment."†

Holiday raises an angry eyebrow. "You had an advance medical directive, did you?"

"A long-standing one: *Leviticus.*"

"The Institute does not tolerate personal vendettas, Scorpion."

---

* SVR [*Sluzhba Vneshney Razvedki*] the Russian Federation's Foreign Intelligence Service, formerly First Directorate of the KGB
† **Negative Treatment**—a Mossad euphemism for assassination

"Considering what our conversation revealed, I judged it to be a security contingency requiring a low-signature remedy."

Her boss glares sternly but motions for her to continue. "Tell me about your *molich?*"

"Cyrus Narsai is an unscrupulous antiquities dealer, the perfect unwitting actor Giraffe needed to make his pitch convincing to Wild Boar. Luckily, Cyrus didn't need much persuasion."

"And that priest you went to see in Boston? You're not thinking about converting, are you? What's his role in the operation?"

"My 'Expert with Handles'.* Our Technion people didn't have the chops to translate that vellum. Father Callan did. One of my professors at Harvard Divinity School," she explains without embellishment. "I needed his help to narrow our search coordinates."

Her boss reads between the lines. "You *do* like to play with fire, Scorpion." Holiday's fingers tap the glass tabletop impatiently. "After Giraffe opened this can of worms, I did some fishing on my own. An American source turned up a classified debriefing of one of Abdul Rashid Dostum's 'Northern Alliance' people in Qunduz, a former gunship mechanic from the 56th Air Assault Brigade, Soviet Frontal Aviation. In 1989, this Uzbek fellow was assigned to a crack helicopter pilot charged with flying Priority One cargo to Chirchik as the Soviets were withdrawing. The mechanic would normally have crewed the mission, but on this particular occasion he was bounced by a Spetsnaz unit. It saved his life, because neither the cargo nor the gunship arrived at its intended destination. Sound familiar?"

"You *know* it does," Sonya admits into her coffee.

"Your father's flight mechanic corroborated the story you were told by the Ukrainian Colonel. He witnessed a number of hard cases

---

* **Expert with Handles**—an outside professional, preferably but not necessarily a *sayan*, either employed or compelled by a Mossad agent to identify documentation in his/her field of expertise

marked 'meteorological equipment' being loaded into the gunship's bay but deduced from the KGB escort that they must have been something a lot more important. A few years later, a Russian defector blew the whistle on the existence of devices he called 'suitcase nukes' and then a former Paratroop unit commander in Afghanistan reported that some of these things had gone missing. The Americans thanked him and stupidly kicked the ball back into Russia's court."

Holiday peers over the top of his sunglasses. "And now, thanks to Giraffe's initiative, word that we're actively looking for these things is on the street. So, we must assume the usual suspects are monitoring what we do about it. *If* these weapons actually exist, then securing them before they are found by the wrong actors takes priority over Wild Boar's retirement. Understood?"

She nods, and her boss looks away. "One other thing…you will no longer report to Giraffe."

"Why not?"

"Because he got sloppy and Wild Boar retired *him*."

The euphemism leaves her breathless. "*Retired?*" Sonya's face flushes hot, but she forces herself to focus. When she finally speaks, her voice is hard and flat. "Impossible. Giraffe's too smart to have exposed himself. He probably had to run a *maulter*. Wouldn't be the first time."

Holiday rubs his thumb and index finger into the corners of his eyes beneath his glasses. "A member of Giraffe's Brooklyn team made the ID. He sent photos. We think Wild Boar made it look like a Chechen vendetta. His twin Dancing Bears learned their trade torturing insurgents in Grozny."

"Let me see the photos," she demands. "Maybe it isn't Giraffe."

"Believe me, you do not want to see these things…"

"He's my *katsa*," Sonya vehemently reminds her boss.

He hesitates then hands her his Blackberry. Sonya scans the images of Shlomo's mutilated body with no more expression than if she were observing some anonymous corpse in a morgue. She gives Holiday back his mobile, wraps her hands tightly around her coffee cup and tries to absorb its warmth through the Styrofoam.

"That's his shirt," Sonya admits quietly as her jaw tightens and the muscles of her shoulders tense.

"Giraffe knew the risks," her boss reminds her coldly. "Nuclear weapons that could end up in hostile countries are one of our main priorities. So, we need to keep Wild Boar in play, Scorpion."

"Yes sir."

"We're in Daylight Condition now. You'll be reporting directly to me on this operation."

Sonya's eyes narrow defiantly as she gestures toward the gruesome images of her former *katsa* on Holiday's Blackberry. "Are you really up to *this* kind of field work?"

Her boss flips up his clip-on shades and stares her down with a cold-blooded savagery that makes Sonya shudder. "Who the hell do you think *ran* the Wrath of God?"*

THURSDAY, 9 JULY 2009 • CAMBRIDGE, MASSACHUSETTS

....

FATHER CALLAN'S ATTEMPT TO WRITE a research grant proposal is interrupted when Cyrus arrives unannounced at his office. He enters without knocking and leans over Danny's shoulder to inspect the 2004 Red Sox pennant tacked to the shelf above his desk.

---

* **Wrath of God** [Operation Bayonet]—Caesarea's *kidonim* hunted down and executed 20-35 PLO Black September operatives believed by Mossad to be responsible for the murder of 11 Israeli athletes at the 1972 Olympic Games in Munich.

"Hell of a game!" Cyrus muses as he taps his fingers against the cover of the velo-bound report in his hands. "Remember that two-run homer Damon dropped on the upper deck at Yankee Stadium? To think I almost scalped those tickets for a lousy three-bills."

Danny's eyes remain fixed on his Mac Book screen but all he can see is red. Without looking up, he asks, "What's Geochron's verdict?"

"C-14 passed muster." Cyrus hands him the thin report bound in clear plastic. Danny scans it quickly, flips to the calibration curves where a raw radiocarbon date is listed. He can feel Cyrus watching in anticipation of Danny's reaction. His eyes widen when he reads the numbers:

$$1,800 +/- 30 \text{ BP}.$$

"BP" [Before Present] is the number of radiocarbon years prior to 1950, when atmospheric nuclear weapons testing dramatically increased Carbon-14 concentrations on Earth. Sonya's document is estimated to be 1,800 years older with a thirty-year variance.

"Congratulations," Danny says flatly, handing the report back over his shoulder without looking up.

Cyrus claps his hands together and laughs. "Listen, Danny boy, this means my client will certainly spring for your expedition to Ish... Ishikosh...wherever the hell you guys are going."

"I'm not going anywhere," Danny replies abruptly. "My role in this play ended Sunday morning, Cyrus. You guys are on your own and, if you'll excuse me, I've got work to do."

He doesn't feel the least bit guilty for enjoying Cyrus' distress.

"That puts me in a very awkward spot, Danny Boy. Remember, *you* are the one who dropped this cherry in my lap."

"Maybe so. But you're the one who ate it." Danny can feel Cyrus smirking behind his back at his flustered double entendre. His face flushing red with anger, Danny swivels in his chair.

"Give me one good reason not to clock you in the teeth."

As the muscles tense in Danny's arms, Cyrus steps back to a safe distance. "Look, I really had no idea you and Sonya were…I just assumed…I mean, Jesus, Danny! You're a *priest* for God's sake."

Danny lowers his eyes, shakes his head. "Just…drop it."

Cyrus sighs heavily, extracts an envelope from the back pocket of his trousers and hands it to Danny. "Before she left, Sonya asked me to give you this."

The sealed Algonquin Hotel envelope is addressed in Sonya's unmistakable hand.

Dear Danny,

I know you don't trust me and I do understand why.
But please know I haven't lied to you, no matter what
you may think. Cyrus can have that vellum for all I care,
and you can take credit for having found and translated it.
The only thing I care about is finding my father —
or whatever remains of him. Can you understand that?
Wouldn't you have felt the same about your brother?
What if it were Pete who'd gone missing? Wouldn't
you have moved Heaven and Earth to find him?
If you are the man I think you are, Danny, I know
you would. Please keep your word. I need your help.

— Sonny

The stationary even smells like her. Danny has to close his eyes for a moment to compose himself.

"You're right," he admits, looking up from the note. "I dropped Sonny in your lap last week and you responded exactly the way I knew you would. I'm not going to hit you for being who you are, Cyrus, but I'm not going to keep torturing myself either. I've got next semester's curriculum to prepare, and a research grant proposal to write. You can help Sonny much better than I can. So, just do what you have to do. You have my blessing—for whatever that's worth."

Cyrus sits on the edge of the desk and leans slightly forward. "Listen to me, Danny. My client can easily fund your research for years to come. You do this for us and you'll never have to write another grant proposal."

That irritates Danny even more and his eyes flash angrily. "Do *what*, Cyrus? You want me to go to Afghanistan and steal manuscripts so your anonymous client can tuck them away in a vault somewhere and wait for their value to appreciate? You think I'm fucking Indiana Jones or something?"

"Look, you know as well as I do these things will either rot away or be destroyed by fanatics unless someone archives them properly— and pretty damn soon. We're not talking about theft, Danny. We're talking preservation."

"And what if we don't find anything to preserve? I lose a month of my time, put my reputation at risk, and your client ends up with zip."

"If this single piece is what you believe it is, we've already got the price of admission," Cyrus assures him. "But more to the point, are you really going to spend the rest of your life wondering what you might have found if you had pursued this? I mean, if that vellum is authentic—and it certainly looks like it is—you'll be rewriting the textbook on Central Asia, Danny. Are you going to let an old flame torch your professional integrity?"

Cyrus looks up toward the Red Sox memento and fingers one of its dangling tie-strings. "What's it going to be, Danny Boy? Game called due to ruffled feathers? Or are you finally going to take a shot at the pennant?"

WHEN CYRUS LEAVES, Danny sits immobilized, staring at the Algonquin stationary on his desk as if it were a summons from the Office of the Inquisition. He reads Sonya's words again and again, studies her clumsy public-school printing in an attempt to read between the lines. But the only meta-message that reveals itself is his completely rational skepticism struggling with a totally irrational desire to believe her.

It occurs to Danny that he has never written Sonya a letter. More surprisingly, he has never even thought about doing so until now. So much of his academic life involved writing to research colleagues and publishing his own papers on anthropological linguistics, stuff that would have put most laypeople to sleep. Even his mother has never read a single one of his published works.

Sonya read them all. During that summer they spent together, she sat for hours in the fragrant grass by the boathouse, wearing his Boston University T-shirt over her distracting bikini and carefully reading through the manuscripts he was submitting for publication. As he sculled the green water of the Charles, she covered his work with a blizzard of insightful comments, hand-written on little Post-It notes, questioning everything from Danny's sometimes ponderous syntax to his basic theoretical premises.

He had never known anyone like her, never imagined he would find such a kindred spirit in such an alluring package. Danny saved every one of those little notes, along with all the others reminding him of the ballet tickets she had bought for them.

Why had he never reciprocated—never put a single word on paper for her eyes alone? He told himself it was a waste of time. He could speak his mind whenever he wanted. But that was a lie. The truth, he knows now, was even worse. He had been a coward, afraid to commit his feelings to paper. That would have made his decision to take a leave of absence from the seminary too real. It would have been like carving a map of his vulnerability on a stele for the world to see. Not something a Southie would ever *think* of doing.

On his desk, a lined yellow note pad taunts him. What would he say to Sonya right now if he had the guts? Would his response be reproving? Ironical? Apologetic? Would he answer obliquely, or drive straight to the bone? He picks up a pen, clicks the point into place, drops it to the top of the pad, and writes in that cursive the nuns beat into him in first grade:

Dear Sonny,

His hand hovers below the salutation—shaking. Danny drops the pen in despair, even knowing that his note will never be placed into an envelope, let alone sealed and stamped. He stares up at the stained acoustic panels on the ceiling of his office and softly speaks the words he cannot bring himself to write, "Why the hell did God send you to me...*again?*"

He didn't tell Cyrus about the voice message on his answering service that morning. The call came in at 8:07 am, as he was rowing to clear his head. Coincidence, maybe, but he had been thinking about the events of July 4th, replaying that trip to Northampton over and over as he pulled his oars through the morning mist.

Danny picks up his desk phone, punches in the code, and listens again to Bashir's lilting voice recorded on the Centrex message center. He begins to sense that something beyond his control is in the works, some Divine plan, maybe. He can only strive to be a better priest— *Ad majorem Dei gloriam*—have faith and walk the path, wherever it is destined to take him.

Danny dials and Bashir answers after three rings. "Father Daniel. You are well?"

"Yes, I'm fine. Have you been able to contact your cousin, Bashir?"

"Not yet. Murad has no Internet service and connections in his town are inconsistent at best. But I have been thinking…I have not seen my cousin in seven years. And, since you are seeking an introduction, perhaps it would be an auspicious time for me to pay him a visit. So, if you are amenable, I would like to go with you to Ishkashim. Perhaps I can be of assistance to your friend."

Danny looks down again at Sonya's note and has to stop himself from smelling it. "Bashir, I need to ask you something. What's your intuition about…my friend?"

Danny hears the little rug dealer sigh. "She is in pain, Father Daniel. So *much* pain. And so deep that no one can penetrate to where it dwells."

"Do you think she's telling the truth about her father?"

"Who can say for sure? But I sense that her heart is good. In any case, finding her father is unlikely, but if that is her real quest, then she *will* try. With or without you."

Danny laughs in sad admiration. "You see right into people's hearts, don't you?"

"It is not always a blessing," Bashir admits. "I see also what this woman means to you, and the pain it has caused you both."

Danny clears his throat, finally gives in to temptation and lifts Sonya's note close enough to his face to inhale her scent. "God must be punishing me."

"Testing you, perhaps," Bashir replies. "But Al-Llâh always is merciful. I believe He sent this broken winged bird to you for a reason, Father Daniel. Perhaps to heal *both* your hearts."

THURSDAY, 9 JULY 2009 · NAMAL TEL AVIV, ISRAEL

....

190 CENTIMETERS TALL in Jimmy Choo stiletto heels, silver cuff bracelets glittering on her wrists and raven-black hair framing her face, Scorpion slips through the young crowd queuing up for the mega-bars packing the Port of Tel Aviv's waterfront promenade. Plunging below a black lace choker, her silk camisole leaves only its label to the bouncer's imagination. He lets her skirt the line of college kids and enter Hangar 19 for the price of a smile. Once inside the Club Galina, she begins to gyrate and whirl to the techno music vibrating everything that is not bolted to the floor.

As her ears acclimate to the pulsing bass, she loses herself in a cascading wall of lights, lasers, and balloons floating in the humid night air beneath the old hangar's steel trusses. Soon her bangs are sticking to her hot, glistening face and eager boys are buying her shots of vodka.

One of them is cute, a real *chatich*—a "nice piece," as the kids say in Tel Aviv. She tosses back the drink he hands her and undulates shamelessly against his sinewy body as the alcohol and throbbing house music numb her brain and banish unwelcome thoughts. All she can feel is the tight muscles in her legs as she dances and the growing hardness in the boy's jeans as he grinds against her. The smell of his sweat is intoxicating. Or is it the vodka? She does not really care which.

It is after 1:00 am when they emerge from the converted hangar onto the still-teeming boardwalk, where Scorpion lets the boy buy another round of drinks and listens to his callow banter at one of the crowded cocktail bars. He has just been discharged from the army, full of swagger and *re'ut*, that macho IDF camaraderie, but embarrassed that he is still living with his parents in Holon. He borrowed their Volvo to drive here. They could sit in the car and talk for a while, he suggests.

Why not? A zip-less fuck is just what she needs.

They make out beside the car in the parking lot for a while, but the boy is so clumsy she quickly loses interest. Oblivious to her protests, he wedges one hand between her legs while kneading her breast with the other like a nesting cat. She suddenly remembers the Seal Point Himalayan her mother had saved from the pound in Leningrad. It looked so beautiful and she had rubbed its soft white belly until it purred in ecstasy. Then, for no apparent reason, the evil creature turned on her, sinking its teeth into her hand and drawing blood, then slinking away as if she had offended it.

"Over-stimulated," Maryna had explained. "Even pleasure can become painful."

The drunken boy reaches for his zipper and tries to press her to her knees in front of him. When she pushes him away, he persists, as any cocky *sabra* who has spent the last two years "demonstrating presence" at strangulation checkpoints in the Territories would have been trained to do. She has drunk far too much and defaults to the coping mechanism she knows best.

Scorpion jabs her knuckles hard into the boy's Adam's apple, and as he gasps for breath, jams the point of her knee into his testicles. He doubles over in agony, and she pivots on her toes, grabs his ears and slams his face into the fender of his parents' Volvo wagon. She hears his pretty nose break with an ugly crunch, then steadies herself against the side mirror.

"*Lo' perusho lech tiz'da'yen!* ['No' means fuck off!]," she slurs.

Scorpion leaves the clueless boy slumped beside the car's front tire, exposed, semi-conscious and bleeding. Without looking back, she walks unsteadily to a taxi kiosk and swings her long legs into the first one in the queue.

In her room at the Diaghilev, she kicks her scuffed stiletto heels across the carpet, tears off her wig and camisole, and staggers into the bathroom. After retching violently into the bidet, she crawls to the tub, still wearing her lace panties and choker, turns the shower on full force and curls into a fetal position. The rushing water saturates her matted hair, turning gold into straw. Mascara bleeds from her eyes, runs down her cheeks and drips onto the white porcelain as she sobs like a helpless child.

The mental image of what those Ukrainian butchers did to Shlomo, the horror she has spent the whole day and night trying to erase, has proven impervious to both alcohol and sexual distraction. Shaking uncontrollably, her alter ego disintegrates beneath the steam and hot water, leaving her fully exposed.

Never in her life has Sonya felt so small and alone.

FRIDAY, 10 JULY 2009 · BOSTON, MASSACHUSETTS

....

MONSIGNOR SEAN DEVLIN WAS APPOINTED Chaplain of His Holiness and handed the fuchsia sash four years ago by recommendation of the Archbishop of Boston. Father Callan knows his mentor's appointment was a reward for adept damage control after a botched transition between Cardinals Law and O'Malley. That, and Sean's artful spin-doctoring with the *Boston Globe* barracudas who had smelled blood in the Holy See when the besieged Cardinal Law was invited to reside permanently at the Vatican, presumably to insure his eminence's continued reticence regarding sexual predators in the Boston archdiocese.

Monsignor Devlin is now installed at the Jesuit Provincial Office on Harrison Street beside the Church of the Immaculate Conception, tucked into a low brick building that hides like a timorous child behind its mother's skirt. His official business has been concluded for the day, and Sean—brooding, as he always does, over the unrelenting controversy with which he has had to contend—seems happy to have his spiritual mentee drop by for a chin-wag.

"It makes me so sick to think of all these wasted resources. 2.6 billion in damages. Six Archdioceses already in bankruptcy proceedings, and rumor has it Wilmington is next on the hit list." Sean lifts the stopper from a crystal decanter on the sideboard. "Bushmills?"

"No thanks," Danny nods toward the rocks glass Sean is pouring for himself. "I thought you gave that up?"

"As you know, bucko, the flesh is often weak."

The comment flicks at Danny's emotional hair-trigger. "Is that a reference to me or my brother, Monsignor?"

Sean pauses with the glass at his thin lips, taken aback by Danny's reaction. "I was referring to myself, Father Callan. I don't sleep well these days. Can't stop thinking about all the lawsuits against the Church, all the good men who've been destroyed by these scandals."

"Not to mention the good altar boys."

"Goes without saying." Sean sinks heavily into one of the paired burgundy love seats. "So, what can I do for you, Danny?"

"A situation has come up, Monsignor. As my Spiritual Director, I felt I should consult with you on the best course of action. I've been offered a considerable amount of grant money if I take on a research project in Central Asia during the next month. I'd return before the semester starts and resume my teaching schedule. But this fieldwork could be the most important I've ever done, and could very well secure the future of my department at the Center for the Study of World Religions. It would also go a long way in maintaining a Catholic perspective at Harvard Divinity."

Sean swirls the ice cubes in his glass. "I'm sensing a caveat here."

Danny holds his mentor's bloodshot gaze. "You remember when I took leave from the novitiate…and why?"

"I do."

"Well…she's going to be on this expedition. In fact, she organized it. A well-heeled antiquities expert with whom I've worked previously is picking up the tab. It looks like a legitimate venture, but not without risk."

Sean's brow furrows.

"I know," Danny acknowledges. "Occasion of sin. That's why I'm seeking your direction on this, Monsignor. If I'd followed your advice eight years ago, I wouldn't be needing it today."

Sean sets his glass on the marble tabletop, breathes deeply, and stares for a long moment at the portrait of Pope Benedict XVI on the wall above his desk as if hoping for an *ex cathedra* pronouncement.

He turns solemnly back toward Danny. "I'm going to be straight with you, bucko. I think you're a gifted teacher and a good man. But frankly, you've never struck me as comfortable in your vocation as a priest. I've read some of your published work, and while it is certainly intellectually rigorous, your conclusions often strike me as syncretistic and sometimes in conflict with Church doctrine. That may be right up Harvard Divinity's alley, but we require unwavering consistency on our side of the Common.

"Of course, there are many ways to serve God. However, if you want to serve as an ordained priest of the Roman Catholic Church, you do so at the pleasure of the Vatican. It's why we Jesuits take that extra vow: obedience to the Holy Father. We can't afford to have our soldiers questioning their commitment to a strict code of behavior, or the Holy Father's infallibility in matters of Faith. The Society of Jesus has got to hold the front line in defense of Papal authority. *And* stand in opposition to those who would destroy the Church."

The Monsignor's blue eyes narrow. "You can't ride the fence, bucko. You need to be all in. Am I making myself clear?"

"Very."

"You know the drill, Danny. You need to meditate seriously on your position and commitment, and pray for higher guidance than mine. You need to decide once and for all where you stand."

Sean drifts into dismissive banality as he moves to the wet bar for a top-off. "As always, the Holy Spirit will guide you."

Danny flattens his palms against his knees, nods earnestly, and stands to leave. "Thank you for your time and advice, Monsignor." Chin tucked stoically into his stiff white collar, Danny starts across the plush carpet but stops short of the oak door. He stares down at the embroidered AMDG as if it is the first time he really sees it.

"You've been like a father to me, Sean, and I respect your opinion. So, let me clarify *my* position: God gave me a mind and I've always believed it would be a grievous sin not to use it. Nothing I've written diminishes my loyalty to the Church or my commitment to serve Christ. And *because* of that, I cannot turn a blind eye to misguided attempts by flawed human beings to interpret and justify God's will …or protect those who abuse the power of their holy office."

Danny pauses, looking up into the Monsignor's reddened face. "You're right, Sean. I have *not* been an exemplary priest, and as a man, I'm as flawed as they come. But I will continue to serve the Church as long as it pleases the Holy Father."

Standing over that once-perplexing monogram, Danny feels as if striving for God's greater glory finally makes sense to him.

"Let me tell you what I've learned about the Holy Spirit, Monsignor. He speaks to us in a 'catholic tongue,' remember? A universal language called 'compassion.' He *invented* syncretism. Why do you think Aquinas used the attributions of Roman Stoics, Neo-Platonists and Muslim mystics to argue his *Summa*? Universality, Sean. The Holy Spirit is truly non-denominational."

Appraising the Monsignor's slack-jawed expression, Danny steps over the line in order to make sure his meaning is not lost.

"He *never* judges us, because he knows we'll always judge ourselves more harshly than he ever would. But here's the thing, Sean: even though he'll lead you to the water, he will never *make* you take a drink. Or stop you for that matter."

....

KATHRYN CALLAN LEARNED A LOT about gentrification after young urban professionals began bidding up the real estate along Dorchester Avenue. A sushi restaurant and upscale bar were going into the block formerly occupied by the Triple O's and Whitey Bulger's gang. Gay couples were snapping up row houses and lofts in renovated industrial buildings. The Town was changing fast.

Kathryn thought the South End lost its soul after Tony's fruit and vegetable shop closed on Shawmut Ave and a trendy art gallery moved in. Now, Frank Faylen, a broker with Conway & Company, is teaching her all about mixed-use, earnest money and flipping. It happened already in Charlestown and Jamaica Plain. Frank assures Kathryn that she is sitting pretty for the next yuppie gold rush.

"Mister Faylen says a one- or two-bedroom condo in a converted triple-decker is going for upwards of $280,000," Kathryn tells her son as she shucks white corn in the kitchen. "Anything that's been renovated half-way decent goes for half-a-million and up. Frank—Mister Faylen—thinks I ought to convert the top two flats to condos."

"And Mister Faylen would naturally get the listing?" Danny sits at the kitchen table sipping Buzzards Bay Lager as she prepares fresh scrod for supper.

"Well, I think he's just being helpful," Kathryn says. "But supposing I did decide to go condo. He'd be my first choice as selling agent. Frank grew up right here in Southie, and you can barely tear him away from that Multiple Listing Service. Who better to negotiate?"

She worries, from the petulant look on Danny's face, that she might have hurt his feelings. After all, he has been her only support since her husband drank himself to death fifteen years ago. Even so, Kathryn is not about to tell her son that Frank Faylen has also shown more than a passing interest in her as well as her family home. She is pretty sure it is not just the menopausal delusion of a 68-year-old widow woman.

Back in the day, she turned more than a few heads. The gonzo boys coming home from Vietnam used to fall all over themselves buying her drinks on Friday nights down at Striggie's. Frank, who suffered from migraines until his forties, never served in the military, but that is just fine with Kathryn. She has had quite enough of brooding Marines, with their dark days and drunken nights reminiscing about "Eye-Corps" and "Charlie." She does not want another soldier in her life after losing two of them back to back. And she is so glad Danny never followed in his brother's footsteps. Still, she hesitates to admit to her son that she has feelings for Frank.

"Just don't sign anything until I look it over, okay Ma?"

"Sure Danny, of course." Despite his clerical duties and teaching commitments, Danny still sees himself as head of the household. He has dinner with her at least once a week and helps with the book-keeping for her rental units. Kathryn has never been smart with the numbers. She feels lucky her youngest boy was born with brains.

Kathryn drops ears of corn into boiling water on the stove and fans herself with a quilted potholder. "It's wicked hot in here, don't you think? Let's have supper out on the piazza."

"Whatever. You pick up that huckleberry pie for dessert?"

"Is the Pope German?"

"Bavarian, actually." Danny slips the starched white tab out of his collar and opens the top two buttons of his shirt. "I should take a look at your books this evening before I leave. Just make sure everything's up to date. You know how you forget to post your checks."

"Does it have to be tonight, Danny?"

He hesitates, "Look Ma, I'm going to be away for a little while. About a month."

"A whole month?" She feels a twinge of apprehension.

"An important manuscript turned up in northern Afghanistan and I've been asked to help authenticate it before the term starts."

"I don't like you going back there, Danny. Aren't we still at war with those Arabs?"

"They're not Arabs, Ma."

"Whatever. It's still dangerous over there."

He laughs. "Don't worry, Ma, I promise to give those evil-doers a wide berth."

Kathryn dredges and breads the whitefish fillets, arranges them on a sheet of wax paper then chops onions as oil heats in the skillet. She has noticed something odd about Danny's behavior during the past week and cannot help but think it is more than just work related. Mothers instinctively know these things. Her son seems troubled in a way she has not seen since his sabbatical from the priesthood.

"You look tired, Danny. Been getting enough sleep?"

"I'm okay," he says. "Just burning the candle on a grant proposal." He pretends to look at the *Globe's* sports section to avoid her maternal scrutiny. "Hazards of an academic life."

"Why couldn't you have been a parish priest, Danny? Stayed closer to home?"

"I'm only in Cambridge, Ma. It's not the other side of the world."

She sighs heavily, and her son rolls his eyes.

"Look, you know I wasn't cut out for the parish life. God puts you where He thinks you'll do the most good. For me it's teaching."

Kathryn frowns, flicks a few drops of water into her iron skillet to test the temperature, then scrapes onions into the sizzling pan. "Believe me, I thank God every day that He led you to the Jesuits rather than the Marine Corps. It would have broken my heart to see you end up like Peter and your father. Promise me you'll be careful, Danny. Stay out of trouble."

"How much trouble's a priest going to get into, Ma?"

Kathryn stirs her onions and arches an eyebrow. "Why don't you ask your old boss at the Archdiocese about that?"

FRIDAY, 10 JULY 2009 · CAMBRIDGE, MASSACHUSETTS

....

CYRUS OPENS HIS DOOR to find Father Callan standing on the unlit porch. The priest's tousled hair is wet from the oppressive humidity; his black clerical shirt is unbuttoned and untucked. Beneath it, a white sleeveless T-shirt is patched with sweat at the center of his chest.

"You look alarmingly at home in that wife-beater, Danny Boy," Cyrus tells him. "And possibly in need of some air conditioning and a drink."

"I know it's late," Danny says, "but we need to talk. Tonight."

Cyrus grins and cracks the screen door. "As long as you don't take a swing at me."

Danny kicks off his Oxfords in the hallway and paces the pine living room floor. Cyrus turns down the volume on a Rachmaninoff concerto and moves to the wet bar.

"I've got a nice Caol Ila if you're in the mood for a 15-year-old."

Danny shoots a scowl in his direction.

"Sorry," Cyrus shrugs. "Bad joke."

Cyrus pours copper-colored single malt into a crystal snifter, drops in a large, spherical ice cube and Danny accepts the offering with lowered eyes. "Thanks, I guess I *am* in the mood." He sips the floral whiskey, relaxes a bit and props himself on the Eames chair's leather ottoman.

"I've decided to accept your anonymous client's offer of grant money," Danny stares into his glass. "But there are a couple of conditions: I want to take a colleague with me on this expedition—Bashir, who helped solve the riddle of our palimpsest. He'll be invaluable with the Isma'ili community. I'll catalogue anything we find and with Bashir's help negotiate to provide archival stewardship. You can retain exclusive brokering rights, but I want your personal guarantee that any indigenous claims of ownership will be respected."

"Done," Cyrus nods and pours himself two fingers, neat.

"One more thing," Danny says. "I want to make sure my mother is taken care of if…if anything should happen to…well, you know what I mean."

Cyrus nods. "You've really got it bad for her, don't you?"

"My mother?"

"Don't be obtuse." Danny draws out a breath, searches his glass for an explanation. He stands and begins to pace again in front of the cast-iron stove. The pain in his voice is so raw that he has to subjectively distance himself.

"After eight years, you almost forget how it feels." Danny stops in mid-stride, bites his lower lip. "Eight years without a single word. And then, out of the blue, she shows up on your doorstep and all that hard work you've done, all the soul searching, all the prayer and meditation and begging forgiveness for breaking your vows goes right down the crapper. You realize you've never gotten over her, just fooled yourself into believing you had. You thought you were a soldier of God, but it turns out you're just another pussy-whipped punk."

"I think you're being kind of hard on yourself, Danny." Cyrus swirls his whiskey, takes a slow sip and drops into the sofa.

"How much do you *really* know about Ms. Aronovsky?"

Danny looks up from his glass. "What do you mean?"

"Her background? Her employer?"

Danny looks confused and Cyrus crosses his legs. "Think about it. This beautiful, enigmatic young lady appears after an eight-year absence with a dubious but incredibly intriguing document and an ingenuous smile. But you and I both know Sonya is no ingénue. She's brilliant, connected and knows how to get *exactly* what she wants. Am I wrong?"

Danny narrows his blue eyes. "You're not doing a good job of convincing me to go on this expedition, Cyrus."

"Oh, believe me, I'd love to get my hands on some rare Kushan manuscripts, assuming they actually exist. But I'll never see a scrap if something happens to you over there in Ishi... damn it! Why can I never remember the name of that place?"

"Your concern is touching."

"Look, I'm just saying, Sonya can be very convincing, but she's never entirely forthcoming, is she? We both sense that. And let's face it, with me being the possible exception to the rule, you give *everybody* the benefit of the doubt when it comes to good intentions. I'm a bit more skeptical than you, so I did some background checking, and I'm pretty sure Sonya works for the Israeli government in some intelligence capacity."

Danny laughs. "Sonny's a scholar, a cultural anthropologist and Arabic translator. I saw her ID from the University of Haifa."

Cyrus cocks his head and smiles condescendingly at Danny's naiveté. "Of course you did. We've both seen exactly what Sonya wants us to see. We're her audience as well as her actors."

"What are you getting at, Cyrus?"

"Come with me." Cyrus leads Danny into his study. The room is surrounded by built-in bookshelves holding a library of art history references and steel case flat files containing prints, maps and drawings. An antique rug from Tabriz covers his floor, and the classic Danish Modern desk in front of a wide picture window overlooks his garden. Cyrus opens a closet door and lifts a small hard-shell case off the shelf. He opens the latches and withdraws one of a matched set of compact Iridium Extreme satellite phones.

"This is the On/Off, two-way nav-key, and this red button on top will send an SOS. It has a Global SIM card with 200 pre-paid minutes. I want you to take it with you. Keep me posted on your progress and whereabouts."

Danny sets his drink on top of the flat file and hefts the rubberized phone with its thick antennae. "And spy on your partner-in-crime?"

Cyrus sinks into the Aeron chair at his desk. "Okay, let's say you actually find a treasure trove of fragile, ancient manuscripts. What are you going to do? Stuff them into a backpack and smuggle them past corrupt border guards and banditos shaking down every foreigner within sight? Or are you going to hope Sonya and her spook employer have an exit plan that includes you? Frankly, Danny, I don't want to see you caught between Scylla and Charybdis with the Golden Fleece in your lap."

Danny lifts the sat phone with two fingers. "Since we're mixing epic metaphors, this is my *deus ex machina?*"

"Direct line to Olympus, Danny Boy."

He shakes his head. "Who *are* you, Cyrus? I mean, really? I know you have a bunch of shady connections, but this has gone way beyond my professional comfort zone."

"Danny, look…"

"Sonny only asked me to help her locate her missing father."

"A Russian helicopter pilot who went MIA twenty years ago."

He looks surprised. "She told *you* that?"

"Oh no. I had to excavate the family tree all by myself. Sonya told me we were in the same business. That she needed an investor to score this manuscript deal. And she was *very* persuasive. But I'm guessing she always is."

Danny looks agitated as he reaches for his drink.

"Look, I'm not trying to rub salt in the wound, Danny. I'm just suggesting you watch your back. Neither of us has figured out what Sonya is really up to, but whatever it turns out to be, I don't want to see you get hurt. *Capice?*"

Danny probes Cyrus' eyes as if trying to parse his intentions. He tosses back the last of his whiskey and slips the satellite phone into his back pocket.

"Point made, Cyrus. I'll send you a postcard from Dushanbe."

"Don't bother. You'll be back before it gets here."

SATURDAY, 11 JULY 2009 • PALMACHIM, ISRAEL

....

THE CONCRETE BUNKER at Soreq Nuclear Research Center has a reinforced steel door that can only be unlocked by scanning the eyeballs of Avner Ron, Professor Emeritus from the Interdisciplinary Center Herzliya, while his right thumb presses onto a glass plate. Sonya squints at the light reflecting off Avner's bald head as he tinkers on a workbench beneath cool LEDs. Her hair is disheveled, her face scrubbed and her eyes red. An oversized chambray shirt covers everything but her black Luminox watch and bored expression.

"*Achla derech le'valot et sof Ha'shavu'a* [Hell of a way to spend the weekend]," she sulks.

Avner, formerly the Institute's go-to-ghoul at IDC, is now their eyes and ears at Soreq. He uses a slender screwdriver to open the side panel of a meter-long cylinder with a conical head. His limpid eyes glare at Sonya through thick lenses. "You know, I have other things I could be doing on *Shabbat* besides giving a crash course in nuclear weapons to a whiny bitch."

Sonya exaggerates a pout. "I had no idea you were such a religious man, Avner."

She gestures toward the steel cylinder. "This one of the pillars of our Samson Option?"*

"I don't know what you're talking about." He raises an eyebrow, smiles sardonically. "But don't worry; it's not loaded."

"That's a relief."

Avner gets excited by things that would bore most sentient beings to tears. He points out the details of his shiny toy with exuberance. "The usual design consists of a deuterium/tritium pump surrounded by fissile material, a tamper encased in an explosive shell, a neutron initiator and detonator, all controlled by a sequencer. A high-voltage source is required for triggering, and the timing is critical to yield. To preclude noise or interference from being accepted as a false positive, the detonation sequence can only be initiated outside the weapon's detonator by a specific arming code passed to the device by a unique signal generator."

He removes the last screw, lifts the hatch cover and exposes a six-digit rotor display panel beside a hexagonal connector socket. Sonya leans on her elbows and pays close attention as Avner adjusts a hex wrench, then carefully removes the cap to reveal a round 25-millimeter opening exposing a set of copper sensors. "J1 socket," Avner snorts. "Of course, nobody uses these dinosaurs anymore."

"Vestige of those halcyon days of Mutual Assured Destruction?"

"Pray those days aren't over," he snaps. "Now, *may* I continue?"

Sonya waves an acquiescent hand.

"The key to building a miniaturized nuclear warhead is a non-spherical core incorporating a two-point detonation system. Because of geometry and size constraints on the warhead, a nuclear artillery

* Samson Option—Israel's still-unacknowledged nuclear defensive strategy of last resort

shell implodes a cylindrical core after a timing-based security protocol has been satisfied." He rummages through his Zero Haliburton
case for the knurled aluminum connector he needs. "An MC4142
should do the trick." Avner wags it in her face and lifts an eyebrow.
"Strike enabled plug."

He fits it onto a 24-pin adaptor and plugs it into the port
on the open cylinder. "The Americans developed the first PAL—a
Permissive Action Link—in the early 1960s when they discovered
how vulnerable their nuclear arsenal was to accident and theft—
especially among careless NATO allies. They decided the world would
be a safer place if this technology were shared with their enemies
as well as their friends. Good idea in theory, but the Soviet Union
declined their magnanimous offer—for the same reasons that the
Pakistanis did forty years later."

"They thought Helga wanted to booby-trap their bombs?"

Avner raises an affirmative eyebrow over his glasses. "The Soviets
developed their own security protocols—probably with some indirect
American guidance. Their version of a PAL system has been standardized since the mid-1980s. This is a very good thing, believe me."

"I always believe you, Avner. Even when I haven't a clue what
you're talking about."

He scowls. "You'll thank me if you ever have to disarm one of
these fucking things all by yourself."

Sonya sullenly props her chin on her hands and listens. She is
no novice to explosive devices but has never seen *anything* like this
one—and never been asked to stop one from doing its job.

....

SONYA'S TENSE MEETING with Holiday the previous afternoon
was clouded by an ugly hangover from her ill-advised outing to

Club Galina. The Head of Operations was seated at his desk with only a single file folder beside his PC monitor. She caught a glimpse of the screen saver before sitting opposite him. It displayed the wistful face of a Dobermann puppy.

Without even a greeting, Holiday launched into a grim soliloquy. "The Iranians just announced they are beginning construction on ten new uranium enrichment plants. In addition to their hardened facility at Natanz, we know they have one carved into a mountain near Qom that can hold 3,000 centrifuges. It will take them ninety years to enrich enough fuel to run a reactor for just a year, but only four years to produce enough highly enriched uranium for a weapon. As if their intentions weren't clear enough, they parade Shahab-3s through the streets of Tehran draped with 'Wipe Israel off the map' banners. We may have no choice but to take unilateral action."

"And we are waiting *why?*" Sonya inquired incredulously.

"Unit 8200 has been working with Helga on a high-tech, low-signature intervention.* Unfortunately, Washington is doing a diplomatic dance with Moscow, which has lucrative weapons contracts with Iran. Since economic interests drive diplomacy, we are once again urged to show restraint in exchange for future considerations."

"Meaning what? Bibi gets to build more gated communities in East Jerusalem?"

Holiday leveled reproving eyes at her through his heavy lenses. "While we wait patiently for Helga to play its Machiavellian game, we cannot chance even one portable nuclear warhead falling into the wrong hands, let alone a dozen of them. Even if some jihadist group

---

* **Unit 8200,** in a joint venture with NSA's Tailored Access Operations [TAO] called "Olympic Games," developed and deployed a cyber-weapon called "Flame," which became known as the Stuxnet [.stub/mrxnet.sys] computer worm. Its 650,000 lines of code attacked the industrial programmable logic controllers at the Natanz enrichment facility and destroyed 3,000 of Iran's nuclear centrifuges before accidentally infecting another 200,000 computers worldwide.

didn't have Russian codes, they could probably find a rogue weapons engineer with the skill to jury-rig a usable device."

"Like we did."

Holiday's face twisted in disgust, "You're beginning to sound like your mother, Scorpion."

"Just stating the obvious." Sonya shrugged. "Don't worry, the bleeding-heart gene is recessive in my DNA."

Her boss swiveled in his chair and spoke to the puppy screen saver. "When he first proposed it, Giraffe's plan for narrowing the gray market weapons' pipeline to Syria and Lebanon made sense: Create a plausible scenario for Wild Boar to acquire tactical nukes, propose an irresistible deal, follow his money trail, hack his accounts and take him out of the food chain before he can broker another SCUD to people who think every Jew should have been shipped to Alaska. We assumed our bait was either fictitious or of dubious provenance." He turned back toward her. "We were wrong."

Sonya sat up in her chair.

"We have two sources that corroborate these missing suitcase nukes, one admitting the KGB deployed some to Afghanistan. We know, from your unauthorized conversation with Bagram's now-deceased commander, that your father flew 'sensitive cargo' out of Afghanistan. We have his flight mechanic's statement that unusual hard cases were loaded onto his gunship. Lastly, we have your vellum note stating the cargo was 'safe.'"

Holiday turned and looked her in the eye to drive home his point. "What we do not know is in *whose* safekeeping or why these weapons have never turned up in the past twenty years. Until we can answer those questions, no one will be sleeping well. Least of all Bibi."

"The Americans have a whole army in Afghanistan," Sonya replied. "Why not let them do the heavy lifting?"

"After all the damage America has done, the Afghans hate them as much as they hated the Russians. Americans are a culturally clueless herd of stampeding elephants. Their idea of swaying hearts and minds is sending Hellfire missiles as wedding presents. They are notoriously loose-lipped and their Intelligence Oversight Committees have more leaks than my roof in Yafo. Until we find out exactly where those nukes are, and under whose control, ISAF* will only get in our way."

"I suppose sending in Shaldag† is out of the question?"

Holiday rolled his eyes. "That's the *last* thing we want to do. You know as well as I do how touchy Helga is about us operating in its theater, which is why we are sometimes obliged to work with freelancers who aren't worried about stepping on the wrong toes."

Without looking down, Holiday's stubby fingers slid the file folder on his left in front of Sonya. "This one is called 'Payload.' An American, unfortunately, but at least he understands how these tribal bastards think. Like your priest."

Sonya scanned the folder and grimaced at the face in the photo. "Looks like someone the Hell's Angels would think twice about," she said. "Why *this* guy?"

"Two reasons," Holiday said. "First: Payload worked with Wild Boar to quietly arm the Afghan Northern Alliance in the run up to the US invasion in 2001. Second: Wild Boar has just retained Payload to track a mysterious young woman who was photographed by a secretary from the Consulate General of Israel in the lobby of a well-known New York hotel having tea with an unscrupulous antiquities broker and one of our retired collections officers."

Sonya stared silently, her teeth on edge.

---

* **ISAF**—International Security Assistance Force in Afghanistan led by the United States military
† **Shaldag** [Kingfisher]—IDF Unit 5101, Air Force commandos operating from Palmachim Airbase

"When Payload gave me a courtesy call, I had the choice of either a lame denial of what we both knew was true, or recruiting him as an insurance policy. Double indemnity. Better to have the bastard working with us rather than getting in our way."

"Giraffe would have applauded your initiative."

"Giraffe is no longer of interest to me," Holiday snapped, leaning into his desk. "But your 'Expert with Handles' *is*. Get this priest to use whatever academic alchemy he has at his disposal to help us locate these goddamn weapons. Payload claims he can arrange extraction to Bagram, at which point we will quietly evaporate from the scene." Her boss paused, exposing his discomfort like an abscessed tooth. "Make no mistake, this Payload is a loose cannon and possibly rogue. We can't trust him any more than Wild Boar can."

Sonya sighed, shook her head. "This just gets better and better."

Holiday's cold eyes drilled into her. "Listen to me very carefully, Scorpion. Ahmadinejad or Assad would pay 200 million US for a single functional nuke. And we both know exactly who they'd target. Bottom line: if we ascertain that Payload's loyalties are even *slightly* creeping in the wrong direction, we will need to terminate our insurance policy and, at very least, make sure those weapons can never be used against us. Are we clear on this?"

"We?"

"You."

....

"THE TRIGGERING MECHANISM for an implosion bomb employs a capacitor bank that's similar to a camera flash unit." Avner Ron lifts a rugged battlefield laptop out of his hard case and sets it on the workbench beside the steel cylinder. "A Krytron-Pac is a gas-filled, specialized cold cathode tube and trigger transformer in a single housing. It gets charged when the weapon is armed, then discharges the capacitors and feeds a high-voltage current to the detonators." He flips open his laptop and boots up.

"The detonator is not a simple contact closure but a complex digital signal. So, a Permissive Action Link relies on both tamper-resistant encapsulation and encryption of the digital signal path. The PAL will lock up if an erroneous bit is entered anywhere in the sequence. The switching system, however, is typically mechanical. You wouldn't want an electrical gate accidentally closed by a stray piece of metal short-circuiting a pair of wires, now would you?"

"Definitely not." Sonya forces a smile as perspiration prickles her forehead.

"Conversely, critical elements of the detonator are *deliberately* weak, designed to fail if exposed to any 'abnormal' environment, say, a fire or an external explosion. If any other than the exact proper detonation sequence occurs, there will not be a nuclear reaction."

Avner looks up to be certain she is following his explanation. His eyeglasses eerily reflect the hanging LED lamps as he taps the six-digit rotor display beside the strike enabled plug and adaptor. "The *only* accessible part of a Permissive Action Link is the interface for entering the arming code—the key that decrypts the timing data." He runs his fingers along the smooth aluminum cylinder toward its conical head. "The PAL's inaccessible part allows the trigger to charge if the code is input correctly. With me so far?"

Sonya nods, wishes she were with *anyone* else.

"At first, Permissive Action Links were externally attached to the electrical circuitry," Avner continues. "But weapon designers soon recognized that it would be relatively easy to wire up a work-around. So, they buried the PAL deep inside the device, making it inaccessible to anyone trying to arm it without authorization. The good news is that a modern Category-F PAL is virtually uncrackable because it encapsulates the entire weapon in a protective skin. Any penetration of the covering results in automatic, irreparable damage. Insertion of too many false codes or an attempt to bypass the PAL will render the weapon permanently inoperable. Even if someone had a set of technical drawings, they would be unable to detonate the weapon without knowing its codes."

Sonya narrows her eyes, "So, if I wanted to neutralize an unarmed device, all I'd need to do is input random codes until its PAL froze up, right?"

"Right..." The professor raises a cautionary finger. "But only on a *modern* device."

"I knew there was going to be a catch," she sighs.

"Prior to Cat-D, circuit components were outside the tamper-resistant barrier—so they *could* be accessed. Someone in possession of a weapon with an older PAL might be able to bypass those circuits entirely, as we discovered thirty years ago..."

He blushes and clears his throat. "Please forget I ever said that."

"Don't worry, Avner. Indiscretion is still the lesser part of valor."

He stares humorlessly at her and continues. "The older PALs had cryptographic rotor settings, like this one, but to change them you'd have to open the sealed environment. If that were done outside the factory, the device would become useless. However, the rotors could be encrypted in an external key, and then changed by way of a micro-computer embedded inside the protective skin."

He taps the hex plug and its adapter. "Like setting an electronic door lock."

"Which means it could be cracked the same way."

"Exactly! You're not nearly as vapid as you look."

Sonya crinkles her nose sarcastically.

"But here's the rub," Avner quickly adds. "A Cat-C PAL accepts multiple six-digit keys. One might be used for training exercises, another to disable the weapon, another to arm it. And there are one million possible ways to write a six-digit numerical code."

"What if the code were alphanumerical? Written in Cyrillic?"

Avner nods appreciatively. "33 characters plus ten numbers—to the power of six. More than six billion possible combinations."

Sonya sighs hopelessly.

"Cheer up! The decryption key has *got* to be present in the actual code—no matter how complex," Avner assures her. "With current micro-processor technology, it is possible to access the central processing unit of an embedded system and tease out its decryption key." He reaches into his hard case and withdraws a printed circuit board about the size of his palm mounted to an electronic device, which looks to Sonya like mating robot spiders.

"With one of these." Avner proudly displays the device, turning it so Sonya can admire its compact elegance. "The Arduino is a microcontroller with on-board flash memory. I've been playing around with them for a couple of years, developing new algorithms for task-specific shields. This one's a Field Programmable Gate Array, which I've configured as an in-circuit emulator."

He attaches one end of a small computer serial interface adapter to the plug assembly protruding from the cylinder; the other end he presses into the Arduino's serial port.

"With this little darling, you can connect a PC to any embedded system and imitate its CPU. We know that the algorithmic language ALGOL 68 and the A68LGU translator were standardized in the Soviet Union, very popular for industrial applications. It's a good bet this is the hardware description language you'll encounter in the field. So, I've programmed the FPGA shield to recognize it."

Avner grins like the naughty hacker he is. "This will allow you to deploy a computer intelligence assembler/disassembler program and reverse-engineer the code key."*

He snaps a USB-2 cord into the Arduino's output jack, plugs it into his laptop and chuckles as if he is about to breech the World Bank's slush fund. Avner motions for Sonya to pull up a chair beside him in front of his laptop.

He types on his keyboard and Cyrillic characters dance across the screen, reflecting in his eyeglasses like a chorus line of fireflies. Avner's face glows with a conspiratorial satisfaction as he enters:

ВЫБ~В~ЛИБО~БЫВ

"ALGOL 68's reverent case statement. Standard protocol for ending a command." Avner explains, adding in English, "'Case, in, out, esac.' That's…"

"'Case' spelled backward?" Sonya smiles ingenuously.

"Very good!" Avner clears his throat. "All right, now pay close attention. I am going to teach you how to crack a Cold War-era Permissive Action Link."

Sonya sighs wistfully. "You really know how to show a girl a good

---

* Computer Intelligence Assembler/Disassembler [**CIASDIS**]—a Forth-based tool that allows a programmer to incrementally and interactively build knowledge about a body of code and re-assemble all disassembled code to the exact same configuration.

INTERPOLATE

....

*"When some American colleagues and military politicians
tell us that they are worried by tactical nuclear weapons,
we say, let's make it clear who should be worried more by it."*

— Yuri Baluyevsky, First Deputy Chief of the Armed Forces
General Staff for Arms Control, at a news conference on the
Strategic Offensive Reductions Treaty [SORT] in May 2002

AYASOFYA WAS CONVERTED from a Byzantine basilica into an Ottoman mosque by the sword in 1453 and demoted to a Turkish museum by political decree in 1935, yet it is still besieged by thousands of ecstatic worshipers. Father Callan watches them crowd its cavernous nave, crane their necks to gaze into its celestial dome and stand slack-jawed beneath mosaics of archangels, intricately painted cherubim and Naskh calligraphic discs glittering in the sunlight that streams through a carousel of arching windows.

Justinian's masterwork was officially dedicated to *Agia Sofia*, the "Holy Wisdom of God." But, for reasons Danny never understood, the seat of Eastern Patriarchy became conflated in the minds of believers with Hagia Sophia, a canonized female Roman martyr. Standing in the basilica now for the first time, Danny decides the irony of that anthropomorphic transposition is chillingly apt. Ayasofya had been stripped by fanatical iconoclasts, raped by avaricious crusaders, ornamented by sybaritic sultans, and desacralized by nationalist zealots. Despite these indignities, "she" remains one of the few places on Earth where Danny has actually felt Divine Presence.

The Supreme Being, by Roman Catholic theological definition, is unknowable. And yet the mystics Danny most admired spent their tortured lives exploring this "great mystery." His own attempts had been fraught with doubt and despair. During his darkest nights, the Trinity had confounded him. He had challenged the Father's authority, rejected the Son's intercession, and screamed in frustration at the Holy Spirit's impotence. God remained silent.

But one night as he lay sobbing on the floor of his room, feeling as if his heart were tearing open, Danny had heard a voice. And to his dismay, it was a *feminine* voice, not the beatific consolation of the Blessed Mother, but the soft reassurance of a celestial lover.

Both pagan Greeks and Christian Gnostics had considered the goddess Sophia the personification of universal wisdom, but to a Jesuit, feminizing the divine bordered on heresy. Still, Danny could not deny the voice he had heard or the presence he had felt. The mystical Beloved had whispered into his heart, given meaning to his struggle and kept him sane in the epicenter of a spiritual cyclone.

It was not something he ever shared with his spiritual advisor.

Distracted now by his surroundings and the fog of jet-lag, Danny walks past the woman wearing a long skirt and lightweight pashmina standing beneath a gilded mosaic of the Christ. She lightly touches Danny's arm as he passes.

"What have your people done to our nice rabbi?" Sonya's voice snaps him back to present time as her wide Semitic eyes gaze upward into the stern Byzantine face of a transcendent Jesus. "And what the hell is a 'pantokrator,' anyway?"

"Greek translation of *El Shaddai*—'God Almighty.'" Danny smiles as he observes her sharp profile. Her blonde hair hidden by the gauzy scarf, Sonya could easily pass for a chaste Muslim girl. "The closest English word is 'omnipotent.' But *pantokratoros* is a more dynamic descriptor. God's power manifesting as a cosmic event."

Her amber eyes reflect Jesus' golden halo. "Like *Genesis?*"

"More like your palimpsest, Sonny," Danny says. "*Kalachakra*, continuous creation through time. No resting on the seventh day."

Sonya looks up at him, her eyes savoring a bittersweet memory. "Oh Danny," she sighs and chases it with an endearing laugh. "How could I *not* have fallen in love with you?"

Maybe it is because they are both out of their element, or maybe just because the feeling can no longer be contained, but when Danny allows himself to look deeply, to fearlessly see the woman he remembers, a seemingly unnavigable ocean that has separated them for eight years is crossed in an instant. He feels a cool breeze caress his face, as if the Goddess Sophia were standing there beside him. In a sense, she *is*. The Russian diminutive of Sophia is Sonya.

Seeing her again like this, Danny knows this moment is all that matters, the truth they will always share, no matter what life throws at or between them. In this moment, out of time and tide, he forgives her *everything*, all the lies she has told in the past and all she will undoubtedly tell in the future.

When he is able to think again, Danny says, "Bashir is with me. Old guy has more energy than I do and the time difference doesn't seem to bother him at all. He's already whirling like a dervish—hobnobbing with his fellow wizards over at the Museum of Islamic Art. Made me promise to bring you over for tea." He catches himself staring at her and looks down. "Bashir's very fond of you, Sonny."

"That little man is a fine judge of character."

"Well, he's the reason I'm here," Danny lies.

Sonya slips on her big sunglasses. "Guess I owe him one."

....

THE SWEET SMELL OF ROASTING CORN wafts from vendors'
carts in Sultan Ahmet Park. Trimmed boxwood hedges skirt the
arching fountain and benches filled with gossiping ladies in colorful
esarp and fitted *ferace*. Beneath the shade of a horse chestnut tree,
a young woman modestly enshrouded in a black *chador* waves soap
bubbles from a plastic wand and gleefully watches them rise on
the hot air currents, obviously one of those "dangerous Islamists"
Erdoğan has warned the nation about, Danny concedes with a smile.

In the ancient Hippodrome of Byzantium, Danny and Sonya bear
right at the Obelisk of Theodosius and enter the former palace of
Ibrahim Pasha, Suleyman the Magnificent's grand *vezir*. Like most
of the Ottoman architectural relics in Mustafa Kemal Atatürk's
domain, it too was re-purposed as a museum of Turkish and Islamic
Art to chasten its imperial hubris.

Shaded by a brick arcade in the cobblestone courtyard, patrons
cluster around café tables sipping apple-flavored *çay* and cardamom-
scented *kahvesi* from plastic cups. Bashir talks animatedly to a short,
stout man with a trimmed black beard and rosy cheeks.

"May I introduce Professor Iskender Arslan from Istanbul University," he says. "One of the few living experts on the Tasawwuf."

"*Teshekkür*," the plump professor thanks his old friend and mops
perspiration from his forehead with a rose-scented handkerchief.
He speaks to the others in Oxfordian English. "Though you embarrass
me with flattery, I am grateful to still be counted among the living."

Bashir takes Sonya's outstretched hand. "Welcome to Istanbul,
habibti! Clearly, Al-Llâh *has* willed that you make your journey."

"And apparently has assigned *you* as my 'spiritual bodyguard.'"
Sonya smiles obliquely and sits in the filligreed chair Arslan holds
for her. "Please enlighten us about the Tasawwuf, Professor Arslan.
Bashir has been frustratingly circumspect on the subject."

"I understand his reticence," Arslan replies. "Sufis have always
generated more questions than answers. Did the Tasawwuf arise in
reaction to the sybaritic excesses of the Umayyad Caliphate, or is their
history rooted deeper than Islam? Perhaps in the *dharma* of India
or teachings of the Biblical Prophets? Some scholars say the Arabic
name derives from *suf*—a 'woolen garment'—others from *safa*—
'inner purity'. Still others insist it comes from the Greek *sofia*—
'wisdom'. Some identify as Sunni, others as Shi'i, but I believe it
is accurate to say all Sufis seek *tawhid*, the dissolution of individual
ego in Divine Presence."

"Are you a practitioner as well as a scholar, professor?"

He touches a hand to his heart. "I study with a living master of
the Rifa'i Tariqah in Üsküdar, Shaykha Çamal Nur."

"*Shaykha?* You study with a woman?"

Arslan bows his head slightly in deference. "Al-Llâh chooses
His instruments, sister."

Bashir, who has slipped off to the café counter, returns with four
cups of gritty *kahvesi*. "Since we are discussing God's instruments,
allow me to introduce Father Daniel from the Society of Jesus and
professor of Comparative Religion at Harvard Divinity School."

Arslan shakes Danny's hand briskly. "An honor, Father Daniel."

"The honor's mine, Professor. Since Bashir acknowledges you as
the 'living expert,' maybe you can tell us something about the Sufis
of Khurasan? Balkh, specifically?"

Arslan places the thick tips of his fingers together in thought.
"*Umm al-Belaad*, the great 'Mother of Cities.'"

"Just out of curiosity," Sonya interjects, "was the 'Mother' a single parent, or did all her cities have a 'Father' as well?"

Arslan sips sweet coffee and chuckles into his cup. "The 'Father,' Miss Sonya, was known as the 'Land of a Thousand Cities,' a vast region that once encompassed Tagzig, Margiana, Bactria, Kapisa, Oddiyana, Olmolungring, Zhang-Zhung, Gandharva and Uyghur. His name comes from two ancient Aryan words: *sham*, meaning 'light' or 'illumination,' and *bala*— 'held high.'"

"*Sham-bala?*" Sonya's voice bridges surprise and skepticism.

"Exactly," Arslan confirms.

"Now you mention it," Danny says, "I *do* recall a Zoroastrian fire temple complex at Balkh called 'Shamis.' Never made the connection."

Arslan nods. "As Gurdjieff proclaimed, 'all roads lead to Balkh.' It was the ancient center of both commerce and religion long before it became the hub of Khurasan. Zoroaster spent his last days there, they say. As for the Sufis, Adham, Shaqiq, Rabi'a, and Rumi hailed from Balkh or nearby."

"Iskender-jan," Bashir uses the Persian term of endearment to address his learned friend, "do you know if there are any surviving *khanaqat* in Badakhshan?"

"Retreat lodges?" Arslan shrugs, scratches his beard. "As you know, Badakhshan is predominately Isma'ili and their traditions are quite different from other Shi'a sects. However, I have heard rumors that the Sarman-Darga is still hidden away somewhere in the Hindu Kush, preserving secret wisdom from the time of Zoroaster."

Arslan seems amused by the idea and explains to Sonya, "It is typical of Sufi orders to incorporate a word play into their name. In Persian, *darga* means 'court' and *sarman* is 'bee,' presumably an arch reference to the precious honey of their tradition, or perhaps their ability to flit easily from flower to flower, drawing spiritual nectar."

"Court of the Bees," Bashir's eyes twinkle as he winks at Sonya.

"*An-Nahl.*" She remembers the *surah* from Al-Qur'ân referenced in her manuscript.

"Gurdjieff also wrote about contacting this secret brotherhood almost a century ago," Arslan adds, "although he referred to them as 'Sarmoung,' an Armenian pronunciation. He claimed they were associated with the Aga Khan in Kabul."

"Head of the Isma'ili sect, isn't he?" Danny asks.

"Indeed. But Gurdjieff is a questionable source to say the least," Arslan sighs. "Frankly, I would not hold out much hope of gathering any 'precious honey' in Afghanistan. I fear these days you will find only fanaticism, grinding poverty and landmines. So please…" the professor looks directly at Sonya and cautions, "*do* watch your step."

....

BENEATH A VINE-COVERED PERGOLA, Sonya sips sweet çay from a tulip glass as the evening cools. The Rossiya shares Ihtisap Agasi, a pedestrian walkway, with seedy disco bars named Jasmine, Melody and Irmak in a district of Istanbul called Aksaray, after Anatolia's famous Silk Road *caravanserai.* In this modern market-place, Sonya observes that the signage appears in both Turkish and Cyrillic, and its shoppers are enticed into ordering off-the-menu Russian delights.

A slender, dark-haired girl sits alone at one of the tables, her Eurasian eyes wide and blue as the Bosphorus, her face made-up to appear older and more sophisticated than she is, but her red strap-less party dress looks cheap and obvious. Stiff as a mannequin, the girl never checks her mobile or orders a drink. A bald, unshaven waiter with a white jacket over his black T-shirt treats her as if she were invisible. The girl slowly scans tables where men cluster in small groups drinking milky licorice-flavored *raki* from tumblers. She arches an invitational eyebrow when one of them notices her, but quickly drops her gaze when she realizes Sonya and her large male companion are keenly observing her stagecraft.

"The 'Natashas' usually hop ferries to Trabzon, then work their way to Ankara and Istanbul," says Eddy Thompson, whose bronzed features appear carved from wood. A thick, rust-colored moustache hides his upper lip, a triangular tuft below his mouth points toward a square, cleft chin and his sun bleached chestnut hair is loosely cinched into a short pony-tail on the crown of his head. He wears a nubby white shirt open to mid-chest, sleeves rolled to his elbows, a leather cord around his neck with gunmetal dog tags and a matching ring in his left ear. The American drags on a Turkish cigarette, sips a bottle of Amstel beer that almost disappears in his enormous hand, and pronounces his vowels with a Brooklyn accent.

"A 15-buck ticket gets all the hopefuls in as weekend shoppers from Odessa, Chisinau, Constanta, Varna or any of the Black Sea ports. Here in Istanbul, they can work legally in the brothels, get a Turkish ID card and access to free medical and social services." The American inclines his head toward the pretty girl who grows increasingly nervous about being watched. "Hotties like that one are picked up by the local *vory* before they get the chance to go legal. They're usually young and stupid, use drugs, lose their passport, get raped, have abortions, and then do as they're told or end up with faces no one ever wants to look at again. You'll find them at most of the clubs in Taksim across the Horn and all over the Aksaray. On any given night you'll see fifty 18-year-olds working the disco at Bacardi and Balance, their Russian pimps stalking like jackals in the corner."

"You seem to know a lot about the trade, Mister Thompson." Sonya replies.

The big man squints in amusement through his cigarette smoke. "Enough to get a blowjob without a shakedown." The corners of his hooded eyes crinkle as he appraises Sonya's unruffled demeanor. "Call me Eddy."

Sonya is already somewhat acquainted with "Eddy Thompson," or whatever his name really is, having read his colorful dossier in Glilot: Operation Desert Storm with US Army Special Forces in Kuwait, Operation Gothic Serpent with Delta Force in Mogadishu, and CIA Special Activities Division in Afghanistan. The codename "Payload" is an arch reference to his incendiary role in crushing the Taliban prison siege at Mazar-i-Sharif. Eddy's last known employer was Blackwater USA, with which he had a falling out after four of his colleagues were shot to pieces, burned, and hung from a bridge in Fallujah, Iraq. For the past five years, he has been a lone wolf, leading private treks for well-heeled adventurers and freelancing below the radar for people who need a delicate situation fixed quietly.

"Do you interview girls for Viktor Kaban, Eddy?"

"Not my specialty, darlin'. While the dogcatchers are combing Trabzon for strays, Vik's scouts are recruiting talent *before* they get on the ferries. He brings them to Istanbul on private boats. Places them in his exclusive club, not very far from here."

"Let me guess. Members all have lines of credit with Akbank?"

Eddy cocks an appreciative eyebrow and shrugs. "What can I say? Business gets done, the girls get protection, and Vik takes his pick of the litter. The most talented move on to porn careers in Prague."

"Guess every girl wants to be a movie star."

Eddy blows smoke toward the dark-haired beauty sitting stiffly at the café table. "Beats taking it up the ass for *borsht* money."

Sonya ignores the provocation. "So, what exactly *do* you do for Kaban, Eddy?"

"Well, Sonya…may I call you Sonya?" She inclines her head and he continues. "I like to think of myself as an entrepreneur."

"Meaning you get paid twice for the same job?"

Eddy drops his cigarette and crushes it beneath a distressed Blundstone boot. "Way I see it, same actors but different plays. Vik hires me to track you and your Persian pal. Tells me this guy, Levi —dude you met up with in New York—was Mossad. I've got a few acquaintances in Universe,* so I start poking around. Imagine my surprise when your boss hires me to keep an eye on you as well, make sure you get in and out of my old stomping ground in one pretty piece. Frankly, Sonya, I do not see this as a conflict of interest."

She appraises Eddy over the rim of her tea glass. "What else did my boss tell you?"

"Same thing Vik told me: Chechens smoked Levi."

She swallows the bad taste in her mouth with a sip of sweet tea. "Did he tell you exactly what we are looking for?"

"Suitcases the Ruskies left lying around."

"Ancient manuscripts, Eddy. Let's stay on the same page."

"Hey, I'm all over this, Sonya. 'Ancient manuscripts' it is!" Eddy winks and his nostrils flare. A crooked smile tells her he is enjoying their conversational sleight of hand. "So, is your Persian boyfriend with the natty threads coming along on our excursion?"

"You mean Cyrus?" Sonya laughs, "No, and he hasn't a clue what is going on. You can tell Kaban that Cyrus is a dead end. Believe me, you're right where the action is."

"Copy *that.*" Eddie glances obviously at the dark-haired girl and she averts her eyes. "I am curious, though. Why did you want to meet down here in hooker central?"

---

* **Universe** [Tevel]—the Mossad department that manages relations with foreign, "friendly" Intelligence agencies

Sonya tosses a few Turkish Lira onto the table beside her empty glass. "Because I want you to take me to Viktor Kaban's exclusive club, Eddy."

He appraises her long, shapeless skirt and loose cotton blouse. "Seriously?"

"Why not? I've already been to church today."

Eddy shakes his head slowly as he laughs. "Well, you definitely have a set of balls on you, lady. But you're not exactly dressed for a walk on the wild side."

She pushes back her chair and grabs her knapsack. "Give me ten minutes to fix that."

....

EDDY THOMPSON ALWAYS had huge hands. In fifth grade at PS 181, he could already palm a basketball. By age 15, Eddy could wrap his fingers around almost anyone's face and make it disappear. He thought that was kind of freakish. Girls thought so, too. Most were spooked when he reached out for their petite painted fingers in the movie theater. But the Army had been happy to make concessions for Eddy's manual monstrosity.

Though he had trouble with tight trigger guards on small side arms, he made up for it by being able to crush a man's trachea without even breaking a sweat. Special Forces had encouraged that talent. So had Delta and SAD/SOG.*

During interminable days on recon in one rag-head country or another, Eddy occasionally daydreamed about doing more creative things with his hands—braiding a lanyard, for instance, or picking

* **SAD/SOG** [Special Activities Division/Special Operations Group]—CIA paramilitary unit comprised of operatives from JSOC—the Joint Special Operations Command: 1st Special Forces Operational Detachment-Delta, Naval Special Warfare Development Group [DEVGRU], Air Force 24th Special Tactical Squadron, and Army Intelligence Support Activity

up loose change waiters left on his café table, or finding that special spot between a woman's legs that made her moan in ecstasy. Sadly, Eddy remained *persona non-grata* in the world of small-motor dexterity. At least he had a reputation for being a generous tipper.

Eddy lights another cigarette while waiting for his baby-sitting assignment to emerge from the Rossiya's restroom. Vik told him the woman in the Algonquin photos was some kind of meeting planner. Did everything but swallow. She looks younger, less experienced than Eddy would have expected. Pretty face but dresses like a model from an LL Bean catalogue. And Christ, that yuppie leather knapsack makes him want to push her in front of a moving Prius. Eddy wonders why this chick is so damn important to Mossad. But, what the hell, shekels are as good as dollars and Eddy only asks questions when he absolutely, positively needs to know. In this case, he frankly does not give a rat's ass.

He watches the dark-haired girl working her program. She is too young for this shit and he has a stupid urge to buy her a ticket home to her mother. But *that* isn't going to happen. In his peripheral vision, he notices a tall, sleek blonde in a very short, very tight olive dress, a wide, beige leather belt around a slim waist and matching lace-up stiletto sandals. The white-coated waiter belligerently blocks her path as if she is walking the wrong side of *his* street. Eddy hears her say something in Russian to the bald man, who glances over at him, then sullenly stands aside.

The woman walks straight toward Eddy's table, her short hair fluffed into a golden aura, her amber eyes set to stun. And that rack—Jesus! Were it not for the yuppie leather knapsack slung over her shoulder, he would never have recognized her.

Sonya stands akimbo, like some kind of super model, and purses her red lips sarcastically. "Ready, Eddy?"

The cigarette hangs limp beneath his moustache. "Okay, I take it all back."

"What?"

"About the balls."

"Premature evaluation, was it?"

He rubs the stubble on his chin. "What did you say to that scumbag waiter?"

"I told him you were a big-shot Hollywood producer and I was your escort."

Vik may have misjudged this one. Eddy reminds himself not to make the same mistake. His squint softens into an appreciative smile. "Okay, Sonya, let's go slumming."

....

ISTANBUL IS THE ONLY CITY in the world that spreads its legs between two continents, so the fact that it has become a natural locus for the sex trade between Asia and Europe is no surprise to Sonya. While she has never had the occasion to visit a sex club anywhere in the world, serendipity and her present company have provided the perfect opportunity to jump in with both feet.

She hooks Eddy Thompson's massive arm and they walk to the corner of Ataturk near the aqueduct. He waves down a taxi and the Kurdish driver proceeds to dodge a phalanx of motorbikes and pimps on a boulevard chock-a-block with bleak hotels and shops sporting the latest Euro-trash fashions. Their driver weaves beneath a maze of overpasses, negotiates streetcar tracks, and turns right on Dagarcik, cruising between a hospital and tree-lined cemetery into a quieter neighborhood. He drops them in front of a gated wall. Behind it, a restored 19th century townhouse gives no indication of its 21st century business model.

To the left of a gate forged of stylized wrought iron tulips, a call box is mounted on the stucco wall. Eddy punches the button. "We'd like a tour of your wine cellar."

A Russian-accented voice replies, "There is charge for tasting."

Sonya watches Eddy glance down at her legs as he informs the box, "Not a problem. We brought our own corkscrew."

The gate clicks open. Dark wooden shutters flank rows of tall, counter-weighted windows on the elegant façade of the four-storied house. At street level, a white marble alcove frames double doors inset with leaded-glass panels. Inside, a muscular black-suited bouncer pats Eddy down, then searches Sonya's knapsack for weapons and badges. All he finds of interest is a tapered, 26-centimeter-long black silicone dildo.

Eddy raises an eyebrow and Sonya shrugs without a trace of embarrassment. *"Ti ponimaesh, devochka dolzna imet eto na vsyakiy sluchai* [Girl's got to have some back-up, you know]," she tells the licentious bouncer. Smirking, he ushers them down a carpeted marble stairway. At the bottom, the concierge swipes Eddy's credit card, hands him a red token and they enter the tasting lounge.

Progressive house music thumps softly over a cocktail bar illuminated by a gauzy web of pin-light LEDs. It is still early but a few young women have already started to entertain businessmen in cozy booths around the room. Three Englishmen in Jermyn Street business attire sit at the far end of the bar sipping martinis and chatting up the exotic brunette bartender wearing a revealing designer knock-off. She breaks away from her admirers to take drink orders from Sonya and Eddy.

After listening to her accent, Sonya remarks, *"Ti is Chelyabinska* [You must be from Chelyabinsk],"

"Ti znaesh [How could you tell]?" The girl laughs.

"Those beautiful Tartar eyes," Sonya admits, noticing one of the Brits reclaim his tip while the girl's back is turned. "I'm from Piter." She uses the colloquial for Saint Petersburg.

"Practically neighbors!" The Siberian girl winks. "What can I get you?"

"Cristal Brut," Sonya continues in English so Eddy can follow. "He's buying."

"Knock yourself out," Eddy shrugs. "Vik's picking up the tab."

"Even better." Sonya scans the room as Eddy orders Blanton's on the rocks with a Red Bull back. "So, how does all this work?"

He tosses back the caffeinated drink first. "Well, Sonya, it ain't exactly rocket science."

"Okay, let's say I'm a Footsie 100 exec in from London on business and want some playtime. Do I just ask the barkeep to pour me a tart on the rocks, stirred but not shaken? Or what?"

Eddy flags the bartender. "Can we have a look at tonight's house specials, darlin'?"

The Siberian girl reaches under the bar, hands him a J3400 electronic tablet and raises a conspiratorial eyebrow in Sonya's direction. "*Karusel?*" She uses the Russian slang for group sex.

"Considering the options," Sonya demurs.

Eddy types his password and swivels the screen toward her. "Here's what the house is pouring tonight." Displayed at the top of the menu are a series of professional head shots with single names beneath: *Alina, Eva, Karina, Marinka, Tatiana…* Sonya clicks on a stunning blonde named *Iryna* with the number 403 beside her name. Up comes a light-box photo gallery of the slender girl modeling lacy lingerie and posing semi-nude. Her vital statistics are displayed below the photos:

Nationality:	Ukrainian
Languages:	Russian, English
Age:	20
Height:	170
Weight:	53
Hair:	Blonde
Eyes:	Blue
Tits:	B
Pubic hair:	Shaved
Orientation:	Bi

Client reviews follow a brief *curriculum vitae* and a rate chart for her services.

"I've heard the boss has his eye on that one," the bartender confides to Sonya.

"For 250 Euros an hour she must be a contortionist! I'm definitely in the wrong business." Sonya points to a list of abbreviations beside Iryna's professional qualifications. "What are all these?"

Eddy glances over her shoulder. "Girls list all their…you know, their 'specialties,' so everybody's clear on the rules of engagement."

"What's GFE?"

"Girl Friend Experience," Eddy explains. "Big fantasy among business men. They don't want to feel like they're whoring, so the GF-thing makes it seem more legit."

"That costs extra?"

"Oh yeah."

Sonya nods thoughtfully. "How about OWO?"

"Oral Without."

"Without what?"

He swirls the ice in his whiskey. "A condom."

"And CIM?"

"Well, that would be the end result of 'oral without,' wouldn't it?"

"Right…of course. So, I'm guessing COB is…" She glances down at her décolletage.

"You're a quick study."

"And I used to think military-speak was complicated," she admits. "What's upstairs?"

"Dining area, private meeting rooms, party central. Third floor's where the action takes place," Eddy offers his arm in a gentlemanly gesture. "Shall we?"

Sonya finishes her champagne, leaves a hundred TL note on the bar and follows Eddy into the elevator, half-expecting to encounter Bosch's *Garden of Earthly Delights* on the third floor. Instead, the elevator doors open on a stylish woman with short, dark hair sitting behind a red-lacquered Chinese writing table in an open antechamber. She wears a black high-collar business suit softened by a red rosebud *boutonnière*. Behind her, golden spotlights illuminate an arrangement of strelitzia potted in an antique Iznik mosque lamp and an embroidered black satin curtain mutes the edgy thump of techno music playing somewhere in the background.

Eddy hands the woman in black his red token. She opens her desk drawer and produces a plastic key card in a red sleeve embossed with the same stylized tulip adorning the front gate.

"You are welcome to enjoy the lounge," she says. "Room 403 is down to your left."

Eddy parts the satin curtain into a pheromone-charged atmosphere accompanied by a throbbing soundtrack. Two girls perform on a circular platform beneath a shimmering wall of blue light. One slides her G-string rhythmically up and down a brass pole with slow precision, while the other, wearing only white lace gloves and panties, demonstrates her skill at fellatio on a partially dressed customer. Around the stage, silhouetted bodies grind and writhe in the perfumed darkness. It is impossible to make out faces, ages or, in many cases, genders. The anonymous clientele lounge on wide futons among mountains of pillows or perform sexual gymnastics atop cushioned blocks like bonobos on Spanish fly.

Sonya floats through the humid *karusel*, more curious than aroused. "Some clients order from the menu," Eddy explains softly. "Some bring their own. But once everybody's in the dark..."

"They learn Braille?" Sonya guesses.

Eddy laughs as they emerge into a narrow corridor lined with paneled doors. He taps one with 403 engraved on a brass oval and gently slips his key card into the lock. Inside the air-conditioned room, Iryna lies on a satin bedspread bathed in rosy light from the ceiling spots. Her lean, pale body is sparsely decorated in black lace lingerie, a garter belt clipped to smoky stockings and crimson high heels. The girl's mouth is painted to match her shoes. Blond hair falls silky and straight; limpid blue eyes open wide with invitation. "Please make comfortable," Iryna urges, picking up an ornate phone on the bed table. "I will call for champagne."

Sonya scans the dark recesses and furnishings of the elegantly appointed, windowless room, checking for surveillance equipment. She spots an obvious two-way mirror on the wall and the unlit, dish-shaped light fixture floating above the bed. Undoubtedly the bathroom mirror also conceals a camera and microphone.

"We just on recon?" Eddy asks, watching her work, "or you in for the full Monty?"

Sonya shrugs. "Why not?"

Eddy wraps a hand around the door jamb behind her head, leans in close and brushes her cheek with his coarse moustache, inhaling her scent. Sonya's palm flattens firmly against his broad chest and pushes back unequivocally. "But only with *her*."

Eddy stands down, teeth flashing. "Not a problem, Sonya. I've got your back."

She wanders to the edge of the bed as Iryna hangs up the phone and smiles like a child trying to project sex appeal. Her features are classically Slavic, angular and sensuous, her eyes beneath the heavy mascara still ingenuous, too young to have hardened into the marble stare of a professional whore. This world is new to her, a naughty adventure with the promise of a lucrative video contract.

Sonya sits beside Iryna's supine body. Her scent is pleasantly cloying, candy-coated, the way teenage girls often smell. "*Tobi diysno dvadtsyat' rokiv* [Are you really twenty]?" Sonya asks.

The girl seems surprised to hear her native Ukrainian.

"*Dosyt' blyz'ko* [Close enough]," Iryna replies with a shrug and takes Sonya's hand. She kneads it gently, places it on her flat stomach and presses it into the warm flesh over three blue stars tattooed just above her panty line. Slowly, she coaxes it upward to the under-curve of her lacy brassiere and Sonya can feel the padding that fills the vacant space around the girl's small breast.

Leaning close to Iryna's ear, Sonya whispers softly, "I've never been with a girl before. Just show me what you like."

....

FATHER CALLAN SIPS gritty Turkish coffee on the rooftop terrace of the Seven Hills Hotel, watching Ayasofya blush as the sun kisses her massive stone buttresses. To the west, the ascending domes and minarets of Sedefkar Mehmed Agha's "Blue Mosque" bask in golden morning light. Sonya sits across from him at their table, pensive and distant behind her sunglasses.

She appears distracted by ferries crossing the Bosphorus as Danny discusses their evening departure. "Bashir says we get into Dushanbe around three in the morning. Nothing but gypsy cabs at that hour. So, your fixer has transportation and lodging lined up?"

"My colleague from Saint Petersburg has had an accident," Sonya informs him, her shades reflecting the red tablecloth and obscuring her emotional state. "I've hired a new guide—an American. He's arranging for visas, transportation on both sides of the border and the gear we'll need in country. I plan to do some shopping today for boots and personal stuff."

Danny feels immediately uneasy about the sudden change of personnel. He stares into his cup, swirls the fine grounds that remain in the bottom and wonders if Cyrus' suspicions about Sonya were so far-fetched after all. A waiter brings figs, yoghurt, and *börek*— torpedo-shaped pastries filled with cheese—and then adjusts a white canvas umbrella to block the oblique morning sun.

"Sounds like you've got it all under control, Sonny. Tell me again why I'm so damn important to this expedition?"

"Because I need someone I can trust, Danny. Women are systematically exploited in this part of the world. They can't even ride a streetcar in Istanbul without being groped by some ignorant pig." She unfolds her napkin and arranges it in her lap, looking down as she speaks. "Men take whatever advantage they can, don't they? Just part of the ancient cultural fabric of civilization."

Danny bites into a pastry and averts his eyes to sea. "You don't really need me, Sonny. Bashir knows the language and the territory much better than I do."

"He's a lovely man but he doesn't have the capabilities I need."

"What about your new guide?"

"Capable, I suspect, but I still don't trust him." She lowers her glasses and glances over the rims at him. "Not the way I trust you."

"Well, since you broached the subject, tell me why I should trust *you*, Sonny?"

"Because I've never lied to you."

"Really?" He feels accusation building behind his eyes. "You told me you hadn't slept with Cyrus."

"Well, at the time, I hadn't," Sonya drops her gaze. "Besides, I don't think it's any of your concern who I sleep with."

"Whom." He petulantly corrects her grammar.

Sonya shrugs. "Arguable either way, professor."

Danny drips golden thyme honey onto his yoghurt, then plays his hand. "You know, Cyrus thinks you're a spook. Some kind of undercover spy."

Sonya quietly dissects a fat green fig revealing its seedy pink center. "Does he?"

"Yeah, Israeli Intelligence." Danny watches for a reaction, waits for her response. Neither arrives. "Well? Is it true?"

"If it were," she replies without looking up, "you don't think I could admit it, do you?"

"Or what? You'd have to kill me?"

"Let's not find out, shall we?" Sonya pops half a fig into an arch smile. Danny is not entirely convinced she is joking.

"Hope I'm not interrupting anything."

A gravelly voice prompts Danny to swivel in his chair. A big man stands on the terrace behind him—maybe six-four and back-lit by the morning sun. He wears military khaki trousers and a navy T-shirt. Beneath a battered blue baseball cap, mirror-coated sunglasses hide his eyes.

"Father Callan, this is Mister Thompson," Sonya says, "our trekking guide."

"Call me Eddy." Dimples cut trenches into his bronzed cheeks when he smiles. A bushy Fu Manchu and soul patch amplify Eddy's irreverence. He stands only a couple inches above Danny's eye level but seems as intimidating as Goliath.

"Call me Danny." He takes the big man's extended hand and feels its crushing grip while glancing up at the New York Yankee insignia on Eddy's cap. "How's Rodriguez doing since the break? I haven't been following the last few days."

"He's slamming the Tigers this week," Eddy grins. "Forget about those steroids."

Danny shakes his head. "I don't know, Eddy. Sox had a three-game lead in the division going into All-Stars. A-Rod might be back on the juice by September."

Eddy tightens his jaw. "Well, I wouldn't bet the parish poor box on another Series at Fenway this year, Padre."

Sonya's fingers impatiently tap the table as she breaks into their conversation. "When you gentlemen have finished urinating on the shrubbery, can we discuss our travel plans?"

Eddy pulls up a chair from the closest table, positions it neatly between Sonya and Danny then sits backward on it like a cowboy in a saloon. "Sonya, you're good to go. No visa required since you're traveling on a Russian passport."

Danny flashes her a questioning look. "Since when?"

"Since I was ten. Dual citizenship."

"The rest of us will need letters of introduction to get double-entry visas for Tajikistan since we'll be going out and re-entering at the same border post," Eddy says. "My homeboy in Dushanbe can set us up with the Taj doubles, GBAO permits—which usually take ten days to process—and visas for Afghanistan."

"What's a GBAO?" Sonya looks up tentatively at Eddy. "Or do I really *not* want to know?"

He chuckles as if it were an inside joke. "Gorno-Badakhshan-skaya Autonomous Oblast. You need special permits to travel in the Pamirs since the civil war. Helps sort out the tourists from the heroin smugglers."

Feeling somewhat excluded from the conversation, Danny probes their guide's credentials. "Mind if I ask who your 'homeboy' is?"

"Attaché to the US Ambassador. Dude owes me a favor or two. He already faxed the letter of introduction we'll need at Immigration."

Danny nods. "Your homeboy throwing in transportation?"

"Land Cruiser turbo V8, with a Ruskie- and Taj-speaking driver." Eddy slips off his shades and props them on top of his ball cap, exposing steely gray eyes and an alpha male stare. "That meet with your approval?"

Danny returns the attitude. "Long as we're not concerned about fuel efficiency, big guy."

Eddy emits a low, good-natured laugh. "Hey, you see Wakefield polishing the bench during the All-Stars game, Padre? That guy *ever* gonna retire?"

....

MUSA DUBAYEV TENDERLY KISSES each of his three daughters, nods to his stocky wife as she washes the dishes and tucks a Yarygin nine-millimeter pistol beneath the waistband of his trousers. He leaves his cramped apartment in Istanbul's Zeytinburnu district, wearing a knitted white *kufti* over his shaggy black hair and carrying a green, pocket-sized Qur'ân. On Fridays, the 33-year-old Chechen immigrant walks through Sümer Mahallesi to the Kubbeli *camii* a few blocks away for prayers. Musa knows any pattern of behavior has inherent risks, but he finds some measure of comfort in both tradition and predictability.

By late morning, the stink of diesel overpowers the aromas of baked bread, ground coffee and pungent tobacco along the hot cobblestone street where he lives with his family. Head down, Musa walks beneath shop awnings, furtively checking the opposite side of the busy street as he passes behind the wooden rack of a glazier's truck. At the corner market, he positions himself behind the sidewalk kiosk and pretends to thumb through the English language newspapers until he is fairly certain he has not picked up a tail. Then he continues on to the *camii* for the *zuhr* prayers.

Payload is the last person he expects to see at the mosque, but the big American is waiting on a wooden bench in the small wedge of greenery outside the whitewashed building. He motions for Musa to join him. He sits cautiously on the gray weathered slats, keeping a lot of space between himself and the intimidating American.

"Hey, Moose, how's it hanging?" Payload seems cheerful. A cigarette bobs in his mouth beneath a thick, drooping moustache as he breaks off bits of a sesame *simit* ring and scatters the sweet crumbs to foraging pigeons. He appears to be smiling beneath the reflective sunglasses that always hide his real intentions. "Haven't seen you since Baku, ol' buddy."

"It is *juma*," Musa sighs heavily. "I am here to pray."

"Don't mean to get between you and the Big Guy, Moose. Just need a little package delivered to Zharkov."

Musa's blue eyes scan the perimeter nervously as he strokes his thick beard. A group of old Turks in tattered gray suit jackets scowl at the gathering flock of pigeons leaving white droppings on the sidewalk. One spits at the birds mingling around Musa's feet as he passes.

Without making eye contact, he tells Payload, "I am not your private messenger."

"Never said you were, Moose. Just figured you'd want to square things after Zona's fuck up with the ENKA* slush fund," he replies. "You know, your little brother would be landfill if I hadn't intervened. Maybe you as well."

Musa checks his watch. "It is almost *zuhr*. If you will excuse me…"

As he tries to stand, Musa feels Eddy's large hand descend firmly on his shoulder. A white Tofas Sahin pulls up to the curb and three

---

* **ENKA** [*İnşaat ve Sanayi AŞ*]—based in Istanbul and Moscow, with ties to the American Turkish Council—builds US embassies in Central Asia and reputedly channeled off-the-books financing from the US State Department to CIA covert operations in the Caucasus.

young men in dark slacks and dress shirts jump out. The driver knifes back into traffic on 67 Sokak and speeds off. One of the men glances at him and mutters, "*Asalaamu aleikoum*," as he passes by.

Payload leans in close to Musa's left ear and growls softly behind a savage smile, "You know, Moose, I do *not* think the Emirate would look kindly on you and your brother smoking your own homies for a Russian paycheck."

Musa's hand creeps beneath the hem of his loose shirt and closes around the hard rubber pistol grip. He glares into Payload's fiery sunglasses as sweat trickles down his sides. He tries to snarl as Bruce Willis does in American films. "How long do you think you would live after they found out?"

Payload leans back on the bench and rolls a slow laugh at him. "I didn't come here for a pissing match, Moose, just a little *quid pro quo*." He pops a piece of *simit* into his mouth.

Musa eases his hand off the pistol. "What is this package you have for Zharkov?"

Payload slides an open packet of Samsun across the bench. Musa pokes his index finger into the foil and feels a plastic object behind the cigarettes.

"What is this?"

"Keeps track of my dental implant, Moose." Payload exposes his teeth in a wolfin grin. "The less you know, the better." Musa tucks the cigarette pack into his shirt pocket.

"Just out of curiosity," Payload asks, "you hear of anybody shopping WMDs lately?"

Musa stares straight ahead and answers in a lowered voice. "There were rumors that Riyadus-Salikhin wanted to acquire a nuclear weapon for bin Laden, but that was more than three years ago—before Basayev was killed. The Emirate is trying to distance itself from his crimes and Umarov has publicly condemned attacks on civilians."*

"For now." Payload tosses a few crumbs to the birds at his feet. "What about Obschina?"

This time it is Musa who laughs. "You, of all people, should know the Community has been in FSB's pocket for years. They decided long ago that drugs are a safer livelihood than politics."

Payload crushes his cigarette out and rubs his unshaven chin. "You hear anything about them hitting a Mossad jumper in New York about a week ago?"

"They are not stupid. The Israeli's have a long reach and a longer memory." Musa stands to leave. "But who can say? These days, there are too many reasons to kill too many people."

"*Ameen*, brother!" Payload flings the rest of his sesame ring to the ravenous pigeons attacking each other in competition for the sticky crumbs. "Go say your prayers and get that package to Zharkov A-sap. He's expecting it. And tell him I'll be leaving town shortly."

"To where?"

"Like I said, Moose, less you know…"

....

VIKTOR KABAN'S VILLA IN BEBEK hides everything but its terracotta tiled roof beneath a thick mantle of cypress atop a slope above the Bosphorus. The verandah off Viktor's bedroom peeks down over the white Rococo turrets of the Âli Pasha Yalisi, an ostentatious mansion that has served as the Egyptian Consulate since Atatürk's tenure. Out beyond the grand *yali*, white luxury yachts bob like champagne

---

* **Riyadus-Salikhin** [Martyr Battalion]—**Shamil Basayev's** insurgents were responsible for the school siege in Beslan, North Ossetia, that killed 385 hostages in 2004. **Doku Khamatovich Umarov,** former president of the unrecognized Chechen Republic of Ichkeria, declared himself *emir* of the "Caucasus Emirate" in 2007.

corks on the chop as an afternoon sea breeze begins to clear Viktor's head of the cocaine and vodka he ingested last night.

Wearing a plush white bathrobe bearing an embroidered monogram, Viktor surveys his manicured tulip garden, breathes in the scented sea air, and watches Marko clean his arsenal on a filigreed cast-iron table—the Glock 25 that caused so much trouble for Viktor in New York, and his Izhmash AK-9 with a long barrel suppressor.

Viktor hates to separate the twins, but now he needs Kyrylo in Brighton Beach to insure his mother's security after the kidnapping, at least until he can find a replacement for Vitali, or a safe place to lock the old woman up. Besides, Marko has to learn to work independently or he will be useless in the future. As long as Viktor keeps him on-task, the boy stays focused. If push comes to shove, Viktor knows his fierce dog of war has only to be unleashed. That comforting thought makes him smile like a proud father.

His mobile phone begins to vibrate and Viktor digs it out of his bathrobe pocket with a scowl.

"Morning, Vik," Eddy Thompson says. "How's tricks?"

"It is afternoon, Eddy. Even *I* am aware of that." Viktor tries to laugh but his head hurts.

"Had a nice time at the Tulip Club last night. Met a sweet little blonde named Iryna. My associate seemed pleased with her talents as well."

Viktor frowns at the thought of Payload fucking his newest interest before he has had the chance to do it himself. "I assume I will be receiving a bill for your...research."

"Naturally. Thought you'd also want to know we're booked on Turkish Air to Dushanbe tonight. If the road isn't too washed out, and the border police don't fuck with us too much, we should cross at Ishkashim sometime Tuesday, maybe Wednesday. One of our party has a cousin on the Afghan side. Oh, and there's a priest along for the ride. Scholar of something or other. Official story is they're researching old manuscripts. My guess is they don't have a fix on that cache yet. Most likely playing it by ear once we're in country."

Viktor scratches his tender nose. "They must be following some sort of trail, Eddy."

"Let's hope. And by the way, here's a news flash, Vik: Forget about that peacock. He was just a smokescreen. Your gazelle, however, is one very smart cookie and no meeting planner, believe you me! She worked with Levi, the guy who tipped you about the cache."

Viktor sighs heavily. "Nothing is as it seems in our business, is it Eddy?"

"You got *that* right. In fact, I'm thinking your mother's kidnapping has Mossad's fingerprints all over it. Bet you haven't seen any deposits into your Akbank account yet."

"Not yet." Viktor's head feels even heavier. "Why would Mossad do such a thing, Eddy? I am an Israeli citizen in good standing."

"You sure about that, Vik? No back-channel deals with people in Damascus?"

"You know I am just a businessman, Eddy, politically neutral. I back no one. I oppose no one. That is why you and I have done business, is it not? We serve no masters, only customers. We can both be trusted not to take sides. Am I right, Eddy?"

"Well, I'm guessing your agnosticism pissed off somebody in Tel Aviv. Levi wasn't in the Big Apple on vacation. He was a jumper running an op."

Viktor decides to test the water. "That must be why the Obschina assassinated him."

There is a pregnant pause before Eddy replies. "I don't think it was Obschina, Vik. Levi was sniffing for nukes, not drugs."

"Then who would have done such a thing?

"Perplexing, isn't it?"

Viktor glances down at Marko adjusting the red dot sight on his Izhmash. "Very."

Another pause. "Listen Vik," Eddy's voice sounds serious, "I gotta be honest with you, pal. We both know this situation has gone way beyond mission scope. Now, I know you're a very smart guy, and I know you're connected, but realistically...I'm thinking you should be looking at an exit strategy right about now."

Viktor notices that he has begun to sweat heavily, even though it is not particularly hot. "You have something in mind, Eddy?"

"Yeah Vik. Something that will keep us *both* alive."

FRIDAY, 17 JULY 2009 • LANGLEY, VIRGINIA

....

COURTNEY KINCAID'S SENSIBLE HEELS click a determined staccato along the polished corridor of the fourth floor between OHB and NHB, the Original and New Headquarters Buildings of the Central Intelligence Agency. Recruited four years ago as an analyst for the Office of Transnational Issues, Courtney reports weekly to the Associate Deputy Director of Intelligence and Foreign Affairs.

A bi-lingual Louisiana Creole with a Tulane University PhD in Greek, Roman and Near Eastern Archeology, Courtney craved adventure after two stultifying years of post-doc research at NYU. To celebrate her 30th birthday, she had traveled to Paris and bumped into a gentleman while browsing the lovely clutter at Shakespeare & Company. Monsieur Genet was an Intelligence Analyst for the International Criminal Police Commission, a *bon vivant* with a penchant for both Honoré de Balzac and Josephine Baker. Over a bottle of Chateau Margeau that evening at La Mère Catherine, he failed to entice Courtney into his *chambre* but did convince her to apply for a position with INTERPOL. It was October of 2001, and everyone was hiring *anyone* who knew anything about the Near East.

Two years later, Courtney was assigned to an Incident Response Team helping UNESCO investigate the disappearance of Gandharan busts and Bactrian Greek coins from the National Museum in Kabul. Shortly after that, a batch of cylindrical seals and cuneiform tablets went missing from the Baghdad museum post-Desert Storm. She enlisted the forensic expertise of Cyrus Narsai, with whom she had an affair after attending an auction of 18th century Ayutthayan temple Buddha heads looted by the Burmese. Working closely under-cover with her silent sleuthing partner in the well-heeled world of black-market art, despite warnings from more officious members of her team, Courtney began to notice similarities in the two wartime burglary cases and meticulously compiled evidence until her conclu-sion was airtight.

She reported to INTERPOL's General Secretariat in Lyon that the Afghan and Iraqi heists both appeared to be not only inside jobs but executed by US intelligence operatives for preservation rather than profiteering, a conclusion that the curators of the respective museums would certainly not have shared. 24 hours before she was scheduled to deliver her brief to UNESCO, Courtney was relieved of her duties for "overstepping IRT investigative authority."

48 hours later, the CIA offered her a job with OTI, ostensibly impressed by her "out-of-the-box investigative initiative."

Courtney continued to consult with Cyrus after relocating to DC. That was why, on his behalf, she started making inquiries about another scholar of Near Eastern studies, a young woman named

Sonya Aronovsky. Courtney told Cyrus she had found nothing particularly unusual in Aronovsky's past, but that was not entirely accurate. INTERPOL had taught her never to reveal her hand before all bets were on the table.

Courtney waits impatiently for an elevator to the seventh floor, flashes her lanyard badge at the duty officer, and enters a window-less briefing room on the top executive level. The Associate Deputy Director, whom everyone calls "A-D-D"—an abbreviation that, in his case, is more than just an unfortunate double entendre—sits behind an open laptop, a smart and a secure phone at the long conference table, flanked by a half-dozen associate assistant liaisons for some-thing-or-other, all shielded behind their respective digital devices like Wall Street traders at an SEC *auto-da-fé*.

Courtney takes her seat at the mahogany table with the self-absorbed ensemble, flips open a MacBook Air and smooths her light-weight skirt toward her knees. Analytic data flashes from a digital projector for the next half hour. Spreadsheets and classified appraisals are shared among the associate assistant liaisons over a secure intra-net. As always, the forty-something-Clark-Kentish ADD seems distracted when Courtney finds herself up to bat.

"PowerPoint or Keynote?" He asks without looking up from the Blackberry on which he is probably rescheduling his next meeting.

"No visuals today, sir," Courtney brushes a wing of straightened black hair back over her right ear, revealing the glittering diamond stud Cyrus had given her. "Sir, I think we may have a developing sit-uation in Afghanistan."

"Got an FYI for you, Court," the ADD replies deadpan while thumbing a text message on his iPhone. "We've had a sit in the Ghan for quite some time."

Snickering circles the polished table.

"Not like this one, sir." Courtney straightens up in her chair. "I have reason to believe KK* is conducting a covert operation in Badakhshan Province."

That gets her boss' attention. "The hell you say! I saw no briefing on that."

"Because they *haven't* briefed us, sir. But there are a number of seemingly unrelated facts that, when you knit them together, form a rather alarming pattern." Courtney interlocks her fingers as she explains, knowing her boss responds better to visual cues.

"Okay Court, spit it out."

"Sir, you may remember my colleague in Cambridge who helped out on those INTERPOL investigations a few years ago." Courtney fills her boss in on Cyrus' chance meeting with Sonya Aronovsky, her solicitation of his partnership, and his suspicions about her actual intentions. "I checked our Universe source and dug up a basic CV: Russian immigrant, Fulbright scholar of Middle Eastern culture and language, IDF reservist who formerly worked with AMAN in Hebron and Khan Yunis. So, I queried AMAN. They had no record of her."

The ADD nods as if he is listening, but his glasses only reflect the e-mail scroll and CNN's news crawl on his laptop screen. "Meaning they *gave* you nothing. So, what?"

Courtney speaks louder and taps up some notes on her screen, "On that Fulbright grant, Aronovsky spent a year at Harvard Divinity School and returned to Tel Aviv on the first flight from Logan airport after 9/11. I requested a scan of her passport from DHS, then checked her past travel itineraries with El Al and her academic record on the University of Haifa's faculty database."

"You've been a busy gal," her boss quips.

---

* KK—CIA cryptonym digraph for Israel

Undaunted, Courtney leans into her laptop screen and reads:

"In April 2002, Aronovsky presented a paper at a linguistics conference in Moscow, then stayed put in Haifa until September 2004, when UH sent her to American University in Amman on a scholarship exchange doing Arabic translations. She stayed until November 2005, then returned in May 2006. On a hunch"—Courtney always uses the masculinized euphemism for intuition when speaking to her boss—"I checked with Royal Jordanian airlines and found a Sofya Antonova flying from Amman to Damascus on September 21st, 2004 and again from Amman to Beirut on May 22, 2006. Russia On line Genealogy lists 'Sofya Antonova' as the name on Aronovsky's birth certificate. She holds dual-citizenship and sometimes travels by that name on a Russian passport. That's when I realized AMAN was stonewalling me."

There is a chuckle from one of the wonks at the table, but the ADD seems not to notice.

"Now, here's the interesting part." Courtney looks up earnestly. "I cross-referenced our database for significant events that coincided with Aronovsky's/Antonova's travels."

The ADD props a hand on his chin and glances sideways at his laptop screen. "Go on."

She pauses, clears her throat and reads her notes. "In April 2002, Anatoly Kuntsevich, who'd been assisting Bashar Al-Assad produce VX nerve agent, mysteriously dropped dead on a flight from Aleppo to Moscow. Turns out Antonova traveled to that Moscow conference via Nicosia, with a stopover in Aleppo.

"Five days after she flew to Damascus in September 2004, Izz al-Din al-Sheikh Khalil, a HAMAS liason with the Iranian Revolutionary Guard, was blown up in his car at his home. Khalil happened to be supervising the shipment of Iranian missile parts to Gaza.

"In November of 2005, during the time Aronovsky/Antonova was at the American University in Amman, an explosion took place at a wedding reception in the Radisson SAS Hotel. 36 Palestinians were killed, including Major-General Bashir Nafeh, head of Military Intel in the West Bank and Colonel Abed Allun, a Preventive Security Forces official."

"That was Zarqawi's work," the ADD says without looking up.

"The bombing *was* credited to Ali al-Shamari, an associate of Abu Mus'ab al-'Zarqawi,* with the alleged intention of 'killing Jews and Crusaders.' Curiously, only Sunni Arabs died in the blast."

"Your point?"

"There were reports that GID evacuated a number of Israelis from the Radisson a couple of hours *before* the attack took place. Shamari's wife, Sajida al-Rishawi, was seen leaving the banquet shortly before the lights went out. She was arrested next day and confessed, under enhanced interrogation at the Fingernail Factory,† to being an accomplice. But the transcript of her statement didn't align with the actual sequence of events and she later retracted her confession. GID's 'official' report claimed the device was a home-made belt explosive, but their *preliminary* investigation concluded that military-grade Semtex had blown out the ballroom ceiling and shattered the windows."

Her boss shrugs. "So?"

"There's some speculation that it was a Mossad false flag op."

"Unsubstantiated," the ADD replies sharply. Courtney glances up to note that his attention is uncharacteristically focused only on her. "Besides, Zarqawi had a long-standing beef with the GID. Often happens after they string you up in cuffs and beat the crap out of you for a couple of weeks."

"Yes sir," Courtney takes a breath and continues. "In May 2006, Mahmoud al-Majzoub—alias Abu Hamza, Commander of the Palestinian Islamic Jihad—and his brother were taken out with a car bomb in Saïda, while Antonova was ostensibly attending that conference in Beirut, just a few miles up the coast."

Courtney looks up from her notes to see her boss showing obvious discomfort. "Let's jump to 2008," she suggests. "On July 29th, Aronovsky flew via Athens to Cyprus for an 'eco-tourist' holiday on the Karpass Peninsula, about sixty miles from the Syrian coast. Three days later, General Muhammad Suleiman, Special Advisor for Arms Procurement and Strategic Weapons to Bashar al-Assad, was shot in the head by snipers at a beach resort near Tartus."

The ADD holds up his palm to interrupt her litany. "Let's cut to the chase, Court. You suggesting this Russian bookworm from Haifa had something to do with all these hits?"

Courtney folds her hands primly on the conference table. "I know it's frowned upon, sir, but I made an unofficial inquiry with a former associate from INTERPOL, currently working SIGINT at OPS2A. They've been picking up chatter from Unit 8200 and EWD* indicating KK is on a hunt for tactical nuclear weapons, small, portable devices the Soviets somehow misplaced as they were pulling the 40th Army out of Afghanistan in 1989. That in itself is disturbing, but the big question is: why *now*? If they recently received actionable intel, why have they not seen fit to share it with us?"

---

* **SIGINT** [Signal Intelligence] at **OPS2A**—National Security Agency's headquarters at Fort Meade, Maryland, also known as "Black House" and "Puzzle Palace." **EWD**—the Jordanian Electronic Warfare Directorate—has an intelligence sharing agreement with the NSA.

Courtney closes her laptop with a satisfying click. "There's also buzz that our counterparts in both Lubyanka Square and Yasenevo* are tracking Antonova's movements. They apparently have an asset monitoring the situation on the inside. We're not sure who."

The ADD has not glanced at his phone since she mentioned her contact at NSA. All the associate assistant liaisons around the table have grown silent as a Lutheran church congregation.

"Dual citizenship, huh?" Her boss rubs his chin for effect. "You think she's stringing for SVR?"

Courtney is not put off by his sarcasm. "Sir, it's more likely that Sonya Aronovsky is a Mossad sleeper, which would explain why we don't know anything about her and why KK doesn't even admit she exists. I think our 'bookworm from Haifa' is their point recon in Afghanistan."

The ADD smirks. "Sounds like one hell of a leap, Court."

"Yes sir."

Courtney glances down at the gold-trimmed Cartier Panthére Cyrus gave her for her 35th birthday in Paris. "Oh, one last thing, sir: According to my former colleague in Cambridge, and verified by Turkish Airlines an hour ago, Sofya Antonova is now on a flight to Dushanbe, Tajikistan, accompanied by a Jesuit professor of Central Asian Studies from Harvard Divinity School, and a rather colorful backcountry guide whom I discovered to be a former Blue Badger[†] in Afghanistan, codename…" she checks her notes, "'Payload'? Could that be right?"

Her boss is no longer smirking.

"Let's take this off-line, Court."

---

* **Lubyanka Square** is formerly KGB and now FSB headquarters in Moscow; **Yasenevo** is SVR headquarters.
† **Blue Badger** is a full-time CIA employee; Green Badger is an independent contractor.

....

BENEATH PITILESS FLUORESCENT ceiling fixtures, a tall, silver-haired man argues with a squat, taciturn immigration official about an unspecified "problem" with the visa he got in Istanbul. Standing in quiet irritation between him and three chain-smoking Chinese businessmen, Sonya counts five Ministry of Internal Affairs security police sporting Czech Kalashnikovs and gray camo stalking the perimeter. The silver-haired man is asked to step into an adjacent office by one of the policemen, presumably to buy his way into the Republic of Tajikistan.

The scene at Dushanbe International Airport reminds Sonya why her mother was so quick to leave the Soviet Union during *perestroika*. Tajikistan, like most countries once shackled by a heavy-handed Soviet system of incompetence and corruption had, upon independence, simply replaced the party *apparatchiki* with lazy and self-indulgent *cheloveki*, "insiders" that embraced both capitalist excess *and* systemic corruption. Sonya hopes that at least their restaurants have improved.

Eventually, she steps up to the bulletproof window, hands the immigration official a Russian passport and sighs. *"Nadeyus' vikup ne ponadobitsya* [I hope that a fine will not be necessary]."

The officer scrutinizes her conservative academic passport photo. He seems particularly interested in those entry stamps that show Hebrew letters.

"You travel often to Israel, Miss Antonova?" He looks as if he is biting into an unripe persimmon.

"I have a research grant at the University of Haifa," Sonya replies.

The officer continues to thumb idly through the pages again and again, as if he might have missed something that could result in a sizable fine. "And what do you research there?"

"Dead languages."

He looks up sharply as an Internal Affairs officer taps his shoulder and whispers while pointing at Sonya. The immigration official scowls and nods toward the senior officer. "You will follow him," he barks, dismissing Sonya and waving the first Chinese businessman forward.

The Consular bureau is a windowless room painted a particularly nauseating shade of green. Danny and Bashir are already parked on folding chairs at a wooden table that looks to be of Stalinist vintage. Sonya is told to wait with her companions.

"Big Eddy's still in the back room," Danny says. "There seems to be a disconnect between our fixer and his Embassy homeboy." He looks tired but sexy in his black T-shirt, and a day's growth of beard. Sonya idly wonders if the Jesuits allow their priests to have tattoos.

She rolls her chambray shirt to the elbows and sinks wearily into the unpadded seat, gazing up at the non-functional ceiling fan. "Any idea what the problem is?"

Danny shrugs. "My guess is that somebody didn't pay somebody enough *bhaksheesh.*"

"*Insha'al-Llâh.*" Bashir's onyx eyes twinkle optimistically. "That, at least, *can* be fixed."

Eventually, Eddy pushes through a steel door, his eyes sullen shadows beneath the cold fluorescent lights. "Sorry for the delay, folks, but we've got a situation."

He slouches into a chair at the table and tucks his big hands into the cargo pockets of his khaki trousers. "There's a security alert in the wake of some former minister of something-or-other getting his ass smoked under peculiar circumstances about a week ago. My contact at the embassy was not able to arrange double-entry visas for us at this time. OVIR, the Ministry of Internal Affairs, will issue single-entry visas and fast-track our GBAO permits, but we'll have to pick them up from the consul in Khorog along with our visas for Afghanistan." Eddy hesitates. "So, here's the deal, boys and girls: after we cross the border from Tajikistan, returning via the same route will not be possible. We'll need to find another way home."

"Sounds like a deal *breaker,*" Danny frowns. "State Department alerts say security in Badakhshan Province has badly deteriorated. Traveling overland to Kabul would be suicidal."

Sonya shows no emotion as she appraises Eddy. "What's our backup plan, Mister Thompson?"

"I call in a favor from my boys at Bagram. Arrange a helo lift and a flight to Turkey. We're out the return tickets from Dushanbe but that's the cost of doing business, right?"

Danny is skeptical. "These more of your 'homies'?"

Eddy exposes his teeth. "That's right. But *these* homies get shit done, unlike the limp-dick desk jockeys our State Department sends to suck air in countries we don't give a shit about. The PJs with the 83 ERQS* have pulled my ass out of the fire on more than one occasion."

"Not quite the same as rescuing stranded tourists."

"All in their job description, Padre. Besides, I've got a couple of markers to call in."

Danny's tight jaw dimples into a weary smile as he shakes his head. "Well, that's a relief. I thought maybe your homeboys were all Yankees fans."

Eddy grins. "In that case, Padre, *you* would be up shit's creek without a paddle."

....

THE US CONSULAR BUREAU rubber-stamps two-week tourist visas and Sonya exchanges US Dollars for Somoni notes. On the other side of passport control, their gear is stacked like logs at baggage claim, zippers askew, indicating it has all been searched for contraband. Eddy lights a smoke, slings an Arc'teryx LEAF pack over his shoulder and pushes through a mob of gypsy cab operators desperate for work. Danny grabs Sonya's duffel and his own as Bashir follows to curbside with two small suitcases.

Around five in the morning, a battered, 1990 vintage Toyota Land Cruiser rattles up to meet them at the curb. The short, barrel-chested driver climbs out dressed in a blue suit jacket with a bogus designer label stitched above one cuff. A half-smoked, unlit cigarette dangles beneath his steel gray moustache as he makes a solicitous effort to load everyone's luggage into the back of his vehicle. "Is okay," he insists many times over in English. "No problem."

* PJs—Para-rescue Jumpers of the **83rd Expeditionary Rescue Squadron** attached to the 455th Air Expeditionary Wing [USAF] at Bagram Airbase, Afghanistan

"Hey, hold up a minute!" Eddy tries in vain to get the driver's attention. "Look, pal, this is not the vehicle we were promised, you understand? Where the hell's my FTV?"

"No problem!" Farkhod reiterates. "Ride very good. You see. Very good!"

"*Po krainei mere ona mashina sdelana ne v Rossiye* [At least it's not Russian-made]," Sonya chides their driver.

"*Nyet problem, bol'shoye spasiba* [No problem, thank you very much]," he says nervously.

"Well, he speaks Russian, anyway." Danny slaps Eddy on the shoulder and suppresses a smirk. "Guess your embassy homie was concerned about gas rationing after all."

"Sonofabitch! I swear I will rip that paper chasing motherfucker a new asshole next time I see him." Eddy glances at Sonya. "Pardon my French," he adds gratuitously.

"*Pas de problème* [No problem]." Sonya sighs and slides into the back seat of the Land Cruiser beside Bashir. "Can't wait to see our hotel accommodations. How big are the roaches here?"

"No roaches, *habibti*," Bashir assures her. "Only bedbugs."

SUNDAY, 19 JULY 2009 · KALAIKHUM, TAJIKISTAN

....

THE ROAD IS DESIGNATED HIGHWAY M41, but Farkhod calls it *Pamirsky Trakt.* Paved in sections, the "highway" extends northeast from Dushanbe across the cornfields and rice paddies of Tajikistan toward a brown haze creeping in from China. Through the cracked windscreen of Farkhod's Land Cruiser, Sonya watches a procession of old Russian Ladas and new stolen Mercedes, petrol stations with no fuel, donkey carts lugging giant bales of hay, stacks of ripe watermelons and mutton joints dangling from roadside racks, lean men in Nike knockoffs and pear-shaped women in brocaded *rumol*, children playing besides open sewers and army trucks rumbling past ubiquitous billboards depicting President Emomali Rahmon cutting ribbons, wearing a white construction helmet and saluting constituents with his signature high-five.

The past 24 hours have been a jet-lagged blur, only slightly mitigated by fitful sleep. Sonya and her companions checked out of the guesthouse Farkhod had arranged, and their driver had his vintage vehicle loaded and on the road by 7:30 am. An hour and a half later, the macadam paving dissolved into dirt, and it soon became painfully apparent that Farkhod's Land Cruiser had a bad rear suspension.

"No problem," he chants like a supplication to the gods of Toyota with each jolt.

The road climbs into brown foothills, and Farkhod stops at a spring to pour water into his radiator and cool the engine before passing beneath a monumental gateway marking passage into Gorno Badakhshan. Approaching a police checkpoint, everyone emerges to stretch their legs and present their passports and GBAO permits to a humorless policeman brandishing an AK-47.

They continue south to meet the raging Panj River at Kalaikhum, where Afghanistan looms in a haze on the far side and ominous signs appear on patches of poplar-dotted fields by the riverbank. The Tajik warning, printed in Cyrillic, is accompanied by a stylized graphic depicting a human leg being blown off.

ЗХТИЕТ БОШЕД! МИНАХО!

"'Be careful! Landmines!'" Bashir translates with a shrugs. "Crude, but effective."

Despite international efforts to clear them, Eddy says many landmines are still buried along the frontier, a grim legacy of the five-year civil war that ensued after the USSR collapsed. As far as Sonya is concerned, it is just one more good reason to avoid any country ending in "stan."

As evening finally dusts the sky with a rosy blush, Farkhod pulls up to what appears to be an old army barracks along the river just outside Kalaikhum.

"*Gastinitza*," he assures them.

The single-story "guesthouse" has thick, whitewashed adobe walls, a corrugated tin roof, cerulean blue trim and its front door broken off the hinges. Inside, bare light bulbs hang by copper wires from the poorly patched ceiling above a narrow corridor. Warped planking creaks beneath their boots as they follow a heavy-set woman wearing a loose brown dress and thong slippers past the open door of a WC to their rooms. The bleak dormitories have dry-rotted casement windows and short steel military bunks covered in faded blue and white quilting.

Sonya drops her duffel inside the door and inspects the sheets on one of the beds for signs of lice. The pillowcases look dingy but smell recently washed. Just the same, she pulls on a watch-cap before lying down, closing her eyes and imagining she is *anywhere* else.

For Sonya, personal survival has always depended upon maintaining an emotional distance from her work. Non-attachment, usually considered a Buddhist virtue, happened to be a Jesuit ideal as well. Danny told her that one afternoon while they were lying in bed, spent from hours of love-making in her tiny apartment on Garden Street that always smelled of vanilla candles and fresh cut flowers. Ironically, if anyone needed a lesson in non-attachment, it was Danny. After all her strategic efforts, she was never able to entice him away from his spiritual vocation for more than a few hours. And in the intervening years, it seems that Danny has grown even more attached to his ideals and naive optimism.

By contrast, she is pragmatic, meticulous, uncompromising and ruthless. All the reasons Giraffe recruited her, and precisely why she is still alive and her *katsa* dead. Giraffe flouted those "Moscow Rules" Sasha Krasny had drummed into both of them: Never expose yourself needlessly, Sasha had warned. Never allow ambition to override caution. And never, *ever*, let things get personal. Giraffe became obsessed with taking Wild Boar down and it had cost him his life.

Sonya refuses to spend another wretched night dazed, drunk and drenched, mourning his blunder. There will be no more tears. Not a single one. By the time a flat toned dinner bell gets her attention, Sonya has almost convinced herself that Shlomo Levi never existed.

Her plate of *shashlik* has bits of organ meat swimming in lentils over rice, accompanied by a liter of Baltika pilsner. Sonya's head is still heavy from lack of sleep, and pointless banter around the table blurs into an unbearable static in her ears.

She takes her green tea out to the concrete stoop by the unhinged entrance and sits on the top step. The oppressive heat of the day has cooled in twilight and the sound of the rushing river dissolves into soothing white noise. She reaches into her shirt pocket and tries to decide if she really wants to smoke the cigarette she bummed earlier from Eddy.

As if having intuited her unhealthy intentions, Danny appears on the stoop, sits down beside her and leans back against the wooden porch post. He tucks his hands into the pockets of his jeans and asks, "You okay, Sonny?"

She hesitates, then shakes her head slowly. "No, but I'll get over it. Just needed some air."

Danny remains quiet for a while, staring straight ahead into the stand of tall poplars that delineates the gravel river road. He begins his confession with a deep sigh. "I'd like to tell you I'm here for altruistic reasons, but you know as well as I do that Cyrus wrote a fat check to make this adventure happen."

"Yes, and that was *my* idea, as you may recall," she reminds him. "You seemed offended at the time."

"Not offended, Sonny. Rattled," he admits. "When you showed up in Boston, I thought I'd be able to detach myself from everything except solving the mystery of your palimpsest. But when you asked me to put skin in the game, help you find your father, I panicked."

"Why? Because you don't trust me and think I'm a lying, selfish bitch?" Sonya sips her tea and watches for his reaction.

He rubs the back of his neck and grimaces. "I know I've been judgmental; not exactly the model of Christian compassion."

Her voice softens. "Even a priest is human, Danny."

"The reason I balked at coming along is not because I don't trust you, Sonny. It's because I don't trust *myself*." Danny's hands implore the air around him for the right words. "I just…wasn't prepared to see you again. Or handle the feelings it dredged up for me. I got stupid jealous when I found out you and Cyrus were…"

He pauses for a slow breath. "Look, you are absolutely right; it's none of my business who you sleep with."

"With *whom* I sleep," she teases.

He turns to face her, and even though she cannot see into the deep shadow falling across his face, Sonya feels Danny's hurt blue eyes locking on to hers. "What I'm trying to tell you is…this really shook me, Sonny. It made me question *everything*…all over again."

Those same questions throb in Sonya's head. She has maneuvered him into this moment, stirred the ashes of Danny's memory to reignite the flame he once carried. Watching the sparks dance now before her eyes, she cannot bring herself to engage. "Maybe you just have to accept the fact that you will never have certainty."

She looks away, unable to bear the feeling of his eyes on her. "Isn't that what your religion teaches? Acceptance of suffering?"

She can feel the frustration in his voice when he asks, "Is that really how you've made peace with the past?"

"The past is just ruins buried in the sand, Danny. As for peace..." she shrugs, "that's the biggest lie of all. An absurd fantasy that human beings can live in any other state but conflict."

"What the hell happened to you, Sonny?" The urgency in his voice penetrates to a heart she has almost forgotten she possessed. "What made you so damn cynical?"

Sonya cradles the teacup in her hands, tucks it beneath her chin and allows the steam to caress her cheeks. A sudden surge of panic accompanies the realization that she can no longer picture her mother's face, as if the mental image has faded like the old Polaroid photos her father had taken.

This is as deep as she can go, as much as she will ever allow herself to feel. "Life eventually wakes you out of your illusions. Truth is: everything and everyone you love either leaves or dies."

She smiles bitterly. "Dust in the wind, Danny. Isn't that how the song goes?"

"My God." He breathes the words like an act of contrition. "We really *are* alike, aren't we, Sonny? Couple of lost souls searching the night sky for a reason to get up in the morning." He stands slowly, walks toward the open door, then turns and speaks to her back.

"No wonder I'm still in love with you."

MONDAY, 20 JULY 2009 · KHOROG, TAJIKISTAN

....

THE PANJ RIVER ROAD IS A SERPENT of rutted gravel hugging a writhing water snake that slithers through walls of rock and shale. Chinese cargo trucks and Russian motorbikes play chicken with flocks of sheep, army checkpoints pop up along the roadside and venal border police in blue camo look for shakedown opportunities. Farkhod keeps a death grip on the leather-wrapped steering wheel as rain spatters against the old Toyota's cracked windscreen. Sonya has watched their wily driver charm his way through checkpoints with American cigarettes as skillfully as he now navigates the precarious loose gravel that threatens to slide them into the raging river.

She is wedged between Danny and Bashir in the back seat of the Land Cruiser, while Eddy rides shotgun in front. Sonya feels completely out of her element in this part of the world and there is *nothing* she hates more than vulnerability—not even the confusion of emotions brought on by Danny's admission last night. It is irritating enough being bounced out of her seat by every stray rock on the road, but having to smell her former lover's sweat and feel his muscular shoulder rub against her all day long transforms that bouncing into a very different form of torture.

She tries to focus on their conversation about Central Asian politics, sort through the complexities of a place that seems as alien to her as the rings of Saturn. Danny thinks a new "Great Game" is being played along the border of Afghanistan, one in which the drug trade influences *realpolitik*. In the former Soviet oblasts of Tajikistan, Uzbekistan, Turkmenistan, and Kyrgyzstan, radicalized Muslim militants now finance their *jihad* against decadent Western values by providing the satanic *kuffar* with all the vices they crave.

"And God bless the fucking US of A for making that possible," Eddy says. In exchange for American aid, the Taliban shut down *tarok*—opium poppy—cultivation in Afghanistan during their draconian rule. But, after the United States-led post-9/11 invasion, the Tajik and Uzbek warlords of the so-called "Northern Alliance" revived opium production well beyond all previous levels with the tacit consent of the "coalition of the willing." It was the same blind-eye policy extended to South Vietnam's Nguyễn Cao Kỳ, who once controlled much of the opium traffic in the Golden Triangle. The CIA's "Air America" had even flown heroin out of Laos for him.

Bashir notes that many of the 25,000 Russian border guards in Tajikistan supplemented their income by smuggling heroin out of Afghanistan. The United States promised an airbase to help underwrite President Rahmon's own corrupt regime, but all he got was another "Friendship Bridge" connecting his country to the Afghan opium fields, courtesy of the US Army Corps of Engineers.

On the outskirts of Khorog, capital of Gorno-Badakhshan, the road becomes intermittently paved again, and Farkhod resumes the role of tour guide to his captive audience. "Before Russians build fort here, was only Bar Panja Qal'a on Afghan side," he says. "But now in Khorog are stadium, hospital and university. Gifts all from Aga Khan. Museum also, and airport just ahead for fly in small plane."

"The Afghan consulate is closed by now," Eddy interjects, checking his carbon field watch. "We'll spend the night here and get our visas first thing in the morning. It's only a four-hour drive to the border crossing at Ishkashim."

Sonya stretches her arms up toward the roof until she hears her vertebrae popping and then sighs in relief as Farkhod turns off the road into a modern compound on the riverbank. Parking in front of the newly constructed, single-story structure with an aluminum roof, their driver beams with civic pride. "Aga Khan has also built this beautiful Serena Hotel for you."

"Please tell him we're thrilled," Sonya jokes. "How does the Aga Khan manage to get so much traction in a corrupt narco-economy?"

"Gorno-Badakhshan has long been an Isma'ili stronghold," Bashir explains. "Also, one of the poorest provinces in Central Asia. Since the Soviets left, His Highness has invested in projects to better the lives of his people and preserve their cultural identity. But he has to compete with the opium smugglers. Khorog is their main entry point from Afghanistan."

Bashir nods in the driver's direction. "I'm sure Farkhod wanted to spare us that grim reality. Bad for tourism."

Sonya rubs her stiff neck. "No worse than the road we've been on for the past two days."

························

HER ROOM AT THE SERENA is unexpectedly elegant. Wooden box-beams form an iris-like skylight above a double bed covered with a thick comforter and brocaded bolsters. A mirrored vanity sits beside the bed, and in the tiled bathroom she finds a tub long enough to stretch out her legs.

Achy and irritable from the road, Sonya soaks in the magnesium sulfate she brought in her kit. Closing her eyes, she drifts lazily in the heat of her bath, soothing the cramps in her abdomen. She was always amused by the medical term her mother used for the discomfort of ovulation, *mittelschmerz*, and fascinated by the vivid sexual visualizations that often accompany it. At this moment, they take the shape of Danny's fingers kneading her tight trapezii and scapulae as her body relaxes into his strong hands. Sonya's imagination guides her own fingers to another destination of Danny's former caresses. She strums her submerged instrument, *allegro non-tropo*, until her entire body arches up out of the water and shudders in crescendo, then lies spent in the warm bath.

When the water grows tepid, she dries off, slips into a long twill skirt and modest cotton blouse, then wanders out onto a garden patio that extends to the bank of the Panj River. The rain stopped more than an hour ago and sunlight teases through the billowing cumulus, paints the rose garden magenta and gilds the ochre hills on the far side of the river. On a low stone wall overlooking the riverbank, Bashir kneels on his prayer rug, dressed in traditional cotton trousers and long blouse, his legs tucked beneath him, his face turned West, presumably toward Mecca. Bashir lifts his gaze and notices Sonya sitting quietly in a white wicker chair below the rose garden. He beckons her over.

"I didn't want to interrupt."

His brown face reflects the sun. "An angel always has permission to interrupt a mere mortal."

"Why Bashir!" Sonya laughs. "Are you being naughty?"

"Not at my age, *habibti*."

She smiles coquettishly and sits beside him on the wall, watching shafts of golden sunlight melt through the cloud bank. "It's too late for the *'asr* prayer and too early for the *maghrib*."

"Ah, yes. I forgot you are a scholar of all things Islamic," Bashir replies with wry smile. "So, you must know that, although Sunnis pray *salaat* and most Shi'a pray *namaz* five times each day, the Nizari Isma'ilis pray only three. We have no *masjid*, no *adhan* and no *wudhu*. Only *du'a*, performed in the *jalsa* position, like so…" Sitting back, Bashir pats both his bent knees.

---

* *Masjid* means a "place of prostration;" *adhan* is the call to prayer; *wudhu* is ritual washing; *du'a* is a personal entreaty to Al-Llâh.

"So, you *are* Isma'ili, then?"

He shrugs, humor dancing in his eyes. "In Mecca, I am Sunni; in Tehran, I am Shi'i. Here in Kuhistoni Badakhshon, I am Isma'ili." He places a hand over his heart, "Beneath all these disguises, I am only a soul longing for the Beloved."

"Well, you're definitely a charmer," she admits. "And quite rakish in your *shalwar kamiz*."

Bashir laughs in delight. "Here, we call them *perahan tunban*." He takes her hand in his. "Tell me, do you still have hope of finding your father?"

Sonya drops her gaze. "Or some trace of him."

"The shell in which we walk this earth is fragile." Bashir pats the back of her hand. "I pray that you will be able to make peace with the truth, whatever it may be." He hesitates a moment. "I pray also for Father Daniel, that his heart may be free of the pain he carries with him. It is no wonder that you were so drawn to each other."

Sonya smiles wistfully at Bashir then turns her gaze toward the unknown on the far bank of the Panj. She feels uncharacteristically safe sharing her heart with this little man. "It's ironic, isn't it? Falling in love with the one person in the world you can never be with."

"Perhaps, *habibti*." The little rug dealer's eyes crinkle as a warm breeze rustles the poplar trees around them, blending into the sound of the river. "But do not confuse irony with destiny."

MONDAY, 20 JULY 2009 · GEORGETOWN, WASHINGTON, DC

....

THE LINCOLN TOWN CAR PULLS UP to the corner of 34th and M Streets NW, where Courtney Kincaid waits curbside beneath a red umbrella in the gentle rain. She wears a little black dress bought that afternoon and charged to her expense account. It is the first time her presence has been requested at an embassy soirée but if she plays her cards right, it won't be the last. As Courtney climbs into the limo's back seat beside her boss, the Associate Deputy Director, is in the process of sending a text message on his mobile.

"Thanks for joining me on short notice, Court. I hate going to these fucking dip functions without somebody I can talk to, and my wife never talks to me anyway, so…" The ADD glances quickly up at her. "You're looking very attractive tonight."

"Thank you, sir," Courtney replies demurely. "New dress, sir. Givenchy. What diplomatic function are we attending, by the way?"

She shifts slightly in his direction, the hemline of her new dress slipping higher above her knees, revealing the clasp of an elegant garter. She pretends not to notice.

"PRC. Fuckers always have cocktail parties on the worst possible nights. Even Chinese restaurants close on Monday, don't they? Anyway, I'm supposed to stand around with my thumb up my ass, pose for their surveillance cameras, pretend I never heard of their fucking Comment Crew,* and field their stupid questions about why we don't ship their goddamn Uyghurs back from Gitmo so they can shoot them all in the head." A Twitter notification chimes on his Blackberry. "Did I mention you look very nice, Court?"

"I don't know, sir. Did you?" Courtney allows her hem to drift a bit higher as the ADD swipes back to his text messages. "Maybe the new Israeli Ambassador will be there tonight," she suggests. "Just across the street from the Chinese Embassy, aren't they? I read one of Oren's books on the history of US involvement in the Middle East. *NYT* bestseller. Predictably idealistic about American foreign policy."

When her boss does not respond to either her display of geopolitical nuance or nylon clad leg, Courtney sighs and watches through a rain-beaded window as the Lincoln turns off Wisconsin onto Calvert and circles the US Naval Observatory. Traffic slows almost to a stop. On the roadside, a DC cop's lights flash red, white and blue as paramedics carry a tarp-covered stretcher from beside a Cadillac limo to an open ambulance. The Lincoln cruises slowly past, but the lingering vision of what she could not quite see leaves Courtney feeling unsettled. She shivers and shifts toward the ADD, revealing goose-bumped flesh between her stockings and crepe dress.

---

* **Comment Crew** [aka: Comment Panda, Byzantine Candor, GIF89a or Advanced Persistent Threat 1] —2nd Bureau of the Third Department of the People's Liberation Army, Unit 61398, a cyber-warfare hacking group operating from a building on Datong Road in the Pudong district of Shanghai

"Still no briefing on KK's adventures in AfPak?" she asks as her boss continues to tap on his mobile. Courtney begins to wonder if she can even get arrested in this town.

Then, in the midst of texting, the ADD replies, "Oren probably doesn't know shit about what Mossad is up to. Nobody ever does until it's a *fait accompli*."

"*Ah, vous parlez Français* [You speak French]," she mutters.

He hits "send" and drops the Blackberry into his suit pocket. "I know you think I don't pay attention to you, Court. I'm just a multi-tasker. Can't help it. But I *am* listening."

"I'm flattered, sir."

"And if you show me any more of that garter belt, I'm going to need a paramedic myself."

"Now, I'm blushing." Feigning embarrassment, she smooths the dress down to her knees.

"Seriously," the ADD assures her, "You pick up on the details my staff misses. And you hit it out of the park at last Friday's briefing. Very impressive analysis." He pauses, tightens his lips in thought then looks directly at her. "So, about your antiques guy from Cambridge…"

"You mean Cyrus? He's a forensic art historian, sir."

The ADD raises an inquisitive eyebrow. "Right…Cyrus. Isn't that a Persian name?"

"US-born, Iranian extraction. He's already got SCI* clearance. When Cyrus told me he was helping his Jesuit friend and Aronovsky arrange an expedition to Afghanistan, ostensibly to retrieve some valuable old manuscripts, I suggested he equip the priest with one of his satellite phones to help us keep track of his progress—and their location."

---

* **SCI** [Sensitive Compartmented Information] a system to protect intelligence information concerning sources and methods

"Good thinking, Court." Her boss stares out the window, apparently considering the possibilities. "Maybe you should invite Cyrus down for an intimate supper or something."

"He *is* fond of 1789."

"Getting access to that sat phone's GPS coordinates short of involving a FISA* court would give us a leg up on whatever Mossad is sniffing out in our theater without shooting our wad to the Puzzle Palace. Your pal at Fort Meade hear anything over the weekend?"

"A lot of buzz about suitcase nukes on the internet, more than the usual paranoid fringe lunatics. MAC† is showing keyword correlation with numbers on the watch list. Jihadist groups and gray arms dealers. Definite trend. Viktor Kaban's name came up. I did some digging and found out we used him as an intermediary to get weapons quickly to Dostum's Northern Alliance fighters before the invasion. Turns out this Payload guy was our asset on the ground and brokered the deal. By the way, Kaban now has Israeli citizenship."

"This is starting to smell like week-old Gefilte fish," he frowns. Anything from INTERPOL?"

"Not since that report about the Mossad case officer murdered by Chechens in Brooklyn a couple weeks ago. According to Cyrus, the incident coincides with Aronovsky's meeting in Manhattan." Courtney pauses for dramatic effect. "Sir, I don't think it's any coincidence that she and Payload are now in Tajikistan."

"What do we know about this priest with the sat phone?"

"Daniel Callan, Jesuit professor at Harvard Divinity School—well-respected, according to Cyrus." Courtney says. "He had an affair with Aronovsky eight years ago when she was there on a Fulbright."

---

* FISA—The Foreign Intelligence Surveillance Act of 1978 prescribes procedures for physical and electronic surveillance of US citizens.

† MAC—Metadata Analysis Center [Project Stellarwind] was developed in 2001 by NSA to keep tabs on terrorist networks by "contact chaining" through US telephone numbers and internet records, correlating them with foreign connections.

"Hmm, think she's still horny or just using him as cover?"

"I think she's very good at using people, sir. Especially men."

The ADD raises an eyebrow as he whips out his Blackberry. "If these TNW rumors turn out to be more than just a Cold War myth and Bibi calls us in for backup, I want to be ahead of the game for a change. Not some last-minute cluster fuck. Especially if Payload's working this op. I just *knew* that swinging dick would go rogue someday. But with the fucking Israelis, for Christ's sake!"

"Well, sir, we're not exactly sure about that. Payload hasn't yet exposed himself—electronically, that is—but SIGINT *has* intercepted mobile calls from a Tajik driver he hired in Dushanbe, placed to the Russian *rezidentura** in Tashkent. For all we know, sir, Payload could be on Moscow's payroll."

Her boss slaps his armrest. "Should have permanently retired that sonofabitch before he hired on with the fucking Black Prince."[†]

"I'll get in touch with Cyrus this evening."

"Outstanding!" The ADD pockets his Blackberry and turns to face Courtney for the first time during their ride. "You know, Court, I think you are being seriously underutilized in OTI. I've been looking for somebody to work more closely with me, somebody smart and proactive. Somebody who can really hit the ground running."

"And do it all in heels?"

He winks conspiratorially at her. "Let's revisit the possibilities over a drink somewhere, assuming I can get through this fucking Chinese fire drill without shooting *myself* in the head."

"Don't worry, sir. I'll restrain you."

---

* ***Rezidentura***—Russian Federation foreign ambassadors are usually undercover agents of the SVR—Foreign Intelligence Service.

† **Erik Prince** is founder of Blackwater, USA, a private security contractor to military and law enforcement that later became Ze Services.

TUESDAY, 21 JULY 2009 · ISTANBUL, TURKEY

....

THE RUSSIAN HAS AN UNMEMORABLE FACE, Viktor Kaban decides. Lean, angular, and not particularly good-looking, but not bad either. Wiry salt and pepper hair hangs loose across his high forehead in nothing anyone would call a stylish cut. It is a non-threatening face that would disappear in a crowd, a definite asset if you are running a hit squad for the Russian Intelligence Services.

Alexander Zharkov recruits Chechen nationals to spy on, and occasionally assassinate, the more radical members of their diaspora community for the pro-Russian Kadyrovites.* Eddy Thompson, who seems to know everyone who kills anyone for a living, made the introduction before embarking on his hunting trip to Afghanistan.

Nadiye, a buxom, dark-haired girl, whose entire family works as caretakers at Kaban's Bebek estate, brings mint tea and a tray of sticky, cheese-filled *künefe* to the garden table. The morning sun dapples Viktor's tulip garden and a gentle sea breeze undulates the pink flowers like a silk pashmina. But Zharkov is uninterested in tulips, the refreshments or Nadiye. He pinches the long, hollow tube of a Belomorkanal cigarette into two flat, perpendicular surfaces, ignites the short, tobacco filled end with a gold Dunhill lighter and inhales the pungent smoke like an opium addict. When he speaks, Viktor notes the discoloration of his teeth.

"*Koroche* [Let me be clear]," he begins. "We understand you are not in possession of our property, and do not yet know where it is located. Neither do we. But, for obvious reasons, we do not want

---

* **Kadyrovites**—a Chechen clan that became separatists after the fall of the USSR, then shifted their loyalties to the Russian Federation in 1999. Akhmad Kadyrov, a Muslim *imam*, was assassinated in 2004, and his son, Ramzan, became president of the Chechen Republic in 2007. They have since enjoyed the support of Vladimir Putin and the Russian FSB.

this equipment to fall into the wrong hands, and that includes the hands of either Israel or the United States. Payload is sensitive to these things, which is why he reached out to us on *your* behalf. We are monitoring his movements in Tajikistan and will provide him with air transport when the time comes. But it would be advantageous if the Russian Federation were not implicated in any actions that might re-open old wounds in Afghanistan or overtly encroach on the American theater of operations."

Zharkov sits back in his chair, the crimped white cigarette tightly clenched between his yellow teeth. He stares at Viktor for a few seconds, then shifts his line of sight to Marko, standing in the Ottoman garden gazebo directly behind Viktor, positioned to put a frangible round into Zharkov's head if he shows any sign of belligerence. "That being said, we are willing to compensate you quite generously for your time and trouble, and also provide you with technical assistance in helping us retrieve our property."

Viktor carefully halves a flaky pastry with a pearl handled knife. "I have heard this 'property' came from a Ukrainian arsenal. Perhaps it would be more appropriate to ask Prime Minister Tymoshenko if she would like to make me an offer to retrieve *her* property. Or maybe I should call NATO. I am sure the International Security Assistance Force would be grateful for any help in keeping this sort of 'equipment' out of the hands of terrorists. That is all of our concern, is it not?"

An arabesque of gray smoke accompanies Zharkov's weary sigh. "I am not here to beg for your cooperation, Mister Kaban. At the request of our American colleague, I have been asked to broker an insurance policy against future...uncertainties. From ISAF, you *might* receive protection, probably in a high-security prison cell. From Tymoshenko, you are unlikely to get so much as a reply. She is too busy these days putting out political fires over Gazprom contracts. However, from the Russian Federation, you would receive a finder's fee of $100 million US. This is more than you would have ultimately gotten from the people who took your mother hostage in Brooklyn. Also, we are prepared to give you special consideration on lucrative contracts we are currently negotiating in your region of influence."

"Are you talking about Assad?"

Zharkov's dull brown eyes reveal no humor when he laughs. "Do you honestly care?"

"You are aware that I am now an Israeli citizen?"

"Perhaps not in such good standing. Let us say that you would be ill-advised to return to either Tel Aviv or Brooklyn at present."

Holding his cigarette pinched between thumb and index finger, Zharkov surveys Viktor's lush tulip beds, opulent villa and bountiful servants, then smiles with only his mouth. "But you seem quite comfortable where you are."

Viktor nods and remembers Payload's warning about an exit strategy. "I will need to relocate my mother immediately," he says. "You mentioned also 'technical assistance'?"

Zharkov squints through the gray smoke as he inclines his head toward Marko. "Many former Spetsnaz, like your employee over there, are now private contractors with Grom.* We can make introductions and provide equipment. But all transactions must go through your accounts—so there is no direct association. This must appear to be a freelance operation. Understood?"

Viktor bites into a honey-soaked *künefe*, feeling like a child caught sneaking sweets as flecks of golden filo rain onto the tablecloth.

---

* **Grom** [Thunder]—a private security company that contracts exclusively to the Russian Federal Government, and employs former operatives from FSB Special Groups Alfa and Vympel, and OMON—a Ministry of Internal Affairs special police unit

"Understood. I will return the Ukrainian property of the *Rodina* [Motherland]* safely for $100 million US…" Viktor smiles through his double-entendre while licking crumbs from his lips. "Each."

Zharkov forces his sneer into a shrug of acquiescence. Reaching across the table, he stubs his cigarette out on the gold-rimmed Kutahya pastry plate in front of Viktor. "Three hundred fifty for the lot." His reply is curt and unequivocal. "And that will also cover your out-of-pocket expenses."

Viktor shrugs. "My mother is tired of Brooklyn anyway. Too much crime."

---

* *Rodina*—the term was usurped by a right-wing, anti-Communist Party political faction, the "Motherland-National Patriotic Union."

TUESDAY, 21 JULY 2009 · ISHKASHIM, TAJIKISTAN

....

A NORTHEAST WIND SWEEPS the 200-meter-wide stretch of no-man's land between Tajikistan and Afghanistan, chases a thick mantle of cumulonimbus into Pakistan and exposes the sharp teeth of the Hindu Kush. Eddy Thompson paces in front of the eight-foot locked gate, beyond which two steel trusses bridge the Panj River. The first span is anchored at a stony embankment mid-stream, where two whitewashed, aluminum roofed huts represent the illustrious Organization for Security and Co-operation in Europe Border Management—when any of its "managers" feel like showing up for work.

At the barracks across the road, Farkhod discovered that the senior officer had been invited to a wedding celebration in town, which meant he would be drunk for days. Thus, the border was closed. Their conscientious driver dropped off his passengers and their gear at the gate two hours ago, in case anyone with a key showed

up by accident, and continued into the Soviet-era town to find someone whose palm he could grease.

The priest and his Afghan friend have taken a short stroll downstream where the burned-out hulks of two Russian tanks rust in
the exposed riverbed. Observing the debris of war, Eddy reminisces
about running advance force ops on the other side of that river, as a
Blue Badger riding horseback with Dostum and Tiger O2 in Mazar-
i-Sharif, and later hunting high-value targets on the porous AfPak
border in the Spin Ghar mountains as a Green Badger with TF11.*
He misses the action but there is a lot to be said for civilian autonomy
and multiple paychecks.

Sonya sits by the bridge gate on a white concrete block painted
with black stripes, impatiently flicking at wisps of hair protruding
beneath a red bandana tied above her forehead. The wide aviator sunglasses and twill grannie skirt give her the aura of a hippie chick from
the Haight-Ashbury. Then Eddy remembers how nicely she cleaned
up that night at Vik's place in Istanbul, how smoking hot she looked
in her white lace skivvies, that long, ripped body stretched out on the
embroidered duvet, working her silicone Steely Dan between Iryna's
spread legs as the Ukrainian girl worked on him with her mouth.

Good times. Eddy smiles at the memory, shakes out a Samsun
and offers one to Sonya.

"Clever ploy you pulled at the airport." She exhales her accusation without looking at him.

Although he knows it is a hopeless task, Eddy attempts to look
ingenuous. "Ploy?"

"Double-entry visa thing. Smooth way of closing the back door."

---

* **Tiger O2**—Special Forces Operational Detachment Alpha 595 from Fort Campbell, Kentucky
were also called the "Regulators." **Task Force 11** was composed of US Army Delta Force and Navy
DEVGRU operators, supported by the 160th Special Operations Aviation Regiment and CIA
"Green Badge" contractors. Its mission was to hunt and kill al-Qaeda and Taliban "in and around"
Afghanistan. The outfit was officially disbanded by US Central Command in July of 2003.

Eddy acknowledges her perceptiveness through the smoke.

"Do you actually know an attaché to the US Ambassador here?"

"Oh, I *know* him, alright. But I wouldn't ask that little shit stain for an MRE if I were starving to death in a dung heap. Good story though, huh?"

Sonya purses her lips and inclines her head appreciatively.

"Our letters of introduction were written by a tour operator in Dushanbe. Dude also hooked me up with Fark. Wasn't exactly what I bargained for, but he's been useful so far." Eddy laughs. "And that bit about the former interior minister getting smoked is actually true. Probably got caught by his mistress screwing his wife."

"I won't ask what arrangements you've made with Viktor Kaban." Sonya looks up and he can feel her eyes x-raying him through her shades. "Candor isn't our strong suit, is it, Eddy? But, whether or not we find what we're looking for..."

"You mean those ancient manuscripts?"

She sighs impatiently. "You'd better deliver on that exfil."

He scratches the stubble on his chin and grins condescendingly. "Oh, you can count on it, Sonya."

"Otherwise, my boss will be pissed off. And believe me, he has a very long memory."

"So I've heard." Eddy grinds his cigarette into the gravel with the toe of his boot.

The priest and Bashir ascend the shale embankment as Farkhod's Toyota appears on the road to the west. Their driver is being tailed by a Russian GAZ armored four-by-four kicking up a cloud of gray dust. Farkhod must have found the right palm.

As the steel gate swings open and the striped barrier arm lifts, Eddy inserts a lithium battery into his satellite phone and makes a call. "Coming through," he says before popping the battery out again.

Farkhod drives across the first span and helps lug their duffels and rucksacks to the Tajik Border Service office—a hut with a gray linoleum floor and matching laminate desks. Sonya counts five 100 Euro notes into his hand and their resourceful driver makes an effusive farewell, scuttles back to his vehicle and disappears across the bridge.

One by one, they step up to the counter and are scrutinized by a bored customs officer. Papers are ceremonially shuffled, notations painstakingly hand-written in a notebook, passports passed back and forth, exit forms collected.

Crossing the second bridge, they repeat the routine with the Afghan Border Police. An officer with thick glasses and a shrill voice transliterates their names into Arabic on an antique computer keyboard. Three ABP soldiers wearing traditional *shemagh* scarves, desert camo BDUs and newer folding stock AKM rifles slung over their shoulders, search each of the duffels for anything that looks like contraband. An officious, bearded guard tears open a box of tea bags to be certain it is actually tea. "Wine?" he inquires with a scowl.

"No wine," Eddy assures him, patting the hip flask buried in his cargo pocket. At last, he is back on familiar turf where he knows the rules.

When the search is complete, the bags are carried across the final bridge to the last gate. Storm clouds have softened into cotton wisps floating across a blue sky above peaks to the south and a swath of cool green orchard that separates the rocky floodplain from the dun colored mountains. On Saturday mornings, Eddy recalls, the barren alluvial plain teems with Afghan merchants who set up stalls beneath sun tarps and haggle with Tajik shoppers over the price of produce and rugs. But today, it is a deserted rock garden.

Eddy has been sizing up the priest, watching him smoothly negotiate the immigration queue, speaking a few words of Dari here and there to the soldiers. He looks very fit in his T-shirt and blue jeans, nothing like any sky pilot Eddy has ever known. Inspecting two camo-painted Polaris ATV quads rusting beneath an overhang of the guard hut, Father Callan frowns and shakes his head.

"Your tax dollars at work," Eddy tells him. "Nobody at ISAF asked these guys if they could read the operating manuals in English."

"Or thought to print them in Dari?"

"Mistakes were made, Padre."

A swirl of dust erupts on the edge of the green belt as vehicles approach rapidly along the rutted road from the border town of Sultan Ishkashim. The whine of a turbo-charged engine catches everyone's attention and Eddy motions toward the cloud with a wry grin.

"Remember that turbo V8 I promised you?"

....

DANNY WATCHES TWO VEHICLES emerge from the dust cloud. In the lead, a white Tacoma four-by-four is tricked out with high-clearance suspension and halogen spots mounted on a roll bar. Two men ride in the cargo bed as if it were a chariot. Then a silver Land Cruiser SUV with a winch on its bumper jockeys past the pick-up as the two vehicles vie for supremacy.

"More of your homeboys?"

Eddy strides into the center of the road. "Colleagues, padre."

Both vehicles skid to a stop in front of him and a black bearded man wearing a distressed leather motorcycle jacket leaps from the filthy Land Cruiser. Goggles perch atop the checkered *shemagh* that wraps his regal head like a turban and piercing gray eyes bespeak his Aryan bloodline.

The tall young man struts up to Eddy and declares solemnly, *"Asalaamu aleikoum,"* placing his head to either side of Eddy's cheeks.

Then, flashing perfect white teeth, he emits a giddy laugh. "Sister-fucking grand to be seeing you alive, Payload! We heard you were beheaded in Waziristan."

Eddy taps out smokes for both of them. "Not friggin' likely, Jam. Can't ransom a head. You boys stringing for McRaven now?"*

"For US dollars," he replies into Eddy's lighter, "we will suck the dick of Uncle Sam."

Eddy chuckles, taps him in the chest with the side of his fist, and motions toward Danny with his Zippo. "Watch your language, Jam. We have a man of the cloth traveling with us."

"What was that he called you?" Danny asks, "'Payload'?"

"Nickname." Eddy says, introducing Jamshid and his crew—Kourosh, Chir and Yusuf—all outfitted in a mash-up of civilian and military gear, rolled *pakul* caps, and scarves.

Jamshid gestures toward their Tacoma. "Look, we find very good Talibanmobile in Qunduz."

Eddy laughs. "Those fuckers all want the HiLux with a Dishka twelve-seven mounted on the roll bar." He peers into the cargo bed. "You bring all the gear?"

"Of course." The young man gestures toward three long, olive drab duffels in the pickup's flatbed. Eddy unzips one, peers inside and whistles appreciatively.

"Fucking A, Jam! Either you won the DEVGRU Texas Hold'em tournament or boosted the ANSF† armory."

Clearly, Eddy is no ordinary trekking guide, Danny decides. He squints ominously at Sonya. "What are you not telling me, Sonny?"

She remains pokerfaced and Danny turns to confront Eddy. "Who the hell *are* these guys?"

---

* **Vice Admiral William McRaven** became head of the Joint Special Operations Command [JSOC] in 2008.
† **ANSF**—Afghan National Security Forces

"Last of the Panjshir Muj, Padre," he says, a cigarette bobbing from the mouth camouflaged beneath his Fu Manchu. "Came up hard after the Russians booked and Hekmatyar turned Kabul into Tombstone. Just kids during the civil war, but they learned how to plant C-4 where it would do the most damage. Rumbled with Mullah Omar and cut Pashtun throats when they got the chance. Mike Spann and I were attached to a Special Forces outfit at Mazar-i-Sharif shortly after 9/11. We found these cowboys riding horseback with Dostum after Massoud got smoked by AQ. They were on recon with me when Mike ran out of ammo at Qal'a-i-Jangi.* Been freelancing with JSOC ever since." He leans into Danny's face and adds, "I'd trust them with my life, Padre, and *that's* saying something."

Danny coolly holds his stare. "So, are you still on the Company payroll, Eddy?"

"Fuck no! I hate those hypocritical cocksuckers." He begins passing duffels up to the bear-like Yusuf in the pickup. "I hate them for fucking over a lot of good people and giving weapons, money and immunity to scumbags who do bad shit to little girls. I hate them even more than those grandstanding ISAF generals looking to score Board of Directors seats with fat-cat defense contractors." Eddy pauses, grins savagely and thrusts his trigger finger at Danny's chest. "And do *not* get me started on the Catholic-fucking-Church!"

Danny laughs. "Why? Were you an altar boy?"

Eddy cracks a collegial grin and cocks his head in Sonya's direction. "Seriously, Padre, you really should talk to the meeting planner about our agenda."

---

* **Gulbuddin Hekmatyar**—the "butcher of Kabul"—was funded by the CIA through the Pakistani ISI during the Russian occupation of Afghanistan. **Johnny Michael Spann,** CIA special operations liaison with General Abdul Rashid Dostum after 9/11, was killed while interrogating Taliban prisoners at the **Qal'a-i-Jangi** prison near Mazar-i-Sharif. Spann was the first US casualty in Afghanistan.

He hoists his heavy LEAF pack into the cargo bed and takes shot-gun position in the right-hand drive Land Cruiser next to Jamshid.

Danny slides into the back of the SUV beside Sonya and Bashir. Through the gap between gaudy crocheted seat covers he recognizes a plastic framed photo hanging from the rear-view mirror—the revered Tajik general, Ahmad Shah Massoud wearing his jaunty *pakul*, a flak jacket over his *perahan* and a Russian AK-47 cradled in his aristocratic hands. The legendary *mujahid* became elevated to martyr status when an al-Qaeda operative posing as a journalist assassinated him with a suicide vest two days before 9/11. Jamshid looks as if he could be Massoud's son.

The Land Cruiser jolts forward and Danny twists the cap off a bottle of water. "What *are* we doing here, Sonny?" He passes the bottle to her without eye contact. "Really."

"Searching for my father, Danny." She pauses to take a sip while staring out the window. "And what he was carrying with him when he disappeared."

TUESDAY, 21 JULY 2009 • SULTAN ISHKASHIM, AFGHANISTAN

....

FIVE KILOMETERS SOUTH of the border crossing at Ishkashim, a swath of green farmland carpets the alluvial plain. Murad Bokhtar's *hujra* emerges organically from a rocky plateau, an adobe-plastered stone house with a flat roof on which hay, apricots and mulberries dry in the blistering sun. A fieldstone wall delineates the compound above the terraced green hillside, and over the lintel of its weathered gate, the great spiral-horned rack of an *ovis ammon poli*—the Marco Polo ram—is mounted like a vestige of some ancient animistic culture.

Murad's daughter, Rukhsana, warmly greets her distant uncle Bashir who makes the introductions. She leads Sonya and Danny through a gate to a courtyard where a concave solar water heater, an insulated storage tank and a battered satellite dish compete for the covetous admiration of Murad's guests. Inside the adobe house, an alcove opens into a large room where five carved wooden pillars support a box-beamed ceiling with the iris-like skylight Sonya remembers from the Serena Hotel. A black iron stove heats a well-worn teakettle in the center of the earthen floor room, around which thick tribal rugs cover a tiered dais. Sonya removes her boots, sits cross-legged on the platform with the others and notices a car battery in the corner supplying electricity to the bare bulbs strung from exposed wires.

Rukhsana places delicate porcelain cups and saucers on a copper tray. The slender, pretty girl looks about 18 years old and not the least bit shy. Her skin is honey-colored, her brown eyes curious and her loosely covered hair cropped above the shoulders. Although she wears a conservative red dress with traditional floral design hand-stitched in golden thread around the neck opening and sleeves, the girl projects an independence and fearlessness that Sonya immediately finds both admirable and intriguing.

Her father finally appears, assisted by a stout woman wearing a floral *rumol*. Sonya guesses she is not Rukhsana's mother and reckons Murad is old enough to be the girl's grandfather. His burgundy woolen cap is banded with colorful embroidery and his old gray suit jacket lends a tattered dignity to the taupe *perahan tunban* beneath. Like Bashir, his short-cropped hair is silver, but the nut-brown face above his white beard shows the roadmap of a very different life.

Murad's movements look pained by arthritis as he embraces his cousin. He slowly lowers himself onto thick cushions sewn from carpet remnants and greets his guests.

"*Khosh amadee, khaneh khodetan ast* [Welcome, and be at home here]," their host proclaims with genuine warmth.

"*Khane-tan bisyar…ah…mughbool ust, sa'ib* [Your home is beautiful, sir]," Danny replies in tentative Dari.

Murad looks pleased with Danny's effort, and gestures to the iris-shaped skylight in the ceiling as Bashir translates. "Murad says his father built this traditional Pamiri *chomah* guided by sacred geometry. The *chorkhona* roof design symbolizes the four elements: earth, water, air, and fire. The five pillars you see around the room represent Imam Ali and his family: Prophet Muhammad, Bibi Fatima, and the two that are joined with the brace are Ali's son's, Hassan and Husayn. The platforms on which we sit are called *loshnukh* and *barnekh*, the two realms of the soul."

Sonya accepts a cup of milky, salted *shur chai* from Rukhsana and places a hand over her heart in a gesture of thanks. As Bashir and his cousin catch up in rapid-fire Dari, Rukhsana and the stocky woman spread a long strip of red cloth between the host and his guests, a *dastarkhan*, or "floor spread," Bashir explains, on which the women serve rounds of *naan* with dishes of yoghurt and pistachio nuts. Rukhsana pours water into her uncle's cupped palms from a copper ewer, and hands him a small towel before attending to the other guests.

When their host has finished his ablutions, Sonya tears off some warm bread and turns to Bashir. "Would this be a good time to ask your cousin if he knows anything about my father?"

Bashir dips his *naan* into a dish of sweetened curd and explains Sonya's request to Murad, who glances earnestly at her from time to time. "He says that during the war, there were Soviet garrisons here in Ishkashim as well as in Zebak near the Pakistan border," Bashir explains. "The *Roussi* soldiers sometimes bought goats and sheep. He remembers helicopters flying in and out regularly, but never met any of the pilots. After ten years, they abandoned these outposts and pulled back across the Panj over the course of a few weeks, leaving garbage dumps, broken telephone lines, barbed wire, and land mines."

Sonya tries to dampen the frustration she feels. "My father's helicopter must have gone down somewhere in the mountains between here and Bagram airbase. He survived long enough to write a note and convince a shepherd to bring it to one of the border crossings."

"There is a *Roussi*-built bridge at Prip as well as here at Ishkashim, another at Khorog further to the north," Bashir translates. "And there was a border crossing also at Zorkol, in the Wakhan. Your father's note could have been delivered to any of these."

"Does he know anyone who might have worked in a hospital here during those years?" Sonya asks earnestly.

Murad again shakes his head. "Injured soldiers were always taken across the river for treatment at the hospital in Ishkashim town." Bashir sighs sympathetically. "My cousin is very sorry, *habibti*. He does not think he can help you find your father."

"Let's look at this from a different angle," Danny suggests. "You said the vellum we showed you appeared to be verse written by a sage that lived here in Badakhshan."

"Nasir-i Khusraw," Bashir confirms.

"Where could something like that have been found?"

Murad's brow furrows. "It is hard to say," his cousin replies. "Nasir is widely regarded as the patron saint of Kuhistoni Badakhshon, 'Mountainous Badakhshan.' His shrine still stands on a boulder at Hazrat Sayyid above the valley of Yumgan to the west of here, where Nasir died in exile. The *mazar*—his tomb—was destroyed long ago by the Mongols and rebuilt several times after being damaged by earthquakes. But whatever writings may have been left there are long gone. Sonya's manuscript is probably a later copy of a verse from Nasir's *Diwan*."

"But what if it's *not* a copy?" Danny counters. "What if it's an original written by the man, himself, on vellum that was recycled?" Sonya watches Danny shift his legs beneath him as he mentally calculates the possibilities. "Since Nasir was in exile, he probably had limited access to writing materials. What if one of his disciples, or students, found some old vellum that had been salvaged from a forgotten library somewhere and scraped it clean for his master's verse?"

Bashir raises both eyebrows as Danny continues. "The question is: where could her father have found it? Nasir's original manuscripts must have been preserved after his death and protected somewhere around here, in an archive or library of some kind."

"Or a fortress, perhaps?" Sonya suggests. "Weren't the Isma'ilis known for their strongholds like Alamut. And their assassins?"

"An Orientalist fantasy," Bashir chuckles. "Hassan-i Sabbah's 'Garden of Paradise,' populated by an army of hashish-eating thugs, was a myth spread by Seljuk Sunnis attempting to brand the entire Isma'iliyyah as heretics. And yes, assassins."

"Myths of Paradise still have enough power to inspire zealots to strap on suicide vests and fly planes into skyscrapers, don't they?"

Bashir's face grow serious. "That is true, *habibti*. Any mythology can be dangerous if accepted without critical scrutiny. Especially if the result is an oppressive nationalistic ideology."

Danny clears his throat. "I believe we were discussing libraries?"

"There is something you both need to understand about the Isma'iliyyah," Bashir explains. "When the Mongols invaded, sacked Alamut in the Alborz and destroyed Balkh in Khurasan, the Nizari Isma'ilis were scattered to the wind. But here in Badakhshan, they went into hibernation, employing a strategy learned after centuries of persecution by the Ghaznavids and Seljuks. They practiced *taqiyya*, hid their identity, pretended to be Sunni and prayed in the *masjid* rather than their own *jamatkhana*. This is the reason many Isma'ilis took refuge with Dervish orders and embraced the tradition of Tasawwuf."

Murad sets down his teacup and taps Bashir's arm. "My cousin says there *are* some fortresses near here. Qahqah dates from the 3rd century BC. Zulkhomor also was built in Zoroastrian times. But these places are in ruins, certainly not suitable to house a library of ancient manuscripts."

"If the Isma'ilis of Badakhshan took refuge with Dervish orders," Danny asks, "wouldn't they have preserved some of their cultural heritage within the lodges?"

"You mean like the 'Court of Bees'?" Sonya suggests.

Danny turns excitedly to Murad and summons his sparse Dari vocabulary. "*Sa'ib, az… Sarman chi shuneedi* [Sir, what have you heard about the Sarman]?"

Their host hesitates in the midst of tearing off a piece of *naan* with his gnarled fingers, apparently taken aback by the question. Murad's gaze drifts toward the skylight and he laughs. "That they are as old as Zoroaster himself," he replies through Bashir. "Isma'ilis call them *Khwajagan*—the Masters."

"A Sufi order?" Danny asks.

"A school of Dervishes founded in the 14th century by *Khwaja* Baha-u-Din Naqshband Bukhari." Bashir winks playfully. "In Balkh."

Sonya remembers Professor Arslan's exposition at the Islamic Museum café in Istanbul. "'All roads lead to Balkh.' So how do we find these 'Masters'?"

Rukhsana has been quietly eating her meal beside the iron stove. She approaches her father from behind, leans over his shoulder and speaks softly into his ear. Murad beckons for Bashir to join the family confab and Sonya watches intently.

"Rukhsana travels occasionally into the Wakhan to buy goats," Bashir explains. "She says there is a place two- or three-days' journey east of here, in the Hindu Kush, where it is rumored the Khwajagan have a secret lodge. The Wakhis in the villages nearby tell stories about great warriors and saints flying through the air and disappearing into solid rock. Rukhsana says they call this place *Aubshaur*, which means 'Waterfall.'"

Sonya feels despair rolling over her like a storm cloud. Has she really come this far only to hit a dead-end of medieval superstition? She must clear her head, plot her next move rationally. Wiping sweet yoghurt from her fingers, she sips the last of her tepid *shur chai* and wishes for a moment that the future might actually be revealed in the dregs of brown tea leaves floating at the bottom of her cup.

Sonya looks up into Bashir's sympathetic eyes. "I'm sorry, but these fanciful stories don't really interest me right now."

"This one might, *habibti*," he ventures. "Rukhsana says one of the legends is about a particular Master at this lodge, a blue-eyed warrior who fell from heaven many years ago, bearing a silver lion— emblem of the Aga Khan."

....

"YOU CANNOT MAKE SHIT LIKE THIS UP." Peering into the back of the Land Cruiser, Eddy shakes his head in dismay at the Afghan girl with a scarlet *rumol* sitting timidly beside Sonya. Rukhsana quickly averts her eyes as if Eddy were the devil incarnate—a possibility Danny has not entirely ruled out.

The devil, Danny decides, lies in Eddy's incongruous details. His Yankees ball cap sits backward on his head, mirrored Oakleys propped on top. His muscular arms bulge from a cut-off sweatshirt with a faded green Dartmouth logo arching across his broad chest. Above his left bicep, the Delta Force insignia is tattooed, a dagger thrusting upward through a triangular lightning bolt. At Eddy's side, an ugly-looking knife in a ballistic nylon scabbard hangs from a khaki web belt, and Danny can only guess what sort of surprises bulge in his cargo pockets.

"Just what we fucking need." Eddy drops the shades back down over his eyes, shuttering everything but the scowl on his unshaven face, then slings his big backpack into the Tacoma. "Another civilian to babysit. And this one telling us fairy tales about flying ragheads."

Sultan Ishkashim's main street is already bustling with three-wheeled Zarang motorbikes, their small flatbeds loaded with everything from kitchen equipment to bags of cement. As merchants unlock ramshackle wooden stalls, pairs of Sunni women, anonymous beneath electric blue *chadri*, peruse colorful garments they can never wear in public draped from the beams of porches, while grizzled men in turbans and *pakul* caps gather around rusted oil drums sipping *shur chai* from small glasses. Tiny burros overloaded with bundles of dry branches for firewood clop along the muddy, rutted road, scurrying diagonally to avoid the Afghan Border Patrol's battered green Ford Ranger pickups with large caliber machine guns bolted to their roll bars wheeling out of the fortified police compound.

Beneath the clear morning sky, wiry Chir, handsome Kourosh and burly Yusuf load crates of bottled water, cans of beans, burlap bags of rice and potatoes, and those olive drab duffels full of God-knows-what, into the cargo bed of their Tacoma as Danny unfolds a narrow topo map on the Land Cruiser's hood. He draws his finger from Ishkashim northeast along a route that hugs the Panj River past the town of Khandud then splits at Goz Khun. The south fork traces a valley bisecting the Wakhan Pamir and Hindu Kush ranges, meandering east to the village of Sarhad-i-Broghil where the road ends. From there, trails wind over high passes that lead south to Chitral in Pakistan and east into the Xinjiang Autonomous Region of China.

Danny says, "The Buddhist Silk Road came right through here."

Eddy hunches over the map and squints. "Where's the chick say this Shriners' lodge is supposed to be?"

Danny has circled a village on his map. To its south, neither trails nor passes can be seen—only glacial tributaries cascading from high peaks that delineate the border of Pakistan and empty into the Wakhan River. He taps narrow elevation lines above the village. "Rukhsana thinks it's up in here somewhere."

"*Thinks?* She's never been there?"

"Apparently not, but she says the place is called 'Waterfall.' The villagers there must know about it."

Eddy scratches a three-day beard beneath his bushy Fu Manchu. "That's only a couple of klicks from the KP, Padre. Khyber Pakhtunkhwa—Pashtun country. Border's porous as an Indian condom."

"Taliban?"

He shakes his head. "Unlikely. They've gotten into Chitral through Kunar but the Wakhan hasn't interested them. So far, anyway."

"Then what's the problem?" Danny asks.

"Opium smugglers. Weren't of much concern until they turned in their old *mush-kush* rat killers and bought new Chinese AKRs in Pakistan. Sons-of-bitches can be unpredictable."

"Guess that's why you get paid the big bucks—'Payload.' Our tax dollars at work, right?" Danny folds his battered map and smiles at the big man's sweatshirt. "You really go to Dartmouth, Eddy?"

"What? You don't think I look Ivy League?"

"Well..."

"Believe it or not, Harvard boy, I have a degree in chemical engineering from Big Green—fucking *Cum Laude*. How do you think I got so interested in blowing shit up for Uncle Sam? Suits me better than sucking up to a bunch of douche bags from Chevron or BP."

"Guess that explains the nickname," Danny says. "Somehow, the military just doesn't seem like the best place for a guy who's got a problem with authority."

"I could say the same about the seminary, Padre." Eddy's moustache obscures what could either be a smile or a sneer. "I heard your old man and brother were both jarheads."

"Yeah," Danny laughs. "Guess I was the family black sheep."

"Well, now that you mention it, you're not what I'd call chaplain material." Eddy turns toward the pickup, hesitates then glances back at Danny. "Listen, I know it's none of my business, but were you and Sonya ever…?"

Danny cuts him off. "Time to saddle up, Eddy."

"*Saddle up?* What are you, Duke fucking Wayne?"

Danny slips into the front seat beside Jamshid, who smells of cardamom and rose hips. The young Tajik raises two fingers to his lips and then touches them reverently to the photo of Massoud hanging from his rear-view mirror as if it were a phylactery.

Danny nods respectfully. "Lion of the Panjshir."

"Fucking damn straight!" Jamshid affects the same arched eyebrow and rakish movie star smile as his *mujahid* hero.

Danny grins. "You must have learned English at Dartmouth, Jam."

Eddy pokes his head into the back seat again where Rukhsana sits safely chaperoned between Bashir and Sonya. Sizing up the girl with the defiant eyes, he scratches his chin. "You sure it's a good idea to bring her along?"

Sonya stares out the window toward the horizon and ties her red bandana around her neck in anticipation of another long day on the dusty road. "She knows the territory better than any of us."

"Just saying, if the shit hits the fan, she's one more liability."

"So far, she's the only one who has a clue where we're going."

In the rear-view mirror, Danny watches Rukhsana reappraise the American *kafir*, her brown eyes softening, curiosity overcoming apprehension. He laughs at the improbability of *that* pairing.

Eddy seems flustered by this infusion of high-powered estrogen. He throws up his hands in resignation and growls at the smooth-faced Kourosh behind the wheel of his pickup.

"What are *you* looking at? Shove over! I'm riding shotgun in your sisterfucking Talibanmobile."

The big man tosses a grimace back at Danny. "Let's saddle the fuck up!"

WEDNESDAY, 22 JULY 2009 • GEORGETOWN, WASHINGTON, DC

....

THE APRONED *SOMMELIER* pours a 2002 Blenheim Chardonnay into Courtney's long stem glass as Cyrus peruses the menu at 1789. The wainscoted Garden Room is pleasantly cool in Georgetown's sultry evening. Low angling sunlight filters through the lacy curtains on Federal-style doors behind Courtney's head, rimming her brunette bob with an auburn halo and painting the white tablecloth with the luminescence of a Vermeer still life. Cyrus notes that she is wearing the Guerlain scent he gave her last time they met for a weekend tryst. It reminds him of all the intimate details he dutifully forgot the Monday morning after.

"We really must start with the Foie Gras Torchon," Cyrus insists. "I know it's terribly un-PC, but one taste and you will swear the goose went out with a big smile on its beak."

Courtney tastes the expensive wine, leaving a perfect pink lip print on the rim of her glass. She nods approval to the *sommelier* while smiling seductively at Cyrus. "You know I never get anthropomorphic about food, *mon chér*. Like we always say in NOLA: *Quel que soit votre bateau flotte* [Whatever floats your boat]."

Cyrus chuckles as the wine flows into his Burgundy glass. "Mine's definitely floating, love. What a delightfully decadent way to celebrate hump day here in our great Nation's Capital. Is this a Company tradition, or have you just been missing mine?"

Courtney bats her long eyelashes over the rim of her glass. "You know the creed by now, Cyrus. There is no distinction made between business and pleasure inside the Beltway. It's all political-theater-as-usual. And happily, I get paid very well to act out."

"I'll drink to that."

"So, darling, before we imbibe too much of this lovely wine and start doing naughty things to each other under the table," Courtney smooths a white linen napkin across her lap, "we should take care of the business part of our stage production. In brief, I'd like access to your satellite phone, and it would be better for both of us if you didn't ask why."

Cyrus hides his cards behind the menu, "This Brussels Sprout salad with the pine nuts and Pecorino Toscano sounds divine…and curiosity demands I ask you for at least a redacted explanation."

"Since dinner is on me, it will be *heavily* redacted."

"Fair enough. But tell me, since you work at spook central, why don't your people just intercept the satellite signal, or whatever it is they do?"

"Good question. As I recall, you're on the Iridium network, Low Earth Orbit technology?"

"I'll bet you remember every word of that very naughty text message I sent you on your birthday last year."

"I confess I had to look up a couple of the Latin terms," Courtney fans herself facetiously. "We can track LEO systems using Doppler shift calculations from the satellite, and with Iridium hardware, it's possible to extract coordinates using Hayes commands."

"Which are...?"

"A series of short text strings that produce commands for telecom operations—you know, dialing, hanging up, changing the parameters of a connection and so on. But we've got to intercept an up-link in progress, and the positioning calculations can be off by kilometers in many cases. We've reverse-engineered voice encryption algorithms, so even sat phones aren't very secure anymore unless you are constantly changing your position. For now, we're not so much interested in what your Jesuit friend says; we're interested in where he *is*. If the phone is turned on, we can determine exact GPS coordinates when you ping him and he responds."

Courtney's expression turns serious. "We think Sonya Aronovsky is running an Israeli operation in our theater. Bad form without briefing your best-friend-with-benefits. If we can keep her on our radar via your sat phone, we can jump in if things get messy."

Cyrus inspects the sunlight reflecting through his glass onto the tablecloth. "So, I was right about Sonya. She works for Shin Bet."

"That's internal security, Cyrus," Courtney sighs into her Chardonnay. "We think Aronovsky works for Mossad."

Cyrus arches an appreciative eyebrow. "Hmm, I just *knew* she was worth watching."

Courtney narrows her eyes playfully, jabbing a perfectly painted fingernail at his naughty smile. "Now, don't you utter one more word about that bitch! Not when I'm buying dinner."

Cyrus raises his glass. "Not another word, love. Scout's honor."

"You never struck me as Boy Scout material, Cyrus."

"Guess I've never been very good at tying knots."

"How about trimming loose ends?"

....

"**CHEW IN MOUTH AWHILE.**" Jamshid tears off a chunk of desiccated mutton with his impressively white teeth while steering the Land Cruiser. His eyes are fixed ahead on the punishing terrain as he passes the muslin-wrapped meat over his shoulder into the back seat. "Spit makes taste like sheep again." Sonya regards both the dried gray flesh and Jamshid's culinary instruction with equal disgust as Rukhsana grabs hold and sinks her teeth unabashedly into the local delicacy.

Danny checks their map. "We're coming up on a village called Qal'a-i-Panja."

"The old capital of Wakhan," Bashir confirms. "The last king had a hunting lodge there. It is probably our best chance of finding a place to sleep tonight."

Since leaving Ishkashim that morning, they have been driving east into the "corridor" negotiated by Great Britain and Russia during the 19th century. Sonya had read up on the "Great Game" imperial brinkmanship during her flight to Istanbul last week.

As Czarist Russia had consolidated control of the Central Asian Emirates and Khanates, British India pressured Abdur Rahman Khan, *emir* of Afghanistan, to extend his kingdom east through the mountainous Wakhi, Shegnani and Kyrgyz tribal lands, creating a narrow but formidable buffer zone between the Russian and British Empires. The 220-kilometer-long salient cut a deep divide between the Pamir and the Hindu Kush mountains, while the Panj River imposed a natural border to the north as far as Lake Zorkul. To the south, a British civil servant, Sir Mortimer Durand, drew his infamous line through Pashtun and Baluch tribal territories in 1893, which became the arbitrary, and largely ignored, border between

Pakistan and Afghanistan. Yet another example of the shortsighted, and ultimately disastrous "divide and govern" policy of Great Britain. Sonya had grown up with its violent legacy in the Levant.

They have covered eighty kilometers of gravel flat and stony wash since breakfast, snaking wildly across a rutted dirt track to avoid potholes and fording a dozen swollen tributaries that flood the boggy sedge and grazing pastures.

At Khandud, the administrative capital of Wakhan, they were obliged to visit the governor, a young Wakhi bureaucrat dressed in an ill-fitting suit, to obtain permission for passage through checkpoints in his province. Even though they already had a permit from the Border Police in Ishkashim, Bashir explained it was important not to ruffle local feathers. They sipped *chai* with the governor and chatted perfunctorily about life in America. Later, they explored the domed shrine of Ras Malak, built in a sparse grove of willow trees on the ruins of an ancient Buddhist *stupa*, while the Panjshir crew strained dirty petrol through cheesecloth into the fuel tanks of their vehicles.

For the past hour, Sonya has been trying to doze as Jamshid negotiates the pitted rocky track through green patches of terraced farmland that form a living quilt between the barren foothills and swollen river. Rain and snowmelt from the mountain glaciers has engorged countless tributaries that claw through the alluvial fan, while the road ahead disappeared into a surge of floodwater.

Jamshid parallels the pickup and Eddy pokes his head out. "Let's winch up," he orders.

Jamshid jumps out, flips a lever on the Land Cruiser's bumper winch to free its spool and manually unwinds the cable. He wraps the braided steel around the pickup's tow hitch beneath a twenty-liter Jerry can and attaches its hook to a steel grommet. The tethered vehicles proceed cautiously into the swollen stream.

Slowing to five kilometers-per-hour, Jamshid is careful not to hydro-lock his engine or short the electronics. Sonya watches his face tighten as he scrambles over large rocks through the quickening current. She grips a handhold above her window, feeling their struts engage as the Land Cruiser's right front wheel attempts to gain purchase on a sloping boulder. The SUV slips, lurches to the left and loses traction, carried for several meters by the fast-moving current before it jolts to a stop in the roaring stream.

Sonya hears their wheels spinning in the slick sand. 15 meters ahead, the Tacoma is almost at the water's edge. She watches Jamshid reach below the steering wheel, shift his transfer case into neutral, squeeze the lock-up and pull the power take off lever toward him. The winch engages and the cable snaps taut. Still, the pickup slips backwards, straining against the pull of the winch, and the Land Cruiser's wheels sink deeper into the sandbar.

"Fuck! We are too heavy," Jamshid growls. "Cable will break!"

Danny leans over the front seat. "We need to lighten the load, Sonny. Grab hold of the door and bumper. We'll use the cable to wade across."

Sonya pushes open her door on the SUV's downstream side. Water surges beneath the side runner as she swings her legs out and lowers her Gortex boots into the stream. The afternoon runoff from melting glaciers is colder than she imagined. She touches solid rock beneath her feet and holds tight to the door frame as Rukhsana gathers her cotton *tunban* around her waist and knots it before entering the spray. Danny and Bashir follow the girl into the river and they begin to inch toward the front of the vehicle.

Sonya watches the rushing water rise to Danny's mid-thigh as he grips the front bumper guard, then guides Rukhsana and Bashir to the tow cable. He stretches out for Sonya's hand as she struggles to hold her balance in the fast-flowing current while wrestling her door closed. Water gathers in her long skirt and drags her backward. Her boots slip off the tenuous foothold and she goes under.

In a surreal moment of terror, past and present collide. Sonya is back in Haifa, her first year in a world as different from Leningrad as she can imagine, scampering along the flat rocks at Dado Beach with Uncle Reuven while Maryna works her shift at B'nai Zion. After a winter storm, the Mediterranean is a calm, luminescent green in the mid-day sun, until a rogue wave rises suddenly and breaks like a roaring freight train on the narrow strip of shingle beside them. Startled by the cold assault, she grabs for her uncle's gnarled hand and squeezes tight.

"You must learn to swim," her mother later scolds. In Maryna's philosophy, it is both a literal and metaphorical preparation for life's inevitable disasters. But to Sonya, the revelation that "dark waves," as Uncle Reuven called them, are always lurking below a deceptively calm horizon, just waiting for her to lower her guard, forever denied Sonya the ability to enjoy the water or trust the world around her. In her worst nightmares, the treacherous surf overtakes her as she fights to escape across the slick rocks, her legs too heavy to run. In a moment of sheer panic, cold claws drag her under water and hold her terrified, where she can no longer hear her mother's admonishing voice or feel her uncle's protective grip.

She cannot see or hear anything but a churning gray liquid that blurs her vision, dampening the sound in her ears, drowning out her cry for help and stealing the breath from her lungs. She cannot feel any ground beneath her as she is dragged toward certain death.

Then, a hand has hold of hers, not the bony fingers of her long-dead uncle, but the strong, sure grip of someone very much alive.

DANNY'S BODY CREATES a downstream eddy, but his grip on Sonya's hand is tentative at best. If he can muscle her closer, it will ease the drag, but he feels himself slipping and his fingers weakening. Then, something catches his belt from behind. Glancing over his shoulder, Danny sees Jamshid stretched from the Land Cruiser's door frame, anchoring them all as he strains against the current.

Realizing what has to be done, Danny grits his teeth and pulls with all his strength. He grabs Sonya just beneath her armpit and reaches under water with his right hand, finds her waistband, rips the heavy twill open at its front snap and watches her kick the skirt's deadly drag free of her boots. The billowing fabric shoots rapidly downstream on the current as Danny reels her in and Sonya scrambles to feel solid rock beneath her feet again.

He pulls her tight against him and yells above the surge. "You okay, Sonny?"

Sonya gasps for breath and turns into Danny's chest, her arms clasping his waist as if he were a life buoy. Shivering, she looks up, eyes glazed with fear, composes herself and nods. He points to the front of the SUV and they work their way around the bumper, Danny gripping the taut steel cable and Sonya clinging tight to his waist. He guides her along the slippery line, across the rapid stream to where the pickup is now on firm ground. Rukhsana waits with a dry blanket as the crew gapes in stunned amazement at Sonya's naked legs below the drenched tails of her chambray shirt.

"Civilians clear," Eddy yells. "Get Jam the hell out of there!"

Kourosh guns the pickup and Jamshid engages the winch. The Land Cruiser extracts itself from the sandbar and lumbers across the tributary to dry gravel.

Shivering in the Tacoma's cargo bed, Danny strips off his soaked T-shirt and catches Eddy grinning at him like a frat boy.

"Way to think on your feet, Padre! Ingenious problem solving. And, I have to admit, a *very* clever way to get a lady out of her skirt. You learn that one at Harvard?"

Danny laughs through chattering teeth, pulls a thermal top from his duffel and slips it over his head. "Old Southie technique, Eddy. Came in handy during summers at Marble Head."

WEDNESDAY, 22 JULY 2009 • QAL'A-I-PANJA, AFGHANISTAN

....

HAIR HANGING DAMP ACROSS HER FOREHEAD, Sonya burrows into her sleeping bag, lying on a bed of pillows sewn from woolen pile saddlebags. Danny hands her a steaming mug of *shur chai* and she returns his gesture with a weary smile. Wearing a black jumper stretched tight over his muscular torso, his sandy hair unkempt and his face unshaven, she cannot remember Danny ever looking sexier.

Sonya makes a weak attempt at humor. "Never imagined modesty would be the death of me."

Danny's blue eyes ease her embarrassment. "That's why fish don't wear skirts. Sonny."

Bashir has negotiated a home stay in a small adobe house near what was once Zahir Shah's hunting lodge. Their Wakhi hostess, resplendent in an embroidered magenta dress, decorative pillbox cap, and a necklace dripping with semi-precious stones, tends a goose-neck copper pot heating over coals beneath the vented ceiling. In a state of post-traumatic clarity, Sonya is ecstatic to be out of her waterlogged clothing, dry, alive and solidly in her body.

"Well, I'm dressing like a boy from now on." Sonya's still-cold fingers linger on Danny's as she takes the mug and recalls his strong hands gripping her tightly in the water. He sits beside her and she remembers how those hands used to explore her body as reverently as if she were a Praxiteles sculpture.

"I really should have learned how to swim," she sighs and sips her salty milk tea, then looks up into his hooded eyes with naked candor. "You saved my life today, Danny."

"Does that buy me a straightforward explanation?"

"Cyrus was right," she says. "About my employer. Lucky guess. Or maybe he's just smarter than I thought."

Danny probes her eyes. "The vellum…is it real?"

"*You're* the expert, professor. All I can tell you is that I found it in my mother's things."

"So, the story about your father is true?"

She feels a twinge of hurt that he still has to ask. "It's true."

The Wakhi woman prods the glowing coals beneath her blackened pots with an iron, dusts her hands briskly on her apron, and smiles conspiratorially at Sonya before she leaves.

When they are alone, Danny asks, "So, why Payload Eddy and the Wild Bunch?" His eyes narrow, probing hers. "What exactly *was* your father carrying when his helicopter went down?"

She hesitates for only a moment. "Tactical nuclear weapons, we think."

"Holy shi—! Are you kidding? Do our people know about this? I mean the military? CIA?"

"Quite often, Danny, *your* people make a worse mess of things."

He considers that for a moment and nods. "Israel is taking the lead on this?"

"Not officially. We don't get involved in other peoples' tribal wars. That said, if some tribe that hates Jews ever got one of these things, it would lead to another holocaust. So, I'm here on what you might call preventive reconnaissance. Eddy and the boys are backup, and hopefully our ride home."

Danny shakes his head and laughs with some difficulty. "And to think I once had you pegged as the quiet, studious girl sitting in the back of my classroom."

Sonya takes his hands, smiles at the bittersweet memory. "Once upon a time."

"Jeez, you're an ice cube." He tries to massage circulation back into her fingers.

"I'm freezing. Hold me until I warm up." She shivers inside her sleeping bag.

"Sonny, I can't…"

"Just hold me, Danny. Please? Just for a little while." Her eyes plead with him. "I'm too exhausted to be wicked—promise."

She watches him pull a deep breath, exhale his resistance and sink back into the pillows. Drawing her close, Danny tenderly kneads her shoulders, neck and back, the way he used to before life got so complicated. She burrows her head into his chest, absorbing the heat of his body, inhaling the smell of him and remembering.

"Thank you," she whispers as his arms encircle her. Then, after a long pause, "Danny?"

"Mmm?"

"I never stopped either."

"Stopped what?"

"Being in love with you."

He does not reply, but she can hear his steady breathing catch in his lungs, feel his heartbeat quicken beneath her cheek.

Sonya closes her eyes and smiles contentedly, feeling safe from those dark waves for the first time in many years.

....

A FEW KILOMETERS FROM the Abkhazia border crossing, two Caucasian *volk-ubiyta*—"wolf-killers"—strain against their handlers' chains on a middle school basketball court. The feisty young Sarbai, a shaggy brown Sarplaninac weighing 55 kilos, is favored to win over Ivan, a massive, black-faced five-year-old Ovcharka. Both animals are undefeated, and the men mingling on the concrete pad know it will be a close contest. Some have traveled from as far away as Svanetia to watch the championship matches. Most have already drunk too much vodka on the road and are betting wildly.

The smell of the unwashed dogs mingles with smoke from grilling meat kabobs and the anticipatory sweat of the spectators. Alexander Zharkov strikes a blue-tip match with his thumbnail, lights a Belomorkanal and adds the stink of sulfur and harsh tobacco to the olfactory mash-up before greeting the Petrenko twins.

The giant bodyguards have just arrived from Sochi International Airport and Zharkov cannot tell them apart. Both stand a full head above him, outweigh him by at least forty kilos, and wear identical mottled gray mil-spec trousers and black T-shirts that barely conceal pistols in their waistbands. The one who calls himself "Kyrylo" scans the faces along the chain link fence-enclosed court with suspicion.

"*Mnye vybirat' svoyu komandu is etih sobakovodov* [From these dog breeders I am supposed to pick my team]?"

"*Vneshnost' byvaet obmanchiva* [Looks are often deceiving]." Zharkov feigns a conciliatory smile, exhaling a stream of smoke through his teeth. "Some are former Vympel, like you, others served with Alfa or OMON. Three received the *krapovyi* beret—best of the best—and one is their *Vityaz* instructor.* In Chechnya and Georgia, all these men have seen as much or more service than either of you."

"And now they clean up dog shit," Kyrylo sneers.

"All of us clean up someone's shit," Zharkov reminds him. "At least these men have remained loyal to the Motherland."

The twins remain humorless granite façades as Zharkov motions toward the impending contestants. "These matches have been banned in Moscow and Petersburg," he says. "But here, you would have better luck telling fashionable ladies they can no longer wear sable coats."

Bets placed, the handlers unleash their snarling dogs and step back as the beasts leap toward each other's throats. The spectators tighten into a circle and bark out encouragement over the shepherds' savage growls. Ivan and Sarbai lock paws and shaggy torsos, rising up on their rear legs like fur-clad wrestlers maneuvering for a take-down. Fangs snap, grab hold of sinew and shake; thick brown ruffs are soon stained with blood.

---

* The *krapovyi* [maroon] **beret** is awarded to the "most professional, physically and morally fit" members of the Spetsnaz. Competition is hosted twice yearly by the *Vityaz* [Knight] instructors. Fewer than 10% of the applicants pass muster.

Zharkov gestures toward the spectacle. "In America, I have seen a seasoned Pit Bull and a young Presa Canario tear each other to pieces for hours. The winner was crippled; the loser shot. They do not appreciate their fighting dogs as we do." He blows smoke slowly out the side of his mouth. "Here, dogs are like members of the family. A little blood is shed, sometimes a tendon severed, but the loser is immediately given medical attention and goes back to tending his flock in the mountains. The winner becomes a celebrity, much sought after for his breeding prowess." He glances toward Kyrylo to be sure the giant Ukrainian has understood his metaphor.

The handlers move in with short wooden poles and attempt to pry the dogs apart. The referee approaches close enough to inspect the bite wounds without exposing himself to bared incisors as the shepherds continue to gnaw and snap. The Ovcharka grabs Sarbai's throat in his powerful jaws and tries to break his opponents' neck. The younger Sarplaninac is intimidated by his opponent's death grip. His eyes glaze over in pain as the referee listens for tell-tale whimpers and watches for a slumping tail, sure signs of capitulation.

"Your boss, Viktor Kaban, has become a liability," Zharkov flatly informs the twins. "Uncontrollable and greedy. No doubt he will want more money than we have agreed upon if he ever gets his hands on our property. But he does not know where these weapons are any more than I do." He pauses for dramatic effect. "I, however, know something he does not."

"And what is that?" Kyrylo snarls.

"He has hired an American, a former CIA black operative, to locate our property for him. A few days ago, we tracked this man known as 'Payload' across the Tajikistan border into Afghanistan, traveling with an agent of the Mossad. It seems the Israelis are also trying to steal our property before your boss can get to it. So, they *too* have hired this same American to help them. Everyone seems to forget that mercenaries have no loyalties except to a paycheck. For the right price, they are *always* for sale. Is that not so?"

Marko stiffens as Kyrylo glares at Zharkov, "What are you saying?"

"I'm saying that Viktor Kaban has outlived his usefulness to us. If he is on Mossad's hit list, the Americans will not protect him. He has no leverage and no country. He cannot return to either Israel or the United States, let alone Ukraine. Perhaps it is time for you to reconsider your options."

Both bodyguards glare down at him. "Meaning?" Kyrylo asks with a clenched jaw.

Zharkov shrugs, grinds his spent cigarette into the concrete. "Your boss has no loyalties either. As you well know, he has a reputation for executing his employees when he gets tired of them. How long before Kaban turns on the two of you, like one of those American Pit Bulls?"

Observing that he has struck a nerve, Zharkov feels emboldened. He steps closer, stares up into Kyrylo's chiseled face. "Do you and your brother really want to waste your most productive years as this madman's bodyguards? Remember, you are both Spetsnaz! Your boss is just a petty Jewish criminal. He was not even deemed worthy to become a full-fledged *vor*." Zharkov turns his attention to Marko. "If you work with us, with the Motherland, you will never again need employment with scum like Viktor Kaban."

The twins exchange glances and communicate volumes in that mysterious way genetically identical siblings do. Kyrylo answers for them both. "What is your offer?"

Zharkov leans closer. "Today, Ramzan Kadyrov has Putin's favor. But there are influential people in Grozny, Russian loyalists, who will never trust the Kadyrovite thugs who change sides at the drop of a hat."

Kyrylo raises a blonde eyebrow, glances over at his brother as Zharkov continues his pitch. "These true partisans are interested in acquiring, let us say, a bargaining chip, a hedge against future uncertainty. And they are willing to pay market rate for it.

"If it appears that Viktor Kaban wants to start an international bidding war with our property, all eyes will be on him, you see? So, for this to look plausible, you and your brother must carry out the operation, but with *my* team. Once you have our property in your possession, it will quietly disappear. Kaban will become everyone's target, and we..." Zharkov turns his attention back to the blood-spattered court and chuckles. "We will all become rich as oligarchs."

Both animals still fight through their exhaustion. Ivan's incisors find Sarbai's left eye and the Sarplaninac lets out a piteous whelp. The referee quickly jams a stick into Ivan's mouth to force his jaws apart. Their handlers struggle to re-chain the dogs and tend to their head wounds. As the victorious Ovcharka backs off with a final snarl, Zharkov opens a fresh packet of Belomorkanals, taps one out and double-crimps the long paper filter.

"You see?" He clenches the cigarette between his teeth victoriously as he searches his pocket for a match. "Size still matters."

THURSDAY, 23 JULY 2009 · KRET, AFGHANISTAN

....

RUKHSANA HAS NOT MET many Americans. Her father told her he had gotten along better with the Russians who were stationed in Ishkashim than any of the Americans who now advise and supply the Afghan Border Patrol. They seemed to think everyone should be grateful for their invasion. Rukhsana had not even been born when the *Roussi* had rolled in to support the *Shorawi* Communist government in Kabul, but she did not like the few Russians who came to visit the *chashmat*, the hot springs near Ishkashim. They were usually rude and haughty and smelled of alcohol. Very few Americans visited her town. Occasionally, one or two crossed the border for a day of shopping at the open-air market by the river, but they seldom ventured any farther. And the American army cared very little about any place the Taliban did not also care about.

So, when this large, violent-looking American with hair the color of a chestnut pony and a bushy moustache that hid most of his mouth arrived with her distant uncle, he was the most interesting sight she had seen in years. Rukhsana cannot understand anything he says, of course, but she senses he is a man who treats people fairly. Although stern and gruff, he seems devoted to the young Tajiks in his charge.

His hands are enormous, and she finds herself staring at them when he tears off pieces of *naan* or holds a cup of *shur chai*, almost making it disappear. Those hands excite her. And his smile, the few times she has actually seen it, is warm and genuine and full of humor. She suspects his eyes are as well, even though they are almost always hidden behind ominous orange glasses or sunken in shadow. She wonders where he lives in America, wonders if he has a woman of his own, or whether he frightens them all away because of how he looks. He does not frighten her.

He converses now with her uncle, nodding and pointing at a map, trying to align its features with what he sees on the jagged horizon. Bashir asks her where she heard the secret lodge of the Khwajagan is located and Rukhsana points toward the great white peak of Koh-i-Baba Tangi. The American stares intently up at the mountain, gesticulates with his big hands and then looks directly at her as if he sees right into her heart.

Like most Isma'ili women, Rukhsana never covers her face. But there are times she wishes she could take refuge beneath the *chadri*, like the Sunni woman in town. It would at least spare her revealing an embarrassing blush. Or having to admit the impossibility of her foolish daydreams.

Then, the big American smiles and his white teeth catch the sunlight. He calls out something sweet to her, something that almost sounds like her name.

....

"YO ROXY, MAKE YOURSELF USEFUL," Eddy tells the Afghan girl whose brown eyes resemble a deer caught in the headlights. "Go along with Uncle Bash and charm the fucking pants off that village headman, will you? We need some good intel right about now."

Sonya laughs, crosses her arms and leans back against the dusty fender of the Tacoma pickup. She is wearing khaki fatigues, a denim shirt knotted at the waist over a black tank top, and a red bandana tied around her throat beneath her disheveled, punked-out hair. Eddy decides the only thing missing from the ensemble is a Harley shovel-head rumbling beneath her boyish ass.

"You *so* know how to sweet talk the girls, Eddy."

"Wha'd I say?" He looks genuinely puzzled, then shrugs.

Eddy scans the rugged topography in the direction Rukhsana has indicated. Above the green patchwork of wheat, millet and broad beans, above the distressed adobe huts and low corrals huddled beneath a stand of dwarf willow and swath of Kashgar tamarisk, above the tongue of glacial moraine pushing boulders and scree through a cleft between the steep cliffs, he focuses his 7x50 Steiner's on a massive wall of ice that merges into shape-shifting cumulus. Above the clouds, the Hindu Kush protrudes like the Earth's ribs through sedimentary rock and shale, its intimidating knife edges painted by evening alpenglow reflecting off the glaciers.

"That is one fuck of an uphill slog," Eddy mutters.

"The peak's over 21,000 feet." Danny says, identifying Baba Tangi on his topo map. "I'm guessing this monastery, assuming it exists, sits just below one of those ridges, maybe 12-13,000, sheltered from wind and well hidden from the valley view."

Eddy surveys his encampment. The village of Kret appears to have been extruded from a hanging glacier onto a convex shelf sculpted by the Wakhan River. Five rip-stop camouflaged dome tents are pitched along a low fieldstone wall delineating the scrubby apricot orchard that belongs to the village headman. Hopefully, Bashir and Rukhsana will swill the traditional three cups of tea with the old bastard and find out something concrete about their target zone.

Eddy leans against the bumper next to Sonya, lights a smoke and passes it to her without making eye contact. She takes a quick drag while Danny is not watching. Clearly, these two have it bad for each other. Eddy smirks at the thought of the meeting planner and sky pilot humping like bunnies on the down-low.

The absurd fantasy eases Eddy's irritation and apprehension. He knows that he can count on his Panjshir crew, but civilians are always a complication. Other than public relations assistance, he cannot expect much from the rug dealer. The priest, he figures, could hold his own if push came to shove and the feisty Afghan girl would bite the balls off anyone who stepped uninvited within her reach. Oddly enough, the one he is least sure about is Sonya. Smart, for sure, but erratic. One minute, she is a frumpy librarian and the next a smoking hot lesbian supermodel or a bitch in biker drag. Eddy cannot figure out which is the "real" Sonya and certainly cannot predict how she will present in a firefight. He is determined to keep command

and control of this mission until they find what they are looking for, assuming they find anything at all. Although Eddy remains skeptical, he knows he will be well paid regardless of the outcome.

Chir and Yusuf collect dry buckthorn scrub and dung patties to build a fire, and young Kourosh cooks up a big pot of rice with re-hydrated mutton, canned white beans and pistachio nuts. Bashir and Rukhsana return in time for supper as dusk inks a deep violet sky behind the black peaks.

"The headman says he does not know of any *khanaqah* in the mountains above the village," Bashir tells them. "He says no one can approach Baba Tangi by that route anymore because the *Roussi* left landmines to discourage anyone trying to cross into Pakistan."

Danny is not convinced. "According to the UN reports I've read, there are no minefields in this part of Afghanistan."

"You calling the headman a liar?" Eddy says.

"Maybe he wants to discourage strangers from poking around in his backyard." Danny turns to Bashir. "Where's the man who told Rukhsana about this monastery?"

"She said they met in Khandud," Bashir replies. "He told her that he was buying supplies for a secret *khanaqah* above his *gheshlaq*, this village of Kret, where he lived. The man wanted Rukhsana to visit him." Bashir shrugs. "It is lonely here without a wife."

Sonya rolls her eyes. "And I'll bet he's at least her father's age."

Danny continues. "So, if the trail is mined, how does this guy get supplies up there?"

Bashir asks Rukhsana for clarification. "He told her he has been making the journey four times a year for over a decade. He must know a safe route."

"Alright." Sonya jumps to her feet, kicks a stone impatiently. "Let's find this old lecher and hire him."

Eddy tosses the dregs of his tea on the ground and wipes his hands. "Bash, first thing in the morning, you try to track this goat-fucker down. Tonight, we'll have to double up in the tents. Didn't expect so many warm bodies on this picnic. Sonya, you mind bunking with Roxy?" She nods. "Padre, you and Bash okay as tent mates?"

"Long as he doesn't snore."

"*Insha'al-Llâh*," Bashir grunts, dusts off his baggies and drags his duffel toward the tents.

Eddy glances from Sonya to Danny. "Have a word with you two?" They park themselves on a flat rock and watch Eddy tend the fire. He cocks a smile, pulls a leather-covered flask out of his cargo pocket and pours a draught into each of their aluminum trail cups. "If we're going to be humping up that hill tomorrow, I need to ditch some weight," he says. "And Bulleit's just the thing for a come-to-Jesus talk. No offense, Padre."

"None taken, Payload."

Eddy leans against his backpack and sips the bourbon. "Way I see it, there's a better than 75-percent chance we won't find zip up on that ridge. No Shriners' lodge; no…ancient manuscripts…"

Sonya interrupts. "No worries, Danny's been briefed."

"Then I'll cut to the chase. No bullshit. My contractual arrange-ments do not require that we find any inventory, fissile or otherwise. But from here on, ops con is mine. Understood? If we haven't located anything that looks like a cache in 72 hours, I'm calling in extraction from Bagram and hope to hell I'm still in somebody's good graces there. If not, we're on our own."

Eddy pauses to survey the towering peaks that surround them. "That's where Jam and the boys come in. If we have to make it over-land to Kabul, it will be a rough ride. Your boss is paying me to get you back to the Holy Land alive and well, and I intend to make good on that. Vik, however, isn't so particular about your health, or any-body else's for that matter. Long as I call in and report he won't get suspicious. We on the same page here?"

"Who's Vik," Danny asks.

"No one you'd ever want to meet," Sonya assures him.

"Trust her on that," Eddy adds.

Sonya looks up from her cup. "We're clear."

"Sweet." Eddy tosses back his bourbon and grins mischievously at them. "Let's get some rack ops, boys and girls. First light is at O-five hundred."

....

TRANSLUCENT CLOUDS GHOST across an indigo canvas spattered with celestial legends called Apus, Hercules and Scorpius. The spar-kling constellations remind Danny that the 21st century is just a blink of God's eye. In this forgotten river valley carved between the Big Pamir and Hindu Kush, modernity feels irrelevant. Here, there is only a soft breeze drifting through black palisades, the fragrance of damp earth and a pungent dung fire, the smooth taste of bourbon in his mouth and the bane of his priesthood sitting beside him.

The last time Danny drank strong spirits was the night he bared his soul before selling it to Cyrus' anonymous backers. He remembers his mother telling him that whiskey brings out the truth in people, and he knows from experience it does not take a regimen of contem-plation and daily examination of conscience to reveal self-deception. Despite what he told his mother and Monsignor Devlin, funding for research is not the real reason he is sitting by a campfire in this remote panhandle of Afghanistan. The transparency of his alibi is clear to everyone, it seems—Cyrus, Bashir and even Eddy. What surprises him now is his utter lack of contrition.

Maybe he should drink bourbon more often.

The night cools off quickly at 10,000 feet above sea level. Sonya shivers and zips her lightweight down jacket up around her neck. She slips off the red paisley bandana, shakes her hair loose and brushes it back off her forehead. Danny watches silently, remembering the thick flaxen mane she used to meticulously work through with a wooden pick and an grimace of discomfort.

Sonya pulls on a black watch cap. Content now in androgynous warmth, she cradles the cup of bourbon in her strong hands as Danny watches her and remembers. Despite how hard she has tried to look like a boy, he still finds her as beautiful as the day they met. He wants to tell her, but fears re-opening a dangerous door to the past. Instead, Danny pokes at the waning fire with a willow branch.

"As much as I hate to admit it," Danny says, "Eddy's right. Even if we find something up there, it may not be what you're looking for, Sonny. You thought about that?"

Sonya stares into the firelight. "I've thought about little else." Her eyes are molten amber and Danny can feel her balancing precariously on a wire between determination and despair. "But failure is not an option in my business."

"Look, I'm not suggesting we pull the plug." Without hesitation, he places a comforting hand on her lower back and she lifts her eyes to meet his. "We just have to get real about this. It's been twenty years, Sonny. Your father may be…"

"Dead?" She laughs bitterly. "He's been calling to me, Danny. That note he left is his voice leading the way, first to you, then Bashir and now here…" Sonya scans the jagged black peaks surrounding them like an impenetrable fortress. "The last fucking place on Earth." She looks up at him soberly. "Intuition tells me that my father is still alive. Does that sound completely crazy?"

Danny holds her gaze and shudders at the confusion coursing through him. What really seems crazy right now is the vow looming like an electrified fence between them. Was he never worthy to be one of Iñigo's soldiers? Never made of the right stuff? Has his life's aspiration been nothing but self-deception? He cannot imagine why God would bring him together again with this woman, so close he can smell the fragrance of her. Is it just to torture him with bitter-sweet memories and a desire so intense he can feel it heating his bone marrow? He cannot believe the Deity to which he has pledged his life, his eternity, could be so malevolent, so unfeeling.

Or maybe Bashir was right after all: A merciful God does not make mistakes.

"You look so beautiful." Danny hears himself say as the fire-light dances across Sonya's face. She seems caught off guard, even though she must know how much he has always wanted her.

Her lips part slightly, smiling at his awkwardness. "Thank you." She blushes like a girl on her first date then laughs. "And you look incredibly sexy when you haven't shaved."

Time folds back on itself. He is standing beside her, watching the lights of Cambridge spill onto the satin surface of the Charles River. It is Halloween, her 21st birthday, and she is nuzzling his chest as he inhales her scent.

Kissing is actually more intimate than sex. Offering your mouth… your tongue…the portal of your survival to someone. It's an immense act of trust…or would you say…faith?

And what the hell *is* the difference, he still wonders? Both require surrender to uncertainty. Trust presupposes something that can be experienced and understood; faith requires belief in that which is *beyond* experience, beyond reason. That Kierkegaardian "leap" across the chasm of skepticism.

I promised myself I wouldn't kiss you.

Danny can hear the words coming from his mouth again, as if played back by some recording device of the heart.

A shared memory awakens in Sonya's eyes and she whispers him back into the present. "Why are you always making promises you can't keep?" Her face tilts upward, her tongue moistening her lips, anticipating his permission.

Danny knows he is standing on the crumbling edge of a precipice as her mouth brushes lightly over his. Some part of him begs forgiveness, but the unspoken supplication rings hollow and insincere. He is, after all, what his Creator made him: *adamah*—a man of earth.

And a man can fight his nature for only so long.

He pulls her roughly against his chest, feels Sonya surrender willingly into his arms, watches her eyes glisten with the same unapologetic hunger as that first night in Cambridge. Melting into her triumph, his mouth renegotiates that broken pact of trust.

Or is it faith?

"HIS NAME WAS ABDUL HADUD," Bashir reports, "an Uzbek trader contracted by a Naqshbandi *shaykh* from Samarkand to transport supplies to Aubshaur. If these monastics are the Sarman Brotherhood Iskender spoke of, then they are also loyal to the Aga Khan, which would explain why the Isma'ilis here protect the secret of their lodge."

"And maybe why the village headman has been so circumspect," Danny adds.

A wry smile escapes Bashir's white beard. "It is also a fact that old men like to gossip more than women. Rukhsana and I visited the village *chaikhana* and were soon wagging chins with the elders of Kret, each of whom was quick to demonstrate that *his* personal knowledge of secret information outdid all his associates."

"Shocking what goes on in a tea house," Sonya tries to clear her still-fuzzy head as Danny pours packets of electrolytes into their water bottles. Spending the night alone in a sleeping bag, on a thin pad covering hard ground at nearly ten thousand feet, after drinking bourbon and making out with the one man in the world who causes her toes to tingle, was not conducive to a restful repose. "So, where can we find this Abdul-the-Uzbek?" she asks.

"Unfortunately, he passed away last winter," Bashir replies wistfully. "They say he suffered a heart attack in Sarhad while trying to kidnap a young Kyrgyz girl for his bride. A time-honored tradition, however, one best attempted by a younger man."

Eddy chuckles as he scrapes the remains from his porridge bowl into the smoldering dung fire. "Geezer couldn't wait for Roxy to come around, I guess."

"That's it, then?" Sonya emits a deep sigh. "We've hit a dead end?"

"Perhaps not, *habibti*." Bashir gestures behind her and Sonya turns to see a line of twelve little burros harnessed together, empty wooden packsaddles cinched to their backs, stepping in sync up the trail from the river toward the apricot orchard. A wiry man with a grizzled beard, outfitted in a cartridge vest over dusty *perahan tunban*, follows the caravan on a chocolate-brown stallion with two chestnut mares on lead.

"While the esteemed Wakhi elders conversed with us in Dari," Bashir explains, "they gossip with each other in their native Khik zik. Fortunately, Rukhsana is fluent. And I might add, quite persistent."

Sonya appraises the girl's defiant eyes. "Doesn't surprise me a bit."

"She learned that this Wakhi *padabhan* now approaching us, a herdsman named Assadullah, took possession of Abdul Hadud's livestock after his demise. I believe there was a debt involved. He told Rukhsana that Abdul often boasted his *khar* had made the journey to Aubshaur so many times they could find their way without him."

"You are shitting me!" Eddy squints incredulously.

"*Insha'al-Llâh*," Bashir replies. "I think we will soon find out if this is fact or feces."

Sonya impatiently dumps the dregs of her tea into the fire pit. "Well, give the Wakhi some Afghanis and let's…" she searches for the expression, "saddle up."

Eddy rolls his eyes at Danny. "Jesus! You two deserve each other."

....

BY 14:00 HOURS, the diminutive *khar* are further dwarfed beneath gear and supplies. With Assadullah bringing up the rear, the caravan clops stoically upward through grassy hummocks laced with milky streams and littered with boulders the size of buses. A west wind has banished enough cloud cover to expose the watershed's source, massive shelves of ice on the north face of Koh-i-Baba Tangi.

Riding Assadullah's stallion, Eddy follows the tethered burros into a steep defile between two spurs of dark schist. The trader, his cotton *tunban* tucked into high rubber Wellingtons, leads Sonya and Bashir on the saddled mares, while the Panjshir crew, the priest and Rukhsana trek alongside. Eddy squints up at the fan of talus extruded by the glacier. Above that, an intimidating incisor of granite and snow pierces the clearing sky over Pakistan.

The burros follow one of several streams of glacial melt for over an hour. Then, as if enticed by a siren song in the wind, the lead jack veers to the right. Sinking into icy water rising over his fetlocks and hocks, the *khar* wades determinedly across the fast-flowing stream and continues his ascent without breaking stride. Eddy watches the rest of the pack follow like lemmings, then swivels in his saddle toward Assadullah.

"The fuck they going?"

The trader shrugs as if his burros are calling the tune.

The priest appears alongside Sonya's mare and grins up at Eddy. "First time you've had to follow a jackass?"

"You've been waiting all day to say that, haven't you, Padre?" Eddy watches the last burro veer at the same spot, cross the swift stream and amble up a narrow corridor on the opposite bank. If he didn't know better, Eddy could swear these jackasses had a GPS. Less than twenty feet ahead of them, just beyond where the lead *khar* diverted, an alarming shape catches his eye.

"Everybody *freeze!*" Eddy raises a hand and Jamshid relays the command in Dari.

He dismounts and steps carefully forward, slips his tactical knife from its sheath and squats over the object. Probing the scree around it with the precision of an archaeologist, Eddy slowly excavates a flexible plastic, olive drab wing from the grit. The thing measures less than five inches in length, with a metal-capped cylinder in the center and a thicker wing opposite its exposed mate. He motions for Danny to join him. "Walk slow. Follow in my steps."

The priest peers over Eddy's shoulder and whistles softly. "That what I think it is?"

"Green Parrot,"* Eddy says without looking up. "Anti-personnel mine. Same design we used in Nam, different explosive. The Ruskies dropped a quarter million of these motherfuckers from helicopters. Kids picked them up because they looked like toys. Blew their hands off. Sometimes their faces." Eddy tosses a grimace over his shoulder. "So much for your fucking UN report, Padre."

Danny grimaces. "You see how the lead burro avoided this thing?"

"I'm way ahead of you, Harvard boy."

---

* The Soviet PFM-1, designated **Green Parrot** by NATO because of its wing shape, was based on the BLU-43 Dragontooth, a pressure-detonated, anti-personnel mine used in South Vietnam and Laos by the US military. The PFM-1 was deployed extensively in Afghanistan and provided major impetus for the formation of an International Campaign to Ban Landmines.

Stepping back from the landmine, Eddy jabs his serrated blade toward the line of *khar* following the stream on the opposite bank and yells, "Listen up! We follow the jackasses. Keep *exactly* in their path. There's live ordnance on this slope, people, so stay alert!"

Eddy mounts the stallion and holds out his hand to lift Danny up behind him. The priest hesitates, stares at the winged landmine as if it were a viper.

"That thing can still kill or maim some kid," he says, as if Eddy needs a reminder. "Can you disarm it?"

Sonya reins in her mare beside them and looks down at Father Callan from her saddle. "Once the fuse on a PFM is armed, Danny, it has to be detonated."

Eddy scratches his beard and surveys the terrain on the other side of the stream. He collars Jamshid and points to the ambling pack of burros heading toward a tumble of white granite boulders about a hundred yards up the slope. "Jam, once we cross the stream, tell What's-his-Ass to park the horses behind those rocks where they won't spook." Eddy grimaces and turns to Sonya, appraising her with a renewed interest. "Padre's right; too many kids been fucked up by these things. And where did you learn so goddamn much about landmines?"

"In my neighborhood, you learn a lot about things that blow up."

Danny slings his pack up to Eddy, grabs hold of the wooden saddle and swings a leg over the stallion behind him. Assadullah leads the horses on foot across the roiling stream and the four riders dismount. Then the herder returns for Jamshid and his crew.

Eddy waits with the priest and the young Tajiks until the *khar* and horses disappear behind the boulders on the slope above them. "Time to suit up." He shrugs the pack off his shoulders and nods to Jamshid. "In case we have company up there."

Eddy zips open the top pouch, extracts a holstered SIG-Sauer P226 pistol and straps it to his right hip. He leaves the customized MP7 machine pistol tucked under the flap. The Tajiks unpack their gear, quickly assemble black Heckler & Koch 416 assault rifles, then lock, load and shoulder them in ready position.

Eddy surveys his platoon, nods like an approving Sergeant Major and draws his pistol from its ballistic nylon holster. He racks the slide, thumbs the safety and takes aim at the Green Parrot twenty yards away. Holding his breath, he gently squeezes the trigger and feels the kick as the landmine detonates across the stream with enough force to amputate a man's foot.

"One less piece of work for the HALO Trust,"* he mutters.

Danny nods and shoulders his own rucksack. "Listen, Eddy, about that jackass thing…"

He laughs. "Forget about it, Padre. I've followed more than a few, believe me."

....

THE ROCKY SLOPE FANNING OUT below the mountain's glacial tongue grows precariously steep, and the riders dismount so Assadullah can walk his horses through the rough talus. Lightheaded and sweating beneath the intense afternoon sun, Sonya strips to her T-shirt and loosens her bootlaces to accommodate her swollen feet. None of that mitigates her abdominal cramping. She lags behind everyone but Rukhsana, who understands what is slowing Sonya down and fusses over her like the caretaker most Afghan girls are trained to be. Every so often, Danny waits for them to catch up on the interminable slope and reminds Sonya to hydrate.

---

* **HALO Trust** [Hazardous Area Life-support Organization] volunteers have cleared more than 700,000 landmines from fields and stockpiles, and ten million items of ordnance from Afghanistan alone.

"We're above 12,000 feet," he scolds. "You've got to force your-self to drink those electrolytes, Sonny. You're sweating all the fluid out of your body." Beneath her rucksack, the dampness between her shoulder blades begins to trickle down her spine and puddle above the waistband of her trousers. Danny taps three ibuprofen tablets from a packet and waits stubbornly until she swallows them with a long draught from her Nalgene bottle. He tucks the rest into her cargo pocket. "Anti-inflammatories help at altitude."

Enjoying his ministrations, Sonya teases, "I've heard Viagra works even better."

"Wouldn't know." Danny blushes and wraps a supportive arm around her as she forces her lug sole boots through the ball bearing-sized scree. Despite her exhaustion, Sonya cannot get the taste of Danny's mouth out of her mind, or the memory of that tingling she felt between her legs last night, the itch she was unable to scratch with Rukhsana in her tent. She wonders if *he* will still feel that pas-sion when they have both returned to the banality of civilization. His stormy love affair with an ethereal Almighty always proved more seductive than any illusions she could conjure. Still, she can fantasize. Anything to help her get up this goddamn hill.

Wind chases afternoon into evening. Echoing off the canyon walls it becomes eerily redolent of a forgotten moment, the winter before her military service began. During Chanukah, Uncle Reuven had driven her and Maryna in his old Renault from Haifa to Abu Ghosh, a village in the Judean hills west of Jerusalem. There, in a Roman Catholic monastery nestled in an Arab village built on the ancient ruins of Kiryat Yearim, where the Ark of the Covenant once resided, she had heard a Jewish choir perform a German Protestant's *oratorio* to a rapt audience of Ashkenazi, Sephardi, Mizrahi, Beta, Druze, and Arab music enthusiasts.

"This is how it should always be," her mother had proclaimed with tears of joy in her eyes as she surveyed the radiantly peaceful, multi-ethnic faces around them. "All of Abraham's family celebrating together rather than blowing each other to bits."

Sonya remembers slumping into the hard wooden pew, bored to tears by Handel's *Messiah*, until the "Hallelujah" chorus exploded through the old limestone church like thunder from heaven, just as the wind now resounds off the rock buttresses soaring above them. That ecstatic moment of vocal synchrony almost convinced Sonya that her mother's idyllic vision of *pax mundi* was possible.

Before the bird woman in Khan Yunis ended her naiveté forever.

When she looks up from her dehydrated daydream, blistered feet and *mittelschmerz*, Sonya realizes that it is not wind but *water* that sings to her. Rukhsana points excitedly to a shimmering cascade gushing through the dark schist, feeding a stream from the ridge above them.

"*Aubshaur*," the girl confirms.

Sonya nods wearily as the burros and horses clamber loudly up the talus to a ledge and, one-by-one, disappear behind the narrow waterfall. Assadullah follows them, then Eddy and the Panjshir boys. Danny and Bashir wait for Rukhsana and Sonya to climb to the cascade's base. Taking Danny's hand, Sonya pulls herself up to the ledge and peers tentatively over the steep drop off. 500 meters below, she can see the silvery vein of glacial melt they had been following earlier in the afternoon. Had the donkeys not changed course, they would never have chosen this precipitous ascent to the ridge and might never have made it through the landmines.

She holds tight to Danny's waist as a cool spray kisses her sunburned face. He has to lean close to her ear to be heard above the rush of water. "Looks like things are about to get interesting, Sonny."

A narrow tunnel was excavated long ago from a natural cavern behind the cascade. Sonya's fingers trace its rough, damp contours as she follows the sound of trickling water, the arrhythmic clop of donkeys' hooves echoing in the tunnel and Eddy's torchlight ahead.

The shaft bears to the right, sloping upward as light seeps in, then widens out into a broad plaza, perhaps 25 meters across by 40 meters long, built into a natural amphitheater of red-gray schist. Inset beneath a jutting ledge at the opposite end of the plaza, rough pillars with reclining lions, stylized camels and blocky elephants define a portico over massive wooden doors. Surrounding the entrance, weathered relief carvings of human figures sporting topknots and haloes peek out from the darkness. Fanning out on either side of the portico, eight standing stone figures, five or six meters high, peer from an arcade of niches carved into the sheer walls. These stone guardians watch silently over an incongruous array of solar collectors angled to the south.

Beneath a scumbled primrose sky, Assadullah corrals his horses and pack animals behind the solar collectors as Jamshid, Kourosh, Chir and Yusuf scan the plaza's walled perimeter, assault rifles at the ready. Danny seems fixated on the ancient monoliths standing in their niches. Sonya watches him approach one of the effigies and reach out like a curious child to caress the chiseled folds of its stone raiment. Bathed in the rosy light of sunset, the reified *bodhisattva* smiles serenely down at him.

Sonya suddenly feels unsteady, as if her mind is moving faster than her body. Her tongue tingles at the back of a parched throat and her head spins. She slips off her backpack, sinks cross-legged to the ground and searches for her water bottle. Twisting off the cap with trembling hands, she lifts the wide rim to her lips and takes short, difficult swallows.

A pale-headed raptor with a three-meter wingspan glides in a lazy circle overhead as if surveying the potential carrion. Sonya takes in the dreamscape as Danny squats beside her, his hand resting gently on her shoulder. He squints up at the great bearded vulture silhouetted against the sky.

"Lammergeier," Danny says.

"Thought it might be one of those flying Sufi masters?" Sonya feels strangely giddy as she sips the electrolyte-fortified water. Some of it spills on the ground between her legs and she notices Danny staring at the wet spot. He reaches down and rubs the damp surface until its erstwhile color and design revive beneath the dust of time. A Greek key pattern mosaic, the type she has seen in ancient temples on the Levantine coast, paves the plaza beneath their feet.

"This doesn't make sense." Sonya hears her own words as if they are coming from someone else. Danny insists that she swallow more ibuprofen and drink until her bottle is nearly empty. "Where are we?" her disconnected voice asks. "What *is* this place?"

His sunburned face glows in the soft twilight, and she fixates on each detail as if seeing him for the first time: his strong, square jaw covered with sandy stubble, his serious mouth articulating a history that excites his sparkling blue eyes. She hears only fragments of what he is saying, overdubbed by her pent-up longing to be held safely in this man's arms again, inhale his sweat, satisfy the hunger she has long suppressed.

The thought simultaneously delights and irritates her. She *does* want to listen to his exposition, share Danny's moment of magical discovery, but it is so hard to focus on anything except his beautiful mouth and what she really wants it to be doing right now.

Until motion along the top of the wall behind him disrupts her delicious delirium. "Who…?"

"Seleucid Dynasty, Sonny!" He misreads her question, excited as a boy on Christmas morning. "Macedonian Greeks that settled here and inter-married with the Persians after Alexander's army left. They controlled this trade route for 300 years before the Parthians and Sakas arrived. And look at those bodhisattvas styled like Greek *kouroi*—Kushan, for sure!"

Sonya blinks as gargoyles appear at intervals along the crenellated walls surrounding the patio like shadow puppets dramatizing Danny's passionate exposition. They resolve into purple-gray shapes of men with guns, Kalashnikov buttstocks with banana clips she would recognize across a battlefield.

"Danny!" she motions urgently toward the armed figures on the skyline. "Who are *they?*"

....

"**EASY JAM. LET'S NOT** get into a pissing match." Eddy steadies the young Tajik as he appraises the ominous silhouettes leveling short-barreled AK-74s at them from the surrounding rocks. "I'm counting twenty-four from ten to two o'clock, and we've got a lot of exposed collateral. Better call for a *jirga*."*

Jamshid never takes his narrowed eyes off the interlopers. Eddy watches Jamshid ease his finger around the trigger of his weapon as the rest of the crew slip quietly behind Assadullah's horses for cover, awaiting his command. "These men are not Pashtun. Maybe *chirik*— Kyrgyz militia."

"Or smugglers," Eddy says. "And very well armed at that. Give 'em a shout, Jam. *Bhaksheesh* beats the hell out of a firefight any day."

---

* *Jirga*—assembly of Pashtun or Baluch tribal leaders that make decisions by consensus, resolve disputes and avert bloodshed whenever possible.

Before Jamshid can speak, Bashir's voice echoes across the plaza. "*Salamat basheyd. Shuneedum ki yek mardeh bozorg eenja zendagi mikonad. Aya mehtaneym hamraysh bisheeneym o gup bezaneym?*"

A slow roll of laughter answers him.

Although Eddy understands a bit of Dari, he can't make out Bashir's formal request. He cocks his head toward Jamshid. "What the hell did he say after the 'Peace be with you' part?"

"He says he has heard that great masters teach here and asks to speak with them."

"Least we know they copy," Eddy mutters, thumbing his pistol grip and doing the math: 24 bad guys on high ground with cover and AKRs packing 30-round mags. Range: about sixty feet, civilians in the open, the only cover a twenty-yard sprint. 15 rounds in his P226 —make that 14 after taking out the Green Parrot—and another twenty in his machine pistol, assuming he can get to it; 120 rounds total in the Tajiks' HKs; they would do some damage but probably not enough. He calculates that it would be over in less than ten seconds, maybe smoke half-a-dozen of the Kyrgyz before everyone on the plaza takes a hit.

Probability for survival: lousy.

Eddy detects motion behind the portico. A bald, red-bearded man in a long, patchwork robe pushes through the wooden doors and strides briskly onto the plaza, his hands raised in a gesture of peace. He calls to the gunmen with a commanding voice, probably in the Kyrgyzcha dialect, then bellies up to Bashir. Red Beard's green eyes soften and he switches to Dari.

"*Eenja mahfooz asteyn. Kaseh hamraytan ghuraz nudara* [You have sanctuary here. You will not be harmed]."

Jamshid translates and Eddy signals his crew to stand down. The gunmen on the walls melt back into the shadows, more like a well-trained platoon than a rag-tag bunch of bandits, Eddy notes. He calls to Bashir, "Tell Red we're much obliged for the hospitality. Ask him if we can bed down here by the solar panels for the night."

Red Beard ignores Eddy's request. Instead, he takes Bashir by the arm and glides toward the columned portico, his dramatic robe fluttering as the little rug dealer scurries to keep up. Eddy decides he will have to reassess Bashir's value to this FUBAR op and hopes to hell he can rely on civilian diplomacy.

But what choice does he have? Sonya is obviously in over her head and everyone else is flying blind. This is when unpredictable shit happens, and Eddy dislikes unpredictable shit even more than fat-ass four-stars and arrogant Company station chiefs.

....

THE SILHOUETTED GUNMEN MELT back into the rocks above as Father Callan squats on the patio beside Sonya, urging her to drink more water. Her flushed, sunburned face reminds him more of a petulant young runaway than the golden-haired seductress who approached him at a boathouse ripper eight years ago. She seems out of her element here, more vulnerable than ever. He wants to protect her, wrap her in his arms and assure her that everything will be okay. But, considering what they have just seen, Danny is not so sure that everything *will*.

"Shit!" Sonya grimaces, shifts her body in discomfort and hugs her knees.

"What's wrong Sonny?"

"Menstrual cramps." She props the dark glasses on her forehead and squints up at him with a weak smile. "Just an inconvenient fact of life for us girls."

Danny nods awkwardly.

Out of the corner of his eye, he sees Bashir following the red-bearded man through the wooden doors into the mountain fortress. He stands and slowly sweeps his eyes across the monumental plaza, assessing its extraordinary provenance.

When the Da Yuezhi were forced out of Western China into Bactria, they settled along the banks of the Oxus River before invading Gandhara, what is now northwestern Pakistan. Their *kushan*, literally a tribal "confederation," usurped the Scythians and Parthians who had migrated into Gandhara a century earlier. According to the Rabatak inscription found in 1993—King Kanishka's proclamation about the extent of his realm—Kushan conquests in the 2nd century reached as far south as India's Gangetic Plain and northeast to Turfan, the ancient Da Yuezhi homeland in what is now Xinjiang. So, the Wakhan River valley, carved between the Hindu Kush and Pamir Mountains, was Kanishka's gateway to Chinese Turkistan, and it became known as the "Buddhist Silk Road."

Danny speculates that the remote fortress was probably one of Kanishka's reconnaissance posts, but those Greek tiles beneath his feet lead him to the conclusion that it predated the Kushans' arrival.

It was common practice for conquerors to build new fortifications on the foundations of their vanquished predecessors. The Buddhist effigies carved around the plaza appear to be from Kanishka's era, bodhisattvas, archetypal beings dedicated to freeing the world from suffering, fashioned in classical Hellenistic-Gandharan style. But the surrounding complex looks to have been built much earlier. Perhaps it had been a temple dedicated to a deity revered by the Greco-Bactrian kings—Heracles, judging by the lions atop the columns. Or maybe it had been a Zoroastrian fire temple, similar to the one Danny saw at Surkh Kotal near Baghlan, carved into a mountain-side. Whatever its age and origin, the construction was apparently solid enough to have survived two millennia of earthquakes that flattened most other masonry structures in the region centuries ago.

Eddy approaches with his usual swagger, props his Oakleys on top of his Yankees cap, looks at Danny and cocks an eyebrow toward Sonya, who rests her head against her knees. "She okay?"

"Altitude," Danny reports. "Dehydration and…female stuff."

The big man rolls his eyes. "Explains the bitchy attitude."

Sonya lifts her face, glares up at him. "Fuck off, Eddy!"

"Well, that's showing some of the old team spirit." He chuckles and squats beside Sonya, rubs his enormous fingers over the patch of partially-cleaned tile in front of her.

"Who were those guys on the wall?" Danny asks.

"Dunno," Eddy lights a smoke and offers Sonya a drag. She takes it without looking at either of them. "Smugglers, probably. Bash went to pow-wow with whoever's in charge."

Eddy rises slowly to his feet, cigarette bobbing beneath his bushy Fu Manchu. He plants both hands on his hips above the low-slung pistol and sheathed knife, scanning the perimeter of the plaza from bodhisattvas to solar collectors. "You see all kinds of crazy shit in this country." He taps his fingers against the butt of his pistol and shakes his head in amazement.

"The hell *is* this place, Padre?"

....

"I AM MIZAN, THE COOK," the red-bearded man introduces himself to Bashir as he leads the way into a durbar hall excavated centuries ago from what appears to be a large natural cavern. Surahs are inscribed in gold and indigo on the ceiling vault, illuminated by a succession of flickering mosque lamps with globe shades of opalescent glass. Well-worn tribal rugs cover a portion of the mosaic floor and a fine Ersari is draped over a wooden dais at one end of the chamber. On the far wall, Bashir notes a carved niche painted with the Greek letter Ω. The *qiblah*, direction of prayer toward Mecca.

Observing the red bearded man's rustling *khirqah*, the traditional patchwork robe of the Tasawwuf, Bashir asks, *"Darvīsh?"*

Mizan nods.

"How has your order managed to stay hidden from the world?"

"We have a rather curious history," Mizan explains. "The *Roussi* learned that Ahmad Shah Massoud was transporting weapons from Peshawar through Chitral into the Panjshir, right under the noses of the Soviet army garrison at Zebak. So, they sent scouts into the Wakhan, looking for a route into Pakistan that would not alert the border patrols. When they found our lodge, they commandeered it for a staging base into Chitral and mined the main route up from the village to secure their position. From here, they sent their commandos out to assassinate the tribal elders who had aided Massoud in an attempt to cut off his supply line from Pakistan."

"That explains the land mines we encountered." Bashir replies with labored breath as he tries to keep up with the wiry mendicant skirting the periphery of the Durbar Hall.

"Our brothers became dependent on the *Roussi* for everything," Mizan continues. "Their helicopters flew in supplies when the weather was good, but in winter, we were cut off from the world with too many mouths to feed. So, they relocated forty of our Brothers to a refugee camp across the river. We received word they were eventually taken in by a Naqshbandi *tariqah* in Samarkand." His hand grasps the iron ring of a small wooden door. "They kept twelve of us here to serve as caretakers. And human shields, I suppose. As one of the kitchen boys, I quickly learned how to cook. *Roussi* stomachs were used to much worse," Mizan wryly admits.

"There were benefits, of course: the sun catchers* and generators. With spare parts and repairs, they have provided us with electricity for almost twenty-five years."

Mizan pauses at the door before knocking. "One day, the *Roussi* just left and never returned. We were curious, of course, until we learned what happened to their empire."

"The inevitable fate of *all* empires in Afghanistan," Bashir replies.

Mizan gently raps the iron ring, hears a voice inside and opens the door. They ease into a small chamber appointed with a rough-hewn trestle desk and a dais covered with pillows made from woven pile saddlebags. A shaft of waning light penetrates a narrow opening cut into the rock wall above an old iron stove. It falls across a slender, white bearded man wearing a gray shoulder-buttoned woolen shirt and black rolled *pakul* cap. He sits slightly hunched behind his desk and looks up from a mottled scroll, his watery blue eyes illuminated by the warm contrast of an oil lamp.

The old man addresses Bashir with a single word, *"Barakah."*

"Tashakor," Bashir replies. "May you also be blessed."

"Our Sarkâr." Mizan says with a deferential nod.

Bashir appraises the wizened old fellow just introduced as the lodge's "Taskmaster," thinking he hardly looks the part as his bony hand motions for Bashir to sit on the pillows opposite his desk.

"Forgive my temerity, sir," Bashir begins. "But for a monastic order, you have quite a lot of guns."

"As do you." The Sarkâr's eyes sparkle in the lamplight. "The men outside are traders from the Shahin clan—the Falconers. They hunt fox and lynx, transport the fur and…other commodities to and from Xinjiang and the Northwest Frontier."

---

* The first gallium arsenide **photovoltaic arrays** were created in the USSR in 1970.

"Smugglers?"

"The Kyrgyz have had a hard life in the Wakhan," the Sarkâr explains. "After the Saur Revolution, their Khan feared his herds in the Little Pamir would be taken for the Soviet state. He led 1,200 of his people over the Waghjir Pass to Gilgit. They moved freely back and forth from Pakistan until the Soviet army sealed Afghanistan's borders a year later. The refugees appealed to America for asylum and were rejected, so they were forced to sell their livestock to survive. Many re-settled in Anatolia—they were originally Turkic people, you know—but a few Kyrgyz families remained in Gilgit. Some resorted to smuggling. Our lodge has become their safe haven and in turn they provide us with certain necessities." The Sarkâr smiles knowingly through his white beard. "And protection from bandits. Better the devil you know, eh?"

Bashir can hear that Dari is not this man's native language but he cannot place the accent. "We are not bandits, sir," he assures.

"Then who led you through the minefield? Only one man knew the way."

"You mean the Uzbek trader, Abdul Hadud?"

"Yes!" The Sarkâr's eyes widen in recognition. "Abdul brought us food from Kret, barley and rice, occasionally a lamb or a goat. We have not seen him for months so there is little to eat. Just some *naan* and that Kyrgyz *chuchuk*—horsemeat. Have you spoken to Abdul?"

"Alas, the gentleman has gone to his eternal reward," Bashir laments. "But his herd of *khar* still know the safe route to Aubshaur. Assadullah is their new master. I'm sure you can negotiate supply shipments with him for the twelve of you."

"There are only eight of us left," the Sarkâr corrects. "Myself and the younger Brothers who have survived the harsh winters and still practice the work of our departed Elders."

"The Sarman-Darga?"

The Sarkâr hesitates. "Would you bring us some tea, Mizan?" When the red-bearded man scurries off, the Sarkâr levels his limpid eyes at Bashir. "It is my turn to ask questions. Who are you and why have you come here?"

Bashir sighs. "A complicated story." He tells the Sarkâr about Father Daniel and the Israeli woman who brought him an intriguing old manuscript, and how he came to be part of their expedition to locate the young woman's missing father. He admits to having developed an avuncular fondness for her, despite the gruff American mercenary and Panjshir gunmen she hired for protection.

Mizan returns with a copper tray, a brass samovar, and three porcelain cups. "It is not uncommon to hire protection in this wild country," The Sarkâr replies as Mizan pours *shur chai*. He pauses while lifting his cup and raises a single white eyebrow. "You say this woman is searching for her father?"

"That is what she says, but…"

"You doubt her honesty?"

"I cannot vouch for it," Bashir sips tea and replies thoughtfully. "There is much she keeps hidden away, even from herself, I suspect. But I believe Sonya has a good heart."

Over the rim of his cup, Bashir notices the Sarkâr's watery eyes widening in the flickering lamplight, as if he has just seen a ghost.

....

WHEN MIZAN AND THE VISITOR have left, the old man resumes reading the scroll on his desk. His weary eyes flutter in the lamplight and he sighs, remembering the days when Mizan would read the Persian texts to him, before he was compelled to learn a new alphabet in order to absorb the treasures stored deep in Aubshaur's caves.

At first, it surprised him that the younger Brothers had so little interest in the ancient texts. Some actually considered them vestiges of a dark age better forgotten. Most seemed quite content to lose themselves in the mesmerizing chant of *dhikru'llah*, remembrance of the names of their God, chased by the "dragon of boundless wellbeing" supplied by the Shahin. The Brothers had spent most of their lives at the *khanaqah* and knew little about the world except what they had learned from Russian commandos and Kyrgyz smugglers.

The Elders, however, had treasured the old texts. Educated men, they had come to the Path through a personal turn of destiny, thrust by circumstance into a harsh existence in the remotest of places. Consequently, they were rewarded with the rare gift of time to contemplate the wisdom of the Masters who had walked the razor-thin Path before them.

Because he too was no stranger to hazard— had literally fallen into their midst—the Elders accepted him into their arcane brotherhood. He suspected his violent history was one of the reasons the younger men looked up to him, despite his cultural differences and physical limitations, or perhaps *because* of them. In turn, he learned from them a new language and an alternative reality.

He had never considered himself a "spiritual" man, but in this harsh crucible he learned that spirituality was not at all what he had been taught in school. It had nothing to do with piety and prayer, or even renunciation. It was more about facing one's inner demons and surrendering to truth, however difficult that struggle might be. The Elders had called it the true *jihad*.

When, by default, he assumed the role of caretaker to Aubshaur's arch and allegorical manuscripts, the younger Brothers began chiding their new "Taskmaster." In truth, they considered the beautiful scrolls and bound volumes—most of which he could still not decipher—

superfluous to their spiritual practice, more distraction than meditation. But he took his moniker seriously, considered it a sacred trust
to absorb as much as he could of the Masters' wisdom and preserve
it for future generations, in the hope that humanity might someday
be able to understand its hidden secrets.

He traces a bony index finger down the edge of one of the fragile,
tallow-colored scrolls, slowly translating an inscribed verse that
causes his eyes to tear up in sadness. It is the poetry of someone
identified only as "Hujjat,"* clearly an exile like himself, a prisoner of
his own sense of failure and despair.

> *Never feel secure from the vicissitudes of Time,*
> *that serpent which devours even the elements;*
> *if one day you manage to escape her tricks,*
> *tomorrow she will be back with something worse.*

When his eyes finally tire in the lamplight, he carefully rolls the
manuscript, sets it aside and opens a long, sandalwood box inlaid
with mother of pearl. Assembling his ivory *vafoor*, he screws the
bulbous *hogheh* into its fitting at one end. From a tin-lined cylinder,
he extracts a waxy ball the color of coal tar and places it on a needle
at the opening of the ceramic bowl.

The *chandu* brought from Xinjiang by the Shahin is far superior
to the harsh *madhak* from Chitral.* A pervasive tradition in the remote mountains of Wakhan, the opium soothed both his physical
and psychic wounds. Even though Aubshaur's library had lifted him

---

* Hujjat [Proof]—the *nom-de plume* of Nasir-I Khusraw
† *Chandu*—refined, concentrated opium that is strained of plant matter, salts and resin, is vaporized
  in a traditional Persian opium pipe [*vafoor*], which consists of a hollow stem, metal saddle and
  ceramic bowl [*hogheh*]. *Madhak* is reprocessed opium with dross scraped from the pipe bowl,
  yielding higher levels of *sokhta*, a harsh residue of morphine alkaloid.

out of the despair of loneliness, *chandu* remained a daily ritual, more a necessity, if he were to be honest with himself.

He angles his bowl into the low flame of the oil lamp, draws the vapors deep into his lungs and a softening begins in his temples, then spreads like warm honey through his body. The edge of tension subsides and he sinks blissfully, as if in a cloud, entering into his own deep remembrance triggered, not by loudly chanting the many names of a God he has never known, but rather by whispering a single name he has not spoken aloud in twenty years.

"Sonya."

TUESDAY, 14 FEBRUARY 1989 • BAGRAM, AFGHANISTAN

AN HOUR BEFORE DAWN, Major Dmitry Mikhailovitch Antonov slipped into his winter flight jacket, pulled a leather helmet liner over his head, snapped a full 9-millimeter magazine into his Stechkin, and tucked it into a holster strapped to his right leg. He jogged quickly along the sandbag revetments and razor wire perimeter toward his commander's barrel-roof *khizhina* as cold stung his face and gravel crunched like stale biscuit rations beneath his boots.

Finally, he was going home. To Leningrad. To his family. To everything that had kept him sane for the past decade. He had not seen them in almost a year, had not spent more than a few weeks at home since his deployment in December of 1979. Two months after Sonya was born, 40,000 Soviet ground forces invaded Afghanistan and he had been assigned to the 56th Air Assault Brigade at Gardez. Ten years later, his once boyish face was cut with canyons as deep as the Hindu Kush, his blonde hair had gone gray as winter in Kandahar and his earnest blue eyes were hardened into glaciers by the horrors he had witnessed in Khost, Kunar and the Panjshir. But he had survived. Now a Major, a decorated "hero," he could retire with all the benefits and make it up to his family for those years of absence.

Antonov found Colonel Yuriy Pashkovsky in his office, pallid beneath racks of fluorescent tubes suspended from the vaulted ceiling. The Colonel had been up all night, shredding and burning documents. All facilities belonging to the Soviet 40th Army military operations were being transferred to the Democratic Republic of Afghanistan that morning and Pashkovsky was responsible for delivering Bagram's assets, but not its secrets. Anything that could prove damaging to the USSR, or embarrassing to Minister of Defense Yazov, had to be vetted and destroyed. A lit Sobranie hung from the sallow Ukrainian's lips as he fed sheaves of typed pages into a shredder. Its motor ground and stalled, forcing him to manually clear a jam of paper spaghetti.

"*Sukin syn* [Son of a bitch]!" The Colonel cursed the machine as an inch of ash fell from his cigarette to the cement floor.

Antonov clapped his gloved hands to coax blood back into his fingertips. "*Mozet poprobuesh s'est eto, Tovarich Polkovnik* [Maybe you should try eating it, Comrade Colonel]."

Pashkovsky kicked the shredder and barked at his young ad-jutant, barely visible behind a desk stacked with files awaiting the petrol drum braziers outside the hangar. "See what you can do with this piece of shit." The Colonel turned to Antonov and shook his head. "830 million rubles worth of equipment and facilities! Heard what the ruble is worth these days? One-*fiftieth* of a US dollar! Najibullah is inheriting a fucking junkyard."

"Ah, but a junkyard surrounded by landmines, Yuriy," the Major wryly noted.

Pashkovsky coughed up a laugh. "Maybe that Pathan bastard will live long enough to sell it all to back to Gorbachev."

Antonov impatiently checked his chronograph. "I'll leave politics to those with stronger stomachs. This morning, I'm looking forward to breakfast in Termez."

Pashkovsky looked as if he had just remembered something he would rather not have. "Come with me." He dumped a folder next to his recalcitrant shredder, grabbed up a torch and canvas flight bag then moved to the hangar walkway, briefing Antonov as they went.

Il-76 transports had airlifted 20,000 troops out of Bagram in the past six weeks. A 60-kilometer-long armored convoy, with the stalwart General Gromov bringing up the rear, had already rumbled through the Salang tunnel and would arrive in a few hours at the Termez "Friendship Bridge" spanning the Oxus River. Ahmad Shah Massoud's stronghold had been shelled by Najibullah's artillery under pressure from Marshal Yazov, and the "Lion of Panjshir" was now roaring for Russian heads. His *mutahareks*—hit-and-run squads of Tajik guerillas—were closing in on the bridge north of Gul Bahar, and no *Roussi*, sober or otherwise, wanted to be left at Bagram when they arrived. One last air transport was being fueled in preparation for evacuation.

In the cavernous hangar, maintenance crews loaded ordnance and ran pre-flight checks on the last three Mil Mi-24Ds, which all the pilots affectionately called *krokodil*. Their "teeth" consisted of a turret-mounted, four-barrel Gatling-type machine gun, four 80-millimeter rocket pods and four anti-tank missiles tucked beneath stub wings. Their titanium-armored bellies could disgorge eight commandos to chew up whatever remained. The Mi-24s had been Frontal Aviation's most effective weapon, virtually invincible until the Americans armed their proxy "holy warriors" with Redeye and

Stinger missiles. Since then, 29 gunships had gone down,* the last only 12 days ago. Both crewmen were killed. That disquieting thought loomed large in Antonov's mind as the Colonel handed him the canvas bag containing his manifest and flight plan.

"You're not going to Termez. I need you to fly some sensitive cargo to Chirchik on your way home."

Antonov stopped in mid-stride. He scanned the manifest and shook his head. "There is no mention of any cargo here." He leveled skeptical eyes at his comrade. "What's going on, Yuriy?"

Pashkovsky avoided the Major's gaze. "The *döshman* are watching Gromov's column push north, waiting like locusts to attack Kabul. So, you will give the Panjshir a wide berth, fly east and cross the Alingar watershed. You'll have eight Spetsnaz aboard and an SU-24 escort. The weather report looks—"

Antonov slapped his route map hard against a tool rack to get the Colonel's full attention. "What the hell does 'sensitive cargo' *mean*, Yuriy? I have a right to know who and what is on my ship."

Pashkovsky squinted through the smoke of his cigarette and urgently grabbed Antonov's arm. "You're the only one I can trust with this mission, Dmitry Mikailovitch." He crushed the cigarette butt beneath his boot and walked quickly through the sodium-lit hangar to a canvas-covered UAZ-469 four-by-four tucked behind the camo fuselage of his gunship.

Eight men in winter combat gear and light blue berets stood at the ready. Although the Captain and his men wore standard VDV[†] Airborne patches on their uniforms as cover, their imperious bearing

---

* The FIM-43 "Redeye" and FIM-92 "Stinger" are shoulder-fired surface-to-air missiles. The CIA supplied at least 500 of these "man-portable air-defense systems" [MANPADS] to Islamist *mujahiddin* in Afghanistan through the Pakistani Inter-Services Intelligence [ISI]. Russian sources report that 29 helicopter gunships were shot down by these weapons.

† **VDV** [*Vozdushno-Desantnye Vojska*]—Soviet Army Airborne Forces

and scoped, short-barreled AK-74s told Antonov who they really were: "Alfa," the elite KGB Spetsnaz unit known for their brutal efficiency. Leading the assault on Tajbeg Palace, they had assassinated President Amin and launched the Soviet Union into this swamp of irresolvable tribal warfare. A bloody decade later, 15,000 men had died on foreign soil. Everyone knew it had been for nothing but kept up the honorable pretense.

The Spetsnaz Captain executed a crisp, tight-lipped salute as Colonel Pashkovsky led Antonov to the UAZ's tailgate. Paskovsky pulled a nylon lanyard attached to a faceted cylindrical key from his coat pocket, threw back the camouflaged tarp covering the truck's rear cargo bed and revealed a dozen olive drab Bakelite cases, each one-meter-long and stenciled with black type:

ХРУПКИЙ: МЕТЕООБОРУДОВАНИЕМ

"Your cargo, Major."

"'Meteorological equipment'?" Antonov stared incredulously at his commanding officer. "Is this a joke?"

The Colonel slipped his key into the lock of the case nearest the gate and turned it until he heard the six latches softly disengage. Antonov watched as Pashkovsky turned the lock 45 degrees to the left, pulled it out a click and then returned it to its original position. He flipped the latches up with his thumb and recited his obviously rehearsed speech just loud enough for the Spetsnaz Captain to hear.

"By order of the Commander of the Soviet Limited Contingent of Forces in Afghanistan, this equipment is to be immediately transported to Chirchik-Andizhan Air Base. Marshal Yazov has charged me to assign our best pilot to this task." Pashkovsky's face tightened as he leaned into his masquerade. "Can the Motherland count on you, Comrade Major?" He paused for dramatic emphasis, "Can *I*?"

Antonov swallowed the bad taste in his mouth. "You always have, Comrade Colonel."

Pashkovsky stared at him for a moment, almost apologetic, then lifted the lid slightly and snapped on his torch. Antonov peered into the case where a bullet-nosed black cylinder, less than a meter long and about 15 centimeters in diameter, lay cradled in high-density polystyrene foam. The warhead was proudly stenciled with a single red star to authenticate ownership.

Antonov felt blood rush to his face and a cold sweat prickle his forehead.

The Spetsnaz Captain impatiently checked his watch and moved toward them. The Colonel stiffened, quickly closed the case, replaced the latches and handed the key to him with a perfunctory salute.

Pashkovsky then gripped Antonov's arm and took him aside, making small talk about meeting in Tashkent in a few days for celebratory rounds of Staraya Sloboda. When the Spetsnaz Captain had moved out of earshot, the Major finally spoke in a low voice.

"Yuriy, please tell me these are not what I think they are."

The Colonel squeezed his eyes shut for a moment, as if pleading for his old comrade to comprehend the gravity of their situation and the consequences of non-compliance. He finally replied, "Just get them to a safe place, Dmitry Mikhailovitch. For God's sake!"

....

LIKE SO MANY AMBITIOUS, competitive women that Cyrus has known, Courtney Kincaid is high-maintenance in every way. She takes an inordinate amount of coaxing before she reaches climax and Cyrus feels his jaw muscles beginning to ache with the effort. Fortunately, his *deus ex machina* issues a buzzing reprieve.

"*Ahh, comme c'est ennuyeux* [How annoying]!" Courtney moans, her cream caramel thighs clamped tight against his ears. Realizing what she is hearing, Courtney springs to attention. "Your sat phone!"

"Damn!" Cyrus tries to sound convincingly annoyed. "Suppose I'd better check." He slides off Courtney's 800-thread-count organic cotton sheets and searches around for his satellite phone in the dim candlelight of the bedroom. He finds it on the Art Deco vanity repurposed as Courtney's workstation. The voice he hears restores a grin to his weary mouth.

"Danny Boy, is that you?"

"You must have heard the pipes a'callin.'" Father Callan sounds in unusually good spirits.

He glances back at Courtney stretched across her queen bed. "From glen to glen, good buddy! We've got a great connection."

"We *should*," Danny replies, "considering where I'm standing."

In the circular mirror, Cyrus watches Courtney arise and slink up behind him, wrap her arms around his waist and press her lean body into the curve of his back. "Is that our priest?" she whispers.

"Did I catch you at a bad time?" Danny asks.

"Not at all," Cyrus tells him as Courtney's hand reaches playfully between his legs. "Just...*ahh*, entertaining a colleague."

"I'll bet," Danny laughs. "Cyrus, you will not believe what I'm looking at."

Cyrus crosses his legs as Courtney slips away to her padded vanity bench, flips open her laptop and launches an application that will track the satellite signal. "Where are you?"

"About 13,000 feet up in the mountains of Afghanistan. I'm standing on a Greco-Bactrian, key pattern-tiled patio surrounded by eight Kushan bodhisattvas carved into solid schist walls. Not on the scale of Bamiyan, mind you, but fully intact. These things are freaking beautiful, Cyrus!"

He whistles appreciatively, plants his butt on the silky duvet at the foot of Courtney's bed, appraising her yoga-toned silhouette, back-lit against the circular mirror of her vanity by the screen of her IBM laptop as it displays moving coordinates on a grid map of Central Asia.

"And I thought *I* had an awesome view."

Courtney rolls her right hand in a clockwise motion to indicate she needs more time to get a fix on the satellite phone's coordinates.

"Tell me everything," Cyrus urges.

"I've never seen anything like this, Cyrus," Danny says. "Appears to be a fortress of some sort, built into a natural cave complex and re-purposed as a monastery with some very unusual features."

"Such as?"

"Well for starters, an array of antique Russian solar panels, LED lighting and a small army of guards armed to the teeth."

Cyrus furrows his brow, lowers his voice. "You're not being held for ransom, are you?"

"No," Danny assures him, "nothing like that. We're in capable hands. Sonny arranged a security escort in Istanbul. Former Special Forces guy. As much as it pains me to admit it, Cyrus, you were right about her. She works for Israeli Intelligence."

Cyrus stifles a laugh. "Really? Tell me more."

"Don't want to use up your SIM card."

"That's what it's for, Danny. Any sign of our manuscripts?"

"Not yet, but we only arrived last night. We'll explore the area today and I'll give you a shout after dinner or tomorrow morning."

Courtney flashes him a thumbs-up and Cyrus leans back on the disheveled bed. "Look, Danny, keep the phone turned on and check in regularly. I want you to keep me posted with any news whatsoever. And remember what I said. Watch your back. You hear me?"

"Loud and clear, Cyrus," Danny replies. "This is as close to heaven as I want to get for the time being."

"*Adiós*, Danny Boy."

The phone clicks off and Cyrus moves to the vanity, standing over Courtney's shoulder. His thumbs begin to knead the tendons of her long neck beneath the black bob he recently messed up. Her screen shows a sharp satellite image of mountainous terrain with a yellow border superimposed over a narrow panhandle that juts from the northeast corner of Afghanistan.

Ignoring his ministrations, she scans to the east, zooms in on a river valley, pushes tighter on a rocky ledge above a cluster of rough structures. Cyrus watches a series of coordinates resolve in a translucent box as Courtney grabs her mobile, speed-dials a number and speaks officiously. "Sir, they're in Wakhan Province...Yes, northeastern Hindu Kush. Stone's throw from the border of Pakistan."

SATURDAY, 25 JULY 2009 · AUBSHAUR, AFGHANISTAN

....

THE DREAM WAS UNSETTLING, one from which Sonya awakens feeling as if she has never slept. As her eyes begin to focus on the rip-stop nylon firmament above her, it becomes clear that what she thought she had been doing could not possibly have happened. Altitude, she suspects—and having to pee twice into a plastic bottle in the middle of a frigid night because of all the goddamn water Danny had forced her to drink on the trek. And then there was the wind, howling and battering her tent all night long like some demon with a hard-on. But none of that explains the dream, lingering like a poltergeist on her shoulder.

She is a little girl in Leningrad, and yet she knows far too much for her age. She knows her father is home on leave from that war no one wants to talk about, in the bedroom with her mother, making love. She wants to please him too, in her way, and so begins to prepare his favorite breakfast, slicing a loaf of dark rye and heating sausages in the skillet. She notices one of his T-shirts draped over a bentwood chair her mother brought from Minsk to make their city dwelling feel more like a country home. She stares at the white cotton as she pours milk from a pitcher, noting that it is exactly the same color as her father's shirt. Then she is holding the shirt in her hands, feeling its texture and smelling him in the soft, worn fabric. She hears her mother's voice from the bedroom. When she turns toward it, she finds herself standing in Maryna's closet, in Haifa. Her father's T-shirt is neatly folded on the top shelf. Her mother has saved it but her father's scent no longer lingers in the milk-white fabric.

Then she remembers with a shock that her mother is dead, her ashes scattered on Har Ha'Karmel. But her father's old T-shirt is still in that bedroom closet—*her* closet now—and she knows that its presence has somehow kept him alive.

Oh fuck! She has to pee again.

Morning frost paints the inner dome of the tent with a crystal-line gloss. Sonya unzips her goose down cocoon to discover that Rukhsana has already left the nest. She uses her pee bottle, wraps herself in a thick fleece jacket and jams her legs into utility trousers with gusseted cargo pockets. Peeling back the tent flap, she laces up her boots in the vestibule, rolls out into a brilliant blue morning and inhales a lungful of chilled, rarefied air.

Sunlight reflects off the array of solar collectors like a golden mirror as Assadullah feeds his burros and horses. Beyond the tents, Sonya discovers Eddy and his crew eating breakfast, accompanied by a faint soundtrack of chanting voices from within the temple enclo-sure. Across the plaza, Danny holds a mug of something steamy in one hand and talks into a satellite phone as he appraises one of the placid guardian effigies carved into the cliff face.

"Did you sleep well, *habibti?*" Bashir appears at her side with a strong cup of *shur chai.*

"Not sure I slept at all." She accepts the hot tea with a grateful hand over her heart. It eases her away from the disturbing dream. "The wind was so fierce."

"Yes," Bashir's eyes reflect the morning sun. "The *djinni* were howling in the darkness. But Angel Jibril quieted them by commanding the moon to rise." He points to the oblate lunar orb still visible above the western wall in deep morning blue. "Or you could say that warm air in the valley below drew cool air across the mountain ridge until the temperature equalized." Bashir offers a wry smile and shrugs. "Whichever story comforts you most."

Sonya savors a sip of the milky tea and returns Bashir's smile. "This morning, I think I prefer your angel."

Bashir motions toward the field kitchen Kourosh has set up beside the solar collectors, shielded by a low wall of white supply bags. "Get some breakfast. You will feel better." The little rug dealer pats her hand and wanders off toward the portico.

Kourosh stirs a pot on his two-burner propane camp stove with the concentration of a Cordon Bleu chef. The young Tajik with a wispy black beard looks up shyly at Sonya from beneath his *pakul*, offering a bowl of muesli thick with pistachios and dried apricots.

"*Tashakor*," she thanks Kourosh with a warm smile, noting both the Old Persian word's derivation from its Arabic root, *shukr*, and the pleasure she takes in learning a new language. At the threshold of thirty, Sonya finds it reassuring that she can always retreat into the world of academic linguistics if she loses her edge. Invincibility, she has painfully learned, is a fast-fading illusion of youth.

Eddy perches in his usual state of hyper-vigilance on a pile of olive drab duffels, a cup of something in one hand and a smoke in the other. Rukhsana sits behind him, her head loosely covered, keenly observing Eddy with a combination of apprehension and fascination. He ignores her because, Sonya knows, Eddy considers the girl just one more unanticipated burden. Danny joins the group and spoons Nescafé into his empty aluminum cup.

Eddy launches into a monologue without so much as a good-morning. "So, this cute, two-hump Bactrian camel is sitting at a bar next to a big ol' Indian elephant, having a couple of cocktails, you know, shooting the shit, hitting it off. 'Something I've been meaning to ask you all night,' the elephant finally says. Camel sips her Cosmo, "Yeah? What's that?" 'Well, no offense,' elephant tells her, "I've just been wondering how you got your boobs all twisted around onto your back like that?' Camel shoots him one of those looks, rolls her eyes like chicks do. 'That's a helluva question coming from a dude with a dick growing out of his face.'"

Sonya sighs wearily and parks herself on a sack of rice, stirs her muesli without looking up at him. "If you are trying to cheer me up, Eddy, it's *so* not working."

"Oh, come on! *That* was funny. Wasn't it, Padre?"

"Guess I've heard worse," Danny anoints his instant coffee with hot water from a dented thermos. "Dartmouth frat thing?"

"You guys are fucking hopeless." Eddy shakes his head in frustration and flicks his spent cigarette across the patio. "Well, the clock's ticking, boys and girls. What's our agenda?"

"Bashir's gotten permission from the headman to show us around the monastery," Danny says. "You feeling up to it, Sonny?"

The muesli and strong tea have revived her spirits. "Good to go."

Jamshid loads a clip into his side arm and squats beside Eddy. "*Chirik* are praying now inside. Maybe later they will be not so quiet."

Eddy nods. "Secure the perimeter. I'll recce with them." Catching Sonya's frown, he adds, "My job is to watch your six, lady. Even if you have *no* fucking sense of humor."

Unzipping one of the olive drab duffels, Jamshid distributes Kevlar vests and a dozen sacks of ammo. Hefting a camo-painted assault rifle with an Advanced Combat Optical Gunsight, baffled suppressor, folding butt-stock and bi-pod, he presents it to Eddy with a broad grin. "Gift from ANSF."

"Where would this fucking country be without American aid?" Eddy laughs and squeezes his thick index finger into the rifle's trigger guard, then lifts his shades to squint through the scope. "Sweet! Come in handy if we need to smoke a sentry."

He presents the weapon for Sonya's inspection. "Ever seen one of *these* bad boys in your neighborhood?"

Sonya lifts the lightweight weapon from Eddy's outstretched hand, checks its safety and breech, "Mark 12 Special Purpose Rifle. Modified M16 developed for SOCOM,* as I recall. Chambers the standard 5.56-by-45-millimeter NATO rounds."

"On the money." Eddy seems impressed as he tosses her a gunmetal STANAG 30 magazine.†

Sonya swings the long barrel skyward, snaps the curved magazine into its port and sights through the scope. "Trijicon 4-by-32." She thumbs the elevation knob, checks its settings. "Night vision, tritium illumination, bullet drop compensation, no manual adjustment…and no battery to fail in the field." She cocks her head toward Eddy and smiles obliquely. "With this thing, I could take *you* out at 500 meters in the middle of the night."

Sonya tosses the sniper's rifle casually back to Jamshid and sips her tea as every man on the plaza stares at her in tacit astonishment. "Boys do love their toys," she says.

"Ever think about teaching a post-doctoral course for the NRA, Sonny?" Danny's boyish grin takes her back to their summer together in Cambridge. His blue eyes sparkle with the promise of adventure,

---

* **SOCOM**—United States Special Operations Command
† **STANAG**—NATO Draft Standardization Agreement 4179 allowed military services of member nations to easily share ordnance.

as if the world were about to display its myriad possibilities to them, as if there were no limit to how exciting and beautiful life might suddenly become. She feels an electricity surging through her unlike anything she has experienced in all the intervening years.

Danny nods in the direction of a muffled, mesmerizing chant bleeding through the temple's massive sandalwood doors. "Well, shall we explore what's left of Shambhala?"

....

AS HIS EYES ACCLIMATE to flickering lamplight within the durbar hall, Father Callan's excitement cools to apprehension. The Kyrgyz smugglers who had surrounded them on the plaza last evening are now clustered on a broad carpet behind seven robed initiates wearing pointed hennins emerging from their turbans. The man with the red beard taps a goblet shaped *tompak* as he leads the devotional chant. The others repeat it louder and louder, swaying side to side in unison as if they are performing some magical incantation that will build to an inevitable prestige. Danny recognizes one of the names of God.

"Al-Llâh, Hu! Al-Llâh, Hu! Al-Llâh, Hu! Al-Llâh, Hu!..."

"*Dhikr*," Bashir whispers, keeping to the shadows as they skirt the ecstatic assembly. "The chant of remembrance." He leads the group into a narrow tunnel lit by a single string of LEDs.

Sonya reaches for Danny's hand in the dim light and he feels a current of warmth replacing his chill. He and Eddy have to hunch down to avoid hitting their heads on the low, arching ceiling as they move into the tunnel. At the end of the string of lights, a short flight of rough-hewn steps ascends on their left into a grotto.

"Almost forgot how much I hate caves." Eddy says. He flashes a fist-sized tactical light into the stepped opening. "Looks like some kind of shrine."

Danny steps up into the grotto and runs his hand over an altar covered with bone-dry sheep pelts. Eddy's hi-beam illuminates the formidable skull of a Marco Polo ram mounted on the wall above, its spiraling rack flanked on either side by the skulls of Pamir Ibex, their scimitar horns festooned with a tattered array of red and magenta flags that are woven into a glittering bandolier of brass machine gun cartridges draping beneath the skulls. On the altar, a carved stone figure, about a foot tall, spreads angelic wings over a battered white helmet with a faded red star emblazoned above the sun visor and an automatic pistol holstered in scuffed black leather.

Danny studies the winged figure with a bird's head and human body. It appears to be Garuda, legendary flying mount and protector of the Brahmanic Lord Vishnu. He watches in silence as Sonya approaches the altar and inspects the odd collection of artifacts. Her fingers glide slowly over the surface of the pilot's helmet, leaving parallel trails in the fine silica dust that covers its hard shell.

"The blue-eyed warrior who fell from heaven." There is a bitter sadness in Sonya's voice. "Hell of a grave marker."

Behind her, Bashir says softly, "Not a grave, *habibti*. In these mountains, you will find *ziyárat*, shrines of visitation, on a trail or at the opening to a valley, where pilgrims are invited to pause and contemplate their quest. The purpose is remembrance of one's true nature and the impermanence of everything but Al-Llâh."

He gently touches Sonya's shoulder. "There is something else you should see."

Bashir descends into the passage and feels his way along the dark wall. "The Sarkâr, headman of this lodge, gave me permission to show you." His fingers find what he is looking for and suddenly strings of tiny LEDs cast a cold blue light over the long, low ceiling of a large cave to the right of the little grotto.

Bashir gestures with a broad smile. "The treasure of Aubshaur."

Danny is first to descend into the cavern. He feels a dramatic drop in air temperature as his flashlight slowly scans left to right, illuminating five rows of horizontal niches, each about five feet wide by 18 inches high, like library shelves carved into the bare rock on either side of the cave, and repeating as far as his beam can reach. Every niche is packed with rolled vellum scrolls and leather wrapped bundles.

A whistle slips involuntarily through his chapped lips, exploding into a jet of condensation that dissipates in the chilly blue air. Danny shakes his head slowly and hears himself mutter in euphoric disbelief, "Uncork the Dom Perignon, Cyrus."

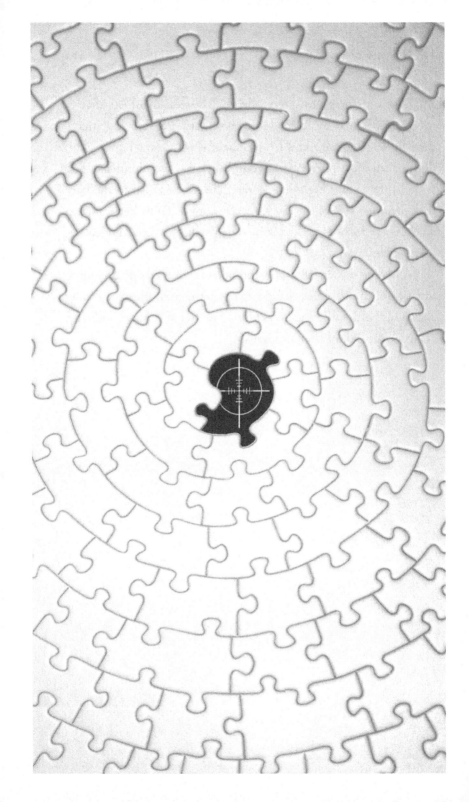

INTERCEPT

....

"It is more likely than not that al-Qaeda, or one of its affiliates, will detonate a nuclear weapon in a US city within the next five to ten years."

— Robert Gallucci, Dean of Georgetown University School of Foreign Service, *Averting Catastrophe: Why the Nuclear Non-proliferation Treaty is Losing its Deterrence and How to Restore it.* May 22, 2007.

VIKTOR KABAN AWAKENS with a splitting headache beside the waifish Ukrainian girl he vaguely remembers sodomizing last night. He cannot remember if she had been a good fuck but, admiring the curve of her white ass, Viktor gives her the benefit of the doubt and slaps the pale flesh with the flat of his hand, leaving a rosy welt. The girl jolts upright as fury ignites her blue eyes beneath a dark smear of mascara; she looks like a child who has gotten into her mother's make-up drawer. When she focuses on him, her expression softens into confusion, then fear, which *really* turns him on.

Viktor hazily recalls how playful and seductive this girl had been at the bar before he brought her to his penthouse suite, the one spot in his opulent Tulip Club not under constant video observation because Viktor hated the idea of anyone watching *him* with his pants down. Examining the girl's smudged face, he can see that he did not slap her around very much, even though he knows the girls always like it a little bit rough.

"*Jak tebe zvaty* [What's your name]?" he rasps, his throat rough from cocaine and vodka.

"*Iryna*," the girl replies. She looks as hung over as he feels.

"How long have you been working here?"

"Almost three weeks."

"You know who I am?"

"Everyone knows who you are."

Viktor emits a low rumble in his chest that vaguely approximates laughter. "That is good." Appraising this naked, disheveled whore, her small breasts covered in goosebumps and dried semen, he wraps his hand around her neck and pulls her matted towhead slowly down toward his growing erection.

"You want some breakfast, girl?"

She looks as if she will gag as he draws back the sheet and that turns him on even more. But his ringing mobile breaks the spell.

No caller ID, but then most of his clients use burner phones.

"You were right about the Russian," Kyrylo tells him.

Viktor motions curtly for Iryna to leave the room. She quickly rolls out of bed without a word and closes the door to the bathroom behind her. "Continue," he says.

"Zharkov says he has buyers in Grozny, some oligarchs who want leverage against Kadyrov. He's brokering the deal behind the scene but wants the spotlight on you. He offered Marko and me a cut of the proceeds if we work with his people and leave you hanging."

"Fuck!" Blood rushes into Viktor's pounding head, exacerbating his pain. He glances down to his hairy belly and below, to where his erstwhile ardor has shriveled into a pink nub. He rubs his face and sighs. "This is Payload's doing."

"Zharkov is SVR," Kyrylo reminds his boss. "Maybe Payload *thinks* he is working for them…or maybe all of us are being lied to."

Viktor grinds his teeth and punches the pillow between his legs. "Payload is too smart to be tricked by this Russian *putz*...which means he must be in on Zharkov's deal." He stares straight ahead in thought, tapping his knee nervously.

"All right, you and Marko will play along. Let SVR graciously provide our equipment and transportation. If you find the cache, deal with Zharkov's men, then move the weapons to our safe drop."

"Understood."

"And Kyrylo, take care of Payload and that Mossad cunt... *C'vysshaya mera nakazaniya* [With the highest level of punishment]." Viktor uses the old KGB euphemism for execution, which brings a sardonic smile to his face.

"With pleasure," Kyrylo replies.

SATURDAY, 25 JULY 2009 · AUBSHAUR, AFGHANISTAN

....

EDDY SCANS THE ROCKY RIDGE that drops precipitously into the Wakhan Corridor more than 3,000 feet below. Even through shaded binoculars, he has to squint into the harsh mid-day sunlight. On the opposite bank of the roiling gray river that bisects the valley, a wall of ochre earth sculpted into undulating flutes by rain and run-off shimmers in mid-day heat beneath white-capped granite peaks of the Big Pamir. Mud-brick structures squat precariously on the alluvial fan, threatened by the unstable earth. Since the wind has died down, the air is warm and still.

Cradling their carbines, Jamshid, Chir and Yusuf keep watch as a solitary lammergeier drifts on gentle thermal updrafts, inscrutably observing their presence. Eddy unbuttons a trouser cargo pocket and extracts his Thuraya phone. He switches to satellite mode and presses a preprogrammed number.

Viktor Kaban answers. "Good to hear from you, Eddy. You have found the cache?"

"Oh yeah," he replies, deadpan. "If you're interested in old scrolls, we've found a whole frigging cave full of them."

"What are you talking about?"

Eddy idly kicks a chunk of granite along the ridge. "I thought your meeting planner was pissing on my boots when she said she was looking for ancient manuscripts. But fuck me, Vik, that is exactly what we found here."

There is an edge to Kaban's voice. "Are you joking, Eddy?"

"No joke, Vik. We're camped out at some kind of monastery in the Hindu Kush—old Buddha statues, chanting dudes in funny robes, caves cut into the mountain. Oh yeah, and there's a small army of AKR-packing banditos guarding the fucking library. But so far, not a trace of what *we're* looking for. Frankly, I'm bummed. I was already planning my retirement in Belize."

"Then what shall I tell your Russian associate, Mister Zharkov?"

Eddy paces the rocky promontory, considering their options. He stops in his tracks and smiles. "No harm, no foul."

"What?"

"Way I see it, Vik, you can walk away from this. You got nothing the Russians would consider their property and Uncle Sam has no beef with you, long as you keep paying taxes. World's nowhere close to being at peace, so you're still in business, wild man."

There is a long pause and finally Kaban says, "I suppose that is some small consolation, Eddy. But what about Mossad?"

"You'll probably have to throw them a bone."

"A bone?"

"Yeah. A name...maybe a buyer in Damascus. Just somebody they'll want to put out of business even more than you."

"That would be extremely dangerous for me, Eddy."

"How's your mom doing in Brooklyn, Vik?"

There is a long silence. Finally, Kaban replies, "Yes, I take your meaning, Eddy. Perhaps we would both be safer under surveillance in Tel Aviv than hiding in Istanbul."

"For now, I'd hang tight. You think of a name we can drop and I'll try to broker a deal in Tel Aviv. Our meeting planner could turn out to be an asset instead of just a pain in my ass."

"I'll give it some thought," Kaban concedes. "But you will keep me informed if the situation changes, yes? If you find anything...more interesting at this monastery?"

"Sure, Vik. I'm your man."

"I knew I could count on you, Eddy."

....

IT IS AFTER NOON when Sonya and Danny emerge from the cold underground library onto the warm plaza, their teeth still chattering. Spotting them, Kourosh pours hot water into plastic basins for each of them to bathe.

In her tent, Sonya strips off thermal layers and squats modestly in her vestibule, washes her hair and sponges herself off. She dresses in clean panties and a sports bra, pulls a tank top over her head and applies sunscreen to her arms and face. Refreshed, she stretches out on a flat rock beside Danny, his bare feet drying in the warm air.

"It can't be more than fifty degrees in that cavern, Sonny. Low humidity, dark storage. No wonder those scrolls are so well preserved."

"And I thought you were joking about Shambhala," Sonya says.

"Only half-joking."

"You think this mythical Aryan kingdom actually existed?"

"All mythology has some basis in truth." Danny rubs circulation back into his white toes. "In the Vedic, Avestan and Bön traditions, this 'mythical' Aryan homeland is described as a utopian paradise situated in a fertile valley, surrounded by alpine meadows and encircled by high mountains. In the *Kalachakra*, its called Shambhala."

Sonya laughs. "Guess that explains why the Nazis went looking for it in Tibet."

"And they made a big miscalculation." Danny excitedly taps the rock beneath him. "It's here, Sonny—right *here*! This place matches the description of a Bronze Age civilization situated directly on the trade routes between China and India, where Tantric and Buddhist practices merged with the Mithraic tradition of Persia."

Danny's eyes are charged with excitement. "Look at that valley below us, tucked between two of the highest mountain ranges on Earth and running right into a third. A dozen civilizations passed through here and left their footprints."

"At the point of a spear, Danny. Hell of a utopian paradigm."

"Maybe so," he concedes. "But we are sitting right on top of an extraordinary, possibly unique archaeological find that could substantiate these mythologies as actual history."

She laughs at his magical thinking. "Congratulations, Danny! You've found the Lost Horizon. And to think you owe it all to Cyrus."

"As much as I hate to admit it." Danny's grin reminds her of the way he looked after winning a boat race on the Charles. "In any case, it will take years to catalog and translate what's in that library. Maybe decades. Sonny, I saw manuscripts this morning that may be from Menander's reign, second century BCE. Some with seals showing an eight-spoke wheel and legends in both Greek and Kharosthi. No one has seen that stuff except on coinage."

Sonya glances over to where Rukhsana and Kourosh prepare lunch in the field kitchen while Eddy and the rest of the crew keep a vigilant watch on the high ground. "You think those boys with the Kalashnikovs are going to let you just walk out of here with sacks of old manuscripts strapped to Assadullah's little donkeys? March them all the way to Kabul, put them on a plane and drop them right into Cyrus' shoe-less living room?"

Danny laughs and shakes his head. "Bashir is trying to arrange an audience with the headman. I'll ask for permission to return next summer with a team and proper equipment, make digital scans and begin the process of cataloging the library."

"Don't be naive, Danny. Cyrus wants to sell off the whole lot to the highest bidder. His clients aren't interested in digital scans."

Danny frowns, hugs his knees petulantly. "So, I'll negotiate, ask for a few samples to take back as proof of discovery. If it serves the greater good…"

"*Whose* greater good? Do you think these dervishes give a damn about the private collections of rich, white Americans?"

"Of course not," he agrees. "But if we found this place, so will others. And the Taliban aren't interested in preservation. You *know* what they'll do if they find this place. I'm sure the Aga Khan Foundation would agree that these documents are in jeopardy and need to be protected."

Sonya lies back on the smooth, warm rock, cradles her head in her hands and closes her eyes. "Seems to me our brotherhood of the Bees here have done a pretty good job of protecting their treasures without any help from us. *Or the Aga Khan.*"

"So far," Danny concedes. "But for how long?"

"**THE SARKÂR REGRETS HE CANNOT JOIN US**," the red-bearded acolyte explains through Bashir. "He is feeling ill."

Beneath the mid-afternoon shade of Aubshaur's portico, Mizan pours *shur chai* from a goose-neck copper pot into four porcelain cups on a serving tray. Sonya, Danny and Bashir sit on pillows sewn from coarse saddle blankets. A red plastic cloth is spread before them for the brittle *naan* Mizan has brought from the kitchen. "I regret we have little to offer you," says the cook.

Danny and Bashir plead the case for cataloging and protecting the library while Sonya listens with some impatience to the Dari exchange, anxious to press their host for different information. But she knows the rules: Tea must be drunk before answers are served.

After the third cup is poured, she collars Bashir. "I'd like to know more about the shrine you showed us with the animal skulls. Ask him where the pilot's helmet came from?"

"The Shahin brought him to us." Mizan's eyes narrow above his bristling red beard. "All the *Roussi* commandos who had been living here left one day without a word. A few days later, the Kyrgyz smugglers arrived with a badly injured pilot after his helicopter crashed. Since we had no contact with the outside world, we did not realize the Soviet Army had pulled out of Afghanistan. This unfortunate pilot was undoubtedly retreating with his comrades."

The emotional impact of hearing the red-bearded man describe her father sets Sonya's teeth on edge. She suddenly notices she is squeezing Danny's hand in furious anticipation.

"Why would smugglers bring him *here* instead of just leaving him for dead?" Danny asks.

Bashir relays the question and Mizan smiles, "The Shahin thought the pilot was a devotee of the Aga Khan because of something they found clutched in his hand. Clearly, they assumed His Highness would reward their good deed with gold or jewels. They were astonished to learn that he has never visited our monastery and is almost certainly unaware of its existence. Since the Kyrgyz no longer had a country in which to take refuge, we came to a mutually beneficial agreement: Asylum in exchange for protection and supplies."

"What happened to the pilot?" Sonya asks urgently.

Mizan inclines his head dolefully, "He is no more."

Sonya narrows her eyes, takes a deep breath and continues, "Was anything salvaged from his aircraft? Any cargo?"

"Not much," Mizan replies warily. "Some ammunition belts, which the Shahin bartered. All but the one you saw decorating the *ziyárat*."

"Nothing else?"

He shrugs. "Only what I have said."

Sonya turns urgently toward Bashir. "The vellum page I showed you the day we met in Northampton must have come from the library here, wouldn't you agree?"

"It is certainly possible, but…"

Sonya continues to press. "Bashir, my father was brought here! He scratched a message on that vellum trying to tell his commanding officer that his cargo was 'safe,' and then somehow got it delivered to a border post."

Bashir looks puzzled. "So, what are you saying?"

She motions with a flick of her head toward Mizan. "I think this man is lying."

....

DANNY CHECKS HIS WATCH and calculates the 8.5-hour daylight time difference in Boston: 8:15 am. In an open area of the plaza, away from the tents and solar array, he makes a call on the satellite phone Cyrus gave him and waits twenty seconds for its owner to answer.

TOM JOYCE

"Little early for champagne, but better get a bottle on ice," Danny says, "We found the Mother Lode!"

There is hesitation and the rustle of fabric, as if Cyrus is hiding the phone from someone within earshot. "That's great news, Danny Boy." His voice is low and tense.

"Cyrus, I've never seen anything like this," Danny continues on a wave of exhilaration. "I'll bet it surpasses the Timbuktu collection.* Bashir and I have presented our case for preservation to a representative from the monastery, and I'm hoping to secure a few physical specimens to bring back for your investors. But here's the thing: we're going to need immediate resources to rescue this library before the Taliban, or some other band of fanatics, finds it and decides to make a bonfire. I've got a few ideas how we can facilitate—"

Cyrus cuts him short. "Danny, shut up and listen to me for a second. You're in serious danger there."

"What do you mean?"

Cyrus' voice drops to an ominous whisper. "I can't get into details right now. Suffice it to say that Sonya is a lightning rod and you are standing way too close for comfort. Do you understand?"

"No, Cyrus. I do *not* understand."

"Danny, I really shouldn't be telling you this…" There is more rustling, and it sounds as if Cyrus is moving as he speaks. "Look, when Sonya first approached me, I asked one of my associates, who happens to work at Spook Central in Langley, Virginia, to find out who Sonya really is. So, to make a long, convoluted story short, it turns out our girl is running a Mossad operation in Afghanistan."

"Yeah," Danny replies without concern. "She told me."

---

* **The Timbuktu Manuscripts Project** at the University of Oslo physically preserved manuscripts as old as the 13th century, digitized them, built an electronic catalogue and made them accessible for research before Islamist rebels destroyed much of the collection in 2013.

"Well, Tel Aviv apparently never cleared their plans with Washington and I'm afraid there will be hell to pay. My colleague is playing it very close to her vest and frankly, I do not trust her employer to give a second thought to your best interests. Or your *life*, for that matter. My advice is to get the hell out of there while you still can."

"Not until I've secured an agreement with the headman here, Cyrus. And I'm going to hold you to your promises when I get back."

"Look, Danny, I'm a man of my word. Just don't do anything foolish—like trying to be a hero."

Cyrus pauses, his voice dropping to a whisper, "And after this call, you'd better turn off that sat phone and pull the battery."

"Why?"

"Because it's broadcasting your location to the goddamn CIA."

SATURDAY, 25 JULY 2009 · BETHESDA, MARYLAND

....

"WE LOST THE PRIEST." Courtney Kincaid delivers the bad news over coffee at Starbucks on Wisconsin Avenue, a few blocks from the Bethesda Metro station.

In his white Izod shirt and khaki shorts, brown hair still hanging damp from the morning's tennis match, the Associate Deputy Director grimaces into his Venti Macchiato. His iPhone begins to vibrate and dance on their faux wood grain table, but to Courtney's surprise, her multi-tasking boss ignores it.

"How the fuck did *we* lose the fucking priest?"

"Well, either his battery died or he turned off the sat phone." Courtney is fairly certain it was the latter and fears it is because Cyrus spilled the beans to Father Callan. But she does not want to ruin her boss' weekend or malign her colleague's patriotism, as long as Cyrus might still be an asset to her ambitions.

The ADD silences his mobile and scrolls through text messages as he stirs granola into his yoghurt with a plastic spoon. "So, what's the *good* news, Court?"

"Payload dropped his drawers," she tells him with a conciliatory smile. "Made a Thuraya network call to Viktor Kaban in Istanbul, picked up by SIGINT at Mazar-i-Sharif."

"They get voice?"

"I had an MP3 of the conversation sent via JWICS."*

"Give me the Cliffs Notes."

"A Russian named Zharkov came up. And a possible deal with Mossad. But nothing about TNWs, just 'ancient manuscripts.' That's consistent with what we were able to pick up from Father Callan."

"'Ancient manuscripts,' huh?" The ADD frowns. "Could be code."

"Could be."

He tightens his mouth and furrows his brow. "I want eyes on this. Roger's the guy we need. He ran the Manson Family at CC-AfPak.† A fucking pit-bull. Meet him up on six this afternoon and give him the download." Her boss picks up his lonely iPhone. "I'd go with you, Court, but I've got this…ah, domestic sit. Priority One."

She arches a conspiratorial eyebrow at the covert implications. "Domestic? Isn't that—?"

"Girls have a swim meet in Chevy Chase. All-state semi-finals."

Courtney feigns sympathy for his suburban dilemma in her cheery patois. "*Laissez les bons temps rouler* [Let the good times roll]."

---

* JWICS—the Joint Worldwide Intelligence Communications System maintains the highest level of encrypted network security.

† **Manson Family**—moniker for the Bin Laden Station at the CIA Counterterrorism Center, Pakistan-Afghanistan Department [**CC-AfPak**] located in Tyson's Corner, Virginia

SATURDAY, 25 JULY • LANGLEY, VIRGINIA

....

WITHIN THE GLOBAL RESPONSE CENTER on the sixth floor of the CIA's New Headquarters Building, the green hills of northern Virginia are as invisible as the afternoon sun. Deep in the maze of glowing computer screens, Courtney finds "Roger," a thin, balding man with a wispy beard, sitting at his desk. Wearing tech conference swag—a red polo shirt sporting an Oracle logo—he remains fixated on his terminal as Courtney's delivers a detailed briefing. She wonders how this wonky data analyst, whose real name is undoubtedly *not* Roger, was once charged with directing the team curiously known as "The Manson Family," dedicated to tracking Osama bin Laden.

Roger seems completely uninterested in everything Courtney says. Until she mentions "small, portable, tactical nuclear weapons."

"'Misplaced,' you say?" His eyes narrow behind thick progressive lenses as Courtney imagines neurotransmitters firing off synaptic connections somewhere in his brain. "In Afghanistan?"

"Or lost," she qualifies. "When the Soviet Army fled."

Eyes bugging like a ferret in attack mode, Roger snaps his head in her direction. "Are we talking about the *'suitcase'* nukes? The ones Alexander Lebed warned us about before Putin had him iced?"

"Pos-s-sibly," Courtney suggests without commitment.

"Well fuck me!" His voice drills into her. "We knew the Ruskies had chemical weapons in Afghanistan. Suspected they had nukes, too. Tactical battlefield stuff, howitzer-fired, or small mobile rockets, like our old Davy Crockett system*—but we could never prove it. You don't just *misplace* shit like that!"

---

* **Davy Crockett** Tactical Nuclear Weapon System—a recoilless gun that fired the M-388 nuclear projectile. Deployed by US Forces in Europe and Korea during the Cold War, the weapon was inaccurate but lethal, delivering 600 rems at 1/4 mile from the blast site.

"You'd think," Courtney agrees.

"Which means they actually *were* lost. If they'd turned up in any of the Stans, you can bet AQ would have tried to get their hairy paws on them. OBL offered the Chechen Mafia thirty mil and two freaking tons of Kandahar Black Jack to boost a single nuke. Nobody would turn down an offer like that if they had the goods."

"You'd think not," Courtney concurs.

"And the Wakhan Corridor would be the perfect place to lose *anything*," Roger continues, nervous fingers tapping on his mouse. "Fuck all up there. Taliban don't even give a wet turd about it. No Pashtuns or poppy fields." Roger turns back to his screen. "Okay. We'll put eyes on the TZ and listen in on their chat."

"What have you got in the area?"

Roger scans his updates. "FOB Chapman shows a free MQ-9 parked at Jalalabad. We can get a Reaper over the Wakhan three times faster than a Predator. RPA teams at Creech will handle the drone once we're on target. Reach-back at D-sigs will monitor the feeds, intercept any comm, and we'll watch the whole ball game here in real-time video. Anything goes down, our Reaper will be packing the appropriate response."*

"Sweet Jesus!" Courtney gasps. "The *last* thing we want to do is detonate a nuclear weapon with a Hellfire."

Roger's moustache becomes a patronizing smile. "No worries. Even a direct hit wouldn't cause a nuke to go critical. Just spread a bunch of radioactive debris. Contaminate the soil—maybe the water supply. Those camel jockeys up there would never even notice."

"Guess that explains the Manson thing," Courtney mutters.

---

* **Forward Operating Base Chapman,** located two miles east of Khost, Afghanistan, is the counter-terrorism hub of CIA's Special Activities Division, providing support for remotely piloted aircraft [RPA], Predator and Reaper drones, in hunt and kill operations.
D-sigs—the US Air Force's Distributed Common Ground System at Langley Airfield is officially known as the AN/GSQ-272 Sentinel Weapon System.

SATURDAY, 25 JULY 2009 · INDIAN SPRINGS, NEVADA

....

FIRST LIEUTENANT SKYLAR "SKY KING" REXROTH wakes up in his Airstream on the outskirts of Las Vegas, showers and dresses in a pressed OD green flight suit. He laces up polished black boots, slips a pair of Bausch & Lomb aviators over his eyes and checks himself out in the mirror next to the grinning photo of Tom Cruise tucked into its frame.

"I feel the need for speed!" he says, preparing himself to unleash his Ninja 650 on that 35-mile stretch of Route 95.

The 17th Reconnaissance Squadron operates from an inner compound at Creech Air Force Base, which even visiting military VIPs are unable to access. The squad transitioned to its new client in 2004 when covert CIA drone strikes began in Pakistan. In the Ops Cell, mission coordinators from the 17th are kept segregated from all the others, and with an aircrew of 300, they can run six simultaneous missions every 24 hours.

At 14:30 hours, Sky checks in with Ops Desk. Staff Sergeant "Princess" Leah Adams has been scheduled as his sensor operator and that desert queen always puts a grin on his face. In the briefing theater, he pours himself a cup of java and drops into the chair beside Princess, a compact brunette with an unappealing green smoothie clutched in her petite hand.

"Phoebe's got worms," she tells him, checking a text message on her phone.

"I'm surprised *you* don't," Sky says, "drinking that slime mold."

"I had to call scrotum face, ask him to take her to the vet today."

"And that, darlin', is why the good Lord made ex-husbands." Sky feels the caffeine beginning to take effect. "So, what's the buzz?"

"Spinning up for a black ops strike," Princess confides. "But you didn't hear it from me."

A projector flashes constant, real-time updates on weather, target data and mission status of every Predator, Reaper and Global Hawk RPA in the skies over Afghanistan. "Red Baron" and "Duck Dodgers," slide in beside Sky for the briefing.

"Left a dozen bug splats at a *jirga* last night, bro," Red brags. "Hope you and Princess can find a wedding party to crash."

Princess rolls her eyes at Red's tired jokes and pumps her fist suggestively. "We all know you boys were getting carpal tunnel watching Lisa Ann gag on a donkey dong last night."

"Girl's got a mouth on her," Duck observes with a smirk.

"And it ain't never gonna touch *your* joystick, flyboy," Princess replies between slurps of green smoothie.

After their group briefing, the two flight teams are ordered to remain. An intelligence analyst enters and projects a series of thermographic satellite images of what appears to be a flat plaza excavated from a rocky mountain ridge. Sky can make out a corral of livestock, an array of antique solar panels and a tight cluster of dome tents. Specks with human heat signatures are noted.

"What do you think?" Sky muses. "AQ ski resort?"

"Check out those domes," Princess whispers with a furrowed brow. "Definitely mil spec. And I doubt those goat fuckers shop at the PX. I'm smelling bad guys, Sky."

The civilian spook confirms that there may be an unspecified high-value target in residence. "But whether or *not* we have positive ID, you will prepare to launch a signature strike," the analyst stresses. "Go-code will be at Langley's discretion. Everyone clear?"

"Roger that, Mike Foxtrot," Princess mutters, playfully elbowing Sky in the ribs.

SUNDAY, 26 JULY 2009 · AUBSHAUR, AFGHANISTAN

....

SOMEONE HAS BROKEN INTO HER HOME and robbed her. The thief could have taken her laptop, her mother's *dreidel* collection or her grandmother's jewelry. Instead, he went into her closet and took her most treasured possession: the white T-shirt that belonged to her father. In tears, she sinks into the gray Chenille chair in her mother's bedroom—*her* bedroom now—and tries to calm herself, consider her options. Call the police? Search every consignment shop in Haifa? Post an ad on Janglo? Before she can decide what to do, the bedroom door swings open and he walks in. As if nothing at all has happened. Wearing his old white T-shirt partially tucked into green twill military trousers, he looks unkempt, bewildered.

"Have you seen my shoes?" he asks. "I can't find my shoes."

Sonya jerks bolt upright in her tent, her sleeping bag damp with sweat, her gasp for breath so loud it wakes Rukhsana out of a sound slumber. The girl leans across the duffel between them to offer assistance, but Sonya brushes her off. "I'm okay…really. Cheyne-Stokes. Never mind. Go back to sleep. Ahh…*nagaram nabash* [don't worry]!"

Rukhsana's eyes close as she mutters an unintelligible response in Dari and relaxes back into her bag. Sonya's disturbing dream still looms vivid in the darkness even as her heavy breathing subsides.

Mizan's redacted story over tea flickers across the synapses of her memory. *The Shahin thought the pilot was a devotee of the Aga Khan because of something they found clutched in his hand.*

"Something in his hand?" Sonya whispers.

She glances over at the sleeping Afghan girl curled up beside her. What was it Rukhsana had told Bashir that evening after dinner at her father's place in Ishkashim?

One of the legends is about a particular Master at this lodge, a blue-eyed warrior who fell from heaven many years ago, bearing a silver lion —emblem of the Aga Khan...

"Master?"

Sonya pulls on a watch cap, fleece jacket and leather palm gloves before slipping out of her bag and into black thermal trousers. She tucks a slim, gunmetal torch into her pocket and laces up her boots in the vestibule, noticing that the moon has not yet crested the horizon.

It is just past midnight and the Milky Way is diamond dust strewn across indigo velvet. The frigid air tastes sharp on her tongue as she inhales deeply, shivers and crawls out of her tent.

Sonya considers waking Danny but decides against it. He would only ask a lot of questions for which she has no logical or rational answers. In truth, only disturbing dreams and vague intuitions guide her movements now.

Sonya skirts the solar array and dome tents, imagining the stone bodhisattvas are following her movements like Cocteau phantasms as she approaches the monastery. Climbing the portico steps, she lifts one of the iron rings, pulls on the heavy door and finds it unbolted. The dry wood creaks as she pries it wide enough to slip through.

Inside, lit by dim oil lamps hanging above the *qiblah* niche, the durbar hall is full of men sleeping on the carpet, awaiting the *fajr* prayer before sunrise, wrapped in their blankets and snoring fitfully. Sonya hugs the back wall, moves quickly through the shadows, passes a smaller wooden door and eventually reaches the passage descending into the library.

Snapping on her torch, Sonya makes her way down the narrow passage, feeling the temperature drop as she presses deeper into the mountain. On the left side of the tunnel near the library, she climbs the steps into the little grotto containing the pilot's shrine.

Sonya paints her narrowly focused torchlight across the bizarre juxtaposition of objects above the altar. In the tradition of her own people, the ram is seen as a sacrificial animal. Here, it is some sort of shamanic symbol. A protector or guardian. But the bandolier seems odd—so out of character. Draped beneath the spiraling horns, festively adorned with scraps of red, magenta and maroon cloth interweaving the brass cartridges, it looks more like a radical art installation, something her mother and peacenik friends would have fawned over for its "powerful anti-war message."

Something they found clutched in his hand. What is she missing?

Sonya approaches the altar and runs her hand over its sheepskin-draped surface. The pelts are coarse and desiccated. She reaches up toward the bandolier but hesitates when LED lights come on in the tunnel behind her. There are faint voices and a rhythmic squeaking of wheels. As the sound grows louder, she shuts off her torch and freezes in the shadow.

Two dark-eyed Kyrgyz men, one with black hair pulled into a topknot, the other with a shaven head beneath a fur cap, Russian Kalashnikovs in both their hands, accompany a white-bearded man in what looks like a hand-made aluminum wheelchair with knobby tires. Wearing a floppy black *pakul* and a rough woolen shawl draped around his shoulders, the older man sits very still beneath the bluish lights and stares straight ahead. Then, as if sensing her presence, he turns abruptly in Sonya's direction.

She inhales, steps slowly out of the alcove's darkness and startles the Shahin guards. The short barrels of their AKRs swing up in her direction. One barks an incomprehensible command, but the intent is quite clear. She holds up her hands to show she is unarmed.

The old man steadies his guards with a raised hand encased in a worn leather glove missing the finger sheaths. As Sonya slowly descends the steps, he wrestles the squeaking wheels of his chair around so he can face her, then looks up and appraises her silently for what seems an eternity before he addresses her.

In Russian.

"*U tebya glaza kak u mami* [You have your mother's eyes]."

Sonya bends down toward the old man's pallid face, deluged by conflicting emotions. She studies his bony features, the eyes that sparkle like a shallow Mediterranean cove in mid-day sunlight. The memories those eyes evoke cause her hands to tremble in a confusion of joy and anger. A single word escapes her throat, a harsh rhetorical question whispered by an abandoned child.

"*Pápa?*"

TUESDAY, 14 FEBRUARY 1989 · BAGRAM, AFGHANISTAN

....

MAJOR DMITRY ANTONOV watched in submissive dread as the Alfa Spetsnaz team loaded twelve hard cases labeled "meteorological equipment" into the belly of his gunship like worker bees feeding their queen. Eight commandos secured the cargo with thick bungee cords to the cabin floor and blanketed the cases in nylon webbing. The hatch doors were locked and the Spetsnaz belted in, back-to-back, on benches in the cramped cabin.

Taciturn Gennady Alyushin reported for duty with his manual case and climbed into his seat on the lower deck of the gunship's tandem cockpit. The Lieutenant's legs straddled a four-barrel Yak-B 12.7-millimeter machine gun slaved to an electro-optical sighting pod beneath the armored-glass canopy.

Stas Bektash, Antonov's flight mechanic, accompanied him on the pre-flight inspection. Bundled in winter coveralls and fur-lined *ushanka* hat, Stas walked the Major around the camo-painted fuselage checking for oil or fuel leaks, anything out of place. When they reached the cockpit step, he looked sadly up at Antonov. *"Rad shto vi nakonets vernetes' domoi* [Glad you are finally going home, sir]."

Antonov clapped his gloved hand on the Uzbek's broad shoulder beneath his ear flap. *"Mi zaderzhalis' zdes' slishkom dolgo, Stas* [We've all been here too long, Stas]. You're getting out soon?"

The Uzbek smiled stoically. "Once all these flying tanks are airborne, I'll be on the last transport. But I'd rather be going with you."

Antonov motioned toward his cargo bay with a facetious grin. "I'm already overloaded with these hitch-hiking bastards and their fucking 'meteorological equipment,' Stas. But your jump seat will be waiting for you in Tashkent, I promise you."

He took the Major's gloved hand and pressed a three-centimeter silver disk into his palm. "This doesn't weigh much." Engraved with calligraphy in the shape of a lion peering back over his haunches, the broach's pin had broken off long ago and its face was burnished by years of wear and handling. Antonov tried politely to decline the heirloom, but Stas was adamant.

"Please, sir! Take it for your daughter."

The Major reluctantly wrapped his fist around the silver broach, nodded with a tight smile and slipped it into a zippered pocket of his flight jacket. "I'm sure my little lioness will treasure this. Thank you, comrade…for everything."

Antonov climbed into the cockpit and took his seat above and behind Alyushin, sensing that he was leaving Stas to the approaching wolves. He stowed the feeling with his flight bag, clipped into the intercom above his right shoulder and buckled his seat harness.

Stas pulled himself up the fuselage footholds and peered into the Major's titanium-armored tub, condensation rising from beneath his grizzled moustache.

"Sir, keep a close eye on your indicators. Both your intermediate and tail gearboxes are overdue for replacement on the maintenance schedule, but new parts requisitions were put on hold, so..."

"I'll mind the lights, Stas," Antonov assured him. "You just get your ass out of Bagram. You hear me?"

His flight mechanic nodded, gripped the Major's hand tightly then snapped the hatch cover into place, sealing the double cockpit. A tractor towed the gunship through hangar doors onto open tarmac as the sky turned gunmetal gray against black peaks on the horizon.

Antonov switched on the electrical and hydraulic systems then fired his auxiliary power unit. "APU engaged..." he told Alyushin, through his helmet mic. Releasing the rotor brake, he opened the fuel cocks and depressed the left engine starter. "Pumps on..." When the tach had climbed to 15 percent, he slid open the fuel shutoff valve, waited for the left turbine of his Isotov TV-2 to reach idle speed then repeated the procedure for the right. As the rotor clocked loudly above his head, the Major monitored the exhaust temperature and hydraulic gauges. "Green bars," he said. "Shutting down APU."

With eight Spetsnaz and heavy cargo aboard, his gunship was pushing maximum gross weight, precluding a hovering take-off. The Major switched radio frequency. "Bagram Ground, Griffon Seven, northeast ramp. Request taxi runway zero-three."

In his earphone, he heard confirmation. Antonov gently raised his pitch control lever, eased his cyclic forward to roll the craft into run-up position and completed the takeoff checklist.

"Bagram Tower, Griffon Seven, good to go at zero-three. Request southeast departure."

Cleared for takeoff, Antonov taxied into position. Both turbo shafts reached full idle and he twisted his throttle, watched the rotor RPMs climb to 97 percent.

"Increasing collective…" Easing his pitch control upward and pushing the cyclic forward, he felt the gunship begin its takeoff roll. As ground speed increased, clean air passed through the rotors achieving translational lift and Antonov's *krokodil* rose gracefully off the tarmac. "Landing gear up." The Major retracted his undercarriage wheels, climbed into a cloudless dawn, heard the familiar pop of his blade tips, then deftly accelerated across the dark patchwork plain of Kapisa toward the Hindu Kush.

His flight plan circumvented the Saricha Road from Charikar northeast through the Panjshir Valley, now littered with the burned-out hulks of BTR-50 troop carriers and T-64 battle tanks. Instead, he flew southeast to Mehtar Lam and banked north into Nuristan as first light cast a silver veil onto the Alingar watershed.

During hunter-killer sorties, he would have paired with at least one other gunship. However, because Alfa was involved, his mission was *chernyy*—"black." High-ranking KGB asses were being covered, which meant that Major Antonov and his Spetsnaz escort did not exist, officially. He looked up through his ballistic-resistant cockpit and caught a glimpse of the Sukhoi SU-24 Fencer shadowing him. He knew its pilot had orders to destroy his gunship rather than allow it, or his cargo, to fall into enemy hands.

Pushing 300 KPH, Antonov dropped into a river valley flanked by snow-dusted mountains. Once he would have negotiated this terrain at an altitude of 1,000 meters or more to avoid small arms fire, but that tactic had changed with the introduction of American Redeyes and Stingers. The Mi-24 had no infrared signature suppression, which exposed the gunship's exhaust to heat-seeking missiles. Heat-dissipators, countermeasure flares and missile warning systems helped, but pilots quickly learned the first rule of survival: shoulder-launched missiles could not be fired downwards from the insurgent hill posts. So, the pilots flew "nap of the earth," hugged the landscape and relied on their speed and armored hulls for protection.

Climbing past Gulcha, between sheer 3,400-meter palisades, the Major was forced to trade airspeed for altitude as he felt the stutter of his blade tips forewarning a stall. His gunship's service ceiling, the maximum altitude at which a 33 meters-per-minute rate of climb could be maintained, was 4,500 meters. With eighty S-8 KOM rockets, four Skorpíon-P anti-tank missiles on his wingtip pylons, 2,980 liters of fuel, eight battle-ready commandos and 350 kilos of tactical nuclear warheads, he was flying heavier than ever with little or no margin for error in that rugged terrain.

The temperature outside his cockpit read minus 25 degrees Celsius and his rotor deicers cranked at full capacity. Antonov relied on his radio compass and altimeter to negotiate the topography, played his cyclic and collective levers against the wind shears and downdrafts that made the mountain passes so treacherous. He inched over serrated ridges at 4,400 meters, eventually tucked into the Togab i-Monjan gorge and followed it north to the Saricha Road, well beyond the narrow Panjshir deathtrap.

Past the threat of Stingers and deadly rock buttresses, the Major breathed more easily at first sight of the Oxus River and the Soviet border ahead. As he glided high over the frozen landscape with his homeland in sight, Antonov could not help but fret over the price his countrymen had paid attempting to prop up the puppet Parchami regime in a land filled with tribes that had not been conquered in a thousand years. He remembered every little village and settlement his Swatters had incinerated, every insurgent his nose cannon had cut to bloody bits as he had soared above the carnage, untouched, invulnerable. It was no wonder Afghans called the Soviet gunships *Shaitan-Arba*—"Satan's Chariots." He could only guess at the price this insanity had cost his comrades and their families, let alone his own Maryna and little Sonya.

Morning sun glittered on turquoise lakes dotting the pristine snowfields that stretched as far as Antonov could see in every direction. At Ishkashim, where the Oxus carved a great trench through the Pamirs of Badakhshan, he would follow the river to Khorog where the M41 highway cut a path northeast through the mountains, and continue to Chirchik-Andizhan airbase at Tashkent. There, he would have a good breakfast of sausage and black bread, strong coffee and maybe a vodka chaser.

Antonov traced a gravel track northeast to where the road terminated on the left bank of fanning glacial run-off and resumed on the right. Above, the recently abandoned garrison of Zebak lay nestled in a narrow green valley. The USSR had established a military command in Badakhshan Province with only a few bases along the Wakhan Corridor separating the Pamirs from the Hindu Kush. The troops in these remote mountain outposts had pulled back to the border garrison at Ishkashim and Massoud's *mutahareks* would soon fill the vacuum. It was rumored the Tajik commander they called "Lion of Panjshir" had traded precious lapis lazuli from the fabled "Blue Mountain" for Dragunov sniper rifles and RPG-7s smuggled in from Peshawar through Chitral. Afghanistan would soon become a blood feud among the tribal warlords.

The Alfa commander's voice crackled through Antonov's helmet mic. "Is that Zebak below, Major?"

"Affirmative."

"Head zero-five-seven degrees. Stay just below the ridges. No more than 3,500 meters."

"Captain, our flight plan—"

"Has just been changed!"

Antonov felt the cold steel of a pistol barrel on his neck beneath his leather helmet flap. The Alfa commander had moved to the flight mechanic's jump seat directly behind him.

"The KGB is now taking charge of your cargo, Comrade Major. Switch off external comm. We are going in dark."

Antonov knew better than to argue with Spetsnaz. He calmly informed Alyushin that they would be maintaining radio silence and banked into the morning sun.

The Major never discovered what the Alfa commander was doing because, just as he could see the juncture of the Panj and Wakhan Rivers ahead, Antonov caught sight of an amber light flickering in the corner of his eye. The chip detector—which meant that a hair-fine sliver of metal had come into contact with a probe extending into the flow of gearbox oil. In a few seconds, the light glowed steadily.

Metallic shavings had been accumulating in his tail gearbox and with routine maintenance, the parts would have been upgraded. But "routine" had gone out the window when the Soviet Central Committee opted to cut their losses in Afghanistan. In all the years Antonov had been piloting helicopters, he had never had a tail rotor go out, and had never imagined it could happen short of a direct hit. The amber light on his instrument panel told him otherwise.

"We've got a *big* problem!" he told Alyushin, heart pounding into his throat with the surge of adrenaline. Emergency procedures flooded his brain. There were only two types of failures, he remembered: drive and control system. The former was far worse—loss of rotating disc area that otherwise acted as a stabilizing fin and enabled the craft's forward flight. Trying to land a spinning helicopter without a tail rotor was every pilot's worst nightmare.

The Major immediately slapped his landing gear down and keyed the cabin intercom. "Captain, we have a serious mechanical situation requiring emergency landing. I say again, we are making an emergency landing."

In a few moments, Antonov felt the pistol jammed hard into the flesh of his neck beneath his helmet liner as the Alfa commander yelled back at him, "Major, you are forbidden to land this craft for any reason until we have—"

A violent shuddering in the tail pylon cut the commander off in mid-sentence and sent a shock wave through Antonov. His tail rotor failed and torque from the main blades caused an instantaneous counter-clockwise rotation of the cabin-heavy fuselage. The craft yawed sixty degrees to the left and the Major instinctively shut off auxiliary servo pressure.

Unable to restore manual control, the gunship was going down fast. Major Antonov knew he was about to lose not only his helicopter but possibly his life, and all the others in his charge, because of a freak mechanical malfunction that his mechanic had seen coming.

"Entering auto-rotation!" Antonov shouted into his helmet mic while he shut off the speed selectors and cut the turbines. Holding his cyclic in a death grip, he fought to maintain a level attitude.

The gunship was side slipping. He knew he needed to increase collective and simultaneously flare, reduce his rate-of-descent and forward speed prior to hitting the snowfield that was perilously close. But it was no good. The overloaded craft was too heavy, the serrated ridge coming up too fast. The wheels hit rock below the snow, the struts collapsed and his gunship began to roll.

He mostly remembered the terrible sounds of the impact as his main rotor sliced into rock: metal shearing, fiberglass splintering. His gunship was tossed like a child's toy across the glittering frozen landscape before it slammed into the mountain's black face, its reinforced titanium hull crumpling like cheap tin.

A single image of the crash burned into Antonov's memory: the sight of Alyushin's white helmet disappearing in a spray of red.

The last sound the Major remembered was his canopy cracking. And then, there was nothing but excruciating pain as his instrument panel snapped down on his legs like a bear trap.

SUNDAY, 26 JULY 2009 • AUBSHAUR, AFGHANISTAN

....

SONYA PERCHES LIKE a wary cat on a stack of pillows sewn from tasseled woolen saddlebags. She cradles a warm cup of *shur chai* one of the Kyrgyz guards brought at his master's behest. Behind the wooden door she passed earlier, in a room carved from a natural grotto, moonlight spills through a narrow window slit and paints a blue band of luminescence across a cot covered with sheepskins and old military blankets. At the foot of the cot is a small, cast-iron stove vented through the window. On the right is a rough-hewn wooden table, its wear-polished surface stacked with yellowed scrolls beside a pair of steel rimmed spectacles, a tarnished brass oil lamp and a long wooden box inlaid with mother of pearl. The man who had impregnated her mother and then left Sonya with nothing but vague memories and disturbing dreams, sits behind the table in his distressed wheelchair, surrounded by all he has left in the world.

After recounting his near-death experience, her father looks up with a dim spark of hope in his limpid eyes, his once steady voice raw with emotion. "*Kak ona* [How is she]?"

"*Ona umerla* [She's dead]," Sonya informs him coldly.

A tear of grief rolls from the corner of one eye into his white beard. "I'm so sorry—"

"Are you?" Her voice is unforgiving. "Then why did you never come back to us?"

He rubs the tears from his cheek with a shaking hand and wheels himself out from behind the trestle table, his arms trembling with effort and emotion. Pulling back the woolen blanket covering his lap, he shows her the extent of his injuries: both his legs, from three inches above where his knees should have been, are missing. His drab gray *tunban* are tied off and tucked beneath him.

"The man you knew as your father died here. Half of him, anyway. The other half...lost his way." It is not a plea for pity, just an honest admission of fact. "Whenever I had thoughts of returning, the *chandu* convinced me I was deluding myself."

"Chandu?"

He points to the box on his desk, its inlay glittering in the lamplight. "Opium."

Sonya closes her eyes, shakes her head slowly.

"The only thing that kept me alive when all I wanted was to die. The *chandu* and I came to an agreement: It showed me the secret of peace, and I promised to be faithful. Forever."

"I would have gladly wiped you from my memory," she snaps, "but the problem is, I knew you were alive. All these years, I just *knew* it. I had dreams...I still have them."

"As do I," he confesses. "And somehow, I always knew you'd find me. That's why I kept this." He lifts the hinged lid of his treasure box and extracts a palm-sized burnished silver disk.

"This is what saved my life," he tells her. "I don't remember much of what happened, but between Mizan's bad Russian and my worse Dari we pieced the story together.

"The Shahin, our Kyrgyz smugglers, were crossing the ridge between Chitral and Wakhan, about a half-day's journey to the west, when they saw my gunship go down. It was very bad, smashed to bits, scattered over the snowfield. The eight commandos were killed when the aft cabin disintegrated. My nose gunner died before my eyes. It was nothing short of a miracle that I survived…or maybe a curse. I think the Shahin would have left me for dead except for this old broach, which they said had to be pried loose from my hand."

He rubs the disk's worn surface like a talisman then passes it to Sonya. She examines the inscription, stylized in the shape of a lion looking back over its shoulder.

"The Aga Khan's emblem, I presume?"

"I had no idea what it was until Mizan told me. It was a gift from Stas, my flight mechanic. To you. He had no children of his own and fell in love with a photo I once showed him of you trying to catch a spider beneath a glass when you were about five. He always asked about you when I returned from leave." Her father shakes his head sadly. "Stas was Uzbek. I have no idea if he made it out of Bagram on that last airlift. At least I've kept my promise to him."

His eyes close for a moment, then look up toward the moon-light beaming through the window slit. "I was almost dead when the Shahin brought me here. One of the monastics had medical training at Kabul University. He amputated my legs before gangrene set in.

"I only remember wanting to die from the pain. They gave me *chandu* to quiet my screams, to help me sleep. When the fever broke, and I regained consciousness, I cursed that man for saving me. Knowing that I would never be whole again, that I could never see you and your mother, never walk up our stairs and hold you in my arms, the agony was unbearable.

"It took many months to recover. Mizan became my legs. He brought me food and read to me, poetry from the library, whatever he thought might lift me out of the dark despair that enveloped me.

As my Dari improved, he taught me how to read the Persian texts for myself. His kindness and those books helped me accept the life I'd been left with."

Sonya drops the broach on the pillow beside her. "And opium helped you forget about Mother and me. You never even *tried* to find a way back home?"

He shook his head, sadness in his eyes. "There was a herdsman who used to bring supplies to the monastery. This hand-built wheelchair came on the back of one of his donkeys. I attempted to get word out through him to my commanding officer.

One day, I tore a page from a volume Mizan had brought me, scratched out a note with a piece of charcoal and bribed Abdul, the herdsman, with my wrist watch to deliver it to a Soviet border post. I had hoped that if Colonel Pashkovsky knew I was alive, he would send a rescue team back with Abdul. But I was careful not to reveal my identity or whereabouts in case the *döshman* intercepted him. Just enough for the Colonel to know it was me. That I was injured and—"

"Your cargo was safe." Sonya finishes his sentence coldly.

Her father lifts his gaze out of a painful reverie to meet her hard stare. His watery eyes dilate in sudden comprehension before clouding with disappointment. "That's the real reason you're here, isn't it, Sonya? That infernal cargo."

Her expression softens but her voice remains uncompromising. "Where have you kept it safe, Papa?"

....

"IT WAS LATE JUNE before the storms subsided that year and the snow pack began to melt." Dmitry Antonov tells his daughter as she wheels him down the narrow passage toward Aubshaur's library. "The Shahin wintered here and in late spring trekked back along their usual route to hunt fox and lynx. They returned a month later with three thousand rounds of ammunition and twelve cases salvaged from the wreckage of my gunship, but clearly had not been able to open them. Mizan convinced the Shahin that the USSR would buy back their salvage and pay a better price than they could get in Chitral. He said I would broker the deal and bought some time by giving them the machine gun belts. I asked to keep a short segment to place on that shrine I built as a memorial to my weapons systems officer, Alyushin.

"Mizan told me that Spetsgruppa Alfa planned to return here. They'd left their solar panels and generators, as well as a small arsenal. Since I was the only surviving representative of the Soviet 40th Army, I exchanged fifty new Kalashnikovs and two hundred kilos of ammunition for those cases, with the assurance I'd cut the Shahin in on any reward for their return to the USSR."

Antonov sighs. "Then I found out there *was* no more Union of Soviet Socialist Republics."

His eyes darken. "Sonya, the wreckage of my gunship should have been destroyed. If the Sukhoi escort had followed protocol, *nothing* would have been left to salvage. That means either the Alfa commander or Colonel Pashkovsky called the escort back before the crash. I really wanted to give Yuriy the benefit of the doubt. I wanted to think he had no knowledge of the KGB's plans. But then I remembered the look in his eyes when he begged me to get those weapons to a safe place. As if he knew something he was not telling me."

They reach the shrine grotto and Sonya switches on the spray of LEDs, awakening both the *ziyárat* and chilly library beyond. Antonov turns his chair laboriously in the silica grit.

"I used to think life was a random event, Sonya, just accident or chance. But here, I've learned there *are* no accidents. Yuriy's betrayal was my initiation—my rebirth." He spreads his arms wide and smiles as he did when he used to beckon for his daughter to jump into them. "What once seemed like a death sentence became my salvation. Here, I found a purpose higher than killing, as both the custodian of precious wisdom and the guardian of unspeakable destruction. It became clear to me that I had been chosen to protect this library *and* to guard these satanic weapons. To make sure neither would ever be misused."

Antonov feels the conviction burning in his eyes. "My brothers here believe a universal disaster is coming. Another world war. They say so many people will die that a bird flying over the landscape will faint in the sky from the stench of all the corpses. They say this apocalypse will happen soon and the Masters have been deputed to save mankind from its path of self-destruction, to pave the way for the establishment of justice and peace among all nations under universal principles. They have convinced me it is a sacred trust, Sonya, something much more important than my small tribulations."

"More important than your family as well."

A deep sadness overtakes him. "I had no way of knowing what happened to you and your mother. I cannot imagine what you must have gone through. But I hoped you would remember me as I was. I never wanted either of you to see me…like this."

His daughter stands in graceful tension, dressed in black like a thief in the night, her eyes hard as agate, her face devoid of compassion, her rigidity masking uncertainty. She bears no resemblance to the child he once bounced on his knees in Leningrad. Looking at her now, Antonov realizes that the curious little girl he has preserved in his memory, like a fly in amber, is just an illusion, an iconic memento of joy in a life of relentless death and sorrow. His daughter has had the audacity to grow up into a fiercely beautiful woman who no longer examines the spiders she has trapped under a glass in the kitchen.

He wonders if she has any more feeling for him now than she once had for those frightened arachnids.

What *are* her real intentions? How could she have known about those weapons? Who else but Yuriy could have told her?

As if reading his suspicions, Sonya shifts uncomfortably on her feet and sighs heavily. "Your commanding officer contacted mother after we left Russia. Felt guilty, I suppose. Pashkovsky sent her the note you'd written to him, probably so he wouldn't have to look at it ever again. Mother never talked about it, but I know it must have tortured her until the day she died. When I found it in her things, I tracked Pashkovsky down in Kyiv and learned what I could about your mission. He never told me specifically what you were carrying for the KGB, but I deduced the details from what he *didn't* say."

Sonya kneels before him in the glittering dust, rim-lit in blue beneath the canopy of LEDs, and takes his gloved hands in hers. "Papa, I can bring you home."

"*Home?*" The word sounds alien to him. "To Leningrad?"

"To *my* home. Where mother lived. You'll be comfortable there. You won't need opium any more. You can reclaim your life."

He stares at her as if she were speaking about some other planet. "This *is* my life, Sonya. What use would I be anywhere else but here? What would become of my library? I'm Sarkâr. It is *my* task now, my duty and destiny to protect the wisdom in these volumes for re-building civilization after the great destruction that is to come. Who else will keep these treasures safe?"

"My friend will," she replies softly, more than slightly concerned about her father's mental state. "He's a Jesuit, a scholar and a very honorable man. We can arrange to have the entire library safely trans-ported and properly archived, where it can be studied and appreciated, as *you* appreciate it. You will always remain its custodian, Papa."

Then his daughter's eyes narrow, drill into him urgently. "Do you know about the Taliban? About their destruction of the great Buddhas at Bamiyan? About their massacre of the Hazara people in Mazar-i-Sharif? About their harboring al-Qaeda murderers?"

He nods grimly. "We received news of the outside world when Abdul Hadud brought in supplies. He told us about the civil war, Mullah Omar, bin Laden, the American invasion. Fortunately, none of that madness ever reached us here."

"Not *yet*, but it's only a matter of time. When the Taliban find this place, they will destroy *everything*. The books, the scrolls, *all* your treasures. That is what these ignorant fanatics do: obliterate their own history so no one can ever revere it."

"As long as the Shahin remain, they won't disturb us."

"The Taliban are monsters! Your smugglers are no match for them." She squeezes his hands tightly and he feels his daughter's desperation amplify her physical strength. Her mother's eyes blaze with determination. "If they find those weapons you salvaged, the Taliban will commit atrocities beyond anything you can imagine. You must understand this, Papa. You *must* believe me!"

Antonov hesitates for only a moment to look deeply into Sonya's eyes, long enough to realize she is telling him the truth. He gently frees one of his hands from his daughter's grip and points toward the *ziyárat* guarded by the horns of the Marco Polo ram and Ibex. "The altar," he says quietly.

Sonya climbs up to the platform, kneels and lifts the sheepskin drape. She unclips the torch from her web belt and focuses its beam into the black void beneath. Antonov watches her spring excitedly to her feet. "I'm going to need help," she says.

A BLACK RUCKSACK SLUNG over her shoulder, Sonya returns from her tent to find her father has pressed his two Kyrgyz attendants into service again. They have already extracted twelve heavy cases from the grotto and set them side-by-side in the corridor for her inspection. Each meter-long olive drab case is stenciled in Cyrillic:

Fragile: Meteorological Equipment.

From the anticipatory smiles on their ruddy faces, the smugglers must think Sonya is that Russian buyer they have long awaited. She runs her gloved fingertips over the scuffed and dusty Bakelite shells then tries several of the steel latches.

"They're locked."

"All but one," her father replies. "Yuriy showed me what I was 'volunteering' to transport for the Spetsnaz. He got nervous and distracted by their commander and never relocked the case he had opened. There is a trick to the latches, so the Shahin never saw what's inside the case."

"Would you send them away?" Sonya motions to the Kyrgyz guards. "I'm going to need privacy."

Curiosity causes the Shahin to hesitate at first, but grudgingly they comply.

Shivering in the chilly corridor, Sonya tries each case until she finds the one Colonel Pashkovsky opened twenty years ago, the one with a lock that turns in her fingers, as her father explains. She drags it from the queue, lays it flat and carefully follows the sequence: 45 degrees left, out a click, then back up to original position until the six latches are freed. As the dry silicone seals crack, she hears oxygen rush into the depressurized compartment. Inset into a gray matrix of dense polystyrene foam, the black warhead stenciled with a red star sends a shock wave of fear up her spine.

Rehearsal is over.

She briefly flashes on a mental image of Giraffe's self-satisfied smile, certain he would be thrilled to learn these horrific things were not just a Cold War myth after all.

Carefully rotating the cylinder, Sonya locates its access panel and unzips her rucksack. She extracts Avner Ron's rugged laptop, a nylon makeup kit and a cellophane-sealed box of She Ultra sanitary pads, an item no Muslim man will touch—let alone inspect—at *any* checkpoint. Unwrapping the box, she removes a thick wad of feminine napkins that has padded Avner's palm-sized Arduino and specially programmed FPGA shield.

Sonya unzips the makeup kit, extracts a slender screwdriver disguised as a mascara tube, and a strike enabled plug fitted neatly into the handle of a soft-bristled blush applicator. She hesitates for a moment, closes her eyes and prays—to whomever it is that Danny always prays to—that Avner knew what the hell he was talking about.

Her father's stern voice cuts through her fear. "Sonya, what are you going to do with these weapons?"

She breathes deeply, beads of sweat already forming on her forehead and upper lip. "Make sure no one can ever use them, Papa."

....

EDDY THOMPSON IS A LIGHT SLEEPER. When he hears his tent flap being unzipped, it takes him less than a second to level his P226 at the intruder's face.

Sonya's voice penetrates the mesh screen of his vestibule. "Put that thing back in your pants and call in exfil."

Eddy lets out his breath, eases his finger off the trigger. "What's up? You find something?"

"Twelve cases, maybe thirty kilos each."

His hooded eyes appraise her skeptically. "You sure they're the real deal?"

"Trust me, Eddy." Sonya sounds tired and irritable. "I really *do* know a lot about things that blow up."

"Okay. I'm on it."

When she has moved away from his tent, Eddy lays his pistol aside and reaches two fingers into his mouth. He wiggles a lower back molar and pries it loose, extracting the crown with a tiny cylinder protruding from the enamel cap. A sub-dermal GPS-enabled radio frequency identification chip has to be surgically implanted and removed. Not so with a dental device. He turns the titanium end a half revolution, pushes it in and a diode glows green at the tip. Transponder activated, Eddy replaces the crown and bites down carefully to secure it.

He pulls on Gortex boots and moves quietly to the tent occupied by Jamshid and Chir. By the time Eddy has unzipped their vestibule, the young Tajiks are up and armed.

"Morning, boys! Pack up the tents and gear before breakfast; then get yourselves dug in on high ground at the south end of the plaza. Oh, and tell old Ass-face to move his animals into the tunnel for safety." He checks his watch. "We're going to have visitors in about two hours and they're going to make a lot of noise."

SATURDAY, 25 JULY 2009 • HAMPTON, VIRGINIA

FOR TWELVE HOURS A DAY, First Lieutenant Justin Mosley mans his workstation in a cavernous secret facility that might be mistaken for the New York Stock Exchange. Except that here, instead of the global movement of wealth, hundreds of hanging monitors stream live video from drones keeping track of enemy movements, suspected insurgent safe houses and American combat units in play as they cruise the skies above Afghanistan, Iraq and the Horn of Africa.

Justin and his colleagues call it "Death TV."

The US Air Force's Distributed Common Ground System at Langley Airfield, is officially known as the AN/GSQ-272 Sentinel

Weapon System, but is commonly referred to as "D-sigs." It employs a global communications architecture combining real-time data collected from U-2 Dragonladies, RQ-4 Global Hawks, MQ-1 Predators, MQ-9 Reapers as well as other intelligence, surveillance, reconnaissance platforms and sensors. The five billion-dollar network produces thousands of hours of video, high-altitude photography and hundreds of hours of TECHINT and SIGINT, including NSA cellular phone call intercepts, monitored by teams of camo-clad Air Force analysts like Justin, peering at their monitors and thumbing trackballs beneath the tubular cooling vents.

At his console in the air-conditioned installation, Justin employs an encrypted instant messaging system to chat with commanders at the front, troops in combat and United States Special Operations Command near Tampa, Florida, sometimes a dozen or more conversations at once. On his headset, he can talk to a U-2 pilot gliding through the stratosphere, an RPA team operating from some desert ground control station, or a high-level kill chain up the road at Spook Central. It is a stressful job, but he gets paid very well for his work and has just put a down payment on his first home. It feels good to know he is making the world safer for his kids, assuming his wife, Brittany, ever does get pregnant.

Three hours ago, Justin monitored a feed from Jalalabad Air Base in Afghanistan—Sunday morning their time—watching a team of Xe Services' contractors fit the six pylons of a Reaper MQ-9 with 1,500 pounds of munitions: GBU-12 Paveway II laser-guided "smart" bombs and AGM-114 Hellfire II air-to-ground missiles. Factoring in the two thousand-pound external fuel tanks, Justin calculated the Reaper could remain airborne for nearly forty hours. On a second screen, he went live with a pilot at Jalalabad who ran preflight checks along-side a technician testing the Reaper's sensors.

An MQ-9's bulging "chin" contains a swivel mount daylight video camera, an infrared rig that detects heat signatures at night, synthetic aperture radar that can literally see through cloud cover and a laser designator. Although the camera system can read a license plate two miles away, it has a narrow field of view, making it most effective when tracking someone relatively close in.

The Jalalabad crew oversaw the Reaper's takeoff and then slewed over to Justin. His job is to facilitate hand-off to a stateside reach-back team at Creech Air Force Base in Nevada then interface between them and his local client. When the mission is completed, he will transfer the MQ-9's controls back to the Jalalabad operators for landing.

The Creech team comes on line and Justin smiles at the familiar voice. "Sentinel, this is Sky King. Princess Leah and I will be your RPA hosts for the evening. Any special requests?"

"Sky King, Sentinel. How's the weather in Vegas?"

"Spinning up for a long, hot night, Sentinel."

"Copy that, Sky."

Justin watches the live feed from the Reaper as it reaches the designated coordinates over a remote stretch of the Hindu Kush mountain range that divides Afghanistan's northeastern panhandle from Pakistan's Khyber Pakhtunkhwa Province. He patches in the team at Creech. "Slewing over Big Boy Seven-O. Your TZ is coming up at four-o'clock."

"Roger that, Sentinel. Confirming hand-off of Big Boy Seven-O. Flight graphics and DVR checked and running. TZ sat images confirmed. Standing by for target designation."

"Copy and stand by…"

SUNDAY, 26 JULY 2009 · AUBSHAUR, AFGHANISTAN

....

THE COOL MORNING AIR IS FRAGRANT with the lingering scent of *ghee*-fried *chuchuk* mingling with *khar* dung. As Assadullah cinches the last of the kitchen gear to his burros' wooden saddles, Danny and Bashir walk the perimeter of the plaza together in sharp, angular sunlight. Danny photographs the stone bodhisattvas in their niches from multiple angles with a small, mirror-less Canon, cataloging the unique sculptural details and estimating the dimensions of each effigy in a little yellow notebook.

Invigorated with a new sense of purpose that eclipses even his vocation, Danny feels as if destiny has stepped in to take charge. It is all he can do to restrain himself from calling Cyrus and thanking him for his manipulative prodding. The archive at Aubshaur is without question the most important find of his professional life and he doesn't want to think about anything else.

He thinks about it anyway.

Danny has prayed to the Holy Spirit for guidance, but neither contrition nor apologia has gotten him closer to absolution. Truth is, he cannot forgive his own human weakness, his broken vows to the Society of Jesus, his discarded vocation or his disgraced family name. The worst part is, knowing what he does about this woman he loves more intensely than his religion, Danny cannot imagine a viable future with Sonya. Her mysterious life, her cynical worldview and her dark profession are diametrically opposed to everything he has always believed. Still, he cannot get the smell of her hair or the taste of her mouth out of his mind.

"These figures are in amazing condition considering their vintage," he tells Bashir, focusing his camera on one of the bodhisattvas' hand mudras as he tries to refocus his thoughts. "The schist here is harder than the sandstone at Bamiyan. Tougher to carve, but a lot more durable."

"And no one has tried to dynamite them," Bashir notes with a wry smile.

"Yet," Danny frowns. "Been thinking a *lot* about that, my friend. If I'm going to make a case for the preservation of this place, I'll need to bring back some sample documents from the library as proof of authenticity. Probably have to smuggle them out of the country but I'll cross that bridge when we come to it. Think you can negotiate permission from the abbot here?"

"The taskmaster of the archive is called 'Sarkâr,' Father Daniel," Bashir replies, "and you can ask him yourself." He gestures toward the portico where a white-bearded man is being wheeled through the wooden doors of the Durbar Hall into the morning sunlight. On the left side of his wheelchair, Rukhsana stands out in her scarlet *rumol,* and on the right, dressed head-to-toe in black, Sonya is a study in colorless contrast.

Behind the weathered doors, morning *dzikhr* is in full swing as Danny ascends the portico steps. The old Sarkâr has a heavy woolen horse blanket spread across his lap and piercing blue eyes beneath his black *pakul.* There is a tough dignity in the old man's face that belies his physical frailty.

Stepping out of the shadowed portico, Sonya squints into the bright blue morning as she pulls off her gloves, slips the watch cap from her head and rubs her fingers briskly through her matted hair. She looks weary, her eyes sunken as she bends toward the Sarkâr's ear and says, *"Eto moi drug, otets Daniel Callan, Iesyitsky ucheny pro kotorogo ya tebe govori.* [This is my friend, Father Daniel Callan, the Jesuit scholar I told you about]."

The old man nods slowly and appraises Danny as Sonya says, "Danny, I'd like you to meet Dmitry Antonov...my father."

Sonya has been telling him the truth all along and Danny feels foolish, embarrassed. His eyes probe hers, tacitly asking forgiveness for having doubted her as he shakes his head in astonishment. His right hand reaches out for the old man's fingerless glove. "Sir...the honor is all mine...you have no idea!"

"He doesn't speak English, Danny. I've already told him your intention is to preserve his library. He trusts that. Says you're free to take whatever you need to make it happen."

There is so much more Danny needs to say to her now, but except for that night in the village below, under the influence of bourbon and the constellations, there has been no time to process the reawakening each of them has felt during this extraordinary journey. He wants to take her aside, somewhere quiet, for just a minute or two. He needs to look into her eyes and tell her everything he has been holding inside for eight years.

Danny reaches out to touch Sonya's arm, but before he can speak his heart to her, apologize for his mistrust, the big wooden doors crack open again. Six of the Kyrgyz smugglers emerge, each lugging two long, slender olive drab hard cases onto the portico and setting them side-by-side.

"You'll need to hurry, Danny. Gather up what you want to take with you." Sonya's eyes are set hard, sharply focused on the task at hand. "We're going to be extracted by air very shortly."

His eyes riveted to the twelve ominous cases, Danny feels his throat constrict with the realization of what they must contain.

"Looks like you've had a busy night, Sonny."

Sonya glances up at him with a weary smile. "You could say that."

A DESERT CAMO HECKLER & KOCH machine pistol is slung across Eddy's chest and the scoped Mark 12 SPR is tucked casually under his arm. He wears snug, half-finger utility gloves, a black Kevlar vest over olive thermal top, khaki fatigues and his baseball cap turned backwards. His coated sunglasses glow alien orange in the morning light as he saunters across the plaza, nods to Rukhsana, Bashir and Danny, then smiles up at Sonya.

Eddy inclines his head toward her wizened father in his wheelchair. "Who's the geezer?"

Sonya bites her lip, marveling at his impeccable lack of social skills. "My pop, Eddy.

"No shit!"

"None whatsoever. You have an ETA for exfil?"

"Any time now, Sonya." Eddy slips the rifle through the crook of his left arm and pulls a battered pack of Turkish cigarettes from his gusseted trouser pocket. He taps one out and offers it to Antonov. Her father's gloved hands continue to grip the wheels of his chair as he stares coldly at the American mercenary. Eddy grunts, grabs the filtered end with his teeth and snaps open his Zippo. "So, your old man really *did* salvage those nukes."

He offers the cigarette to Sonya and she takes a drag despite her father's disdainful look. "At no small cost," she says, lifting a corner of the blanket that covers his lap and missing legs.

Eddy nods respectfully. "After what he's been through, Ruskies should give him the fucking Order of Lenin."

"They stopped awarding those when the Soviet Union collapsed, Eddy. Besides, Major Antonov will not be going back to Russia. He's coming with us."

Sonya's ears prick at a dull sonic stutter increasing in volume until it becomes the sound of a distant helicopter cutting through the air.

"Sounds like our ride home," Danny observes.

"Not exactly, Padre," Eddy replies through a ghost of smoke drifting through his moustache. "This bird's only collecting lost baggage."

Sonya glares up at him, hands on her hips. "What the fuck…?"

Eddy's hand slides back toward his trigger guard. "Here's how this goes down, Sonya. A Russian special ops unit will be landing in about three minutes to take possession of these weapons. *We* will not obstruct or challenge them in any way. Understood?"

"Seriously, Eddy? The Russians are paying you too?"

"Way I see it, Uncle Sam has no claim on Soviet nukes. Neither does Cousin Bibi." Eddy scratches the heavy stubble on his chin and appraises Sonya coolly. "By default, they're still the property of the Russian Federation, which has as much reason to keep them away from bad guys as we do."

"I'm sure Mister Putin will be grateful," she scowls. "More so than my boss."

"Look Sonya, my contract with your boss is to provide security and exfil for *you*. No skin off his ass whether these weapons get to a safe haven at Bagram or Sevastopol. The idea here is to keep them safe." He flashes his teeth at her. "Am I right?"

Sonya takes a final drag and passes the cigarette back to Eddy. "What about Kaban?"

"Believe me, I'm doing Vik a favor. If he got hold of these things, he'd start a fucking bidding war and end up on every kill list in the world." Eddy's moustache accentuates his cynical grin. "But you and Levi already knew that, didn't you? Now, if you play your cards right, Vik could be very useful. He knows a lot about who's running who in Damascus."

"Whom, Eddy. Running *whom*. You've almost got me convinced you're an altruist."

TOM JOYCE

He grins as the thudding rotors grow louder. "Don't get your hopes up."

Danny crouches down beside Sonya's father and places a reassuring hand on his bony arm. "Sonny, please tell him not to worry. I'll take good care of his library until he's ready to resume his duties." She translates Danny's promise and her father nods just as a big gunship appears over the high Pamir to the north.

"I'll meet you back here in fifteen." Danny says, pulling open the big door to the durbar hall.

Sonya observes that the chanting inside has stopped. She scans the plaza. Assadullah is quickly herding his loaded burros into the tunnel and the Panjshir boys are digging in beneath camo netting on high ground opposite the cave complex. She signals for Bashir and Rukhsana to wheel her father back inside. Slipping her watch cap back on, she observes Eddy tensing as he squints skyward.

"Expecting trouble?"

"These Spetsnaz fuckers like to come in hard," he says. "That's just how they roll, and I don't want to give them any reason to get nervous." Eddy extends the Mark 12 rifle to Sonya with a tight smile dimpling his ruddy, unshaven cheeks. "I also like to hedge my bets."

Sonya takes the weapon, checks its breech and magazine, then glances down at the neat row of Bakelite cases sitting in plain view on the temple steps. "So do I," she says.

Turbulence from the gunship's rotor blades rakes the plaza and rattles the old solar panels. "Pick your spot and cover me." Eddy yells over the high-pitched whine of the helicopter's twin turboshafts. He lifts his Oakleys and peers over his shoulder at her, his predatory eyes seeking professional reassurance.

She can barely hear his gruff voice call out, "Tell me you really know how to shoot that fucking thing."

Sonya gives him a thumb's up. He nods and steps down onto the dusty plaza.

"Eddy," she calls after him, for some reason unclear even to her. "There's something I think you should know..."

But he can no longer hear her above the shrill whir of the rotors.

....

"**LOOKS LIKE AN MI-17,**" Roger gestures to the eight-foot plasma video display on which a massive helicopter gunship is shown easing its fuselage into a small excavated plaza on a mountain ridge, narrowly avoiding what appears to be an array of solar panels.

Roger nods appreciatively. "The sonofabitch flying it is a shit-hot pilot to set that big fucker down in that iddy-biddy space."

Courtney, acting as the ADD's eyes-on, has been monitoring the MQ-9's video feed with Roger at the Global Response Center all evening, communicating simultaneously with D-sigs "Sentinel" at Langley Air Force Base, the RPA team at Creech and her boss, patched in from who-knows-where. She sips tepid coffee from her Starbucks to-go mug and moves in closer to the big screen.

"Isn't that a Russian helicopter?" Courtney asks.

"Yep, export version of the Mi-8," Roger confirms. "See those dust shields on the air intakes and tail rotor to port? Best of breed for high-altitude emergency rescue. Sucker can carry thirty passengers or 9,000 pounds of cargo and still ceiling at twenty grand." Roger squints up at the screen through his thick glasses. "This baby looks like a One-V mod. See the gun pods mounted on those hardpoints?"

"Question is," the ADD's disembodied voice chimes in on speaker, "what the fuck is it doing up on the AfPak border?"

"We've been using Mi-8s and 17s for training in the Ghan," Roger admits. "JSOC deployed them to obscure special ops after the MCWG was adopted. We also gave a few 17s to Kayani last month for his CT ops in South Wazi… So, it could be one of the Paks.'"*

"'These guys are a long way from FATA, Rog."

"Maybe they really *are* Russian," Courtney suggests.

SUNDAY, 26 JULY 2009 • AUBSHAUR, AFGHANISTAN

....

THE BLACK GUNSHIP CUTS its twin turbo engines and the whine diminishes as its long rotor blades clock slowly to a full stop. Sonya lies flattened on the portico's edge, hidden between two, meter-high stone carvings. The sniper rifle is steadied on its bi-pod, the padded stock snug against her shoulder.

The Mark 12 feels reassuring in her hands, a reliable tool. Her index finger rests against the inside of the trigger guard. With both eyes open, her field of vision takes in everything between the gunship's forward hatch and the cross-hairs of her ACOG scope as the fundamentals of battle sighting flash across her memory. In a perfect world, she would have already logged data from previous engagements,

---

* **MCWG**—the Military Cooperation Working Group was established in January 2009 to identify mutually beneficial areas of military cooperation, coordinate work on international security and develop military contacts with the Russian Armed Forces. In June 2009, the United States delivered four Mi-17s to Pakistan's Chief of Army Staff, **General Ashfaq Parvez Kayani** after his urgent request to the State Department for helicopters to assist his counter-terrorism efforts in **FATA**, Pakistan's Federally Administered Tribal Areas.

zeroed the optics by firing three consecutive rounds within a three-centimeter square at 100-300 meters and referenced the reticle for holdover or under. But Sonya does not have that luxury under the present circumstances. Fortunately, her weapon is spec ops state-of-the-art and her target is only 25 meters out.

At the moment, that target is Eddy, his legs apart on the plaza, hand resting on his machine pistol, barrel pointed down, waiting.

The helicopter's side hatch slides back and two large Spetsnaz wearing black balaclavas, dark glasses and ballistic vests leap from the fuselage before the steps are lowered. One of the point men moves cautiously in Eddy's direction, while the other takes a wide tangent toward the solar array. Sonya keeps the former in her scope while tracking the latter's motion in her peripheral vision. Both carry short Izhmash AK-9s with barrel suppressors, and she knows their 9 x 39-millimeter subsonic cartridges, created especially for silenced firearms, can penetrate Kevlar body armor. She feels beads of sweat forming on her forehead as she zeros her cross-hairs on the bridge of the commando's wrap-around shades.

Eddy nods to the first Spetsnaz giant, a curt acknowledgment to his brother warrior, and gestures toward the Bakelite cases lined up atop the portico steps. The point man signals his craft and the helicopter's rear clamshell cargo doors swing open. Six more commandos emerge and make a dash for the cases. Both point men focus their attention on Eddy, their weapons at the ready.

Sonya cannot see the olive drab cases from her position but hears one of the Spetsnaz attempting to open latches. "*Zapertyy* [Locked]," he grunts in Russian. Another tells him to "quit fucking around. Our job is to bring them back, not inspect the contents."

The six commandos heft two cases each and tote them to the waiting gunship. Eddy remains tense but cool, watching the operation go down like clockwork. The tail doors fold in and only the point men remain on the plaza. The first looms half a head above Eddy and outweighs him by at least twenty kilos. He appears to relax and extends a gloved hand, as if to congratulate Eddy on a mission accomplished. It seems natural enough and Eddy lifts his own right hand from his machine pistol to accept the gesture.

As the commando grips Eddy's extended hand, there is barely a moment of hesitation before a long, matte-black knife appears, thrusting upward toward Eddy's throat with shocking speed.

The former Delta Force and CIA special operator reacts just as Sonya would have expected. Eddy pivots to the right and grasps his opponent's knife hand in the same motion. The blade narrowly misses its mark as Eddy twists into the momentum of assault and rips free from the commando's grip. He locks both of his powerful hands around his opponent's and tries to break his wrist, but the giant throws his mass into a body slam and knocks Eddy off balance. Before he can recover, the Spetsnaz swings his AK-9 up for the kill.

In a nanosecond of hyper-clarity, Sonya recalls the instruction given by her sniper team leader in Unit 188: A shooter's tendency when engaging a fast-moving combatant, he said, is to focus on the target rather than the tip of the weapon's front sight post—its "iron sight." And then she remembers the price of her hesitation in Khan Yunis.

Training trumps regret as Sonya calculates the angle of movement in the space between two heartbeats. She tracks smoothly across her target while maintaining sight alignment, leading him by one-half POA, the natural "point of aim" calculated to minimize the effects of motion. She holds her breath and squeezes off four 77-grain rounds. One finds the opening of the commando's balaclava, shattering his left cheekbone just beneath his dark glasses.

Sonya perceives the result of her shot in what feels like a slow-motion ballet. The giant's head arcs sideways with the impact of the high-velocity bullet; his shades somersault through the cool air; pink mist catches morning sunlight like a halo around his disintegrating head; the short assault weapon drops from his useless hands and dangles on its ballistic nylon tether. The Spetsnaz is already dead before his legs collapse beneath him.

Eddy dives to the paving stones and rolls behind the commando's massive corpse for cover as Sonya pivots toward the solar array to locate the second point man. He has spotted her position and now moves diagonally in a low crouch, weapon aimed. Before he can fire, a high-caliber fusillade erupts from the helicopter's side hatch and the second big Spetsnaz goes down like a slaughtered bull in a hail of jacketed lead.

Then all hell breaks loose.

SATURDAY, 25 JULY 2009 · LANGLEY, VIRGINIA

"ARE YOU GUYS SEEING WHAT I'M SEEING?" Courtney watches through the Reaper's eye as its chin camera makes a slow sweep of the plaza. Eight black-clad figures have emerged from the helicopter gunship; six scurry like ants across the patio, carry back what appear to be long, heavy cases and load them into the hold. There is an altercation; two go down, then a third. The camera pans further to the right, revealing a contingent of fighters on high ground above the patio, dug in among the rocks, their weapons trained on the gunship.

"Sentinel, Roger. Zoom in on that ridge at three o'clock."

"Copy that," Sentinel replies. There is a slight lag before the daylight camera pushes in. Courtney can make out at least twenty fighters in native dress, crouching behind hard cover and, judging by the recoil of their Kalashnikovs, actively engaging the helicopter.

"Don't appear to be friendlies," Roger concedes.

"Any way to contact that helo?" the Assistant Deputy Director asks over his comm-link.

"Negative," Sentinel replies. "They're silent running."

"They've got the cases," Roger confirms. "I counted twelve. That fits Lebed's debrief."

"But we have no way of knowing if the crew is American, Pakistani or Russian," Courtney adds cautiously.

"Doesn't matter," the ADD says. "We've got unidentified hostiles attacking either our guys, our allies or friendlies. All members of the nuclear club. We have to assume worst-case scenario. No way are we going to allow possible terrorists to get their hands on twelve TNWs. This is clearly a Section 413 sit.* You agree, Rog?"

"All the way," Roger confirms.

"Then make the call."

"Sentinel, Roger. Hostiles at three-o'clock are your target."

"Roger *that*," Sentinel replies.

SATURDAY, 26 JULY 2009 · INDIAN SPRINGS, NEVADA

....

FROM 18,000 FEET, Princess Leah can watch a group of Pashtuns kicking a soccer ball across an open field. Her infrared camera can still detect their heat signatures on cold ground after they have left

---

* **Section 413(e)** under Title 50 of the United States Code designates the CIA as sole discretionary authority for engaging in "covert action" under the 1991 Intelligence Authorization Act. Executive Order 12333, *United States Intelligence Activities* issued by President Ronald Reagan in 1984, defined *covert action* as: "special activities, both political and military, that the US Government can legally deny."

the area in pitch darkness. From 5,000 feet, she can tell what type of sneakers they are wearing and follow them home to their *hujra* without them ever knowing she is watching. If they light a cigarette, she will see a phosphorescent flare, and when she targets them with her laser, it resembles a bolt from heaven. A Ranger once told her they call it "the Light of God" because of how her laser looks through night vision goggles.

It is a heady experience and Leah Adams loves her job.

After her divorce, six months of imagery analysis and air corps school at Holloman got her off the Vegas blackjack tables and into a cushy ergonomic flight seat in a USAF air-conditioned freight container, where she now gets paid very well to play the ultimate video game. Here, in Ground Control Station 12 at Creech Air Force Base, Princess wields the awesome power of Wonder Woman.

"Sky King, Sentinel," she hears on her headset. "We have targets at three-o'clock on that ridge above the plaza. Counting 24 hostiles. Confirm eyes on."

Sky eases his joystick to the designated location. "Pilot copies, Sentinel, Eyes on target."

"Sensor copies," says Princess.

"I'm coming hard about to reduce the range and give Princess a better shot." Sky says.

"Sensor confirms."

"Princess," Sky says, "lock up target with Big Boy Seven-O."

"Copy."

Sentinel requests a weapons check.

"I'm showing six AGM-114s and two GBU-12s on Big Boy Seven-O," Sky says.

"Sky King, Sentinel. Expect to be cleared hot on target."

"Copy that."

TOM JOYCE

Sky gives Princess a thumbs-up. "Okay, let's spin-up a couple of those AGM's."

"Pre-launch checklist." Princess runs down her routine, tapping keys on her console.

"PRF code?"

"Entered."

"AEA power?"

"On."

"AEA bit?"

"In progress…passed."

"Weapon power?

"On."

"Weapon bit?"

"Passed."

"Code weapon?"

"Coded."

"Weapon status?"

"Weapon ready."

"Pre-launch checklist complete." Sky confirms.

"Sky King, Sentinel. You and Sensor are cleared to engage target at your discretion."

Princess furrows her brow. She has no problem smoking bad guys, but sometimes mistakes are made. Just last month, 67 people were turned into dog food in a strike attempt at a funeral gathering in South Waziristan. The target, Baitullah Mehsud, was unfortunately not in attendance.* Princess consoled herself with the thought that most of those guests were probably terrorists—or would have grown up to be.

---

* **Baitullah Mehsud,** leader of the Tehrik-i-Taliban, was eventually assassinated in a CIA drone strike in August 2009.

The blast radius of an AGM-114 II is about 65 feet. She calculates which direction the "squirters"—survivors trying to escape after the first explosion—will likely go and determines where to place her second Hellfire for maximum impact.

"Launch checklist," Sky says. "MTS auto track?"

"Established." Princess replied.

"Laser?"

"Laser selected."

"Arm your laser."

"Laser's armed."

"Master arm is hot. Go ahead and fire the laser."

"Lasing…"

An operator's command takes 1.2 seconds to reach the drone via a satellite link. A box pops up on her screen and Princess sets her laser designator on two target points, locking in on those pixels that look like people.

"Okay, I've got 'em," Princess confirms. Her computer calculates the trajectory, distance and speed then estimates the time until impact.

"Within range," Sky says. "Three…two…one… Rifle! Rifle!"

She squeezes her joystick's trigger. "Time of flight, eight…and twelve seconds."

Sky King covers his mic and winks at her. "Alpha Mike Foxtrot."

"Adios mother fuckers." Princess Leah grips her stick, holds her breath and waits for it.

SUNDAY, 26 JULY 2009 · AUBSHAUR, AFGHANISTAN

....

THE CONCUSSION FROM THE BLAST knocks Sonya flat, smacking her face hard against her rifle's stock and pressing the air from her lungs. Blood tastes metallic in her mouth as a second blast rips the air four seconds later, raining loose stone and dust over her head. She has not felt anything like this since Gaza City.

Sonya assumes the Russian gunship is firing its Swatters, but when she catchers her breath and raises her head to look, the helicopter has lifted off the plaza and is banking sharply to the north. Her ears, still ringing from the two blasts, never heard its engines firing up. By the time the conflagration is over, the gunship is beating a line across the Wakhan River valley toward the white peaks of Tajikistan. Shaken and bleeding from her lip, Sonya eases from beneath the portico to assess the situation.

Eddy has scrambled toward the damaged array of solar panels where the second point man is sprawled amidst debris and broken glass, bloodied but still alive. He jams his knee into the commando's chest and draws his knife to finish the job.

"Wait!" Sonya sprints across the plaza and crouches beside the dying Spetsnaz. She pulls off his glasses, lifts the balaclava over his head and recognizes the square, Slavic jaw and blonde crew-cut. It is a face she remembers targeting through her laser scope in an abandoned Red Hook factory only a few weeks ago.

"He's one of the Petrenkos, Kaban's bodyguards." Sonya motions to the massive corpse ten meters across the plaza. "His twin brother, judging by the size."

She grimaces, shakes her head. "His own men shot him, Eddy. This doesn't make any sense."

"True that!" Eddy snarls, holding his serrated blade pressed firmly against the commando's throat. "Before I give him a trach, why don't you ask this motherfucker what's going down."

She backhands Petrenko's face to get his attention. "*Pochemu tvoi strelyali v tebya* [Why did your own men shoot you]?"

His glazed eyes stare up at her. "*Eto ludi Zharkova* [They're Zharkov's men]," Petrenko rasps, bleeding from his nose and mouth as the life leaks out of him onto the paving stones beneath his useless ballistic vest. Then his face contorts into something approximating grisly amusement. "Too late for all of us, bitch! Those fucking things are on their way to Chechnya."

Petrenko's final attempt at laughter coughs up frothy blood that spatters against Sonya's cheek. Her eyes snap back toward Eddy. "I need your sat phone."

He hesitates, waiting for a translation or at least an explanation. Instead, Sonya springs to her feet and levels the Mark 12's baffled suppressor directly at Eddy's face.

"*Now!*" she screams.

If her voice had not convinced him she is dead serious, the rifle does. Eddy lifts his knee off the Russian's chest and stands slowly. He fishes the Thuraya out of his cargo pocket, switches it on and hands it to her without a word.

On her left, Sonya notices that Jamshid and the Panjshir crew have emerged from their camo cover at the far end of the plaza and are running toward the solar collectors. They stop short and raise their weapons when they see that her rifle's business end is pointed at Eddy's head. He motions for them to stand down and nods for Sonya to proceed. She punches a number with her thumb, her lip bleeding onto the satellite phone's keypad.

"Get down and cover your eyes!" she yells.

Eddy knows better than to question "drop and cover." He loudly relays that command to the Tajiks and they all hit the deck as Sonya presses the send button. She flattens herself against the cool paving stones as an intense burst of light overwhelms the morning sun, followed by an ear-splitting sonic concussion.

SATURDAY, 25 JULY 2009 · LANGLEY, VIRGINIA

....

"**WHAT THE FUCK JUST HAPPENED?**" Roger leaps to his feet as his screen at the Global Response Center suddenly blows out white.

"Sentinel, Langley. Sit rep!"

"Langley, Sentinel." Justin Mosley replies at D-sigs. "Checking status... Sky King, Sentinel. Confirm operational status of Big Boy Seven-O."

"Affirmative, Sentinel. We are operational but experiencing severe turbulence and loss of visual. Adjusting pitch and switching to IR..."

As Sky King regains control of the Reaper, its camera aperture widens and a bleached out infrared image gradually resolves on the screen into an orb of light mushrooming against a dark sky over the mountainous landscape.

"Sensor, Sentinel. Confirm you did *not* engage those GBUs?"

"Negative, Sentinel," Princess confirms. "But something real hot took out that bird."

"*Hot* is a fucking understatement!" Roger switches off his mic, tries to regain composure and addresses the disembodied Assistant Deputy Director as Courtney stares at their monitor with a horrified expression. "We'd better contact AFTAC,"* Roger grimaces. "Looks like one of those frigging suitcases went critical."

There is brief but pregnant lag before the ADD responds with near-sociopathic detachment. "This is in your wheelhouse now, Rog. But copy me on your report to Blair,† will you?"

---

* **AFTAC**—US Air Force Technical Applications Center operates the Constant Phoenix program responsible for confirming underground or atmospheric nuclear tests by collecting air samples and debris to detect telltale traces of radioactivity.

† **Dennis Cutler Blair**, Admiral US Navy, became Director of National Intelligence in January 2009.

SUNDAY, 26 JULY 2009 · AUBSHAUR, AFGHANISTAN

....

EDDY RISES CAUTIOUSLY TO HIS FEET and scans the plaza after the blinding flash and shock wave have subsided. The solar array is damaged by rubble scattered across the plaza from the first two blasts. HEAT weapons—high-explosive anti-tank warheads judging by the stink of propellant lingering in the air. Most likely Hellfires.

Squinting up into the sky, Eddy catches the glint of a drone's wing as it descends for damage assessment. But that third explosion was *not* an Air-to-Ground Missile, a Guided Bomb Unit or a Joint Direct Attack Munitions. It was like nothing he has ever heard before.

Over the mountains to the north of the valley, an ugly gray cloud billows ominously into the stratosphere and a chill of comprehension shudders through him.

"Holy-y-y-*shit!*" He breaths. "What the fuck just happened?"

"I just saved your ass, Eddy." Sonya picks herself up from the paving stones, returns his sat phone as if disposing of a dead rodent and casually brushes the gray dust off her fleece. "Seems your old pal, Viktor Kaban, double-crossed you. And somebody named 'Zharkov' cut him and the Petrenko boys out of the deal as well."

"Sonofa-*bitch!*"

Eddy grimaces at the two giant Spetsnaz brothers sprawled in expanding pools of blood as his Tajik crew jogs across the plaza. The second point-man still claws at the pavement, gasping for shallow breaths. Eddy nods to Jamshid who dead-checks Petrenko with two head shots. His face twitches, his massive body spasms only once and then lies still as the stone plaza beneath his corpse.

Sonya continues without flinching. "Petrenko told me Zharkov was flying those nukes to Chechnya," she says. "For obvious reasons, I could not let that happen."

Eddy appraises Sonya's dirty face and bloodied lip. His eyes drop to the Mark 12 cradled as naturally in the crook of her arm as if she had been born with it in her crib. He finally comprehends why Mossad's Head of Operations finds this brilliant, deadly chameleon so valuable. Eddy lifts the iridescent lenses from his eyes and squints at her in a confusion of disbelief and admiration.

"You *armed* those fucking things?"

"Only one."

....

DANNY HAD JUST FINISHED carefully sealing twelve samples he considered exemplary of Aubshaur's archive into heavy-duty ziplock bags. They will have to pass scrutiny by acknowledged experts and analysis with the latest technology before their pedigree can be verified, but Danny had no doubts. He would wager the contents of his rucksack held more than enough to endow his program at Harvard Divinity School for at least the next decade.

When two consecutive blasts shook the grotto with the force of an earthquake, he flattened himself against one wall of niches and instinctively recited Loyola's *Anima Christi*, expecting boulders to rain down on his head and send him to his Maker at any moment.

"Soul of Christ, sanctify me. Body of Christ, save me…"

To his relief, only a fine layer of grit drifted down like snow flurries. Danny regained his composure and remembered that the cave complex had withstood many centuries of tectonic volatility, massive earthquakes endemic to the Great Pamir Knot. He suspected that his salvation was more attributable to structural integrity than Divine intervention. Even so, he was more than willing to give the Father, Son and Holy Spirit the benefit of the doubt. Those explosions were clearly *not* a natural seismic event.

Then he remembers Sonya is still up on the plaza.

Danny scrambles out of the library and up through the access tunnel until he reaches the deserted durbar hall. Stoic Rukhsana assists the ashen-faced Bashir with Major Antonov's wheelchair, while Mizan and his brother monastics stand frozen in dread as a third explosion diffuses the mosque lamps' glow with silica dust. This one sounds farther away, but it sends a sonic shock wave through the whole mountain, rattling the lamps on their chains and reverberating through Danny's bones.

Pushing through the heavy wooden doors onto the dusty, sunlit portico, Danny's heart pounds as he looks frantically for Sonya. A few of the solar panels have been shattered by falling stones, one of the lion capitals has collapsed, the ledge above the portico is cracked in several places and large chunks of schist are scattered near the entrance. To his relief, the bodhisattvas still appear to be intact.

Down on the plaza, Eddy is talking on his satellite phone and checking his watch. Weapons at the ready, the Panjshir crew scan the perimeter as Assadullah runs toward them, babbling frantically, something about "Satan's chariot."

Danny is frozen in place by the sight of two large, inert bodies lying in patches of dark blood on the pavement. Out of the corner of his eye, he spots Sonya, the camouflaged sniper's rifle tucked under her arm, approaching him with the steady gaze of a seasoned hunter. He swallows his initial revulsion at what he can only guess has transpired and runs down the steps toward her.

"Thank God you're okay, Sonny!"

She looks relieved to see he is safe. "I doubt God had anything to do with it, Danny."

He hesitates, then touches her cut lip tenderly. "What the hell happened here?"

Sonya glances down at his hand brushing her dirty cheek and her eyes tell him she is remembering another time and place. Danny cannot imagine what she has just been through. Ignoring the weapon she still holds, he moves to instinctively protect her from a situation he still struggles to comprehend. Then his attention returns to the sound of rolling thunder echoing through the valley to the north.

Danny turns toward the rumbling sound to see what he can only comprehend as a surreal scene out of *Dr. Strangelove*. A mushroom-shaped cloud rises into the cumulus layer over the mountains across the valley. Transfixed by a sight he never imagined he would see in his life, Danny feels Sonya take hold of his cold hand and press it against her warm cheek.

She sigh. "I know…it's complicated, Danny. I promise I'll tell you everything on the way home."

....

"**SHE-IT, PAYLOAD!**" Captain David "Dutch" Van Agalen lifts his goggles, slips past a GAU-17 swivel mounted Gatling gun in the open hatch of his Sikorsky MH-60G PAVE Hawk, hops down onto the dusty plaza and grins into a Texas drawl. "Think you could have gotten your ass stranded anywhere more fucking remote?"

"No easy day, Dutch." Eddy wraps his gloved right hand around the pilot's as Van Agalen unsnaps his helmet's chin strap.

After activating his dental implant to alert Alexander Zharkov that the missing Soviet tactical nukes had been located, Eddy burned through his Thuraya SIM card to pull in a favor. Homeboys from the 83rd Expeditionary Rescue Squadron came through with flying colors. These USAF Special Operations Pararescue Jumpers, cruising in gunships equipped with long-range external fuel tanks, can cover 800 klicks, fight their way in and out of an active troops-in-contact situation and return with three tons of cargo or casualties.

Dutch pulls off his flight helmet. "How long's it been, anyway?"

"Twenty-O-three, as I recall," Eddy replies. "Parrot's Beak. That nasty HVT scalp hunt in Spin Ghar—just before CENTCOM shut us down."*

"Well, what did you snake-eaters expect after pissing on the big kahuna's boots, good buddy?"

"Do *not* get me started, Dutch." Eddy flips his spent cigarette toward the damaged solar array. "But I surely appreciate the exfil. It's been one hell of a morning."

Captain VanAgalen rubs his sweaty brown crew-cut as he surveys the rubble, refugees and pack animals now assembling on the sun-baked plaza. He spots the two black corpses laid side-by-side and a trail of dried blood marking the path where one had been dragged. "Still making friends wherever you go, I see. Good thing we brought some body bags."

Eddy watches Dutch do a double take as Sonya approaches the helicopter. Stripped down to her black athletic tank top and thermal trousers, her blonde hair back-lit in warm sunlight, and that Mark 12 carried with military swagger, she cuts an impressive silhouette.

"Well, hell-*lo* there, ma'am!" Dutch grins.

Eddy makes the introductions, then adds, "I would be very careful what you say to this lady, Dutch. Sonya's got no sense of humor and she'd just as soon shoot you as give you the time of day."

Sonya slaps the sniper rifle into Eddy's hand with a sarcastic smile then aims her feminine charm, and her pouty, swollen lower lip at Van Agalen. "Don't worry, Captain, I'd never shoot anyone who is offering me a lift home."

* **Parrot's Beak**—the mountainous Kurram District of Pakistan's Federally Administered Tribal Areas jutting westward into Afghanistan south of Jalalabad and north of Khost. In the 1980s, this porous border region was one of the primary routes for smuggling weapons to the American-backed *mujahiddin*. After the Tora Bora offensive in 2001, Osama bin Laden escaped into Kurram over the **Spin Ghar** mountain range and was hunted by US special operations units like Task Force 11.

"Well, ma'am, I would *surely* like to take you all the way, but I'm afraid Bagram's going to be end of the line for me."

"Guess I'll have to get a rain check for door service," Sonya winks at Van Agalen and saunters back toward the plaza.

"*She-it!*" Dutch shakes his head in slow appreciation.

"And just imagine how she cleans up," Eddy assures him.

Dutch sighs and turns his attention to the thunderheads already building over the mountains of Tajikistan. "RC North* has been picking up reports of drone activity in the area," he says. "And one motherfucker of an explosion near the border."

"That's affirmative," Eddy replies.

"Spook Central?"

"Now Dutch, you know I can't talk about that shit. Let's just say we're all under the radar here. Bunch of archaeologists that got into an altercation with the locals and called for evac. You copy?"

"Loud and clear, good buddy."

"I owe you a bottle of Black Label when we get back to base."

"And Sonya's phone number."

"Believe me, Dutch, you do *not* want to go there."

....

RUKHSANA'S UNCLE HELPS TO BROKER a deal between Mizan and the taciturn *padaban*, Assadullah, to transport future shipments of food, supplies and replacement parts for the damaged solar array. Rukhsana watches the tall, golden haired woman dig deep into her money belt and hand wads of banknotes to Mizan for repairs to the *khanaqah*, and then to Jamshid, Kourosh, Chir and Yusuf for their services. She slips a few to Assadullah, presumably as an incentive

---

* **Regional Command North**—International Security Assistance Force [ISAF] headquartered in Mazar-i-Sharif, the provincial capital of Balkh. Germany is RC North lead nation.

not to renege on his agreement. Lastly, she approaches Rukhsana and tucks more cash into her hand than she has ever seen in her life.

"*Lotfaan* [Please]—" Rukhsana tries to decline the offering, but the golden-haired woman insists, closes her fingers tightly over the bank notes and then embraces her as she would a sister.

"*Tashakor*, Rukhsana. If it weren't for you, I'd never have found my father again. There's no way I can possible repay you for that."

She understands only her name and the word for "thanks," but the gratitude in the woman's eyes transcends language. Rukhsana places a hand over her heart. "*Khoda hafez* [May God protect you]."

The woman smiles warmly at her then walks briskly toward her handsome man with the sad blue eyes. Rukhsana turns her attention to the big American mercenary helping two of the helicopter crew zip the dead Russians into black bags and load them aboard the waiting craft. Violence is nothing new to her. She has seen the blackened hulks of vehicles pushed off the road after a feud between Sunni and Isma'ili clansmen in Ishkashim, and women wailing over the shroud-wrapped bodies of their men. But what happened here this morning, the horrifying explosions and gunfire, is beyond her experience.

However, it is not revulsion that churns in her stomach. It is something else, something she has never felt before.

Rukhsana stands rooted now like a poplar tree, staring at the big American with his heavy moustache, the color of a rusted water barrel, and that silly cap turned backward on his head. She watches him embrace each of his Panjshir friends, clap them on the backs in a stiff-armed dance of masculinity. She realizes that he is going to get on that helicopter with the other Americans and she will never see him again. Now, she understands why her stomach feels sick.

He and the four Tajik fighters are walking toward her, smiling conspiratorially. He stands in front of her, towering and smelling sour from sweat. Rukhsana's face flushes; she wants to turn away but cannot. Something seems to be forcing her to stare up into the American's eerie glowing sunglasses with defiant courage.

"*Tu adami badrang-i khush ruy asti* [You are a beautiful ugly man]," she hears herself announce boldly. Then, before she can hold herself back or remember her place, Rukhsana throws her arms up and around his neck. She feels like a child trying to wrestle a bear as the Tajiks behind her howl in laughter. But the fierce beating of her heart has made her forget all about her stomach.

....

EDDY GENTLY PEELS THE AFGHAN GIRL off his neck and holds her at arm's length. "Jam, take this little marmot back to her old man's *hujra* before she stows away on our bird."

He catches Kourosh eyeing Rukhsana like a slobbering puppy dog. "And I want your personal assurance, on the Holy Qur'ân, boys, that Roxy will still be a virgin when you get her home." Eddy scowls at each of his Panjshir brothers-in-arms. "Or you will answer to *me*, sisterfuckers! Understood?"

"Of course!" Jamshid suppresses a smile. "We are all men of honor. Until our next war, Payload, *Khoda hafez*."

"Back at 'ya, Jam," Eddy grins and salutes him. "Keep the moondust out of your boxers."

As Jamshid respectfully leads Rukhsana away, Eddy catches the wistful smile she throws over her shoulder.

"Jeeesus," he mutters. "Fucking Ruskies were bad enough."

....

AFTER THE PANSHIR CREW, Rukhsana and Assadullah's donkey caravan have departed through the waterfall passage, six of the robed monastics begin to clear debris from the portico. Sonya and Danny join her father in its shade and Danny places each zip-locked manuscript he has selected on her father's lap for inspection.

"These are the documents I'd like to take with me," he explains as Sonya translates. "As soon as I can get funding, I'll return for the rest. I'm sure any university in the world would be thrilled to acquire this collection. But I promise, *you* will be the one to decide where it gets archived."

Sonya relays Danny's assurances but her father is clearly distracted, watching in agitation as the younger monastics clear debris from the damaged portico. His eyes are glazed from fatigue, his expression anxious and disoriented.

Sonya takes Danny aside and whispers. "I think those explosions triggered some kind of post-traumatic stress reaction. No wonder, considering the hell he's already lived through. Help me get him into the helicopter before he changes his mind. Leaving this place and his friends is going to be very painful for him."

Danny nods and tucks the sealed documents back into his rucksack. "Yeah," he looks away. "I have a pretty good idea how he must be feeling…about abandoning his people, I mean."

Sonya takes his face in her hands as hesitation parts her lips. "Danny, listen…I would never ask you to forsake your vows. After what I've done, I have no right to ask you for *anything*…but I'd be a liar if I told you I didn't care what happens now…or how good I think it could be if we can just find a way…"

Her unfinished declaration and golden sunlight paint Sonya's face with the possibility Danny once saw there. He wraps his arms around her, surrenders to her familiar smell, to her strength and the uncharacteristic vulnerability she is showing him. It banishes any remaining doubt left in Danny's mind, any hurt lingering in his heart.

"I've had a hard time thinking about anything else, Sonny," he admits. "Let's continue this discussion on the way home."

"Agreed." Her face flushes with anticipation and she kisses his mouth quickly. "Damn that hurts!" Sonya laughs. "You just don't appreciate your lips until you can't use them properly."

Together, they roll her father's wheelchair down to the littered plaza, toward Bashir waiting in the gunship's bay. Eddy tosses his gear into the helicopter as the pararescue crewmen lift Sonya up into the craft. Danny passes his document laden rucksack up to Bashir as the PJs grab hold of Antonov's arms from above. Danny grasps both wheels of his chair and lifts from below.

"Seems I owe you an apology, Payload." He grunts under the wheelchair's weight. "Your homies came through after all."

"Fucking A, Padre," Eddy grins down at him. "And speaking of homies, you see any of those Kyrgyz smugglers after the Russians landed? I got a little distracted out here."

Danny shrugs. "If they were smart, they ducked and covered."

....

THE BOY'S MOTHER NAMED HIM *TAALAY*, meaning "Lucky." As he claws out from beneath a tangle of bloody limbs, some still attached to the bodies of his clansmen, Taalay wonders if it is luck or a curse that he has survived the fire that came out of the sky. The rest of the Shahin hunters were destroyed in an instant, as if Al-Llâh had pointed His punishing finger at each of them.

Taalay's grandfather, Myrzakan, had predicted this would happen. The old man had been a *manaschi*, a teller of his peoples' epic, and he had long ago warned the Shahin that the black medicine they brought from Chitral and Xinjiang was evil. It was forbidden in Qur'ân and would bring Al-Llâh's wrath down upon them.

His grandfather had been right.

Taalay gazes in horror at the carnage on the ridge above Aubshaur. It looks like the end of the world, as if he were staring into the Gates of Hell. The torsos, legs and heads of his older brother, uncle and cousins are scattered among the rocks, along with the torn bodies of Aybek and Sukhrab, men with whom he had hunted for twelve seasons. He cannot think clearly, cannot feel anything at all until he tries to stand and stumbles. Looking down, he sees that one of his boots is mangled and bloody. Then he notices more blood dripping from his chin onto his chest. Reaching up, his fingers touch the sticky wetness on the side of his face but he finds no ear where one should be.

His body begins to shudder violently as feeling returns with the pain. Then, he hears another of those *Shaitan-Arba* beating the air and anger replaces his fear and grief. Taalay pulls himself slowly, painfully, toward the edge of the ridge until he can look down onto the broad plaza below. As the big machine lands, he remembers the gunfire, the blinding flashes from earlier. His ears still ring from the deafening explosions and his head still throbs like a drum.

Kalashnikov rifles are everywhere among the rocks, some twisted and broken, some burned and others lying about like discarded toys. Taalay pulls himself across the rocks, nearly fainting from the exertion, until he finds one intact. Hands shaking as his body bleeds out what remains of his strength, he manages to chamber a round and claw his way back to the ledge overlooking the plaza. He aims his rifle toward the ugly flying machine and tries to clear his head.

Men in camouflaged uniforms are pulling long black bags into the craft's gaping side. Taalay sees two of the intruders wheeling someone across the plaza. He recognizes the legless old man they called "Sarkâr," the taskmaster who had read to him when he was just a boy.

His older brother, Zhyrgal, was one of the old man's helpers. Now, his brothers are all dead. Taalay is sure he will soon follow them across the great gorge to *Tengri Tagh*—the Mountains of Heaven. Before he does, he must avenge all the Shahin hunters who died here today.

Taalay sights along the barrel of his rifle. Hands trembling, he steadies the wooden grip on a rock and aims at the broad, dark back of one of the men taking the Sarkâr prisoner, pushing him up into the open belly of the beast. If nothing else, he can strike a blow for the old man who showed him kindness as a child.

He remembers his grandfather's prayer as blood and the taste of revenge fills his mouth and explodes from his lips. *"Al-Llâh-u-akbar!"*

....

SONYA WATCHES DANNY'S FACE contort in shock even before she hears the report and sonic turbulence of AKR rounds hitting armor plate and pavement. His mouth gapes, as if the breath has just been sucked out of his lungs. Danny's hands slip from her father's wheelchair, his legs buckle beneath him and he collapses onto the paving stones.

"Man down!" Eddy yells as he drops over Danny's back to shield him with his ballistic vest.

The two crewmen quickly pull her father to cover on board as Sonya squats behind the armored fuselage, scanning the perimeter for the source of the gunfire. On the ridge above the temple complex, she spots movement and sunlight glinting off a rifle barrel. "Up there!" she points. "Sniper at eleven o'clock!"

A slow-motion ballet unfolds before her eyes. One of the crewmen grabs the dual-handle GAU-17, swings its six-barrel rotary muzzle in the direction she is pointing and unleashes a 6,000-rounds-per-minute fusillade. Everyone still on the plaza scrambles for cover as spent shells rain onto the pavement through the weapon's ejection tube. In ten seconds, there is only stillness on the ridge.

The other crewman leaps to the ground with a medevac litter. He and Eddy roll Danny onto it and quickly slide him up into the craft, semi-conscious and gasping for breath. Blood has soaked into the paving stones where he fell.

The twin turbos are already cranking to life as Eddy yells, "Get us airborne, Dutch!" He slams the hatch closed and kneels to assist the crewman tethering Danny's litter to grommets on the cabin floor.

The crewman bends close to Danny's ear and yells over the din of the engines. "How you doing? Talk to me! *Talk to me!*"

In shock, Danny cannot speak. His eyes flutter as he struggles to breathe. Eddy rolls him onto his side as the crewman performs a finger check of his throat and a blood sweep of his torso.

"Airway clear," the crewman yells as he flips open a tactical knife and cuts away Danny's thermal shirt. "I'm seeing two missile wounds in left mid-thorax but no exit wounds. Not good."

"Temporary cavitation," Eddy frowns. "Fucking AKRs."

The crewman inserts a peripheral IV into Danny's arm and a pulse oximeter on his finger. "Get a drip over here and some O_2 on him." Eddy places an oxygen mask over Danny's mouth and nose as the second crewman extracts a liter of saline, clips it to a carabiner and slides it across the fuselage zipline.

Bashir squats tensely against the pilot's bulkhead beside Sonya's father. Both men watch the paramedical routine in stunned silence.

Eddy slips headphones over his own ears and Danny's. "Come on, Padre, hang in there." Sonya can barely hear him above the whining turbos. "I swear to God, I will personally take you to a fucking Sox game when we get Stateside. Box seats at Fenway. Just hang in there with me, pal!"

Sonya remembers her IDF emergency medical training as she watches the Pararescue crewmen scramble to pack each of the bleeding balloons protruding from Danny's mid-back with combat gauze impregnated with kaolin for quick clotting. One PJ tapes them down for compression as the other wraps a monitor around Danny's arm and checks his vital signs.

Eddy tosses Sonya a headset and she hears the crewman feeding information to the Captain.

"BP: eighty over sixty, heart rate: 140, respiration: 30, pulse-ox: 80…" There is a brief pause. "Better throttle up, Cap. This guy's an Alpha—Tango One!"

As one of the crewmen prepares an injection of intramuscular ketamine to ease Danny's pain, Sonya kneels beside him, takes hold of his hand and feels a weak grip. His shallow breath barely inflates the oxygen mask bladder as she hears Captain Van Agalen through her headset.

"TOC, This is Cisco. Current heading is two-thirty degrees, one-twenty klicks east of Ishkashim. Proceeding one-nine-zero knots to CJTH. We've got a US civilian aboard, Cat Alpha Tango One. MIST: two GSWs, probable internal bleeding…"*

When he finishes his report, Sonya breaks in. "How long to Bagram, Captain?"

"We're racing that golden hour," he tells her with professional calm. "Max speed is 224 miles-per-hour and Bagram's about 280 miles away…I won't lie to you, ma'am; it's not looking good."

Sonya feels a surge of adrenaline overtake her, face flushing and hands trembling in the aftermath of violent action. She fights to

---

* **TOC**—Tactical Operations Center • **CJTH**—Craig Joint Theater Hospital at Bagram Airbase **MIST** [Method, Injury/Illness, Signs/Symptoms, Treatment]—first responder protocol to prep the medical team for an incoming trauma victim • **Category Alpha** is the most critical battlefield injury; **Tango One** requires immediate surgery • **GSW**—gun shot wound

remain steady but there is a frantic edge to her voice. "Captain, just…
please, just do your best."

"You can count on that," Van Agalen replies.

She moves in close so Danny can see her face, squeezes his limp
hand in an attempt to reassure him. The Ketamine anesthetic glazes
his eyes, relaxes the tense muscles of his jaw. "I'm right here with
you, Danny. Right here…Just stay with me. *Please*, stay with me…"

....

THROUGH THE MARINE LAYER, Danny can see a watercolor silhouette of Boston painted on the diaphanous veil of mist. His scull
slips over the still, gray water of Hingham Harbor, gliding toward
the causeway at World's End as sunlight teases through the haze.

This is the place he loved most as a boy, the "Irish Riviera" his
parents had called it, not all that far from the boisterous streets of
Southie and yet a cultural universe apart. It is the place where he
began to appreciate the solitude of nature long before he discovered
the idyllic paeans of Henry David Thoreau or Edward Abbey's "green
rage." He remembers his Dad telling him that this pristine peninsula
had been considered for both a United Nations headquarters in 1945
and a nuclear power plant in the 1960s before it was finally preserved
as a public park.

Danny's father brought him here for the first time when he was
only eight years old. The boys left Mom to her shopping on Saturday
morning and drove to Nantasket, where his Dad rented a couple
kayaks and strapped him into the front seat of a double. Pete was
already 15 and experienced enough to pilot his own craft across the
Weir River inlet at Rocky Neck.

Danny never felt so close to his father as when he sat in the front
of that kayak, the sun warming his arms and face, the briny smell

filling him with an incomparable joy as he inhaled the sea air. They paddled around the northern tip of the peninsula, beached their hulls on the sandy causeway and hiked the trails to an overlook where the city's crenellated skyline glittered like Oz in the distance. When they returned to the Nantasket pier in mid-afternoon, his Dad treated him and his brother to lobster, then brought a big tail back for their mother. Danny thought this was heaven, or at least what God must serve for dinner.

He feels light as a feather now, the muscles of his arms pulling effortlessly, his oars gliding silently across the bay's silver surface, completely at peace for the first time in...he cannot even remember when. A flock of sea gulls cruise in the mist above his head, noisy apparitions chattering to each other about what they are spotting in the water below. Danny takes a deep lungful of sea air, watches the world awaken to a perfect summer morning and thinks that heaven cannot possibly be any more beautiful than this.

The sea birds somehow remind him of Sonya and he smiles, remembering their weekends together on the Cape, their toes in the warm sand, the song of the gulls and smell of the ocean. That feeling of unlimited possibility when he looked into her eyes, held her taut body in his arms and heard her breathy voice as they made love.

Stay with me...

Bringing his scull about, he tucks his oars, side-slips toward the familiar causeway. Over his right shoulder, he spots two male figures standing on the beach, dressed in khaki, softly back-lit against the gauzy greenery of World's End. One of the men waves to him, and when Danny recognizes the tall, broad-shouldered Marine, a smile breaks across his face like the sunrise.

"Hurry up, Pee Wee," he hears that familiar voice calling out to him. "Been waiting for you all day."

THE TURBOPROP WHINE IN HER EARS drowns out the scream-
ing in her brain as Sonya tears off her headset and lets it fall into her
lap. All color seems to have bled from the cabin, rendering the grim
tableau in sharp focused black and white. She follows the glistening
beads of sweat on the crewmen's faces as they "package" Danny into a
black rubberized bag for delivery to Bagram alongside the Petrenko
twins. She watches Eddy's massive fist slam in impotent rage against
the bulkhead as his steel gray eyes stare into the cold space between
them, and her white-bearded father's head bow reverently as Bashir
raises his palms and recites the lyrical *al-Fatiha*.

"*Bismillah, Ar Rahman, Ar Rahim. Al hamdu lilahi rabbil 'aalameen*
[In the Name of the One, the Compassionate, the Merciful, all praise
to the Lord of the worlds]..."

She wants to cry, to scream, to rip something or someone to
shreds. But no tears soften her eyes; no sound escapes her throat.
She feels only a shroud of numbness closing around her heart.

As one of the crewmen zips the body bag up toward Danny's
chin, Sonya stays his hand. Looking a final time into the now so
peaceful face of her forever love, she reaches behind Danny's head,
gently lifts the medal of Saint Christopher from around his neck and
nods for the crewman to finish his work.

SUNDAY, 26 JULY 2009 • BAGRAM, AFGHANISTAN

....

EDDY THUMBS THE WHEEL OF HIS ZIPPO, lights a Marlboro he
bummed from a noncom and offers it to Sonya. She sits beside him in
a folding canvas chair on the concrete stoop of a two-story, mustard
color barracks re-purposed from shipping containers. The sun has

dropped behind the western foothills of Charikar, softening the barren brown landscape to the east with a rosy hue. The roar of jet turbines and turboprops on the flight line has subsided during the mid-evening lull.

Sonya takes the cigarette and glances over at her father who no longer reacts to her bad habit. He looks drawn and pallid, a lot older than his sixty years. Sitting passively in a new, hi-tech wheelchair, Antonov silently stares out over the corrugated rooftops at the rugged Hindu Kush in the distance, rocking gently back and forth, his watery blue eyes glazed over in what Eddy figures must be culture shock exacerbated by opium withdrawal.

"Bet your old man never thought he'd see *this* place again." Eddy stretches his boots into the stony drainage trench below the concrete pad. It feels good to be wearing clean boxers. "Must have looked very different twenty years ago. No frigging Popeye's or Pizza Huts."

Sonya's hair is still damp from her shower. Beneath wide aviator sunglasses, her face is scrubbed clean and her swollen lip quivers as she drags on the cigarette. She wears a loose, white T-shirt, and baggy utility trousers rolled below her knees. Eddy notices that Sonya is idly fingering Father Callan's holy medal hanging from a military ball chain around her neck as she speaks.

"I've made arrangements with Danny's friend in Boston to have him transported back to the States as quickly as possible. I know it can take a long time for military channels to handle these things."

"Welcome to *my* world, darlin."

"I just didn't want him lying around here for months in a deep freeze..." Sonya's voice falters as she passes the cigarette back to him with a slightly trembling hand. She glances nervously toward her father who seems to be growing more agitated. "Where's that Oxycodone, Eddy?"

"Corpsman should be by shortly." He picks up a sweating bottle of Budweiser from beside his chair and takes a pull, then crosses his legs and squints through tobacco smoke. "You really should get some sleep."

"Are you fucking serious?" Her manic laughter tells him she is trying desperately to hold it together, remain the stoic professional.

"Frankly, Sonya, and I say this with great affection, you look like hell. Knock off for a while. Problems of the world can wait. I'll make sure your old man takes his pills, okay?"

"I need to know what happened back there, Eddy. You owe me that much."

He exhales smoke through his nose and taps the long neck of his beer bottle. "SOCOM operates in the tribal areas, but we were outside their theater in the Wakhan. That drone strike had to be CIA."

"Why would they call in a strike on a monastery?"

"Good question. They sure weren't shooting at the Russians."

"At *us* then?"

"Not *us*." Eddy glances toward Sonya. "Did Mossad give their friends in Langley a heads-up about your operation here?"

Sonya lets the holy medal drop from her fist and narrows her eyes. "Apparently someone informed them. Was that you, Eddy?"

He shakes his head and snorts a laugh. "The Company and I got divorced long ago, Sonya. Who else other than Vik knew what you were doing here?"

She hesitates, blinks and then lets out a slow breath. "Cyrus had his suspicions. That's why he gave Danny a satellite phone."

"Sat phones are a great way to track people. If Langley had eyes on our TZ, they'd have watched the suitcase transfer go down. The black bird was unmarked but clearly Russian, and there would be no reason for them to waste Hellfires just to slap Mossad's hand." Eddy takes another slug of beer and squints down at the label. "Without reliable HUMINT, those bright boys and girls in SIGINT *have* been known to misread the situation on the ground. I'm just guessing here, but maybe someone decided those Kyrgyz gang-bangers above the temple were bad guys and called in a strike."

"You're saying it was a *mistake?*" Sonya glares at him through her impenetrable shades. "A fuck-up that cost Danny his life?"

Eddy flicks his cigarette butt into the dust beyond the concrete pad with a grunt. "Maybe."

She broods for a minute, then asks, "Who's Zharkov, Eddy?"

"Long story, Sonya. Maybe I'll tell you someday."

A corpsman arrives with a vial of white pills and Eddy slips him some cash. Sonya explains to her father what they are and opens a bottle of water to help him swallow one. The old man relaxes into a sigh of resignation and drifts back into a troubled nostalgia.

"He's lucky to have you," Eddy says, passing his beer to Sonya and pausing as both their fingers grasp the bottle. "So was Danny," he adds, holding her gaze.

Sonya's face remains a death mask beneath the dark aviators. But Eddy notices her left hand is once again clutching the burnished holy medal she took from Father Callan's corpse, as if it still retained the warmth of his body.

"I was the worst thing that ever happened to him, Eddy." Sonya lifts the beer to her swollen lips and passes back an empty bottle.

....

IN THE SEVENTH-FLOOR BRIEFING ROOM, Courtney Kincaid projects a Google Earth feed from her MacBook Air and shows the Associate Deputy Director of Intelligence a satellite image of the Pamir mountain range bulging on the cusp between Afghanistan's Wakhan and Tajikistan's Gorno-Badakhshan provinces. Courtney circles the area with her cursor.

"Sir, we just received confirmation from Roger that AFTAC deployed Constant Phoenix yesterday to carry out an air-sampling mission along these coordinates. The 45th Recon at Offutt has this specially sealed WC-135 that uses external flow-through sensors to sniff out xenon in the atmosphere. Apparently, it doesn't bind easily to other elements, which leaves a smoking gun in the event of a nuclear explosion." She glances over at her distractible boss and wrinkles her nose. "In this case, I guess it's more of a smoking plume."

"Thanks for that clarification, Court." The ADD doesn't look up from his Twitter feed. "Don't we have eyes in the area?"

"Yes, sir, but with heavy weather and debris in the atmosphere, we're having trouble getting good ground sampling and radiometric resolution. Roger says they're working on it."

Her boss glances up at the plasma display panel and squints through his readers, impressed by what he is seeing. "Wow! Civilian sat rez is almost as good as ours these days."

"Better. Silicon Valley doesn't have Congressional oversight."

The ADD grunts. "So, what did our Phoenix team smell?"

"Usually, they try to detect underground tests," Courtney says, sipping the remains of a skinny latte from her aluminum to-go cup. "But this was clearly an air-burst. Last time Constant Phoenix had to track atmospheric radiation was Chernobyl. Preliminary assessment points to a low-yield neutron weapon, probably a kiloton or less, and luckily in an unpopulated area. Apparently, neutron bombs that rely on fission primaries will still produce fallout, but a comparatively cleaner and shorter lasting effect in an air-burst. Little or no radiation would be deposited on the immediate area. It would just become diluted global fallout."

Courtney likes to remind her boss how well she has done her homework. "We're monitoring reports that nomadic herders found debris from a helicopter. Roger says the Russians are pushing President Rahmon to allow a Liquidator Team* into the area. Obviously, they know where the helicopter in question originated."

"Undoubtedly, rubles are changing hands as we speak," notes the ADD. "Any further dope on Payload and the Israeli woman?"

"They're at Bagram, sir," Courtney says. "83rd Rescue brought them in with several casualties." She hesitates and her boss looks up. "One was the priest we were tracking."

* Liquidator Team—term coined by the Soviet Union for the 600,000 civil and military personnel sent to clean up the Chernobyl nuclear meltdown in 1986

"Dead?" he asks.

She nods solemnly.

"Shit! Tell ISAF to throw that rogue, snake-eating sonofabitch in the brig."

"Actually, I inquired if we could detain them both. Ten minutes later I got major push-back from the DNI's office. Seems Payload is… 'untouchable' was the word used. I was told *not* to ask why."

"Mother *fucker!*"

"But I suppose we could have Aronovsky put on ice," Courtney adds hopefully. "Send her to Gitmo on suspicion of aiding terrorists? Maybe reinstate water-boarding?"

"Negative." The ADD chuckles, sighs and slaps his Blackberry against his palm. "Our relationship with the Israelis is complicated. Kind of a combustible mixture of intimacy, caution and distrust."

"In other words, KK gets US COMSAT access and reciprocates with dirt on every other intelligence service in the Near East— friendly and otherwise?" Courtney raises an eyebrow and waits for her boss to admonish her for getting too cozy with Fort Meade.

"Truth is, there *are* no 'friendly' intelligence services," the ADD admits. "Just those we do business with and those we don't. 8200 shares SIGINT on our Arab friends and *they* feed us intel on KK.* Five will get you ten, they also feed it to fucking HAMAS."

"So, you're saying Aronovsky is 'untouchable' as well?"

"Welcome to the dark side, Court." Her boss returns to Twitter as she broods into her latte.

---

* Not only does the US National Security Agency routinely partner with the Jordanian Electronic Warfare Directorate to collect SIGINT on the Palestinian Security Forces, they collect it on Israel as well. According to documents leaked by Edward Snowden, NSA's 2007 Strategic Mission List named Israel as one of the leading threats for espionage directed *against* the US government's Intelligence community, military, science and technology sectors, as well as financial and banking systems. The NSA considers Israel an "electronic warfare enabler."

THURSDAY, 30 JULY 2009 · TEL AVIV, ISRAEL

....

THE TAYALET, A SCENIC PROMENADE that runs north from Yafo to the Tel Aviv marina, is packed with strolling couples in shorts and bikinis, cyclists on beach cruisers and tourists making videos of storm petrels that dance in the sand around loggerhead turtles at the Mediterranean's edge. Sonya blends seamlessly into the summer crowd, just another nondescript university student with shaggy blonde hair, khaki shorts and white canvas sneakers. No one would ever suspect that her black Cordura rucksack contains a GD Itronix 8000 laptop recently used to arm a tactical nuclear weapon.

Leaning on a latticed wooden railing overlooking an array of beach gazebos, the Institute's Head of Operations wears an open-collared dress shirt, gray trousers and thick-soled loafers. Mercifully, Holiday's judgmental eyes are hidden behind his signature clip-on sunglasses because Sonya cannot bear to look at them just now. Instead, she looks out toward the white yachts and sailboats moored on the quay, their masts bobbing arrhythmically against the teal-green sea.

Holiday speaks softly, which only exaggerates his wry sarcasm. *"Mazal tov, Akrav. Hit'aleta al bitsu'echa be-Amman* [Congratulations, Scorpion. You've outdone your performance in Amman].

"The US Air Force detected radiation from an apparent nuclear event on the northeastern border of Afghanistan last week, happily in an unpopulated mountainous region. They report that debris from a Mil gunship was found by nomads in the area. The Russian Federation has dismissed allegations about their involvement, suggesting that an 'inexperienced American crew' probably botched a training exercise in one of their technically advanced rescue helicopter purchased from the illustrious Rosoboronexport."

"Those commandos were Russian Spetsnaz," Sonya replies. "I still don't understand why they killed Wild Boar's body guard. The one I *didn't* shoot. Before he died, Petrenko said someone named Zharkov was shipping those weapons to a Chechen group. Although Payload wouldn't confirm it, my guess is that Zharkov is either FSB or SVR, possibly rogue. But I still can't suss out his game plan."

"We may never know what it is." Her boss grips the railing as if he were choking a serpent. "But our part in this dance is finished. Regardless of what Payload uncovers, the Institute will steer clear of both the Americans and the Russians. Understood, Scorpion?"

She nods, slips the black rucksack off her shoulder and places it against the railing between them. "Could you return this to Avner for me?"

Holiday leans his thick, hairy arms on the railing and cocks his head in her direction. "I thought Avner was going to teach you how to *disable* those damn things."

She sighs. "I only had access to one. Alarmingly, it turns out the older weapons are easier to *arm* than reliably disable. Common cryptographic algos of the 1980s, like DES or RSA, had this glitchy property: Get a probe anywhere into the device, monitor any bit-plane during the computation, and you can recover the encryption key," she explains. "There was also an inherent flaw in the older IBM cryptoprocessors that Soviet weapons designers fancied for their permissive action links. Avner told me the application programming interface would allow an attacker to send the host security module a series of commands that caused it to leak the crypto key."

Holiday raises a single eyebrow above the rim of his clip-ons.

Sonya shrugs. "Turns out Avner was right! It used to take a long time to crack, but modern microprocessors have sped things up considerably. And once you're in, you can reprogram the code; reset the rotors and connect the relay from your cell phone's vibration circuit to the detonator's timing switch. The Roshan cellular network has a surprisingly robust signal in the Wakhan. An incoming call—say from a borrowed sat phone—triggers the Krytron-Pac, discharges the capacitor bank and...*poof!*"

Sonya fans her fingers outward in front of her face as if she were describing a celebratory fireworks display. "Termination of threat."

Holiday stares at her with a humorless expression. If she did not know better, Sonya might have thought she detected a shiver running through him. After a moment, her boss nods briskly. "Avner should be commended for his comprehensive instruction."

"I suggest you nominate him for the Israel Security Prize."

"And approve a bonus for you?"

"Nothing extravagant. Blank gift certificate to Gershon Bram?"

Holiday grunts and looks away. "Sorry to hear about your priest."

Sonya stares quietly at the passing sailboats floating like white gossamer angels on a blue-green sea, hoping her boss does not see the moisture building in her eyes. "Fortunes of war," she replies in a flat voice. "Like Giraffe."

"That New York consulate attaché, Spektor, has been recalled to Tel Aviv. Appropriate disciplinary action will be taken."

"You're much kinder than I would have been," she assures him.

"I know." Holiday places a conciliatory hand over hers on the weathered railing and stares out to sea, either at the passing sailboats or nothing at all.

"And what about Wild Boar?" she asks.

"Not enough hard evidence for a Red Sheet," Holiday says to the passing boats. "But we've got a tradition at the Institute. When someone takes down one of our own, we do *not* turn the other cheek."

Sonya glances inquisitively at her boss. "Sir?"

"*Leviticus*," he reminds her. "I've heard both Payload and Wild Boar are in Istanbul. Why don't you take some time off, Scorpion. A vacation to the former Ottoman capital might clear your head."

"I've got a couple personal issues," she says. "I need to get my father into a rehab program."

"I know the Director at Sheba Medical Center," he tells her. "I'll make a call if you like."

She nods gratefully then turns away before he can see her eyes. "And I have a funeral in Boston."

Holiday gives her hand an avuncular pat and picks up the ruck-sack containing Avner Ron's laptop. "Black suits you," he says.

FRIDAY, 31 JULY 2009 · HAIFA, ISRAEL

....

ACRES OF SODIUM LIGHTS illuminate gigantic cranes looming like Trojan Horses against a black satin sea. Dmitry Antonov sits quietly in his new, comfortable wheelchair and stares out over the tree-covered slope of Mount Carmel to the busy port below. In the flat that belonged to his late wife, in a place he would never have imagined living, he feels almost naked in a light cotton shirt, his hair cropped short, his beard trimmed and his body washed with fragrant soap. Only the vellum manuscript in his lap, one of twelve with which his daughter's Jesuit friend intended to buy Aubshaur's preservation before meeting a senseless death, has a familiar smell to it.

Dmitry made his peace with death long ago. Since that day his gunship went down in the Hindu Kush and the Shahin found him barely breathing, he has come to realize how random existence seems from a human perspective. He imagines his daughter cannot fathom why her old father's life was spared and her young priest's taken away, or what rational explanation there can be for how she came to find him, after a twenty-year absence, in one of the most remote places on Earth. But, here he is all the same. He knows it is no more accidental than those twenty years he was compelled to spend in retreat at Aubshaur.

Sonya appears behind him, the muted reflection of a beautiful young woman superimposed on the industrial landscape outside the window. She hands him a glass of water and a green tablet. It is a poor substitute for his beloved *chandu*, but better than the harsh alternative of total withdrawal. He shivers as Sonya places a comforting hand on his shoulder.

"*Tebe ni holodno, Pápa*[Are you cold, Papa]?" she asks. "I can pull the drapes, warm up the room if you like."

"*Nyet*," he says. "I enjoy the lights. It reminds me of Leningrad."

"They call it Saint Petersburg now," she reminds him.

He swallows the opiate. "That's what they *used* to call it."

He watches his daughter's reflection knead the tension from his shoulders, remembering how broad and strong they once were. "Russia has changed since you left," she says. "The *apparatchiki* are out; the oligarchs and gangsters are in control now."

He snorts cynically. "Doesn't sound like *anything* has changed."

"Look what I found in Mother's closet." Sonya reaches over him, unfurls an old white T-shirt and drapes it over his lap. It takes a few moments to realize it once belonged to him. In his current emaciated state, two of him would fit in it now.

"My God! Why would Maryna have saved this rag, of all things?"

"Probably because it smelled like you," Sonya replies. "At least for a while. Smell fades with time—like pain." Her eyes look sad in the window's reflection.

"But not love," he reminds his daughter, reaching up to touch her hand on his shoulder.

"Papa, I can't keep getting these pills for you," Sonya blurts in frustration. "You need to be in a treatment facility. There's one near Tel Aviv where I can visit while you recover."

He sighs deeply, knowing she is right but dreading the eventuality. "What will happen to my library now that your friend is…" Feeling her tense, he leaves the sentence unfinished.

"I'll speak to someone in America who can help us. Danny said these manuscripts are priceless. We should have no trouble finding money for their preservation. When you've gotten your strength back, you can direct the project from wherever you like. On the Internet, you can communicate with anyone, anywhere."

Dmitry nods, not really understanding what his daughter is talking about but assuming she is telling him the truth. Turning back toward the window, he squeezes her hand. "So, this is what your mother saw every night when she returned from hospital."

"She always closed the drapes," Sonya tells him. "Mother was funny that way. A relentless social activist who needed to shut out the world so she could feel secure."

He squeezes her hand, moves his old T-shirt aside and slips the fragile manuscript back into its plastic bag. "Security is a beautiful illusion, isn't it?"

....

WITH OUTSTRETCHED ARMS, the Good Shepherd, attended by supplicating angels, welcomes Sonya like a wayward lamb into the Church of Saint Ignatius of Loyola near Boston College. Even in her most conservative black dress, she feels somewhat hypocritical, a secular Jew with disdain for any form of religion entering a Roman Catholic house of worship accompanied by a little Muslim mystic in a scally cap and an unapologetic playboy in a bespoke charcoal suit.

"His mother wanted to have the Mass said at Saint Peter's in the old neighborhood," Cyrus reminds her as the three of them enter through oak doors beneath the sculpted limestone arch, "but the good Monsignor Devlin convinced her that Danny would want to be sent off here, surrounded by his Jesuit cohorts. Even offered to do the honors. How could she refuse?"

"The Monsignor is right," Bashir agrees with down-turned eyes. "I'm sure Father Daniel would approve of this venue."

Sonya feels her skin prickling and not just from the oppressive heat. "Oh Cyrus, I don't think I can sit through this."

"Just pretend you're at a *bat mitzvah*," he says, squeezing her arm.

"That won't help, believe me."

"By the way," Cyrus adds, "Mrs. Callan thinks the State Department arranged to bring Danny home."

"Let her continue to believe that," Sonya says as they step into the outer narthex.

Bashir and Cyrus enter to find a free pew, but a table near the aisle catches Sonya's eye. A folded white stole, gold cross and the chalice with which Danny used to say Mass are displayed beneath a gaudily framed portrait of a young priest with optimistic blue eyes, neatly combed sandy-colored hair and formal church vestments. None of it is representative of the man *she* knew, the formidable athlete, the brilliant, idealistic academic, the passionate lover. But it was obviously an important part of the man she never understood. *This* man was his mother's son, the Reverend Daniel Callan, Society of Jesus, a beautiful and tortured soldier of God.

The only man she ever allowed into her heart.

To the left of the nostalgic display, there is a guest book with space for condolences, which Sonya does not sign. Then she tries very hard not to look at the open photo album on the right side, but finds herself drawn to it like a traffic accident. The tipped-in snapshot on the left shows two boys, a teen and his younger brother wearing Red Sox baseball caps and standing on a pier beside their lanky, square jawed, Black Irish father. The boys hold fishing rods and proudly display their catch of the day. The old Kodacolor photo is fuzzy and faded, but the body language speaks volumes about the man's relationship with his sons. One of them would follow in his father's violent footsteps and adopt the Marine Corps' code of honor, a code that could never accept the man he was, but for which he would give his life. The other boy, subsequently abandoned by his father's inconsolable guilt, would become the troubled teenager on the page opposite, the steely-eyed boxer brandishing gloved fists in the corner of a ring. Raised by a grieving widow, he would spend his life trying to answer all his unanswerable questions about a God that allowed so many bad things to happen to good and honorable people.

Turning away from the album, Sonya notices an older woman with dyed auburn hair and a simple black dress stepping through the door accompanied by a paunchy, silver-haired man in a Navy-blue suit. Dreading the moment, Sonya knows this will likely be her only opportunity to speak.

"Mrs. Callan…" Sonya approaches the woman and towers over her. Her male companion nods politely. "I'm so sorry for your loss."

"Thanks." Kathryn Callan looks up. "Do I know you?"

"We met a long time ago. At your home…on Thanksgiving," Sonya reminds her.

Kathryn's puffy eyes probe Sonya's until her memory accesses a file she must have thought she long ago deleted. "Oh, yes," she says. "I remember you now. The Jewish girl. The one Danny nearly left the priesthood for."

Sonya swallows her pride, remembers she is speaking to a grieving mother. "His good sense prevailed in the end," she replies. "That was a difficult time for us both."

"I'm sure it was," Kathryn agrees condescendingly. "But I want to thank you anyway. For leaving him…I'd better get in for Mass."

As she turns away, Sonya blurts out the words before they choke her. "I was there with Danny when he died, Mrs. Callan. In Afghanistan. I thought you'd want to know that your son was every bit as brave as his brother or father."

Kathryn eyes her with a contempt that blurs into bitter laughter. "Oh no, Danny was *much* braver than Peter or my husband. He gave his life to God long ago. None of the rest of us ever had the guts to do that. You don't have to tell me that my son was heroic, young lady. I've known it from the time he was a little boy. And whatever he's done since, whatever temptations he had to fight, whatever sins he may have committed, I *know* he'll be welcomed by the angels."

Her eyes overflow with the fathomless sadness of a mother who has lost everything. "But I will miss my Danny…I loved him dearly."

"So did I, Mrs. Callan." Sonya holds Kathryn's stricken gaze and submits to her scorn. "No matter what you may think of me."

She lifts Danny's medal from her slim purse and holds its ball-chain gently between her fingers. "I came here to return this to you."

Staring at the tarnished reminder of her life's greatest tragedies, Kathryn Callan pulls herself back from the edge of grief, shakes her head and looks Sonya in the eye with defiant dignity.

"No thanks," she says. "You keep it. Saint Christopher didn't protect either of my boys. I'm done with him. Maybe he'll bring you better luck."

SATURDAY, 8 AUGUST 2009 · CAMBRIDGE, MASSACHUSETTS

....

CYRUS NARSAI TOSSES HIS MOHAIR JACKET over the back of his leather sofa, tugs at the knot of his silk knit tie and practically rips open his Egyptian cotton shirt collar. Trying not to look like an excited kid on Christmas morning, he dons folding reading glasses, slips on cotton archivists' gloves and examines the contents of the twelve zip-lock bags Sonya has placed on the coffee table. She sits quietly beside him on the white sofa, her black dress the perfect complement to his motif. After a cursory look, Cyrus pulls the readers off the bridge of his nose, jumps to his feet and practically dances around the room.

"Oh, Danny Boy, you *really* came through! My God, these pieces are incredible!" He notices Sonya staring down at her lap, arms tightly crossed over her heart, remembering, of course, the terrible cost of acquisition.

Bashir Bokhari sits solemnly across from them in the leather Eames chair, sipping chamomile tea. "Clearly, Father Daniel chose these manuscripts because he felt they represented the breadth of the collection," he explains. "From what I have seen, that library contains documents dating back at least two millennia. The Sarman brothers and their ancient predecessors were determined to preserve wisdom from many ancient sources: Vedic, Zoroastrian, Hellenic, Buddhist and Muslim. The environment in that mountain cave is perfect for that, assuming, of course, Aubshaur is never discovered by the *wrong* Muslims."

"Or destroyed by 'friendly' drone strikes," Sonya adds, extracting from her purse the Iridium satellite phone Cyrus had given Danny. She lays it on the coffee table beside the fragile documents. "Yours?"

Cyrus stares at the sat phone as if it were a smoking gun. "Look, I had no idea things would happen as they did, Sonya. I was only trying to protect Danny. Mostly from *you.*"

"I thought you were trying to protect your investment, Cyrus."

"I told Danny to turn that damn thing off when I suspected the CIA had a different agenda than I was led to believe." He plants his hands on his hips and levels an accusatory stare at her. "And since we're pointing fingers, love, maybe you should have been straight with me from the beginning about what you were really after instead of playing me like a mark. Hmmm?"

She sighs and looks away. "Straight talk isn't something either of us do very well, is it, Cyrus?"

He shrugs and softens his voice. "I promised Danny that his mother would be cared for. And he won't be forgotten either. We'll set up an endowment in Danny's name for the preservation of that library at Harvard Divinity."

Sonya stiffens and looks up at him. "My father will be the one to decide where the library will be archived. Bashir has agreed to serve as his intermediary and handle the negotiations."

The little Afghan inclines his head. "I'm sure that is what Father Daniel would have wanted."

Cyrus spreads his arms imploringly. "But, Sonya, I thought we were partners."

"We are," she assures him. "With what's in those plastic bags. But the library they came from has been under my father's protection for the last twenty years and it will remain so." She finishes her tea, stands to leave and smooths out her dress.

"Can you drop me at my hotel?" she asks Bashir.

"Certainly, *habibti.*"

At the front door, Cyrus exchanges contact information with Bashir, shakes his hand officiously and watches him descend the steps to his gray Prius in the driveway. Then, Cyrus finds himself finally eye-to-eye with the "real" Sonya, and bereft of a clever exit line.

"You really *were* in love with him, weren't you?" he says.

"Once upon a time," she sighs. "The tortured Catholic boy and his neurotic Jewish girlfriend had amazing chemistry, Cyrus, We *fit* each other, intellectually as well as physically. Back at Harvard, before the world fell off its axis, I had this crazy thought: Why *shouldn't* we have a life together? I knew I could win over his mother eventually. Mine would be happy I was finally doing *something* normal people do!

"I actually dreamed about our wedding. We'd have two of them: first, under a *chuppah* in Jerusalem. Danny would step on a glass and Mother would try not to cry. We'd have another at the cathedral in Boston where I'd wear a long, white dress, lift my veil on the altar and we'd kiss so passionately it would embarrass the priest. Danny's mother would finally welcome the heathen girl into the family and his drunken cousins would get into a dust up at the reception…"

Her voice wavers and she bites her lip before continuing. "Then, I envisioned us years later. We'd be that international couple, invited to speak at prestigious conferences on linguistics and Near Eastern history, dining with dignitaries and gossiping with celebrities. And I thought it really *could* happen if only…if only we could stop the fucking world and say, 'No more! It's *our* turn now.'"

Sonya's eyes well up with tears Cyrus never expected to see from her. Then she pulls herself back, soldiers up and forces a smile. "But happily-ever-after doesn't happen in the real world, does it, Cyrus?"

He shakes his head in anguish. "I don't think I will ever forgive myself for pushing Danny to go on that expedition."

"Don't feel guilty," she says. "I never saw him happier."

He pulls his hands from his pockets, places them on her tight shoulders and holds her gently. "That's because he was right where he always wanted to be. With you."

Sonya folds her arms around his neck, rests her head beside his and sighs. "You know, Cyrus, despite all your incredibly obnoxious behavior, I'm beginning to like you." She manages a weak laugh as Cyrus feels her damp cheek against his.

"From you, love, even a back-handed compliment is welcome."

He takes Sonya's right hand and raises it to his lips. His thick goatee brushes the back of her hand as he gazes into her liquid amber eyes with genuine affection. "*Mazal tov…*Sonny."

Sonya wipes her tears away, steps onto the porch and breathes in the lush New England summer as if it is the last time she will ever smell its fragrance. She looks back at him, smiles almost wistfully. "Well, my darling Mephistopheles, guess I'll see you somewhere on the other side."

Cyrus feels a wave of nostalgia wash over him as he watches her descend the porch steps into his driveway. Sonya slips quickly into the Prius beside Bashir without looking back and they disappear into the traffic on Brattle Street.

In his air-conditioned living room, Cyrus sinks into his Roche Bobois sofa, dials his encrypted phone, and dances through the usual security protocols before a familiar voice answers.

"Hi, love," he says. "If you promise to stow your brass knuckles and return my other satellite phone in working condition, I will promise *you* dinner at 1789 and some very interesting conversation over dessert. How does hump day sound?"

"Divine," Courtney coos. "I can almost taste that chocolate hazelnut torte."

"Funny," Cyrus replies with a nostalgic sigh. "I just had an intense craving for mussels."

....

BASHIR PULLS UP to a refurbished Queen Ann B&B on Remington Street around 5:00 pm. He reassures Sonya that her father's wishes will be honored. She listens, nods and holds on to his outstretched hand rather than getting out of the car.

"Danny thought the world of you, Bashir."

Sonya hates that her voice always cracks when she speaks his name. "He…he didn't deserve to be taken away so soon. If there really were a God, he should have been kinder to Danny."

"Al-Llâh is the *source* of all kindness." Bashir's onyx eyes reflect a profound wisdom that can only emanate from a broken heart. "He has given Father Daniel the greatest gift of all: an end to suffering. It is you and I who are still fighting our *jihad*." He squeezes her hand and smiles sadly. "With all my heart, I hope the 'great struggle' will bring you peace."

"*Tashakor.*" She hugs him, allowing her heart to open and her tears to fall for the first time since the funeral. "*Khoda hafez.*"

Bashir's sad smile beams in the dashboard lights as he touches his heart with his palm. "*Shalom, habibti.*"

In her room, Sonya hangs her funerary dress on the bathroom door and then showers under cool water. Wrapped in a white towel, she leans back against the bed's padded headboard, her eyes still stinging from the summer heat and the day's emotions. She cannot believe that she dredged up those wedding fantasies for her parting soliloquy to Cyrus. How foolish and unprofessional.

Sonya squeezes her eyes shut as the William Morris-inspired floral wallpaper becomes an ominous tangle of thorns. Projected onto the back of her burning eyelids, she imagines overflowing trays of *asida* dumplings and *mansaf*—lamb cooked in yoghurt—brought through a kitchen door to a dozen floral-decorated tables in a crowded ballroom beneath a brilliant rank of chandeliers.

She watches an *al-zaffeh* procession make a grand entrance from the lobby. The young bride wears a modern white dress and a diaphanous veil instead of a traditional *tatreez*-embroidered *thobe* and gold-festooned *al-suffeh*. Her clean-shaven groom is resplendent in a black suit and bright red tie.

Accompanied by a posse of *zaghareet*-ululating women, the bride and groom take their places on a dais within the wide arc of tables. Poetry is recited: Ziad, Tuqan, and of course, Darwish. Vows are exchanged, and the bride declines to perform *tajalay*, an assertion that she is still a virgin and has not humiliated her family. Everyone knows they are a thoroughly modern couple. Men of all ages, some wearing suits, some dressed in traditional Arab garb, dance the *dabke* to flute and *tablah* drums, their hands linked, their footwork synchronized. A satin scarf is placed on the bride's lap and the family members from both sides approach gleefully to bestow checks and gifts.

"*Mabrouk!*" everyone congratulates.

Sonya notices a stocky young couple exchanging nervous glances at the rear entrance to the ballroom. The bearded man wears a bulky suit coat and a checkered *kaffiyeh* draped like a shawl around him as he points adamantly to the hotel lobby and then moves toward the center of the room. His visibly distraught companion in white *hijab* scurries quickly in the direction he has indicated.

In the midst of all the festive dancing, drumming and boisterous conversation, no one seems to notice the tall woman wearing a forest green silk *abayah* who casually extracts herself from the crowd and pauses by a bank of light switches near the swinging kitchen door. A small mobile phone is clutched in her neatly manicured hand as her narrowed, amber eyes, just visible above a green *niqab*, calculate the timing. She flips all the light switches at once and pushes through the kitchen door. A moment later, the ballroom disintegrates into flying metal, splintering wood, glass shards and horrified screams.

Sikul memukad, Holiday called it, "targeted preventive acts," a sanitized euphemism the Institute had coined for sanctioned killing. No one had anticipated the policy might result in embarrassment and disarray for the entire government of Israel.

Prime Minister Netanyahu had demanded HAMAS heads after their brutal *shahid* bombings in 1997. The Institute had scrambled to present him with candidates for the "Red Page," but there was one

small problem: all the senior leaders of HAMAS were safely shel-
tering in Amman, Jordan, well aware that Israel had signed a treaty
with King Hussein three years earlier. That didn't stop the Institute.

"Operation Cyrus" was their ill-conceived attempt to poison
Khaled Mashal, HAMAS' political bureau chief in Amman, and it
was a cluster-fuck from day one. It ended with a beleaguered King
Hussein pressuring Netanyahu into a lopsided prisoner exchange,
which included Shaykh Ahmed Yassin, founder and guiding light
of HAMAS, for the lives of six Caesarea operatives holed up at the
Israeli embassy and two in GID custody. To add insult to injury, one
of the Institute's *sayanim*, code-named "Dr. Platinum,"* had been
forced to hand over the antidote to save Mashal's life. Things could
not have gone worse. Consequently, the head of Caesarea was booted,
as well as his *kidon* team leader, and the Institute was compelled to
reinvent its operational tactics on the eve of a second *intifada*.

So, when the Mukhabarat, after torturing a few of their usual
suspects, discovered Abu Musab al-Zarqawi's plot to embarrass the
Jordanian monarchy, they saw a unique opportunity and decided to
share intel with the Institute. GID wanted a legitimate excuse to
crack down on dissidents and this was just their ticket. An al-Qaeda
attack against PLO dignitaries in Jordan, assuming it wasn't botched,
would buy public outrage against their supporters, Palestinian sympathy for Hussein and insure Israel's *quid pro quo* downstream.

What could be bad?

A list of auspicious wedding guests was leaked to the Institute,
and the ball was handed to a young upstart, Shlomo Levi. It remains
unclear whether anyone in the Melucha expected him to succeed.

---

* **Dr. Platinum**—the female anesthesiologist brought in to sedate the whistle-blower, Mordechai
Vanunu in 1986, after he had photographed a nuclear weapon at the Dimona lab, sold photos to
the *Sunday Times* in Britain and was lured to Rome by Mossad agent, Cheryl Ben Tov. Vanunu
was spirited back to Israel, tried and imprisoned.

Keshet's *neviotim* were cleared to perform "maintenance" on the ball room by a hotel employee with a large gambling debt, and no one noticed the packets of Semtex strategically placed behind the ceiling panels. Or the tall woman in a flowing green *abayah* who slipped quickly through the kitchen, circled around to the lobby while the panicked hotel employees were tending to the carnage in their ballroom, walked casually out the front door and hailed a taxi before the Jordanian security forces arrived.

Weddings and funerals.

Sonya has had enough of both to last her a lifetime. Shlomo and Danny are dead, and all she has left is a crippled father she has never known—the high price of a violent career predicated on a 2,500-year-old directive from the Tanakh's Book of *Leviticus*:

> *As he has done it shall be done to him,*
> *fracture for fracture, eye for eye, tooth for tooth…*

Sonya opens *her* eyes, shudders and boots up her VAIO laptop. She places a Skype call to "irynatimko-365." There is no answer, so she types a text message:

> Привіт. Прибудтя до Стамбулу на наступному тижні.
> Я гадаю, ми могли би повечеряти. Можна з ночівлею…

Hi. Coming to Istanbul next week. Hoped we could have dinner. Maybe a sleepover…

....

"REMEMBER THE GANG OF EIGHT?" Beneath the brim of his cap, Eddy Thompson's vigilant gray eyes appraise a three-tiered fountain in the rose garden outside the Revan Köşkü.

"You talking about the August Putsch in '91?" Sonya asks.

"Bingo!" He grins. "That's where this story almost ended."

Summer rain has dissuaded tourists from mobbing the Topkapi Palace this afternoon and Sonya finds the Fourth Courtyard's water-color landscape a welcome departure from weeks of jet-lagged travel, emotional trauma and funerals. She and Eddy ascend the granite staircase to a fig and cypress-lined plaza, where a sunken pool is surrounded by an Ottoman arcade. Wear-polished paving stones glisten in the rain as they take shelter beneath the ornate, teal and golden-tiled portico. Sonya lowers her red umbrella and leans back against the cool, gilded stone of a pedestal supporting the pillared arch. She turns down the damp collar of her linen shirt and looks up at the man whose life she saved only three weeks ago.

"Why don't you tell me where the story *began*, Eddy."

And so, he does.

Vladimir Alexandrovich Kryuchkov was chief of the Soviet PGU,* foreign intelligence branch of the KGB. A staunch supporter of General Secretary Leonid Brezhnev, Kryuchkov became one of the most vocal proponents for the Soviet invasion of Afghanistan. In 1988, Mikhail Gorbachev appointed Kryuchkov 7th Chairman of the KGB, which made him arguably the second most powerful man in the USSR.

When Gorbachev's policies of economic restructuring and political openness led him to repudiate the hardline "Brezhnev Doctrine," Kryuchkov felt betrayed and decided to hedge his bets. PGU had controlled its own arsenal, including small, portable tactical nuclear weapons designed as howitzer shells and virtually maintenance-free. A dozen of these so-called "suitcase nukes" were secretly shipped from Ukraine to Bagram, in case America decided to escalate the war in Afghanistan. Chairman Gorbachev was never informed of this because Kryuchkov was already conspiring to oust him.

"When the Soviet 40th Army was ordered to withdraw from Afghanistan, Kryuchkov sent a squad of Spetsgruppa Alfa, PGU's rapid reaction force, to take possession of those nukes," Eddy says, lighting a smoke. "He wanted them under his personal control to insure the eventual transition of power—in his direction.

"My guess is the Alfa squad at Bagram was supposed to rendez-vous with Kryuchkov's team at their secret FOB, our monastery in

---

* **PGU** [*Pervoye Glavnoye Upravleniye*]—First Chief Directorate of the KGB has been succeeded by the Russian Federation's SVR, in charge of foreign operations. FSB is tasked with domestic affairs and internal security.

the Wakhan, then quietly transfer the weapons to a secure location near Moscow," Eddy suggests. "But something went wrong."

Watching rainwater drip from the slate roof and spatter against the paving stones, Sonya takes the cigarette from Eddy and inhales deeply. "We now know what that 'something' was, don't we?"

Two-and-a-half years later, in the midst of food and fuel shortages, factories unable to pay their workers, independence movements in the Baltic States and Caucasus, and political upheaval throughout the USSR, the Gang of Eight made their move and tried to force Gorbachev to declare a state of emergency or step down. When he refused both options, the KGB confined him to his *dacha* in Crimea and Vice-President Gennady Yanayev declared himself acting president of the Soviet Union, with Kryuchkov's blessing.

"Shit hit the fan," Eddy grins. "'Operation Thunder': Tamanskaya and Kantemirovskaya tank divisions, 700 combat vehicles and 2,000 soldiers, along with Alfa, Vympel, OMON and the 106th Airborne roll into Red Square. Boris Yeltsin hoists his drunken ass up onto a frigging T-72 in front of the Parliament building and addresses the crowd through a bullhorn. Marshall Yazov orders the Spetsnaz to attack, but the illustrious General Alexander Lebed talks them down. Yazov relents, Gorby returns to dismantle the Soviet Union, Kryuchkov and his conspirators get adjacent cells in Lefortovo—"

"*Perestroika* wins the day, oligarchs make billions and Putin rises to power. A regular Russian fairy tale," Sonya adds bitterly.

"And this is where Alexander Zharkov enters our story."

Sonya returns Eddy's cigarette. "So, who *is* this guy?"

"Kryuchkov's golden boy in the KGB, one of the trusted few who knew about those TNWs deployed to Bagram. After the August Coup failed and Kryuchkov was put on ice, Zharkov hitched his wagon to the new rising star. He became one of Putin's 'mechanics'

in Saint Petersburg and ended up running a 'wet works' unit when
Vlad took the reins in '98."*

"What's his connection to the Chechens?"

"He kills them," Eddy says, "at least the ones Ramzan Kadyrov
doesn't like. They call it the 'Berlin Group': Chechen, Georgian and
Azeri hit teams, a joint venture between FSB and GRU, with a little
input from SVR. Zharkov handles recruitment from the dissident
diaspora community in Eastern Europe and Turkey. Pulls the trigger
himself occasionally, just to keep his boys on their toes. Al figured
those suitcase nukes still had to be around somewhere and knew
what they'd be worth on the open market."

Sonya glares cynically at Eddy. "So, when your old gun-runner
pal, Viktor Kaban, hired you to track me and locate those weapons
for him, you decided to do a little deal on the side with the Russians
through Mister Zharkov, right?"

Eddy shrugs. "I assumed Putin would want to secure his long-
lost property before bad guys got hold of it. So, yeah, I contacted
Zharkov through a back-channel, got him to offer Vik a fat finder's
fee. Figured everybody would end up happy campers."

"Oh, I'll bet you did." Sonya doesn't try to hide her disgust. "It
still doesn't make any sense that an SVR operative would want to sell
nukes to either Kadyrov *or* his enemies? That would be suicidal."

"True *that!*" Eddy narrows his eyes. "No amount of money would
keep Zharkov alive if he even thought about going rogue. Putin would
track him right into the shitter and cut his throat. So, there's obviously more to this. But I won't know what until I have a come-to-
Jesus with the motherfucker."

* **Mechanics** [*chistilshchiki*] were assassins for the Administration for Special Tasks in the Soviet
NKVD [*Narodnyi Komissariat Vnutrennikh Del*], later incorporated into KGB's Spetsbureau 13
—Department of Wet Affairs [*Otdel Mokrykh Del*]—and now into SVR's Department V,
known simply as the "The Wet Works."

Sonya's eyes drill into him. "Who do you *really* work for, Eddy?"

He glances over at her and inclines his head in acknowledgment of the invisible thread that connects them.

"Officially, people like you and me don't exist...do we Sonya?"

....

THE SLENDER, GLOWING MINARETS of Eminönü point toward the misty heavens like medieval missiles awaiting countdown. From the rain-slick balcony of Galata Kulesi, Alexander Zharkov listens to a doleful *adhan* cascading from loudspeakers on every street corner of the old city, overlapping echoes awakening the Golden Horn to prayer. The tower's restaurant is not particularly crowded due to inclement weather and the observation deck is already closed to all but those with dinner reservations. Only a few tourists brave the rain pattering against weathered stone spheres mounted on the balustrade circling an open balcony, and their eyes are focused on the glittering, storybook mosques dotting the mouth of the Bosphorus.

Zharkov steps out to the overlook, opens a black umbrella with a curved bamboo handle and wanders around to the northern side of the conical Galata tower overlooking the terracotta roofs of Karaköy fifty meters below him. The eerie sodium lights of Taksim Square glow yellow in the distance and a large, lone figure is silhouetted against the urban sprawl of Istanbul. He wears a navy military style rain jacket over blue jeans and rubber soled leather shoes. When he turns to greet Zharkov, his dark brimmed cap shows an American baseball team insignia on the front.

"Hey there, Al," Payload greets him without a smile. "Long time, no see."

"You might have picked a more pleasant place to meet," Zharkov complains. "One where they sell alcohol and allow you to smoke."

"We'll celebrate later," the big man replies humorlessly. "You bring my paycheck?"

"What paycheck? You did not return the Russian Federation's property as agreed."

"Well, that's not the way *I* see it, Al." Payload lowers his hirsute face toward Zharkov, teeth flashing between his drooping moustache and the triangle of hair below his lip. "Your crew took possession of the entire inventory. Apparently, they weren't taught how to handle it properly."

Zharkov shrugs. "I do not know what you are talking about. No property, no…"

The sound is abruptly cut off in his throat by an enormous hand before he even sees it move. Fumbling with his umbrella in one hand, Zharkov tries to pull the PSS silent pistol* he has been gripping in the pocket of his raincoat, but Payload's other hand intercepts it before he can fire a round into the American's gut. Breathless and on the verge of panic, Zharkov launches a knee toward his adversary's groin, slips on the slick stone tiles and feels himself shoved back against the waist-height wooden railing.

"Calm down, Al," Payload counsels between clenched teeth. "I want *all* my clients to be satisfied with my services, so I'm sure we can work something out." He backs off, the pistol a child's toy in his hand. "Haven't seen one of these little fuckers in years."

Zharkov clutches his throat, coughs and considers his options. Through the arched window behind Payload, a middle-aged couple bends in conversation over Turkish coffee and an arrangement of mottled roses in a white vase, completely uninterested in whatever is happening outside.

---

* **PSS** [*Pistolet Spetsialnyj Samozaryadnyj*]—semi-automatic firing a unique 7.62 x 42mm noiseless cartridge with an effective range of 25 meters; developed in 1980 for KGB and Spetsnaz black ops

"So, clue me in," Payload says. "What did you work out with Vik?"

"As we discussed…" he rasps, "I offered Kaban a finder's fee and technical assistance… The Petrenkos were to lead a group of contractors from Grom to recover…the Russian Federation's lost property."

"That's it?"

Zharkov tries to clear his throat as he gauges the distance to the restaurant's doorway. "I offered his bodyguards a sweetened deal to work for their former employer… They accepted."

"That so?" Payload glares at him, a half-smile, half-sneer raising one corner of his moustache. "And why do you suppose one of those bodyguards tried to put a shiv in me?"

"I do not know why…" He coughs then stifles a nervous laugh. "Perhaps you seemed threatening."

Zharkov feels the slippery, varnished wooden balustrade at the small of his back. Behind it, a chest-high steel railing provides some safety, but he can see it would not be difficult to push someone under it. The mesh safety catch between the observation deck and the lower floor of the restaurant might not be enough to keep a man from falling to his death. He wonders if this had been Payload's plan all along. Why else would he want to meet in such a boring tourist trap after closing time?

"And *you* didn't tell your boys from Grom to smoke both of Vik's bodyguards after the inventory was recovered?"

Zharkov feels his sweat mingle with cool rain on his face. He shrugs and tries to calculate how long it will take him to draw the 25-centimeter dagger blade from his umbrella handle and how close he needs to be for an effective strike to Payload's throat just beneath the ear.

"You must know that Moscow is not very trusting with their tactical nuclear weapons, especially not with a notorious Ukrainian

Jewish arms dealer and his proxies," Zharkov admits with a forced
laugh. "Besides, from what you have just told me about the aggressive
behavior of Kaban's bodyguards, our preemptive actions may well
have saved *your* life."

Payload narrows his predatory eyes below his cap's brim. "Well,
you may be right about that, Al." He pauses and cocks his head. "And
you may also be doing a deal on the side with Kadyrov that Mister
Putin would not be pleased to know about."

Zharkov spits a laugh. "That is absurd!"

"Yeah, I would have thought so too. But that's exactly what one
of Vik's boys confessed before he died."

Understanding flickers in Zharkov's eyes and he moves a step
closer. "Ah, now I see why you are confused, my friend. This is the
cover story we told the Petrenkos. In truth, our deal is not with the
Kadyrovtsy. It is with the *Vostochniki*."

That elicits a raised eyebrow from Payload. "Vostok and Zapad*
were disbanded last year, Al. Word on the street is that Kadyrov had
both the Yamadayev brothers hit a few months back."

"That much is true," Zharkov smiles modestly. "I saw to it personally. But Vostok was never *really* disbanded by the GRU, just re-
purposed. There is mounting political pressure to redeploy them."

"Pressure from Grozny?"

"From Moscow."

"But *why*, Al?" Payload looks truly baffled. "Why would your boss
want to disrupt his own hand-picked, bought-and-paid-for regime
in Chechnya?"

---

* **Special Battalions Vostok** [East] and **Zapad** [West] were GRU units comprised mostly of ethnic
Chechens by Sulim Yamadayev, who joined the Russians in 1999 to fight against Arab jihadists. The
Yamadayevs were bitter rivals of Ramzan Kadyrov, also a former Chechen separatist who pledged
loyalty to the Russian Federation and conspired with Vladimir Putin to become president of
Chechnya. In 2008, both Special Battalions were deployed to aid Russian separatists in Abkhazia
and South Ossetia, then disbanded a few months later by Kadyrov, whom INTERPOL suspects
had Ruslan and Sulim Yamadayev assassinated in 2009.

"Oh no, my friend, this has nothing at all to do with Chechnya," Zharkov breaks into laughter at Payload's misunderstanding. "This is about Crimea and Donbass. About reunification. What Gorbachev tore apart, Putin is now stitching back together."

"Are you serious? Vlad would actually deploy tactical nukes to a separatist militia in Ukraine?"

Zharkov shrugs. "Think about it. If Kiev"—he uses the Russian pronunciation—"were to learn that our patriots in their eastern provinces possessed weapons of mass destruction, would Moscow not be forced to intervene and avert a catastrophic confrontation? The Motherland would have no choice but to welcome *Novorossiya* back with open arms. What is that American expression…?"

"Plausible deniability," Payload nods. "Like last year's gambit in Abkhazia and South Ossetia. NATO gets cold feet and backs away."

"Ah well, that is all water under the bridge now, is it not?" Zharkov grips his umbrella with both hands, casually steps closer to his target. "We shall have to see how the politicians work things out, no?"

Payload snorts a cynical laugh. "Business as usual."

"Precisely." Zharkov's fingers tighten around the curved handle of his umbrella as he prepares to disengage the blade with his thumb. "I am quite sure the Russian Federation will continue to consider you a valuable business asset. Now, if you will return my *pistolet*…"

Payload takes a step back, ejects the pistol's magazine, snaps it open, clears its breech and tosses it over the railing. Zharkov hears his PSS clatter into the steel mesh just below the balcony's lip as he thumbs the catch to his blade.

"Oh Al, don't make me have to take that umbrella poker away from you, too." Payload drops the pistol's little magazine at Zharkov's feet, flashes him a final warning and a savage grin.

"I'd hate to see you get wet…*tovarich*."

SATURDAY, 15 AUGUST 2009 · ISTANBUL, TURKEY

....

IN HIS PRIVATE PENTHOUSE SUITE at the Tulip Club, Viktor Kaban pours another frosted tumbler of Beluga Gold from a bottle chilling in an ice bucket on his bed stand, splashing some on Iryna, his current favorite. The waifish Ukrainian girl is very drunk and feels tighter than usual as she slumps on the bed, her ass in the air awaiting his pleasure. He drools some of the oily vodka mixed with his saliva into the cleft between her buttocks and tries to enter her again as her raven-haired girlfriend watches with a salacious smirk.

At the foot of the bed, wearing only a black lace choker around her throat, black satin gloves and a gold stud in her belly button, the full-breasted slut would be a natural for the porn industry, Viktor decides. He was delighted when Iryna suggested a threesome, and thoroughly enjoyed watching this exotic, amber-eyed whore pleasure both herself and Iryna with an impressive dildo. Soon, it will be time to test her skills himself.

The last two weeks have not gone well and Viktor is in dire need of stress relief. Akbank decided not to extend his line of credit and the girls he was expecting from Moldova were deported by the SGK when he refused to pay their exorbitant bribe. His request to be issued a diplomatic visa in New York was ignored by young Spektor—the fucking little *pereguznya* never even responded to his email or text messages. His mother has refused to leave Brighton Beach and he is having a hell of a time finding a competent minder for her.

Worst of all, Kyrylo and Marko have dropped off the face of the Earth, leading him to assume that Russian bastard, Zharkov, made them an offer they could not refuse. Only a deal with Syria looks promising, if he can secure enough isopropanol to make Sarin.

How difficult could *that* be?

Iryna's face is burrowed in a down pillow. From her ostrich-in-the-sand position, she slumps like a rag doll across the king bed, groans and passes out as Viktor reaches for a clear vial of pre-cut cocaine beside the ice bucket. The room shifts like a 3D video without the special glasses and he leans back against the headboard for support. Attempting to focus, he spoons out a measure of the snowy powder and inhales it into his already numb sinuses.

The blow ignites a delicious idea in Viktor's vodka-addled brain as he stares at the identical sluts with black silicone dildos gliding suggestively between their lips. He scoops a tiny silver spoonful of cocaine and tries to deposit it, with little success, on the ridge of his drooping penis. Looking up at the two overlapping, black-haired, four-breasted girls undulating at the foot of his bed, Viktor wipes his running nose, grins and gestures proudly down toward his sugar-coated handiwork, slurring his demand for lip service.

"*Sosy moye huy, suka* [Suck my cock, whore]."

The stereo porn stars crawl slowly across the bed over sleeping Iryna until they merge into a single Amazonian goddess with glistening olive skin, smudged red lips and intense golden eyes radiating from within a dark smear of mascara. Rising up on her knees in front of him like a defiant *Kama Sutra* Kali, she slaps the long faux-phallus against her left palm and licks her lips in sweet anticipation of her next trick.

Then magically, there are *two* dildos. One flashes like a bolt of heat lightning through the air before entering his throat just below the left ear. Suddenly, the oxygen flow through his trachea is cut off and his vision snaps into sharp focus. The last thing Viktor sees before his life fades to black is the raven-haired whore staring coldly at him. The way one might look after exterminating a rat.

"*SAM VIDSOSY* [Suck it yourself]," Scorpion hisses, while maintaining pressure on the 15-centimeter *tanto* blade the tech ghouls had fitted neatly into her silicone sex toy. After severing Wild Boar's carotid artery, it takes only twenty seconds for his spasms to cease, his eyes to roll all the way back in his head and the gurgling sound in his throat to grow silent.

Scorpion's satin glove is soaked with arterial blood as she withdraws the blade, reaches down between his once powerful legs with her left hand and takes hold of his flaccid penis and scrotum. With an upward radial stroke of the razor-sharp *tanto*, she castrates Viktor Kaban's corpse and inserts the limp, bloody organ into his gaping mouth—a Chechenskaya Obschina "calling card," he had informed her a few weeks ago in a Brooklyn warehouse, after cutting his own employee's throat.

Iryna is mercifully out cold from the rohypnol Scorpion slipped into her drink thirty minutes ago. The girl will be unconscious for six hours and convincingly horrified when she awakens. No one will suspect her of anything but having been in the wrong bed at the wrong time. Scorpion tenderly covers Iryna with the gore-spattered duvet, walks calmly to the bathroom and strips off her bloody satin gloves.

In the travertine shower, she washes off Kaban's sticky blood, scrubs smeared mascara from her face, and then rinses her whole body, her gloves, choker and dildo with the hydrogen peroxide she brought for the occasion to destroy Kaban's DNA.

After drying off with a plush Turkish towel, Scorpion locks the *tanto* blade back into its steel-lined silicone sheath and places all the wet items into a water-proof nylon pouch in her leather handbag. As a final precaution, she splashes bleach from the housemaid's closet over the shower, sink and bathroom floor. Her DNA could still be found on the bed, and on Iryna, but what would that prove?

In the bathroom mirror, Scorpion freshens her eye shadow and lipstick, then slips back into her panties, a form-fitting red Lagerfeld and matching Louboutins. Opening the louvered French doors to the balcony, she takes a deep breath in the warm, humid night and conjures the vision of a sadistic Chechen assassin scaling the faceted stone wall to Wild Boar's suite, anticipating cold revenge for a cocaine deal gone wrong.

At the Seminary, she had studied Edmond Locard's Exchange Principle: *Every contact leaves a trace*, the 20th century pioneer in forensic science had written. In Amman, Scorpion had discovered the corollary to his principle: *every trace implies a contact*, and that deflecting responsibility in a spectacularly convincing manner is what elevates the craft of low-signature interception to performance art.

Her hands are steady when she opens the hallway door. The bald, muscular bodyguard is still at his post and obviously new at his job. He stares down into her cleavage with lust in his eyes as Scorpion gingerly closes the door behind her.

"*On speet* [He's sleeping]," she whispers. "Small wonder after all the vodka he guzzled."

"I will need to check your purse," the burly young Russian says apologetically. "He thinks the girls always steal from him."

She smiles, opens the red leather handbag and allows the guard to sift perfunctorily through its contents. He pats the lining for secret pockets, unzips the wet pouch and inspects her gloves and choker, sniffs her Tokyo Milk perfume atomizer, smirks at the foil packets of ribbed condoms and finally withdraws the black, parabolic sex toy, lifting an eyebrow the way men always do when they see it.

And then his blue eyes narrow as he runs a forefinger over the silicone where the head curves gracefully into the long shaft and examines a watery red smear it leaves on his skin.

Scorpion looks up at the Russian with ingenuous eyes and bites her lower lip in embarrassment.

"It gets a little rough sometimes," she confesses.

The guard's tight lips curl into a conspiratorial sneer. "As I've heard." He replaces her instrument of pleasure and hands back the purse. Scorpion's white-tipped fingernails linger against his hand as she takes it from him.

"Next time I'll show you how it works," she promises, throwing an anticipatory smile over her shoulder as she slinks down the hall.

Outside, the club's marble steps are slick from an earlier rain shower and the cooling night air is fragrant with the mingling scent of rose and jasmine. A carbon colored BMW E9X waits on the street just beyond the wrought iron tulip gate through which the club's owner will never again enter.

Scorpion opens the car door, slides gracefully into the passenger seat and accepts a lit cigarette from the chestnut-haired driver who impressively fills out a black T-shirt. She drags deeply, exhales a slow stream of smoke toward the convertible roof and passes it back. Eddy Thompson tucks the lipstick-stained cigarette into a sardonic smile implied by the arch of his moustache, then nods to her with the kind of acknowledgment only one professional can give another.

"All good, Sonya?"

"As good as it gets, Eddy."

Engaging the shifter, he lets out the clutch and pulls away from the Tulip Club's gate as Sonya closes her eyes, leans back against the black leather headrest and surrenders to an impenetrable darkness inhabited by the bittersweet memories of weddings and funerals.